"Adler is a household name to fans of romantic suspense."
—*Library Journal*

"Entertaining. Lust, greed, and murder keep readers on their toes. Adler is expert at digging deep into her characters' psyches and showing what makes them tick. Her villain here is wonderfully portrayed—as are all the other characters in this well-plotted, entertaining work."
—*Publishers Weekly*

"Spellbinding. Adler is a true genius."
—*Affaire de Coeur*

"A fun read!"   —*San Francisco Examiner*

"Gifted storyteller Elizabeth Adler proves once again why she is truly a master of sweeping, intense, and dramatic novels."
—*Romantic Times*

NOW OR NEVER

"Top notch . . . one of the best from the author of *The Secret of the Villa Mimosa*, combining tension, sensuality, and great characterization. Highly recommended."
—*Library Journal*

"The novel definitely packs a wallop."   —*Booklist*

"Will keep her romance audience securely hers as she leads them into new territory."
—*Kirkus Reviews*

"Mesmerizing."   —*Internet Bookwatch*

"Intense, engrossing and exhilarating are just a few words that describe Elizabeth Adler's new release. Ms. Adler's novel brings a wonderful cast of characters vividly to life!"
—*Romantic Times*

THE RICH SHALL INHERIT

"Rises above the genre to surprise, fascinates . . . genuine pathos, humor, and inventiveness."

—*Publishers Weekly*

"Not to be missed! Interesting characterization and exciting plotlines. A modern detective story, a family history, and a murder mystery all at once. Worthwhile reading."

—*Rendezvous*

"Told with charm, wit, warmth, and a good deal of raw suspense. The climax is satisfying. The way things should happen in big, glitzy novels."

—*Rave Reviews*

"Fascinating!"   —*Orlando Sentinel*

"Engrossing. The identity of the true heir will literally taunt you until the end."

—*Macon Beacon* (Georgia)

"Elizabeth Adler weaves the saga and mystery genre together. Elaborately plotted. Dauntless enough to entertain."

—*Kirkus Reviews*

"A juicy detective yarn glossier than Dulux and sexier than suspenders."

—*New Library*, London

"Thriller, romance and rags-to-riches saga beautifully bound together."

—*Oxford Mail*, England

"If you like nothing better than a spellbinding saga to get wrapped up in, this novel is an absolute must. Highly readable. Don't miss it!"

—*Liverpool Echo*

"There is death, violence, passion and the mystery is not solved until the very end. And by that time I was entranced by Elizabeth Adler's latest book, and once again, find myself longing for her next."

—*Reading Post*, England

PROPERTY OF A LADY
"Adler's evocation of fleshpots like Manhattan and Hollywood is admirable . . . wide screen romance/intrigue."

—*Kirkus Reviews*

"A sweeping romantic epic that will absorb readers until the novel's conclusion, when all of the characters and events come together in a rich and fulfilling resolution."

—*School Library Journal*

"Briskly plotted and well researched."

—*Publishers Weekly*

PEACH
"A well-paced story full of rich characters."

—*South Bend Tribune*

"Enthralling. Utterly satisfying."

—*Rave Reviews*

ALSO BY ELIZABETH ADLER

The Last Time I Saw Paris

In a Heartbeat

All or Nothing

Sooner or Later

Now or Never

The Secret of the Villa Mimosa

Legacy of Secrets

Fortune Is a Woman

The Property of a Lady

The Rich Shall Inherit

Indiscretions (writing as Ariana Scott)

Fleeting Images (writing as Ariana Scott)

Peach

Leonie

SUMMER IN TUSCANY

ELIZABETH ADLER

St. Martin's Paperbacks

SUMMER IN TUSCANY

Copyright © 2002 by Elizabeth Adler.
Excerpt from *The Hotel Riviera* copyright © 2003 by Elizabeth Adler.

Library of Congress Catalog Card Number: 2001058858

ISBN: 0-312-98937-7

Printed in the United States of America

St. Martin's Press hardcover edition / July 2002
St. Martin's Paperbacks edition / June 2003

St. Martin's Paperbacks are published by St. Martin's Press, 175 Fifth Avenue, New York, NY 10010.

10 9 8 7 6 5 4 3 2 1

For Anabelle

TUSCANY . . . Vineyard-covered hills, silvery olive groves, fields of dazzling sunflowers, old pastel-colored villas and ancient stone villages, cool archways flashed with sunlight, and the village of Bella Piacere* on the crest of the hill. Paradise . . .

*Bella Piacere was named in the sixteenth century, or round about then, by an Englishwoman who spoke only a couple of words of Italian. Fortunately, though not grammatically quite correct, the two words expressed her emotions on first seeing the lovely hamlet in the Tuscan hills—Beautiful Pleasure. And, anyhow, the name sounded better than "Bel Piacere."

CHAPTER ONE

GEMMA

Let me tell you right from the start, you wouldn't want to know me. Especially on a Saturday night. Why? Because that's when it's toughest here in the emergency room, and the only reason you would ever get to meet me is if you were wheeled in here on a gurney. Then it would be my face looking down at you under a glare of white light, saying, What's your name? . . . Where does it hurt? . . . Who did it? . . .

I'm Gemma Jericho, resident-in-charge at New York's Bellevue Hospital Trauma Department, and Saturday night is always hell on wheels. Right now I'm forging through the usual weekend mayhem of stabbings, shootings, and road accidents, wailing women and haggard drunks, overdosed addicts and a poor limp baby in a frantic mother's arms. I'm on an adrenaline high, calling instructions, going from victim to victim: an intubation; a CAT scan; another shot of ephi; tending the comatose baby; paging the pediatric surgeon.

Sometimes I ask myself, What am I doing here? How did I get here? Why are most of my Saturday nights spent like this? Where's *my* life? Then I catch a glimpse of myself and I see the answer.

I'm wearing scrubs and the equivalent of a plastic shower cap over my hair, sneakers, and a white coat. I've been on duty for eight hours already and with a few more still to come. I'm tired, tousled, and cranky, and I need a shower. Plus this face is never going to launch any thousand ships, even though my mom tells me I'm a bit Meg Ryanish, albeit on one of Meg's bad days, but that's just my mom talking. The truth is that besides being an emergency physician, I'm thirty-eight and divorced, with a teenage daughter to support. And that's reality talking.

Add to that, I have a secret that I'm not telling, a horrible secret guilt that will haunt me all my life, but it explains why I believe no one would want to *really* know me. The true me that lurks beneath this efficient, noble, white-coated doctor exterior.

Sometimes, before I leave for the hospital, I look in the mirror longer than the minute it takes to make sure my face is still there and that my hair has at least been combed, and instead of seeing reality, I remember when I was in high school and thought I might be reasonably pretty.

Gemma Jericho, the Dancing Queen, that was me, and boys were my main interest and girlfriends the center of my life. I remember my mother trying to drill some sense into me, the way I try now with my own daughter, telling me to think about my future and not just throw it away on the high school football hero. Which, of course, is exactly what I did. But that's another story.

Those teenage years are long behind me now. I mean, thirty-eight is awfully close to forty, don't you think? *The Big Four Oh*. It seems so far away when you are only sixteen. How many of us ever really think we will get there? Certainly not me . . . or do I mean "not I"? Whatever, forty is forty. Right. And *plain* with it. Plus I probably rate a zero in "style."

What do I really look like? Okay, so I'm on the skinny side and, as my mom tells me every Sunday when we go to her place for lunch, I could use a bit more meat on my bones. Actually, bigger breasts might help. Maybe I should think about that? I used to stuff my bra when I was younger, but I gave that up long ago. Anyhow, I'm a leggy five-ten, but that doesn't make me "elegant." I'm a bit of a klutz, really, and somehow prone to accidents, except when I'm working, and then I'm a fine-honed speed machine.

Last time I looked I had blue eyes, usually hidden behind horn-rims, the kind that swoop up at the sides. I'm so nearsighted it's pathetic, and without glasses I practically have to grope my way around. You would have thought, me being a medico and all, I would have succumbed to the lure of laser eye surgery by now, but who has the time?

My hair is a sort of subdued natural blonde, short, wavy, and choppy (choppy because in moments of panic looking in that bathroom mirror, I tend to chop chunks off it myself). Plus it seems to have a will of its own—it stands up in a kind of awful springy halo no matter what I do, and it's always untidy because when I'm frantic, which is most of the time, I have this habit of running my hands through it.

The rest of me? Let me think. Ah yes, I have a nose of the usual sort, with a bit of a bump in the middle from a whack with a tennis racket when I was thirteen that seems to have gotten bigger over the years and gives me an arrogant look that, I can assure you, is absolutely not justified. Oh, and I have kind of a smiley mouth that turns up at the corners even when I'm not really smiling, but it makes the patients feel better, so that's okay.

Let me tell you about my marriage to him-who-is-better-not-spoken-of. You'll gather from that, that my ex is not exactly Mr. Popularity around here. Actually, in my high school days, when I was considered fairly cute and a great dancer, I had quite a few boys after me, including "the football hero." I'm sighing as I say this because, as I tell my own daughter now, it gets you nowhere except maybe to the prom.

Anyhow, I was hanging out with this teenage football hero, and oh how I worshiped him. I would have kissed his sweaty feet when he pulled his boots off after the game had he wanted me to. And oddly enough, he was hot for me. *So* hot, we married right out of high school.

Then I went off to college, and so did he—me north, him south, though I gather he spent more time in poolrooms than in class, while I suddenly got this fixation on medicine. I had a goal, he had none. We lasted on and off until, when I was still in med school, I got pregnant. And then he just took off.

That was fourteen years ago. I have never seen him since, and he has never seen his daughter. I divorced him, and I've never taken a cent from him. Not, of course, that he *offered*. I struggled on through medical school, working and studying, and I raised Livvie by myself. And if you ask is there anything I'm proud of, the answer is yes. I'm proud of Livvie.

I have this picture of her in my mind, silhouetted against the bright sunlight: long skinny legs, big feet in clunky platform shoes, narrow hips, wide shoulders, long giraffe neck, and hair that looks as though it's been run over by a lawn mower, especially when it's tinted green with that spray stuff from the drugstore, which it sometimes is, though usually it's just bleached banana-blond.

Livvie is fourteen and into the latest in Outrageous, and you never know with her what you are going to get. Still, I figure this post-punk image is all a phase and that sometime soon she will grow out of it. I've drawn the line at body-piercing and tattoos, though. I mean, I couldn't sit opposite her at dinner knowing she had a *ring* sticking through her tongue or a rose embossed on her behind. My stomach churns at the thought, and as a doctor, my heart simply turns over at the risk.

The third member of our small family is my mother, Livvie's grandmother, Nonna. Of course, *nonna* means "grandmother" in Italian, which is what she is . . . an Italian grandmother. That's her profession. And she does it at full pressure.

Nonna has lived in the same small suburban town on Long Island for forty years, and it's where I grew up. Her shabby old house is a startling Mediterranean blue and stands out from the other gray suburban houses like a scrap of summer sky on a cloudy day. She had it painted this color because it reminded her of Bella Piacere, the village in Tuscany where she lived until her family emigrated to New York. She has never returned, and I doubt she even thinks about her homeland or "the old days" anymore, though she still keeps the photos in silver frames on her mahogany sideboard to remind her.

There's a picture of my immigrant Italian grandparents there, caught forever in blurred sepia, sitting on the stoop of their Bensonhurst apartment house.

There's also a photo of me and Livvie, taken at a Little

League game when Livvie was about seven and still just a simple little blond kid whose only dream was to hit a home run, and I was about thirty and not so simple anymore and my dream was still to meet Mr. Right. Life offered infinite possibilities back then. The home run. The right man. And you know what? It almost came true. And you know what else? I don't want to talk about that.

Then, of course, there's my favorite picture of Nonna, only she wasn't Nonna then. It was taken in the fifties, before she married, when her name was still Sophia Maria Lorenza Corsini. She was seventeen, tall and pretty, with flashing dark eyes and a mass of dark hair flowing to her tiny waist. In the photo, she's wearing a flowered dress with a sweetheart neckline and platform sandals with wedge heels. I can hardly believe this fashionable vision was my mom.

Now Nonna is sixty, a widow for twenty years, in the basic black of the Italian grandmother with sturdy shoes, a little white lace collar, and glasses perched on the end of her arrogant nose. She's usually to be found standing over the stove cooking up the big ritual Italian Sunday lunch, just the way she has for decades.

Nonna is tall, still with generous curves, but she swears that at her age no man would look at her twice. Unless he's after a good meal, that is, she'll add with a disparaging sniff. Hair pulled back into a neat bun, she still has those flashing dark eyes and a flashing temperament to match, and she keeps us in order with a hard stare or a cutting remark.

So that's who we are. The Jericho family. Oh, plus there's Sinbad, the fattest ginger cat you ever saw. Sinbad is enormous, but he eats so fastidiously, polishing his face with a well-licked paw between bites, you never notice how much he's really consumed. He's also close kin to a dog. He brings his ball—a beat-up Ping-Pong ball, much squashed and bitten—for me to throw. This cat plays catch like a wide receiver—he's up there with the football greats—and he has the neck to prove it.

Actually, he's Livvie's surrogate dog, the huge Newfoundland I promised her when I still believed in that future dream of a house in the country. Because there was a time, you know, not so long ago, when life could have been different . . . a time of "might have been." A time when that country house loomed as a bright possibility, filled with a normal, happy family unit: husband, wife, a few kids, dogs and cats. . . .

What am I thinking? I'm not supposed to go there. *He* isn't supposed to *be* there. I've trained myself never to talk about him, never to think of him. And yet there he is in my memory, larger than life and twice as handsome. Cash Drummond, the man who brought magic into my life. And changed it forever.

CHAPTER TWO

I don't quite know why, but what I'm remembering right now is the time we were in his car, the two of us, taking a quick vacation together. I was at the wheel and Cash was beside me, map reading. We were lost and I was annoyed. I said it was his fault and he laughed and said he was sorry and how about we stop and have lunch somewhere. And just like magic, which was the way it always seemed to happen when I was with Cash, we practically tripped over this sweet little country inn. We drove past, screeched to a halt, backed down the winding lane to check it out, and saw the sign RESTAURANT.

We piled out of the car, a little old red sports model (what else would Cash have had?), and walked hand in hand into a New England wonderland of dark-paneled walls and braided rugs and potpourri. There were antlers and wall sconces, throw pillows, flowered chintz and rickety side tables full of bric-a-brac, and a grizzled, sleepy Labrador who opened one eye to check us out and then went back to his snooze.

A kindly blue-haired lady behind the desk smiled at us over her bifocals. "Lunch?" she asked.

Cash squeezed my hand tightly. "Actually, we were wondering if you had a room."

He caught my surprised gasp, and so, I know, did the woman. "Of course," she said. "Let me show you."

I clutched Cash's hand as we headed up the stairs. "I thought we were lost and just coming here for lunch," I whispered.

He threw me a look over his shoulder, already two steps in front of me—as he somehow always was—and I felt myself melt. Did I mention that he was blond and handsome in that strong-jawed all-American, or should I say all-*Texan,* way? Sort of cowboy crossed with Malibu surfer? And I had seen that look before and knew what it meant. In fact, that's the way our relationship had started.

Actually, it started with a pickup in a Starbucks where I was sipping an illicit frappuccino (illicit because, though I know how much sugar there is in those things, I still can't resist). He gave me a smiling glance in passing, and our eyes locked. Then he said in an exaggerated Texas drawl, "Hi, how're y'doin', ma'am?" and I giggled because nobody had ever called me "ma'am" before.

"Actually, it's Doctor," I said primly, because I don't usually go around talking to complete strangers except at the hospital, of course, and then they're on a gurney, and the dialogue is hardly racy.

"How're you, Doc?" He hitched himself onto the stool next to me. I nodded okay, staring out the window, anything to stop looking at him, because they just didn't grow them like this in New York City. His long shaggy blond hair gleamed with lights my own did not possess, his tanned skin glowed with health, and his blue eyes were ten shades lighter than mine and looked surprisingly world-weary.

This guy is no hick from Hicksville, I warned myself. He knows where he's at, all right. All muscular six-four of him, with shoulders whose breadth owed nothing to the old suede shirt he was wearing. I sneaked a glance at his feet. Thank God he was not wearing cowboy boots; that would have been just too much.

"Come here often?" he said.

I glanced skeptically at him out of the corner of my eye and took another sip.

"Okay, then, how d'you like those frappuccinos?"

I stared out the window at a dog-walker with a tangle of leads and what looked to be about sixteen Chihuahuas.

"Just got in from Dallas," he drawled, as though I were even listening. "Don't know too many folks here in the Big Apple."

Oh, *puh-lease* . . . I rolled my eyes. Did he really think I was going to fall for that one? And then he started to laugh, a rich, rolling laugh, natural as spring water and just as refreshing. And I found myself laughing too.

"I'm Cash Drummond." He held out a sun-kissed hand dusted with tiny blond hairs, and so help me, I took it.

"Cash?" I couldn't believe it.

He lifted an amused eyebrow. "It could have been worse. I was called after my grandfather, Wilbur Cash."

I laughed then. "Your mother was a wise woman."

My frappuccino was almost gone, and I was due back at the hospital in ten minutes. "Gotta go," I said, hitching my oversized black tote onto my shoulder.

"That bag looks mighty heavy for a little lady like you," Cash Drummond drawled.

Now, this bag contained my *entire* life: my wallet, credit cards, driver's license, Social Security card, and hospital ID, plus a collection of pictures of Livvie from babyhood to the previous week (she'd turned nine that very October). There were my checkbook and the latest dismal bank statement; my mother's recipe for braised lamb shanks, which I had meant to give to my friend Patty; a clean pair of underwear, in case I had to work late and needed a shower and a change and not for any other reason you might have imagined; and a lipstick that was too pink for my pale autumnal face, plus a comb, rarely used.

"Let me help you," Cash said, reaching for this bag. And this is how moonstruck I suddenly was. *I just handed it to him. Me. A New Yorker.* I *trusted* him!

My eyes locked with his, and I could feel the sap rising in me, so to speak. "Where are you heading?" he said.

"All the way downtown," I replied, "to Bellevue."

"Then let me give you a lift." He slung my bag onto his shoulder and held the door open for me. "By the way," he added, "you didn't tell me your name."

"It's Gemma," I said, my eyes still locked with his as we stood in that drafty doorway at Starbucks. "Gemma Jericho."

And that was the way it started—with lust and love and romance, leading up to the minivacation I was telling you about, actually no more than a long weekend, when we got lost and stumbled across that old inn.

The attic room the blue-haired lady showed us had a steeply sloped roof, a dormer window with a flowered curtain, and a view onto a spring meadow dotted with sleepy-looking horses. The bed was a double with a Victorian iron frame painted white, a multihued patchwork quilt, and half a dozen rag dolls propped against banks of pillows.

We bent our heads and leaned on the window ledge looking out at that meadow for a full thirty seconds before the brass rings of the flowered curtains rattled on their metal pole, the six Raggedy Anns hit the floor, and we were wallowing in that feather bed the way only true lovers do. Hot and ready for each other the way we always were. Then.

I pushed away that forbidden past and came back to the present with a thud. I had told myself I was never going to think about Cash Drummond, never talk about him; but every now and then he just popped into my head, unbidden. I'd swear I'd put it all—*him*, I mean—behind me. I had built this blockade against him, against any feeling. But sometimes I thought he would never let me go.

The dream was over. All that remained was a secret guilt, to be hidden forever, even from myself, because I know I can never face the truth. It's over, that's all there is to it. And now I am a dedicated ER physician, a single mom. And a woman with ice around my heart that no man will ever be allowed to melt.

CHAPTER THREE

In my job, I'm sort of like the captain of the ship—everyone looks to me to lead them. Tonight, as usual, the ER phones are ringing off the hook, my pager is beeping, and the wounded, moaning and wailing, are lined up on hard gray plastic chairs and gurneys. My aim is to get them out of here, on their feet, walking, talking, living.

It's a stormy night and the rain is bouncing down hard as rivets. We all know what that means: more road accidents. And right now I have the sad duty of "calling it" on the first one: a young male victim of a motorcycle accident whose eyes have closed for the final time.

My team had worked on him for almost an hour. We had given it our all, and now I just stood there, defeated, amid the discarded plastic tubes, the drips, the bloody debris of our battle for his life. I felt myself spiraling emotionally downward as I looked at him: so young, so cute with his spiked blond hair. He had everything to live for . . . he must have a mother . . . a lover . . .

I told myself I was cool, I was a physician, I could handle this . . . then suddenly I turned and bolted down the long tiled corridor, through the automatic glass doors, out into the night. The rain bounced down, turning the roads into flowing streams. I was shivering, gasping what passed for fresh air in Manhattan, pacing to the place where the hospital lights didn't reach, to the edge of darkness, and back again. Pacing, thinking. Telling myself *not* to think.

Eventually my heart quit doing a nervous salsa and slunk back into neutral. And as if on cue, my pager beeped and I was running back inside, back to the trauma room.

"You okay?" The charge nurse glanced anxiously at me.

"Sure, I'm okay. I just can't stand the sight of blood, that's all," I said, and we both laughed. It was a way of coping, the laughter. Except now I was the one who had to tell his family. It's the worst job of all.

So. I had been on duty for ten hours already. It had been a long night, and it wasn't over yet. My pager beeped again. This time it was Livvie, who had a couple of friends sleeping over. I'm always worried knowing she's at home without me. Right now our Filipina housekeeper was in charge. She's not much older than Livvie, and she's surely not the world's greatest cleaner, but she is reliable and responsible and she laughs a lot and she keeps an eagle eye on my daughter, so what do I care about a few dust bunnies under the beds?

I called Livvie back, flinching as my eardrums were assaulted by hip-hop at full volume with heavy bass.

"Livvie, turn the sound down," I yelled over the phone. "What are you girls up to?" I was anxiously eyeing a passing gurney bringing in a shooting victim, a female, screaming her lungs out, cursing, thrashing in pain . . . I was already running.

"Mom, I can't go to Nonna's tomorrow," Livvie yelled over the bass boom. "I have a date."

"What *date*? You know you're not allowed out on dates alone. Besides, we *always* go to Nonna's on Sunday."

Livvie's voice was one big groan as she gave me her *omigodmom* reply, but I held my ground, said a quick good-bye and love you, and raced after that gurney. It was just another chaotic Saturday night at Bellevue.

An hour later, the ER was suddenly quiet. The stream of broken people had stopped for a minute. A glance at the wall clock told me it was already tomorrow and that the ritual Italian Sunday lunch was only hours away. Sleep-deprived or not, dates or not, we would go. We always did.

I rested my aching back against the shabby industrial-green wall and took a sip of the boiling brown liquid we all pretended was coffee. Fatigue washed over me like a high tide, and I closed my eyes, hoping for at least a minor caffeine rush.

"Hi there, doll, how're y'doin'?" someone said. I knew without looking it was Patty Sullivan, my best friend and colleague. I turned and smiled at her.

She was leaning next to me, one foot lifted like a resting horse taking the weight off. Patty is redheaded, Irish, and plumply pretty with pink cheeks and greenish eyes and ginger lashes that always remind me of Sinbad, though of course I would never tell her that. We've known each other for fifteen years, been through emergency room training together, through life, loves, deaths, divorces, and, in Patty's case, remarriage.

"Haggard," I said to Patty. "That's how I'm doing. Or at least, it's the way I look."

"Haggard?"

"As in *hag*."

Patty grinned. "After a Saturday night here, you're entitled."

"What d'you think, Patty?" I asked, still worried about Livvie. "Am I in the wrong business? Maybe I should get out of here, take up a rural practice somewhere, get Livvie out of the city, make a better life for us."

But before Patty could reply, I was paged, and I was off at a run again.

"You're like Pavlov's dog," Patty yelled after me. "They call—you run. They hurt—you fix 'em. You can't get away from it."

You know what? She's right. I was just dreaming.

CHAPTER FOUR

I hurried out of the hospital's automatic doors at 5 A.M., yawning as I sat in the subway train, gazing blankly at the early morning darkness outside the window, oblivious to my fellow passengers. It wasn't just the fatigue that was getting to me, it was the terrible emotional letdown that everyone who works in this job gets. One minute you're up, working like that fine-honed speed machine I told you about; the next you're crashing into a black void of what might have been, what could have been, what *was*. And always with that eternal question ringing in your brain: Why? *Why,* oh *why,* did these terrible things happen to people?

I wondered whether I should think seriously about that country practice, get myself and Livvie out of this urban rat race we have come to believe is normal. But the truth is I know I can never do that. I am who I am. *This* is my life. And when I think of moving my street-smart pop-diva daughter to a land of meadows and streams—well, forget about it.

"Home" is a small apartment in one of those flat-fronted, faceless stone buildings, with a doorman, Carlos, who is my saving grace and a friend to all.

He was on the early shift this week and called a cheerful "Hi, Doc, how're you this fine morning?" as he held the door for me.

"You mean it's morning?" I gave him a grin as I walked by, and he laughed at my familiar quip. Well, shoot, a girl couldn't be expected to be original and witty at this ungodly hour, could she?

In the elevator I turned my back to the mirror; looking at myself would have been just too depressing. My cream-painted door on the tenth floor was exactly the same as the six others. I turned the key, stepped inside, closed the door behind me, and threw on the dead bolt.

I leaned against my urban barricade for a moment, listening to the soft dawn silence of my sleeping household, those tenuous peaceful moments when time seems suspended. Then I took a step forward, and of course I tripped over Sinbad, who leaped into the air with a screech that could wake the entire building.

"Jeez, Sinbad, I'm sorry." I stroked his thick ginger fur, though I knew it was really his ruffled feelings I was soothing. He gave me a reproachful green-eyed glare, then hunkered down again, huge paws tucked under.

I peeked in at Livvie. She was sprawled across the bed, wearing an old 'N Sync T-shirt. Her face was squashed into the pillow, but I could see the still-baby curve of her cheek and the curl of her lashes, her soft mouth. I wondered tenderly why it was that no matter how grown-up they seem when they are awake, when they are sleeping our children always look about three years old.

I checked the two lumps tucked into the other bed, who were Livvie's sleepover friends, picked up an empty pizza box, and left the door open a crack so that Sinbad could reclaim his place next to Livvie. Then I walked on down the hall to the kitchen that's like a ship's galley, long and narrow with a window at the far end through which the gray dawn light was rapidly becoming a lighter gray. I checked the refrigerator but was too tired to decide whether I was hungry or not.

Five minutes later, showered, hair still damp, snug in my Victoria's Secret flannel pajamas, my head was on the pillow and I was tumbling over that black abyss into sleep. Only to dream of the young motorbike victim, with his spiky blond hair and his smooth unlined face, who'd had a girlfriend somewhere and all his life in front of him.

I grieved for him as I slept.

CHAPTER FIVE

NONNA

Nonna Jericho was busy cooking that big ritual Sunday lunch. It was what she did best and the preparations kept her busy all week. Right now, though, she wasn't thinking so much about her tomato sauce. She was worrying about Gemma.

She thought Gemma worked too hard, that the hours were too long, that she was under too much stress. Gemma used to be such a joyous, bubbly, flirty girl, full of energy and joie de vivre. There had been many prettier girls in high school, but there was just something about her; all the boys had been after her, and of course she had chosen, and married, the wrong one.

Even that bad experience hadn't gotten Gemma down, though. That had come much later, on a cold winter night three years ago, to be exact. But Gemma never talked about that. Sometimes Nonna wished she would, but Gemma just kept it locked away inside her. Yet what happened that night had taken away the laughing, vital young woman and left only the responsible, dedicated emergency room doctor.

Nonna gave the tomato sauce a thoughtful stir, pushing

back a strand of dark hair and bending her face over the pan to catch the aromas of garlic and oregano, as well as of the half bottle of Chianti she had tipped into it to give it some guts. It smelled good. And so it should, it had been brewing for two days. Ten more minutes and she would turn off the heat and let it stand, allowing the flavors to blend and soften.

She straightened up and, quite suddenly, the room was spinning around her. She clutched the wooden kitchen chair, then sank into it, her head in her hands, waiting for the faintness to pass.

This had happened several times in the past few weeks and the doctor had told her she should rest. He had also told her she had a congenital mitral valve condition and that her heart was weak. This was not Dr. Gemma talking, of course. This was her own doctor, the one she hadn't told Gemma about. Anyway, she didn't know whether to believe him or not. *Congenital* meant she'd had this condition since she was born—right? So why hadn't she had any symptoms before?

It happens, the doctor had told her, when you get to your age. *Mamma mia,* she was sixty and he was talking like she was an antique! Anyhow, she certainly was not taking to her bed and becoming an invalid. She would take daily medication and continue as though nothing was any different. And she wasn't telling anybody about it, especially not Gemma. Life would go on, day by day, as it always had. Until one day it didn't.

The blue airmail envelope was on the table in front of her. She ran her finger slowly over the familiar postmark, the foreign stamp, the carefully written address. Then she took out The Letter, pushed her glasses up on her nose, and began to read it. One more time.

CHAPTER SIX

GEMMA

The smell of garlicky roasting meats wafted down Nonna's street as we got out of the car. Livvie sniffed the air eagerly, like a hound at the hunt. She reached into the backseat to get Sinbad, who always came with us on his lavender, rhinestone-studded leash—Livvie's choice, not mine, and certainly not, I'm sure, big butch Sinbad's.

She tugged her miniskirt down to a more acceptable level before she went in to see her grandmother, and of course she also tucked that eternal cell phone into her jacket pocket, still hoping, I knew, for a call from the "dream date," who might turn out to be only a dream. Then, with Sinbad under her arm, she ran up the steps to Grandma's house.

The rain clouds had cleared, and a cold sun was peeking through. I noticed a black Jeep Cherokee parked across the road. My friend Patty and her husband, Jeff, had beaten us to it. My spirits lifted. I always loved to see them, and I also loved these Sundays "at home."

Livvie bounced through the kitchen door—nobody ever used the front door at Nonna's; the kitchen was where the action was. Then she was enfolded in Nonna's bosomy hug and kisses were showered on her face.

"*Carina,*" Nonna said, smiling, and Livvie beamed back; her faux grown-up defenses were down, and she was just a little kid again. "I missed you this week, Nonna," she murmured, still hugging.

"And I missed you, *ragazza.*"

This was their usual preliminary. Later, the sparks would fly, as they always did when the two of them met. One young, one old, both opinionated and stubborn—what else could it be?

I was next in line for the hug, then Nonna pushed me back and took a good long look at me. This was what she always did and I knew exactly what was coming.

"You look tired." She pronounced her usual verdict, and I replied, as I always did, "Yes, Mom, I am tired, I've had about four hours' sleep." Then I waited for the inevitable lecture on how I should quit the trauma ward and think more about myself and about Livvie, get my hair done, and buy some new clothes. But today, surprisingly, it did not come.

Patty was putting plates and silverware on the table, and Jeff was leaning against the sink, sipping Chianti, watching. I went over and gave them both a kiss. Then, as always, I was drawn like a magnet to the stove. I lifted pot lids, checking with my nose on what they contained, then I tore off a crust of hard Italian bread, dunked it in the tomato sauce, and tasted it. Forget gourmet restaurants, this was my idea of gastronomic heaven.

Steam clouded my glasses and I took them off and wiped them on a towel, glancing nearsightedly around. I caught Patty in the act of checking me out. She said, "You don't look like a hag to me, honey," and we laughed remembering last night, but I could tell from her eyes that she thought I looked beat.

Jeff poured the Chianti, his smoothly shaven cheeks already pink from the heat of the kitchen, and Nonna flung open the window, to let out the steam, she said, but Patty said she'd bet it was so her neighbors would get an envious whiff of that roast and know that Sophia Jericho had done it again.

Watching them together, I knew Jeff was Patty's soul mate. No doubt about it. They even looked alike, both with red hair, though his was paler than Patty's, and with ginger lashes like Sinbad's, who, by the way, had established a beachhead close to the wooden cutting board where the roast leg of lamb drizzled succulent juices into the grooves.

Jeff is a UPS driver and that's how Patty met him, on his regular daily stop delivering parcels to the hospital. She'd told me he was tall and hunky in his brown shorts and crisp shirt, and it was immediate head-over-heels time. They were still holding hands now, seven years later, and even as I watched, Jeff dropped a kiss on Patty's upturned face.

I turned away, sighing enviously. "What can I do to help, Mom?"

"First thing is you can remove that cat from my table." Nonna glared at Sinbad, who stared back unfazed. He yowled piteously, though, when I picked him up and dumped him on the floor.

"And Patty, you two stop smooching," Nonna added. "Jeff, I need you to lift this pot."

"Sì, signora." Jeff grinned, and Patty smoothed down her skirt like a guilty teenager caught making out.

Livvie came in from the porch, letting the screen door slam behind her. *"Madonnina mia!"* Nonna snapped. "All these years, Olivia, and you still haven't learned to close a screen door properly?"

"Sorry, Nonna." Livvie slumped into a chair and hauled Sinbad onto her lap. "Poor kitty, did Nonna shout at you then?" she asked in a loud whisper, giggling as her grandmother snorted.

I carved the lamb while Jeff and Nonna and Patty served up the ravioli in that famous sauce *and* the *vitello tonnato and* the baked eggplant with mozzarella *and* the little potatoes roasted with fresh rosemary *and* the salad *and* that crusty bread I loved so much. More wine was poured and Cokes were popped open. Conversation rattled around, about the usual things—work, food, wine, school, boy bands, neighbors—while Livvie surreptitiously fed Sinbad under the table.

Then the *torta della nonna*, the "grandmother's cake" with the special chocolate filling, which I think Livvie still believed was a cake only *her* Nonna made, was placed on the table, on the same gaudy red-and-green-flowered plate we had used for at least thirty years. Ice cream was fetched from the freezer, the coffee set to brew, and the *vinsanto* poured.

Everything was exactly the same as it always was. You could print out a scenario of our Sundays at Nonna's and use it every week of the year. Nothing ever changed. At least, not until now.

"Allora, bambini," Nonna said.

I glanced suspiciously at her. She only ever called us *bambini* when she was up to something.

"I have a surprise for you." She pulled a crumpled pale-blue airmail envelope from her apron pocket and held it up for us to see. "A letter," she said, as though we hadn't already guessed. "From Bella Piacere," she added, smiling proudly.

Livvie and I glanced at each other, brows raised. Bella Piacere was Nonna's old village. We didn't even know that she knew anyone there anymore.

"Attenzione!" She adjusted her glasses and looked sternly over the tops to make sure she had our attention. Then slowly and carefully she unfolded The Letter and began to read.

"Signora, sono Don Vincenzo Arrici, Parroco della Chiesa di Santa Caterina nel vostro Paese e mi onoro di scrivervi queste notizie—"

"Mom," I said, "we don't speak Italian." She threw me an irritated glare.

"Huh," she said. "Maybe I should have married an Italian after all. Then you would have spoken. And Livvie, please remove that cat from the table."

Livvie grabbed Sinbad. "Oh, go *on*, Nonna," she said.

" 'I am Don Vincenzo Arrici, priest of the parish of Santa Catarina in your home village,' " Nonna read. *" 'It has taken several years for us to find you, signora Sophia, and I am the one chosen to have the honor of telling you the good news about your inheritance. You have been left some property by an old family acquaintance. It is in your interest, signora Sophia, to come to Bella Piacere immediately and collect what is rightfully yours. Before it is too late.' "*

We looked at each other, amazed. Then Livvie said, "Does that mean you're going to be rich?"

Nonna smiled back at her. "Possibly," she said, and my heart sank, because somehow I knew she thought this was true.

Nonna refolded The Letter carefully, but I could tell from its crumpled state she had read it many times. She pushed up her glasses again and looked at us.

"I came to New York when I was thirteen years old," she said. "Before that, I had never left Bella Piacere. I had never seen Florence, let alone Rome or Venice. *Allora*. Now I am going home. I'm going to Italy to collect my inheritance. I intend to see Bella Piacere one last time. Before I die."

We stared at her, stunned into silence, as she put The Letter safely back in its envelope. And then she threw out the second bombshell. "And you, Gemma and Livvie, are coming with me."

Was she *crazy*! She *knew* I had a demanding job. She *knew* I needed that job. I had responsibilities. I didn't even have time to go to the movies, let alone go to Italy!

"You know we can't do that, Mom," I said. "And I don't think you should go either. You don't even know anyone in Bella Piacere anymore. Anyhow, this has to be some kind of hoax."

"A priest would not lie," she said firmly.

"Why not just call this Don Vincenzo and ask him exactly what the property is?" Patty said.

Nonna clutched The Letter to her heart as though she had been stabbed. "You want to take all the joy out of my surprise?"

"Oh, sorry . . . No, of course not," Patty said, bewildered.

Nonna looked me firmly in the eye again. *"We are going,"* she said.

"But I *can't* go," Livvie cried. "Besides, I don't *want* to go to Italy with all those boring foreigners. Anyhow, I've got stuff to do, and I've got school . . . and, like, there's this really cute guy I might be dating—"

"We will go in your summer break." Nonna cut her off in the middle of her protest. "And besides, it will be educational."

Livvie's pretty Italian-brown eyes rolled up in her head.

"A trip to Italy sounds pretty good to me." Jeff tried to arbitrate. "Nonna would get to see her old home and find out what her property is, and Gemma, you and Livvie will get to know your roots. Besides," he added, looking at me, "you could use a break."

"Remember me?" I said. "The single mom? I have to make a living."

"You haven't taken a holiday in three years," Patty put in. "You must have quite a few weeks' vacation time stored up by now."

I glared at her. She was undermining my position. Then I said to Nonna, "The only sensible thing to do is to give this Don Vincenzo a call and find out what he's talking about."

Nonna did not look at me. She didn't look at any of us. She just got up and began removing the coffee cups from the table. She paced silently to the sink with them. Then she paced silently back again. Our eyes were fixed anxiously on her as she silently cleared the table.

She sank back into her chair and stared reproachfully at me. She took off her glasses, and I caught the glitter of a tear. "So," she said wearily. "So, this is how *little* my family thinks of me. *My family. The only family I have left in the world.*" Her voice dropped a tone, and she added dolefully, "Except for maybe a few cousins still in my old village of Bella Piacere, where I now have property."

"M-o-m." I could hear an echo of Livvie's exasperated whine in my own voice. But I was still absolutely firm about this. "I have responsibilities. I can't just drop everything and go on some crazy wild-goose chase. It's impossible. We're not going to Italy. And that's that."

CHAPTER SEVEN

So, of course, here we are in Rome. We are in a taxi on our way from the airport known as Fiumicino, with a driver who has a death wish, weaving through a tangle of traffic that beats Manhattan's and is twice as noisy. Leaning on the horn seems to be a way of life here, and driving is a macho one-upmanship contest that has Livvie on the edge of her seat, Nonna with her eyes closed and probably praying, and me clinging to the strap as we swerve around roundabouts and dart down narrow side streets, missing other vehicles by a whisker.

I'm beat, not only from the long journey but from the stress of having to rearrange my carefully planned life and take four weeks of my accumulated vacation days to accommodate this trip. And the only reason I am here is not because of this foolish "inheritance," which I believe can only amount to a couple of cows in some tumble-down barn, but because I got the feeling that for some reason Nonna really wanted to visit Bella Piacere. She wanted to go home again.

It is dusk, and Rome's lights are switching on in a zillion sparkles, bathing the city in a golden glow, illuminating domes and ancient monuments, ruins and piazzas, and twinkling in trees full of very noisy starlings. Could that really be the Colosseum, trapped by traffic and somehow looking smaller than it did in *Gladiator,* when hunky Russell Crowe braved tigers and soldiers as well as that wicked emperor, cheered on by a crowd of thousands? I turn my head to look as we whiz by. This is almost reason enough to come to Rome, though I guess I'm unlikely to find Russell Crowe among the ruins.

The great dome of Saint Peter's, which no doubt we would visit tomorrow, glows over the city like a beacon, and the famous Spanish Steps are jammed with tourists spilling into the piazza below, milling around as though waiting for something to happen. I think somebody should tell them that nothing will happen, but then that's just me talking, the mean-spirited, reluctant tourist.

Not for the first time, I'm regretting my weakness in saying yes to this trip. I was so determined not to come. All I want is to be back in New York, back at Bellevue, back doing what I did best. Safe behind that barricade I built for myself.

The taxi jerked to a stop and we heaved a collective sigh of relief. *"Buona sera, signore."* A top-hatted doorman threw open the door. We stumbled wearily out and were immediately surrounded by a crew of liveried porters and bellboys. They had our battered duffel bags and Nonna's ancient Samsonite, the one she has had for at least thirty years, loaded onto a gilded cart in a flash.

I stared, stunned, at the imposing facade of the Hassler Hotel, and then accusingly at my mother. She avoided my eyes, but she knew darn well what I was thinking—*that this place must cost a fortune*. And I was thinking it even harder in the ornate marble lobby, surrounded by old-master paintings and crystal chandeliers and huge displays of fresh flowers. I was also thinking of my poor AmEx card, and praying.

I collapsed into a gold brocade sofa, fumbling in my purse, trying to work out the necessary tips in lire, wondering why Italian money had to have so many zeros—even a taxi ride cost millions here. Livvie flopped down next to me, muttering that the place was like a museum, attempting futilely to dial friends in New York on her cell phone, quite oblivious to the fact that people were staring at her. I didn't blame them: her red crocheted shawl was more holes than wool, her cropped hair was banana-blond tipped with lime, and her fingernails were the red of dried blood. She could have been an extra in *Nosferatu.*

Meanwhile, Nonna headed for the reception desk and announced our arrival to the youthful dark-haired Adonis in charge. She leaned on the counter, friendly, smiling at him, as she told him who we were and that she would like an upgrade.

My jaw dropped. I didn't even know she *knew* about upgrades. I mean, Nonna hasn't been farther than Manhattan in twenty years, and that only for a Macy's sale.

"I was born in Italy," she said to the desk clerk, "and you know what? I have never seen Rome. Imagine! Not only that, I've inherited property in Bella Piacere," she added, as though he could possibly know the tiny village in Tuscany.

But the desk clerk was leaning on the counter, hands clasped in front of him, beaming at her as though he had all the time in the world. "Congratulations, *signora* Jericho," he said finally. "This will be a memorable visit. You will enjoy your stay here, *signora.* And of course, we have put you in one of our two-bedroom deluxe suites. It is already arranged."

"Bene, bene, e grazie, signore Antonio."

She patted his hand as though he were her own son, and I held my breath, praying she wouldn't kiss him, but no, she turned, all smiles, as the bellman escorted us to the elevator and we were wafted upward. We trailed down a plush-carpeted corridor and waited while he flung open a pair of tall double doors. Then we stepped into an earthly paradise of gold and rose-pink luxury.

We stood like country bumpkins, staring at everything, while the bellman rushed around switching on lamps, opening curtains, pointing out the view, the two marble bathrooms, the minibar, explaining how things worked. Finally I pressed what I hoped was a hefty tip into his hand and said *grazie,* and he smiled, gave us a little salute, and departed.

I turned and looked accusingly at Nonna. "Do you have any idea what this must be costing?"

She straightened a silk cushion, avoiding my eyes. "Of course I know. I booked the hotel, didn't I? And let me tell you, this is a bargain."

"Yeah," I said dispiritedly, "the Heiress got us an upgrade."

She gave me a nonchalant shrug. "Don't worry," she said. "I have decided to sell my new property. And I'm going to spend the money now, instead of leaving it to you in my will. So enjoy it, Gemma. Just enjoy."

And with that she strode into her elegantly silk-curtained bedroom, leaving me with my mouth open.

Oh my God, I thought, panicked. At best the inheritance is going to be a barren plot of land with a couple of ancient olive trees and a few clucking hens. And now she thinks she can sell it for *real* money. And what's more, she's *spending* that money now.

I could hear her murmuring appreciatively in Italian as she discovered the delights of her marble-and-gold bathroom, the rose-shaded bedside lamps, the waffle-cotton robe and matching little slippers, and the white linen mat placed precisely next to the bed so that she need not sully her bare Heiress feet on the beautiful carpet.

And meanwhile, I was wondering how I could double up on my hospital hours when I got back. Somebody was going to have to pay for all this.

CHAPTER EIGHT

I did not want to go to dinner in the Hassler's smart rooftop restaurant. It was late, and I was tired and sulky as I lingered in the shower, wondering how I could get out of it. But Nonna was lively as a cricket and ready for anything—and dinner was what she wanted, whether we were dropping from jet lag or not.

I sighed wearily as I washed my hair and fluffed it dry with my hands. The little black dress I'd bought in a swift half-hour foray into Banana Republic was creased from being packed in a hurry, but it was too late to do anything about it. I dragged it over my head, powdered my nose, gave a token flick of mascara, and applied the same innocuous lipstick I'd been wearing for years.

"Come on, Gemma, hurry up." Nonna's voice had an excited lilt to it. I put on my glasses, took one last disconsolate look in the full-length mirror, and went reluctantly to join them.

The elegant rooftop restaurant overlooked Rome, sparkling below like a New Year's fireworks display. Alabaster urns brimmed with flowers, a bartender in a white jacket jiggled martinis in a silver shaker, and candlelight flickered on crisp table linens and gleaming crystal glasses. A smart maître d' eyed us from behind a polished

wooden lectern. He didn't actually do it, but I could almost feel him raise his eyebrows as he looked at Livvie.
As usual, she was as out of place as a tropical fish in a
pond of elegant swans.

Nonna said, *"Buona sera,"* and told him who we were
and that we had a reservation. This time the maître d's
eyebrows really did rise, and like the young Adonis at the
desk, he beamed at her. "Of course. You are the lady who
has inherited property in Bella Piacere. Congratulations,
signora. I hope you will enjoy your stay in Rome, and our
wonderful restaurant." Then he picked up a sheaf of
menus, said, "This way, *signore,* please," and led us to a
prime table near the windows.

We sank into striped silk chairs, and without missing a
beat Nonna ordered Bellinis for the two of us and a Coke
for Livvie. Then she opened her menu and began to study
it with a pleased little smile. *"E allora,"* she said happily.
"First a little antipasto, don't you think? But no, no,
maybe not. Perhaps some soup, then something delicate,
very light, since we have been traveling."

I stared wonderingly at her. She was to the manner
born. All these years and I never knew my mother was really a rich woman in disguise. Meanwhile, Livvie
slumped tiredly in her chair, still trying unsuccessfully to
reach New York on her cell phone, until Nonna snatched
it away, informed her once again that it was impossible to
get New York on a cell phone, and told her to remember
where she was and to behave like the lady she was
brought up to be.

Livvie glared huffily out the window, and I took a gulp
of that Bellini. *What am I doing here?* I asked myself one
more time. *All I want is to go to bed, or even better—go
home. This is madness.* I took a second gulp of the cham-

pagne and peach juice, letting the flavors prickle my tongue. I had to admit it was delicious. Actually, I thought I could get very used to it. Fatigue filled my eyes with a kind of fog, but I sat up and took notice when the Italian movie star made an entrance. And what an entrance!

He was in his forties, I'd guess: dark hair brushed smoothly back and silvering at the temples, tall and rugged, elegant in black tie, and *very* attractive. He was holding the hand of a little girl, aged perhaps eleven: black velvet dress, long blond hair, velvet headband. *She* was a princess. And *he* was something else.

I felt sure my mouth had dropped open as I watched them walk to a nearby table. They were so remote from the reality of my own life it was like watching an Italian movie, and *this* was definitely a Fellini moment. He was Richard Gere, and any minute Marcello Mastroianni would make an entrance with Sophia Loren or maybe Catherine Deneuve on his arm.

"That kid's a geek." Livvie's lip curled contemptuously as she watched them. "Like, where did she get that dress? And a *velvet headband*!"

"That is a very well brought up child," Nonna said.

"Oh, and I'm not, I suppose?" Livvie glared at her grandmother.

"Of course you are, but *her* mother has better taste."

I drained my Bellini and summoned the waiter for a second one. I was beginning to feel maybe I needed it. I wondered if Bellinis would become a fixture in my life. *Maybe in Italy, but not in your real life at Bellevue,* a little voice in my head reminded me as I took another sip of the cold, sparkling drink. *Too true*, I thought, with a tinge of something that felt almost like regret.

I took off my glasses and let my fuzzy myopic gaze

rest on the movie star and his daughter. He was studying the menu, nodding gravely as she made her choices, treating her the way he would a grown-up. And the little girl sat up straight, elbows off the table, attentive, polite, and well behaved. Where did he find a child like that? I wondered. Not in my neck of the woods, that was for sure.

"Where do you suppose his wife is?" Nonna said. "My guess is that she's probably in the hospital giving birth to his second child, and that's why he's here alone with his daughter."

I contemplated this version of a perfect little dream family, forgetting for a moment about Bellevue and the high-tension life-or-death scenes that made up my own daily life.

"And he," Nonna added with an admiring sigh, "is a true Italian gentleman. The kind they don't make anywhere else in the world. And she is such a little lady. Just look, Livvie, at her beautiful long hair."

Livvie's lip curled again. "That's not a kid, it's a Barbie," she said.

I took my daughter's hand with its bitten blood-colored nails and kissed it, just to show love and support. Livvie had good manners when called for, but she would never wear velvet and act like a princess, whatever Nonna said.

By now we had finished our second Bellinis and the waiter had become Nonna's new best friend. He was pouring a white wine he had recommended. "A simple Pinot Grigio from the Veneto, *signora*," he said to her. "It will be *perfetto* with the fish, very light."

I tasted the wine, nibbled on the delicious bread, sipped the tomato soup with fresh basil that was my first taste of real Italian food and which was like manna from the gods, but then I could get no further. Only Nonna managed to finish the fish. Jet lag and sheer bone-aching weariness took over. I signaled the waiter for the check. When it came I didn't even bother to read it, I just signed it. Hey, what did it matter? Nonna's inheritance was going to pay for this, right?

I checked the Italian movie star's table. He was on his feet and had his tired daughter by the hand. On their way out, they passed by our table. For a moment, his eyes met mine. I was suddenly aware that I had no lipstick left and that my little black dress, which no doubt had cost a fraction of his daughter's black velvet, was severely creased. Yet somehow, in that brief instant, he managed to make me feel that I was the only woman in the room. Then he nodded, said a brief, polite *"Buona sera,"* and they were gone.

I felt that hot blush rushing up from my neck to my cheeks, the way it used to when I was the teenage Dancing Queen and the best-looking guy in the room had asked me to dance. I hid my blush behind my table napkin and heard Nonna say, "I just wonder *who* he is."

She satisfied her curiosity on our way out by asking the headwaiter, and was told that he was an artist.

"Of course," Nonna said triumphantly, as though she had known it all along. "Another Michelangelo."

"But no, *signora,* his name is Ben Raphael," the headwaiter said. "And he's American."

I laughed, thinking, *So much for the Italian movie star.* This Michelangelo was probably from Long Island.

CHAPTER NINE

It was early, but due to jet lag and the time difference we were up and about, strolling lethargically down the Via di Minerva toward the Pantheon in search of culture, which was what Nonna wanted, and breakfast, which was what Livvie wanted. Personally, I would have preferred a few more hours in bed, but Nonna had said where did I think I was? New York? We were in Rome for one day: there were sights to see, monuments to visit, and shopping to be done. There was definitely no time to be wasted. Which was a pity because I was suddenly feeling like wasting some time—something that hadn't happened to me in years. Maybe Rome was getting to me after all.

We were walking down a narrow side street when I was stopped in my tracks by a sudden vision. The sun was bouncing off an ancient wall, a heap of crumbling stones, turning them to gold. A little plaque informed me that this was what remained of a temple built by Marcus Agrippa in something B.C. I clutched Livvie's hand tightly. Long-ago history lessons flooded my brain.

"Wow, Mom. Oh, wow," Livvie said, impressed. "Do you, like, *believe* these Romans? They're just walking by as though it's just, like, y'know, *normal*!"

We wandered into the Piazza della Rotonda, another of

those breathtaking cobblestoned piazzas Rome seems to
have by the hundred, lined with cafés on three sides and
with the ancient domed Pantheon on the fourth. By now I
could smell coffee, and we followed the scent to its
source, the Caffè d'Oro.

Let me tell you, those Italians surely know how to
make a cup of coffee. At the d'Oro they grind their own
beans, luring a girl with the tempting aroma and also with
the smell of freshly baked sticky-buns filled with custard
and crusted with sugar. Plus there's the extra added attraction of a couple of dozen handsome, tanned, smart-
suited Italian businessmen standing at the counter,
knocking back an espresso on the way to the office. I sat
up and took notice because, as you know, the only men I
get to see are those in green scrubs or lying naked and
comatose on a gurney.

"Forget decaf," I said, recklessly ordering a plate of
the sticky sugar buns and a double espresso with cream
on the side, which together probably added up to more
calories than I ate in an entire day in New York. I enjoyed
this like nothing I could recall in recent memory, along
with the very nice view, human as well as antique.

Nonna approved of my order. "Put a bit of flesh on
your skinny bones," she said. "See how feminine the Roman women are?"

Nonna was right. The women were chic, accessorized
to the hilt, not a hair out of place as they strode through
the bustling streets in their fashionably brief silk dresses
and towering heels. I had thought sneakers were more
practical for maneuvering Rome's slippery cobblestones,
but these women didn't even seem to notice. Years of experience, I guess. A tall, elegant woman in stilettos went
running by; a particular high-stepping kind of run, pick-

ing up each foot like a deer so her four-inch heels wouldn't get stuck between those lethal cobbles. I said it must be a trick Roman women learned as girls, and Livvie said admiringly that she looked like a gazelle about to leap a fence and that perhaps she ought to get some stilettos too and try it, and we laughed and told her to forget about it.

I just sat back and went with the flow, sipping my espresso, contemplating the Roman scene, past and present, from the café terrace. I looked at my little family, at the bustling, bountiful, sunlit piazza. And at that moment I was suddenly, inexplicably, for the first time in years, completely happy.

Seven hours later, I stumbled alone back up the Spanish Steps, laden down with bags and packages. We had seen the Pantheon, where on the steps outside, Livvie had encountered a tiny old crone. She had looked like something out of a Hans Christian Andersen fairy story, shrouded in black and bent as a pretzel, tottering along with a stick. With tears of pity in her eyes, and before we could stop her, Livvie had taken her money from the little purse attached to her belt and given it to the old crone. It was her savings, her birthday and Christmas money, which she had meant to use to buy a pair of Italian boots. And the "old crone" had scampered off like a triathlete as soon as she grasped the dollars.

"How could a granddaughter of mine, a street-smart New Yorker, not know that that was a Gypsy boy in disguise?" Nonna demanded. And Livvie, who still had tears in her eyes from sympathy for the old crone, cried more tears because she had been duped, and besides now she had no money.

So to cheer her up, we took her for ice cream to the famous Caffè Giolitti, which believe me is no Baskin-Robbins. This is a large, high-ceilinged belle epoque structure, with fluted marble columns and crystal chandeliers and waiters in smart white jackets with brass buttons and epaulettes. Nonna had a banana split and Livvie an Eiffel Tower with "the works," and I recklessly ordered a *tartufo,* a chocolate dome almost as exquisite as that of the Pantheon, topped with a fluffy cloud of whipped cream.

The thin chocolate crust crackled under my spoon, like black ice on a Manhattan winter day, as I sought the tiny nuggets of chocolate hidden in the rich ice cream depths. I was in heaven. It was almost as good as sex.

Wait a minute! Did I really think that? That ice cream was almost as good as sex? I know it's been a long time, but I must be losing my mind.

Anyhow, after the second indulgence of the day, we skipped lunch and visited the Vatican and Saint Peter's, where we looked around hopefully but did not see the Pope. I have to confess that Rome was passing before my eyes like a dream. I was not really taking it in. It was remote from me—and I was divorced from it. I was simply going through the sightseeing motions.

Later we visited the Trevi Fountain and threw coins in like all the other tourists, then sat for a while in the Piazza Navona over icy drinks, resting our feet before heading off to the Via Condotti. And the shops.

Of course, I hadn't really been shopping in years, and this was Nonna's opportunity. "Choose whatever you want," she said magnanimously. "I'm buying." *Oh god*, I thought, *the Heiress is back with us,* and I said, "Thanks, Mom, but you get something for yourself." And she said, "What do I need? It's you who needs the pretty clothes."

So then I pointed out some very nice handbags in Gucci, and she said, "Maybe," and, "Perhaps," but finally went in and purchased a plain black bag with a bamboo-look handle, which came enveloped in its own soft little white sack and was probably the most expensive thing she had ever owned.

By then Nonna was really into shopping mode, and we headed across the street to Prada, where she bought Livvie her first handbag (other than a Miss Kitty one when she was seven), a flat black satchel that Livvie thought the last word in cool. And then Livvie saw a pair of bright red boots on sale in another boutique, which meant they were only in the low millions of lire instead of the zillions, plus then there were these cute little T-shirts and sweaters . . . and like that, if you know what I mean.

I bought a great handbag for my friend Patty at a much more reasonable price in Furla, on the Piazza di Spagna, and tried on a soft, silky wisp of a red chiffon dress in a boutique called Alberta Ferretti. It looked almost cute on me, and I was almost tempted. Except then I thought, What am I doing, trying on little silk dresses? When would I ever *wear* a little silk dress? And anyhow, then I saw the price and I almost fainted.

By now I was exhausted. Shattered, in fact. So I left Nonna and Livvie to it and, laden down with all the packages, headed back to the hotel and—oh thank you, God—bed. *Heavenly* bed. My feet felt about ten sizes larger than they had that morning.

A bellboy came running to take my packages, but I

waved him away. It was really more effort to untangle myself and give them to him than it was to carry them that extra few minutes it would take me to get to the room. I pushed the elevator button with my elbow and waited, shifting from foot to aching foot. Was the elevator never going to get here? I turned impatiently away, scowling at the delay. Then there was the little ping and I swung around again, stepped into the elevator, and, klutz that I am, tripped over someone's feet.

I staggered back against the elevator wall, shedding parcels like a pack mule on a mountain bend. "Oh, shoot," I said, kicking the nearest bag crossly. "Damned shopping, who needs it!" And then I saw The Feet.

They were in expensive brown suede loafers, probably from one of the smart shops we had just patronized, and they were worn, I noticed, with pale yellow socks. My eyes traveled upward, past the immaculately pressed pants, taking in the dark blue short-sleeved linen shirt, the steel watch on a very masculine arm with black hairs tangling around it. Up the strong golden-tan neck. And into the eyes of . . . the Michelangelo of Long Island. I felt that blush again, rising like the sun in a fiery glow.

His eyes were gray—or were they hazel?—and flecked with golden lights, and they were not smiling at me. "Let me help you," he said coolly.

"Oh. I didn't realize there was someone in the elevator. I'm sorry. That was so clumsy of me." Conscious of my own scuffed sneakers and dusty appearance, I knelt among the dropped parcels while he pushed the stop button, then bent and helped me pick up my stuff. Our eyes met again over the Prada bag.

"Yes, it was," he said as we stood up and he piled parcels into my outstretched arms.

"Was what?"

"It was clumsy of you."

"Oh!"

Michelangelo stepped out of the elevator, then turned back and said, "What floor?"

"Oh. Seven, please."

He pushed the seven button and stood staring at me as the doors slid closed. I thought there was a hint of laughter in his eyes, but I couldn't be sure. What I could be sure of, though, was that I felt like a fool.

Back in the suite, I flung the packages onto the sofa, then stalked into my room, pulled off my sneakers, and flung myself onto the bed. Fuck Mr. Perfect Know-It-All, I thought, suddenly angry. Who did he think he was, laughing at me, anyhow?

I closed my eyes, and suddenly my head was back at the hospital, my safe place, where I was too busy even to think about myself. This trip is just an interlude, I reassured myself. It'll soon be over. My job is my life, my identity. Without my doctor's coat I'm just another single parent, Livvie's mom, trying to do the right thing. I have my work and I have Livvie. I need nothing more. Or do I?

I thought of the Michelangelo from Long Island and his gray-green eyes, flecked with gold. I thought about his beautiful little daughter and his probably beautiful wife and about their certainly idyllic life. And suddenly loneliness loomed in those sun-filled piazzas, and sleep refused to come.

CHAPTER TEN

I stomped into the bathroom, ran a hot bath, flung in about half a gallon of the Hassler's fragrant bath oil, then slumped in the water up to my chin. This Rome thing was too much for me. I felt like a transplanted alien, thrown into a life of ease and luxury where time had no meaning. I was too used to living on the knife edge, to always having to be alert, to be ready for the next emergency, to juggling time as though it were something precious to be meted out sparingly: so much for this one, so much for that, and none for me. Now all of a sudden I was wallowing in a bathtub wondering what to do next.

This was all wrong. I shouldn't even be here.

I grabbed the hand shower and washed my hair, scrubbing my scalp vigorously as if to stimulate my benumbed brain into action again. Then I climbed out of the tub, wrapped myself in the hotel's white waffle-cotton robe, and twisted a towel into a turban over my wet hair. I rummaged through the packages, which were still on the sofa, and found what I was looking for—an expensive tube of face mask guaranteed to remove those aggravating little lines and snap open pores tight shut. All you had to do was smooth it over your entire face, leaving two holes for the eyes, then wait fifteen minutes and rinse it off.

I smeared it on, then took a long look at myself in the mirror. Did the green clay mask make my eyes look bloodshot? Or were they *really* bloodshot? Maybe I'd better go easy on the Bellinis, though, in fact, the thought of one right now sent a pleasant little tingle down my spine. There you go, I said to myself. One minute you're complaining that you shouldn't be here and that you can't cope. The next you're putting on face mask and thinking of room-service Bellinis. Who *are* you anyway, Dr. Jericho?

I rang room service and ordered that Bellini. Then, remembering the green mask and my nakedness under the robe, I told them to leave it outside my room.

Five minutes later the bell rang. I gave the waiter a couple of minutes to make it back down the corridor and into the elevator before I opened the door. I saw the little cart just to the left with a silver bucket and my Bellini nestling on the ice inside it. Smiling, I stepped outside, reached for the ice bucket, and heard the door slam shut on me.

I swung around and almost strangled myself. The belt of my robe was caught in the door. I tugged, but it wasn't giving. I tugged again. No luck.

Sighing, I slipped the belt from the loops on the robe and tried the door. It wouldn't open. Maybe it was stuck because of the belt. I pushed the handle again, gave the door a shove. Nothing.

Panic swept like a hot tide up my spine. My beltless robe gaped open, and my face was frozen inside a crisp green shell. This couldn't be happening to me. Not me, Doc Jericho, the cool emergency room physician. No, of course it wasn't, I told myself bitterly. *This* was happening to *Gemma,* the queen of klutz. I gave the door a kick, then wished I hadn't. Now my foot hurt like hell.

I glanced behind me. The hallway was long and empty, softly lit and silent. Our suite was at the end of the hall, and the elevators were about midway. Opposite the elevators was a marble console with a big bouquet of flowers, a house phone, and copies of today's newspapers.

I stared longingly at that phone; it was the answer to my prayers. But between me and it was a long stretch of corridor with many doors, plus the elevators waiting to spring unwary guests and shock them with the sight of me, half naked and looking like the Phantom of the Opera.

There was nothing else for it. I adjusted my towel turban, gripped my robe around me, and sped barefoot down the corridor. I glanced warily at the elevators as I grabbed the phone and dialed. I told the man who answered that I had locked myself out of my room and could he please send someone up with a key immediately, it was urgent. He said, "*Sì, signora,* right away." I heaved a sigh of relief. And then the elevator pinged.

Horrified, I sank into one of the little silk chairs next to the console, grabbed a newspaper, and held it up to my face. I crossed my legs and prayed that whoever it was would not even notice a barefoot, half-naked woman in a green face mask with eyes like those proverbial holes in the snow and a dangling towel turban, pretending to read a newspaper in Italian.

I heard the doors slide open and someone step out. The doors slid shut, and still the person did not move. I looked down under the newspaper and saw a pair of feet in expensive brown suede loafers and yellow socks. It was a wonder the face mask didn't crack right off my face, my skin was so hot from the terrible blush.

"By the way," his amused voice said, "you're reading that paper upside down."

I lowered the paper and glared at him. "I locked myself out, that's all," I said in a dignified tone. "I'm waiting for the bellboy to bring me a key."

He was grinning at me now. "Better keep that robe closed," he said. "It's kind of chilly with this air-conditioning." And then he turned and walked off down the corridor. I could hear him laughing all the way.

I sped back to my door, grabbed the Bellini, and took a gulp, cowering in the corner until my savior appeared with the key. He was politer than Michelangelo; he did not even look at me, let alone laugh. And then I was safe inside, rinsing off that stupid mask that hadn't removed a single wrinkle, let alone snapped my pores shut, and, damn it, my eyes were still bloodshot.

I flung myself onto the sofa and slurped up that Bellini. I prayed I would never see that self-satisfied jerk again. I'd had it with Rome and smart-asses from Long Island.

CHAPTER ELEVEN

That night we had dinner at Il Volte on the Via della Rotonda, a smartly casual trattoria with a busy outdoor terrace bordered with greenery and soft lamplight.

It was a hot night, and the purple sky was studded with stars. People thronged the streets, escaping their hot apartments, carrying bright-eyed babies, whisking small children from under the wheels of noisy little Vespa motor scooters, sipping wine in cafés, eating *gelati*, talking loudly on cell phones, embracing friends, kissing in doorways. Being Romans.

Tables were crammed close under the blue awning, and there was music in the air and the smell of pizza margherita, a waft of garlicky clam pasta, the cool taste of white Frascati wine, and a bubble of laughter from a wedding group at the long table next to ours.

The bride was English, beautiful in a skintight white lace dress. Her flowing veil, a cloud of tulle and lace, cataracted carelessly over the terrace. Her new husband was Irish, pink-faced and with his jacket off and his collar unbuttoned against the heat. He had his arm around her shoulders, and there it stayed all night. I watched them with wistful memories of my own long-ago wedding day when, at the last minute, even I had not wanted to be there.

The wedding party was a mixture of European nationalities, and they were laughing, feasting, drinking champagne, having a great time. I caught the bride's eye and lifted my glass to her. "Good luck," I called, and she gave me a glowing smile and said, "Come join us."

"We decided to get married only last week," the bride told me, still thrilled. "We thought it would be so romantic, and Rome was a good meeting point for all our friends. So we just called them. I bought a frock, he bought the plane tickets, we booked the hotels—and here we all are."

We laughed with them and toasted to their health and happiness, then returned to our own pizza margherita and *caprese* salad with tomatoes that tasted as if they had been really grown in hot summer fields, and the bottle of light red wine that had a tiny touch of bubbles in it, the kind the Italians call *frizzante*.

How lucky they were to find such happiness, I thought enviously.

BEN

Ben Raphael, the "Michelangelo from Long Island," watched Gemma from a corner of the terrace. His daughter was eating *fragolini*, the tiny, lusciously sweet wild strawberries that are a specialty for a short season in Italy, and which she nibbled as though they were precious as pearls. Ben felt glad that in spite of her mother's thin-is-better attitude to life, Muffie had inherited his own love of good food.

He glanced again at the American woman, hidden behind those swept-up glasses that matched her swept-up cheekbones, eating pizza with the teenage daughter with the cropped yellow hair and quirky clothes, and the grandmother in her best black.

Odd was the right word to describe her, he thought, shaking his head and smiling as he recalled their encounters that day. But he also remembered when he had first seen her, just last night. For a second there, she had stopped him in his tracks, made him think for a moment how *real* she looked: un-made-up, uncaring, her exhaustion showing.

He'd been struck by how different she was from the glossy women he knew. Looking at her now, in her simple white shirt and skirt, with sandals on her bare feet and her golden hair haloed by the lamp behind her, he wondered who she was and why she looked as though she wasn't enjoying herself, and whether it was just her accident-prone clumsiness that made her seem so vulnerable. Somehow he didn't think so. And somehow, too, she had just stuck in his mind.

CHAPTER TWELVE

GEMMA

The next morning we were speeding north in a car like a silver bullet, a flashy and, since I was with an "heiress," horribly expensive Lancia. The powerful engine hummed soft as a lullaby, the leather had that wonderful new-car smell, and the dash with its high-tech display dazzled. I was in automobile heaven. The signs said FIRENZE, but I almost didn't want to get there. Driving this car was the closest thing to bliss—and bankruptcy—I could imagine. But Nonna had informed us she intended to return to her old village "in style," and how could I say no to that?

The traffic was a nightmare. Cars charged up behind me, lights flashing, forcing me over, then passed at speeds I knew must be illegal, while the truck driver in his lumbering *camion* coming at me on the other side of the road flashed *his* lights, warning me to get over, until I wondered if maybe I should just leave the road to them.

But soon we were out of the city sprawl, passing signs that said URBINO and PIENZA, driving down roads lined with umbrella pines and hillsides dotted with cypresses, past tumbledown farmsteads and through tiny hamlets, mere straggles of houses and barns, with old men sitting in the shade, leaning on their sticks, watching the world flash by.

"Almost there, Nonna," I said, wondering what she was thinking, now she was almost "home."

Nonna was staring worriedly out of the car window at the passing countryside. I guessed she thought she remembered it, but it had been so long, and she had been only a child.

This was meant to be the big event of her life, of *all* our lives, going back to our roots, visiting long-lost relatives, seeing the old village and the humble little stone house where Nonna was born. Now, though, I thought she looked uneasy. What if her village was not the way she remembered it? What if no one was there from the old days? What if there was no one left who even remembered the Corsini family? I saw her take off the large Hollywood sunglasses she had bought in Rome and wipe her eyes. Oh god, she was *crying*. Perhaps this was a mistake after all.

I could swear we had been circling the same route for the past half hour, following Nonna's erratic directions. "Are you sure you've got this right?" I asked her finally.

"You think I don't remember my way home?" She sounded hurt.

"Mom," I said, "I think you haven't been here in almost fifty years and you just don't remember *exactly* where Bella Piacere is."

Livvie got out the road map and studied it one more time. She glanced toward a distant town set high on a crag and said that must be Montepulciano. Then Nonna said to drive on, she would know it when she saw it.

I sighed at her logic as we wound slowly up powdery white roads, with Nonna sitting on the edge of her seat, peering through the windshield like a soldier on military reconnaissance.

"There!" she said suddenly. "Left at the crossroads, the one with the Saint Francis shrine."

I swerved left at the little plaster roadside shrine with the statue of Saint Francis, arm upraised as though he were blessing the jar of plastic flowers someone had placed at his feet, then followed a narrow lane lined with shady poplars, threading ever upward, past a tiny farm where a lone white cow peeked solemnly at us from a stone barn.

I looked around me. So *this,* I thought, is Tuscany: vineyard-covered hills, silvery olive groves, fields of dazzling sunflowers, old pastel-colored villas and ancient stone villages, cool archways flashed with sunlight, and the village of Bella Piacere on the crest of the hill. Paradise.

Oh *puh-lease,* I thought. *This is too good to be true. It's a picture-postcard place, a setup for tourists and Kodak moments.* But there were no tourists around, no cameras clicking. Only silence and a feeling of peace.

I parked in the little cobblestoned square, and we got out of the car. We held Nonna's hands and looked at where we were. At the place we came from.

Bella Piacere dozed peacefully behind closed green shutters in the hot sunshine of siesta. Pink and terra-cotta houses lined the cobbled square; a tabby cat slumbered behind a pot of tumbling scarlet geraniums, bead door curtains clattered in the sudden breeze, and there was a lingering aroma of lunchtime basil and garlic. From the cool dark interior of the tiny honey-colored church came the smell of incense and flowers, and in an alley, a flight of stone steps curved mysteriously upward. There wasn't a soul in sight, and you could almost hear the silence.

Tears suddenly flooded down Nonna's face. We flung our arms around her and stood in the middle of her village square in an emotional clump. This was Nonna's homecoming, and I, for one, was wondering why she had ever left. Because now Bella Piacere tugged at my own heartstrings.

I asked myself, was it was because this was where my mother came from? Because it was my family's, my own roots? Or was it the peace, the stillness, the sense of stepping back in time?

CHAPTER THIRTEEN

The Albergo d'Olivia was a faded pink stucco building facing onto the cobblestoned piazza, where a fountain sprayed over a pair of chipped stone cherubs holding aloft a dolphin. Not so many years ago, Nonna told us, the *albergo* had been a cow barn. Tuscan cows were traditionally kept indoors and groomed like prize horses, and in the old days they often had better living quarters than the peasants who owned them. Now, though, the barn was a tiny inn with wide arched windows where the big doors had once been. There was an ornate wrought-iron sign in the shape of an olive tree over the entrance, and a little terrace bar, just a few metal tables and chairs spilling casually onto the piazza.

Oh come on, I thought, ever the skeptic, *this is too cute to be true. I mean, if you had a picture postcard of the dream Tuscan village inn, this was it!*

We pushed through a bead door curtain into a long, low-beamed room with terra-cotta tiled floors and the original stone walls. To our left was a dining room, just a half-dozen tables with bright green cloths and little jugs of frilly pink carnations. On our right was a small sitting area with a beat-up green leather sofa, two hard-looking high-backed chairs, and an assortment of little tables topped with dinky lamps and a small TV set. A row of stunted cacti stood under the windows, and on the far wall we could see the iron feeding troughs from when the inn was still a cow barn.

"Buon giorno," Nonna called, pressing the bell near the door. It clanged loud as a fire engine in the silence, and a young girl hidden in a cubbyhole under the staircase shrieked and leaped about two feet into the air.

She was small and skinny with round brown eyes. Her black hair was short and uneven, her skin was so pale she might never have seen the light of day, and her mouth was a small pink O of surprise. She looked exactly like an urchin in an Italian movie.

"Sorry. Didn't mean to startle you." I smiled.

She waved her hands wildly in the air. *"Prego, un momento, signore,"* she cried, then shot past us and through a door at the back marked CUCINA. In a second the door flew open again, and another small round woman shot out. She was a replica of her daughter: same round dark eyes, same round little mouth, same uneven haircut. But this woman was fat, and she was very much in charge. She squeezed herself behind the pine counter under the stairs, drying her hands on her apron and looking expectantly at us. *"Prego, signore?"*

Nonna frowned. She leaned over the counter to get a closer look. *"Scusi, signora,"* she said, "but I know your face. You must be related to the Ambrosinis. Carlino and Maria Carmen. They lived at the top of Vicolo 'Scuro."

"Sì, it's true. They were my grandparents. I'm Amalia Posoli."

Nonna clutched a hand to her pounding heart. "I went to school with your mother, Renata. We lived next door. I haven't seen her since we were girls. I was Sophia Maria

Lorenza Corsini then. Now, of course, I am *signora* Jericho, and a widow. I've traveled from New York to visit Bella Piacere, my old village, again. Before I die," she added, as I noticed she always did, a hand still clutched dramatically to her breast.

Livvie rolled her eyes at me, but Amalia thumped an enthusiastic fist on the pine counter, making it tremble. "What a surprise my mother will have to see you again, *signora* Jericho. Welcome home, welcome. Mamma will be so excited. She married Ricardo Posoli. Remember him?"

"*Ricci* Posoli?" Nonna beamed. "Of course I remember him, long and skinny as a string bean, and Renata was short and round."

Amalia laughed, because it was true. "I'll show you to your rooms. I have the reservations right here." She pointed to the school exercise book that was the hotel register. "Then, when you are ready, I will take you to see Mamma. She will be so excited. *Madonnina mia!* What a surprise it will be."

Nonna had a big square room with a window overlooking a grape arbor and an overgrown garden, where tiny tomatoes clung like scarlet roses to the hot stone walls, looking ready to burst with ripeness, and zucchini in rampant yellow bloom triumphed over a patch of struggling lettuces. Livvie had a cute flowery room at the front, and my own room, linked to Livvie's by a bathroom, was all white. White walls, white lace curtains, white linen coverlet.

Like a virgin's room, I thought, bouncing on the bed to test it. And of course it might as well have been. I grinned as it squeaked and groaned. Nobody could lose their virginity in here without half the hotel knowing about it; I'd have to hold my breath every time I turned over for fear of waking other guests.

I peeked into the bathroom and saw white tiles with little pink flowers, a deep tub with a flimsy handheld shower, and a pink plastic shower curtain with stars on it.

Back in my virgin's room, I went to the window, pushed open the rusty green shutters, and stuck my head out. To my left, on the crest of a rounded hill, I caught a glimpse of the grandiose old Villa Piacere, half hidden behind the trees, and home, so Nonna had told me, to the counts of Piacere for more than three hundred years.

Livvie leaned companionably next to me, looking out at the silent square, at the hillsides covered in vines, at the groves of olives. The soft sound of the fountain filtered into the room, and the air was winey and clean. The sun felt hot on our faces, birds twittered, the church clock struck three, and somewhere a dog barked.

"Whatever do people *do* around here?" Livvie whispered.

CHAPTER FOURTEEN

Amalia was taking us to meet her mother, and Nonna had dressed for the occasion in a new black silk outfit, purchased at a Macy's sale just a few weeks ago for what she had then considered an outrageous eighty-five dollars. It had a high round neck, a row of shiny jet buttons, a narrow belt, and a box-pleated skirt that sat nicely a few inches above her ankles. It seemed to have Plain but Good, Suitable for a Sixty-Year-Old Grandmother stamped all over it. Her shoes were plain black pumps with low heels, and she carried the expensive new Roman handbag, large, black, smooth, and shiny. She had scrunched her hair into its usual bun, and to top it all off she wore the large dark Hollywood sunglasses. She looked like the widow at a Mafia funeral.

Livvie and I walked on either side of her, arms linked in hers, like the mourners. Livvie was in her usual miniskirt, black this time, with a clinging white T-shirt and sneakers, and for some reason Nonna had insisted I wear my "best black" too, only now it was even more creased from being flung into my duffel bag at the last minute.

We were surely an odd trio, following Amalia up the steps by the church that led from the piazza to the 'Scuro, as Nonna called it, by which she meant Vicolo Oscuro, or Shady Alley, a narrow, cobbled little street that wound its way tortuously up the hillside in a series of steps.

The tiny iron Juliet balconies of the stone houses were crammed with pots of geraniums and jasmine, and lines of laundry fluttered unashamedly overhead. The long lunchtime siesta was over and life had started up again. Women were emerging from their houses with mesh shopping bags over their arms, small children scurried underfoot yelling at each other, and an old man sat in a doorway weaving a basket from some rushes.

"I remember this," I heard Nonna mutter to herself. "Oh, yes, *I remember*." The hill was steep, and she was breathing heavily. I suggested we stop for a while, but she insisted on keeping up with Amalia, who was leaping ahead of us like a plump deer.

Finally the narrow cobbled street leveled out into a sort of wide ledge immediately above the church, and we were looking down over the little copper verdigris dome with its big cross, at the Albergo d'Olivia opposite, at the fountain in the piazza, and at people like stick figures in a naive painting, strolling and shopping at the general store, the bakery, the butcher, and at the *salumeria* with the big plastic boar's head stuck outside just so you would know they also sold wild boar salami. It was a microcosm of life, perfect and self-contained, a little world of its own.

On this little cul-de-sac overlooking the village was a row of six small stone houses, each with two windows downstairs and three up. A single scrubbed stone step led inside, while in front a mismatched collection of garden chairs and patio tables was set among a conglomeration of pots, wooden tubs, and old olive oil cans filled with bougainvillea and jasmine, begonias, lobelia, and geraniums. It was picture-postcard-Tuscan-village time again.

Amalia looked back to see where we were, waiting for Nonna to catch her breath.

Nonna's face was pale, but then she smiled, a smile so joyous and contagious, I suddenly saw where I had gotten that bubbly, happy personality, the one I'd had when I was young, the one that seemed to have gotten worn down with time. The one that had finally disappeared forever when Cash Drummond disappeared from my life.

"Ecco, bambini," Nonna said, throwing her arms so wide, Livvie and I had to dodge to keep from being whacked in the head. *"Now* I am home." And she walked right up to the very last house, pulled aside the bead curtain, and called out, "Is anyone there?"

Amalia thrust us out of the way and yelled at the top of her lungs, "Giuseppe, Maria, come meet Sophia Maria Lorenza Corsini Jericho, here all the way from New York to visit her old home before she dies. She used to live in this very house. She's a friend of my mamma's."

Giuseppe—about twenty-five years old, in blue jeans, with black hair curling out of his white tank top and a wide white smile—appeared in the doorway carrying a *bambina* wearing only a diaper and a red bow in her hair. And behind him was Maria, young, dark-haired, and olive-skinned, her pretty face showing surprise and pleasure as she welcomed my mother into her home, embracing her as though she had known her all her life.

Nonna stood silently, looking around at her old home. Everything had changed. Where there used to be a hard dirt floor and an open fireplace for cooking and simple wooden chairs to sit on, now there were ceramic tile and a stove and upholstered furniture. But somehow it was still the same: the same feeling, the same memories.

Word had already spread, and familiar faces, grown older, were crowding in the doorway. Everyone remembered the Corsini family; everyone wanted to meet Sophia's daughter and her granddaughter and hear about her life in New York. Checkered cloths were already being flung over the tables outside, more chairs dragged up, and wine bottles opened. Olives and bread were brought out and cheeses and tomatoes and *biscotti* and more wine. Livvie was holding the *bambina,* and tinny music blasted from a radio. All of a sudden there was a party going on.

We were all sitting around watching the sun set over Bella Piacere, and Nonna, who had discarded the Mafia widow look along with the sunglasses, was holding her old friend Renata Posoli's hand and catching up on about fifty years' worth of news.

I caught a tender smile lurking in Livvie's eyes as she watched her grandmother, and I knew, despite my previous doubts, that coming to Bella Piacere had been absolutely the right thing to do. Sophia Maria Lorenza Corsini Jericho was home again.

CHAPTER FIFTEEN

It was late when we returned to the *albergo*. Lights were on in the square and in the church, and in the grocery store window, illuminating the dusty bottles of wine and crates of melons and shiny red peppers. The MOTTO sign over the single-pump garage with the dark little workshop in the back glowed neon green. Next to it, the smoky Bar Galileo, with faded ads for grappas and beers stuck all over its window, was doing good business. From inside came the crackle of the TV with a soccer game turned up loud and the roars of the patrons as Juventus scored again. The *gelateria* opposite attracted evening strollers and small children with its sign saying *granita fatta a casa,* homemade ices, and gnarled old men played bocce on the dusty court overhung with umbrella pines, urged loudly on to victory by the idlers outside the bar.

The lone figure of a priest in a black robe and wide-brimmed hat waited on one of the little metal chairs outside the *albergo*. He was plump, with a pink face, round wire glasses, and an anxious expression. He stood as we approached.

"*Signora* Jericho?" He offered his hand. "I heard you had arrived. I am Don Vincenzo Arrici."

Don Vincenzo was authentic all right, right down to

the holy ring on his finger, the old black soutane, and the scuffed black shoes of a rural parish priest.

Uh-oh, I thought, as we arranged ourselves around the small table and ordered grappa and San Pellegrino water and generally took each other in. *This is moment-of-truth time. Now we get to hear about the worthless little field with two olive trees and a couple of clucking old hens.*

Don Vincenzo spoke practically no English, so Nonna had to translate for us.

"I will get to the matter of importance right away, *signore*," he said, taking a sip of his grappa and beaming at us over his little round glasses. "It happened this way. One winter, many years ago, *signora* Jericho, your father risked his own life to save the youngest son of the count of Piacere from drowning in the rain-swollen river. That son never forgot his fear of death, nor did he forget his savior. The years passed, and the Piacere family dwindled, until finally this son was the only one left. He never married, he had no heirs, and so, when the time came to meet his maker, he left the Villa Piacere and all its land to the family of the man who had saved him."

"La mia famiglia?" Nonna clasped that hand to her heart again, as though to still its astonished beating.

"Sil, signora, la Sua famiglia. The Villa Piacere and all its contents now belong to you."

"Dio mio," she said, stunned.

I suddenly realized this was no hoax; it was for real. I took a gulp of my grappa, choking as it hit my throat like fire. I wondered why anybody drank the stuff, although it was surely strong enough to cure the common cold. But it didn't help the shock.

Livvie was staring, bug-eyed, at me. "Does that mean we have to live here?" she whispered, horrified.

I shook my head. "Of course not, baby. It's just some old neglected villa nobody wants." But then I thought, What if Nonna really did want to live here? What would I do?

"You must meet with the attorney, *signor* Donati," Don Vincenzo was telling Nonna. "He has the details of all the little . . . complications."

We stared at him, too stunned to even take in that ominous word . . . *complications*.

"It will be necessary to speak to this attorney in order to make an appointment to inspect your villa," he continued. "But at the moment, *signor* Donati is . . . out of town."

The priest twirled his grappa glass between his fingers, avoiding our eyes. "There's one other little matter," he added. "The Villa Piacere is rented out for the summer to a tenant who has been coming here for several years. This means you will not be able to take possession for some time, even when all the complications are straightened out."

"But," he added, smiling now, "every year the *signore* at the villa throws a big Fourth of July party. He invites all the locals, the villagers as well as the grandees. Everyone is invited. The party is this weekend. It will give you an opportunity to visit your property."

Nonna ordered more grappa to celebrate, and I slumped back in my uncomfortable little metal café chair, staring at the bocce players and the greenish copper cross on the honey-colored church and the chipped cherubs in the mossy fountain. The villa would have to be sold, that was all there was to it. But how many buyers could there be for a no doubt run-down old Tuscan villa that I'd bet needed an expensive new roof and probably new plumbing, to say nothing of the wiring? I groaned inwardly. I was looking at a bottomless pit.

And anyway, *who* was renting the place? And for *how much*? I perked up a bit at the thought of income, but then reality returned. Any money coming in would go out just as quickly to maintain the place. The Villa Piacere, I thought gloomily, was a white elephant.

But Nonna obviously didn't think so. She was aglow with the news, already chatelaine of a three-hundred-year-old villa. Long Island and the blue house with the porch had disappeared into the past, I just knew it. And I also knew that dissuading her meant my work was cut out for me.

CHAPTER SIXTEEN

The next afternoon I was sitting under a shady grape arbor in an old wicker chair in the overgrown garden in
back of the inn. There was a book on my lap and a glass
of fresh lemonade on the table next to me. Tiny hard
green grapes the size of raisins dangled over my head, the
yellow-flowered zucchini conquered the plot of lettuces,
and I could smell the sweetness of those rosy tomatoes
radiating from the hot stone wall. In the distance, up on
the hill and through the trees, I caught a glimpse of the
coral roofs of the Villa Piacere glittering like a mirage in
the slanting late-afternoon sunlight.

I closed my eyes and sighed. As if life were not complicated enough, now we were stuck with a big old crumbling house. We would be liable for the taxes, and heaven
only knew what taxes were in Italy. Not that we could afford them, unless the summer rental brought in enough,
which somehow I doubted it would.

A few days ago, in Rome, I had been wishing I'd never
come here, but despite all the new problems, I felt suddenly at peace with the world. At least for this afternoon
I did.

I could not remember the last time I had spent an entire day doing absolutely nothing. This morning I had

slept late. I had showered, then breakfasted on bread still warm from the baker's oven and fresh-roasted coffee with hot frothy milk. I had waved good-bye to Nonna and Livvie, who had driven off to Florence, with Nonna confidently at the wheel, to shop for new dresses for the Fourth of July party. I'd refused to go with them. Instead I had resolved to contact *Signor* Donati, the attorney, and sort out the "complications" that came with the villa.

I had already tried to call him, but the number Don Vincenzo had given me did not answer. Now I tried again. Still no answer. I walked over to the church, where I caught the father in mid-prayer while at the same time dusting the brass altar candles with his handkerchief.

"*Signor* Donati is probably in Lucca," he told me cheerily. "He does much business there. Try him *domani*, why don't you?"

Why don't I indeed? I thought, getting into the lazy Italian mood. Tomorrow will probably be just as good.

I wandered around the square, stopped every now and then by new friends, met just yesterday, who wanted to clasp my hand and inquire as to my health. I beamed back, struggling to say in Italian, "I am fine. We are all fine. Thank you for your hospitality." I groaned with the effort. How was it I knew how to diagnose a brain aneurysm and yet had gone my whole life without learning to speak my mother's native tongue? Resolve number two that day: learn Italian.

I peeked into the bar. A tiny black-and-white TV with a rabbit-ears antenna blasted a soccer game, even though the place was empty. I backed quickly out, crossed the square, and bought a delicious pistachio ice cream cone at the *gelateria*. Licking my ice cream, I inspected rows of mortadellas and salamis and the fragrant Parma hams and cheeses in the *salumeria* and came back in a slow circle to the *albergo,* where I took up residence again in my wicker garden chair. I had thought I would try to figure out a few of my problems. Instead I promptly fell asleep.

It was maybe the most restful day of my life. And for once I did not even think of Cash Drummond.

CHAPTER SEVENTEEN

The next day was the Fourth of July, the day of the grand party at the villa. Of course, I would have preferred to linger in the shade of the grape arbor with my book, but now I was forced into some semblance of dressing up.

When Livvie and Nonna had returned from Florence late the night before, they had been laden down with smart shopping bags, but they'd refused to show me what they had bought. Wait and see, they'd said mysteriously, though Livvie couldn't suppress a giggle. So now was to be their "unveiling."

I put on a pale blue linen dress that was definitely last-yearish or even older, added a dash of lipstick, and ran my fingers hastily through my hair. It stood on end as though I had been zapped by lightning, and I quickly slicked on some hair gel and brushed it into submission. I stared, dismayed, at the result in the mirror. I had put on too much gel and now every strand was clamped to my skull. Disgruntled, I grabbed my sunglasses and headed downstairs. The only reason I was going to this party was to see that darned villa. *Nonna's* villa. I figured I might as well know the worst.

Nonna and Livvie were waiting for me in the front hall. At least I *thought* it was Nonna. *Was it? Could it be?*

She had on an elegant green silk dress with a low neckline and a cinched waist, high heels, and a big upswept hairdo. She looked like Sophia Loren at the Oscars. Even the glasses were gone, dangling on a gold chain around her neck, to be put on only when she needed to "inspect" her villa.

"*Omigod*," I said, using my daughter's favorite line. "Mom, is it *really you*?"

Sophia Maria Lorenza Corsini—for this was who now stood before me—patted her upswept hair, smoothed her green silk skirt, and smiled at me. "Do you like the lipstick?" she asked. "The girl in the store said it was exactly right with this green."

I was stunned almost into speechlessness. "The lipstick is fine," I managed. "*You* are fine. . . . You look *great* . . . just like your picture on the sideboard when you were seventeen."

She smiled as she picked up the big black bag, plopped a black straw hat with a large shady brim on top of the hairdo, checked the pearls in her ears and at her neck, and said, "Let's go, girls, we're going to be late."

Livvie, who thank God still looked like Livvie, only Italian style, all legs and big feet and budding breasts in a clingy tie-dyed T-shirt, a brief little white skirt, and clunky platforms, followed meekly, and so did I. At the door Nonna turned and gave me that same up-and-down Sunday-lunchtime look she always gave me.

"Must you wear that dress, Gemma?" she said. "Blue was never your color, and linen creases so." And with that, the fashion-plate heiress and chatelaine of the Villa Piacere swept out the door to her silver chariot, and I, her devoted chauffeur, got behind the wheel and drove us to the party.

It was an idyllic day with a sky bluer than my unfortunate dress. Red-tailed hawks hovered motionless as tiny kites, and a hot sun dazzled the backs of my eyes. The long, potholed sandy lane circled up the hill behind the village, past groves of gnarled old olives whose silver leaves rustled like taffeta in the breeze, all the way to a pair of tall ornamental iron gates, one of which hung drunkenly off its hinges and was embellished at the top with the initial *P* in a wreath of iron laurel leaves. We jolted along an overgrown driveway. And then—there it was. The Villa Piacere. And for me, it was love at first sight.

It sat atop the crest of its hill at the end of an allée of cypresses, large and square, flanked by twin towers, and glowing like a ripe golden apricot in the sun. Its tall windows were hung with shutters whose paint had faded from blue to silver. To the left was an arcaded loggia with thin graceful columns supporting a copper roof that had weathered to a grayish-green patina. A separate building to the right was called, I remembered Don Vincenzo had told me, a *limonaia,* and was where they put the delicate lemon trees to protect them from the winter frosts.

In front of the steps leading to the front doors was a massive fountain where bronze fish leaped with lions, and Neptune complete with his fork gazed at Venus arising from her shell, in a dazzle of mixed metaphors from some long-ago sculptor who had gotten carried away with his theme. Water splashed onto the gravel, and moss grew thickly over the stone pond where goldfish fluttered gauzy little fins in the greenish murk.

A double flight of stone stairs led to enormous doors made of weathered wood, flanked by twin lemon trees in huge terra-cotta urns, dripping with yellow fruit. In front was what had once been a formal parterre garden with low clipped box hedges and neat gravel pathways that were now lost under a riot of weeds and grasses, with here and there a tall marble statue sticking up.

We sat in the car as though zapped by a stun gun, mute with awe. Then Livvie said, *"Omigod,"* and Nonna gave a huge sigh.

My heart sank as I looked at the undulating roofline that I knew spelled trouble, at the unkempt grounds, at the peeling stucco, at the sheer *size* of the place. I ran my hands worriedly through my hair. There was nothing written in concrete that said you had to *accept* an inheritance, was there?

Cars were parked on the overgrown front lawn, and another of those Italian urchins with skinny legs and huge eyes, in a baseball cap and Reeboks, directed us to a spot. Nonna pressed a sheaf of lire notes into his hand, just like the rich lady of the manor, and then we climbed the dozen stone steps to the house.

When I first stepped inside the Villa Piacere it seemed mysterious, filled with history and old furniture and the remnants of people's lives. Suddenly I could barely remember the emergency room with its sounds, its smells, the stress. It was another lifetime away.

The entrance hall ran the entire width of the house, with sets of French windows at the far end leading onto a terrace where dozens of people milled around, glasses in hand. Local girls in black dresses and frilled organdy aprons offered silver trays of hors d'oeuvres, a man in a white dinner jacket played cocktail piano in the hall, a string quartet mumbled over Mozart on the terrace, and in a gazebo on the back lawn, the local youth gyrated to disco music.

An enormous hot-air balloon, starred and striped in red, white, and blue, was tethered to the grass, and a long line waited to take a short trip over the hills. A huge barbecue was fired up, ready for an endless supply of hot dogs, burgers, and chicken, and long trestle tables sporting both Italian and American flags were arranged on the grass.

The party was in full swing, and soon Nonna was surrounded by old acquaintances exclaiming at how beautiful she still was. She took it all in her stride. The Queen Mum had nothing on her. Then Livvie disappeared to "explore the scenery," namely boys, and I was on my own.

I stood for a moment, savoring the fact that this place belonged to us, to the Jerichos. I thought of my Italian grandfather, whom I remembered vaguely as the bearded old man in that sepia photograph on the sideboard, and of how he had jumped into a raging winter torrent to save the life of a boy. And of how that same boy, when he too became an old man, had given all he had left in life to his savior's family.

I wandered through the French doors and out onto the cool colonnaded terrace that gave onto the gardens and an endless view of those vine-covered hills, soft and round as breasts, in an artist's palette of burnished gold, umber and burnt sienna, olive and viridian. I stopped and looked. *Really* looked the way I never had before, really *seeing* it. This *place. This paradise.*

All of a sudden my heart did a double flip. All thoughts of expense and new roofs and property taxes disappeared. This was beautiful. It was Tuscany. It was *ours.*

After a while, I pulled myself out of my dream, went

back inside, and began what I had come here to do: an inspection of our property.

The black-and-white-tiled entry hall soared into a musty rotunda; a marble staircase swept up to a sun-filled mezzanine; the parquet floors were scuffed, the apple-green Lucca-silk walls in the *gran salone* were faded and the oriental rugs worn. There was a tattered air of neglect about the Villa Piacere that tugged at my heartstrings; it was an aging beauty in need of tender loving care. Yet someone had cared enough to fill it with flowers, to touch up the dusty gilt Cupids that punctuated the cornices in the *gran salone,* to whisk the dust from the antique spindly-legged tables, and to place floppy old silk cushions carefully over the torn patches in the faded gilt-wood sofas.

Somebody cared, and I wondered who.

I came upon a large octagonal room that instantly charmed me. The walls were painted with a trompe l'oeil frieze of what I guessed must have been the Piacere family's pets through the centuries. A trio of King Charles spaniels frolicked in a translucent green stream; a tiny golden Pekingese chased a red ball; a Great Dane snuggled on a too-small sofa, huge paws dangling and one soulful eye checking the unknown artist; and Siamese cats crouched on the backs of red brocade chairs, using them as scratching posts, staring out at me with intelligent blue eyes. Those same chairs were still in this room, the red brocade shredded by the cats' claws: a living memory.

In a central alcove was pictured a gaudy parrot, electric blue and green and scarlet, sitting atop a jeweled golden cage. Its expression was haughty, its legs ringed with rubies, emeralds, and pearls.

From the corner of my eye, I caught a flash of movement, of color, and then I realized that I was looking at the original of this painting. That same parrot was sitting by the window in his golden cage, ancient head bowed, feathers molting, his legs still beringed with jewels.

I read the name on the plaque attached to the golden cage. *Luchay*. What, I wondered, was Luchay's story? And who had so adored him that they showered him with jewels? It was a mystery I would have to solve. I wondered if we had inherited him, along with the villa.

CHAPTER EIGHTEEN

"My dear," an English voice said loudly in my ear, "isn't this just the most divine party?"

I almost jumped out of my skin. A woman was standing so close to me I was drowning in her heavy perfume. I took a step back, then I took another look. It was *quite* a sight.

"Hello," she said, smiling. "I'm the Contessa Marcessi. Maggie to my friends, and you, my dear, may call me Maggie."

Her nearsighted face was in mine, and I backed away again.

"Of course I'm Margaret really," she said. "Maggie Lynch that was—before I met the old count and came up in the world. I'm the original showgirl made good, darling, straight from the Follies to mistress not only of the count, though of course he married me and made it all legal later, but mistress of my own domain. The Marcessi estate. You know it, I'm sure? It's over on the next hill— and the next, and the next. More hills than you can possibly count, my dear. Though now, of course, I've sold off bits of them with those dinky little farms and old shepherds' huts the English have converted into 'desirable residences.'"

"Lord knows why. I think they just don't understand how cold it is here in winter when the *tramontana* blows and Jack Frost nips at your nose. Now isn't that a song? I seem to remember warbling it at Christmastime, while covered in the appropriate places with bits of white ermine and wearing a white fox hat that was twice the size of my head.

"Jack Frost nipping at your nose," she sang suddenly in a faltering soprano. "I remember it now. Not too appropriate, though, is it, my dear, for a Fourth of July bash?"

My new best friend stopped talking for a second. She stared nearsightedly into my face, then took out a gold lorgnette, held it to her eyes, and peered even closer. I shuffled my feet, feeling like a specimen under a microscope.

"And who are *you*, my dear?" she asked, looking so surprised to see me, I wondered if she had thought I was someone else.

"I'm Gemma Jericho," I said, taking her in. She was eighty if she was a day, taller than I in her towering gold heels, and hefty with it. Her plump thighs were squeezed into skintight Pucci silk capris and her breasts squashed into a sparkly sequinned stars-and-stripes tank top that even Livvie would have turned down. Her hair was redder than a fire engine and back-combed into a stiff beehive adorned with what looked to be diamond brooches, and she wore what I could swear was a rope of real emeralds around her plump neck, plus an assortment of massive diamond and ruby rings. She was obviously of the "if you've got it, flaunt it" school of thinking, but her long horse face was kind and her faded blue eyes gentle.

She caught me checking her out and gave me a friendly little shove with the hand holding the lorgnette.

"Bet you've never seen anything quite like me, Gemma Jericho," she said. "Come on now, tell me. Have you?"

"No, ma'am . . . er, Countess, I certainly have not."

"And I've never seen anything like you. My dear, didn't anyone tell you this was a party? Girls are supposed to dress up, you know. That's how they catch a man."

I laughed out loud. "Is that right, Countess?"

"Trust me." She nodded. "I caught four of 'em, each one richer than the last. You want to know my secret? Just be yourself, my dear. The hell with their titles and their money, you just stick out your tits," she winked at me, "and tell 'em what you think. Straight out, just like that. Trust me, they'll fall down at your feet and worship you. And that's a very good position to have a man in—at your feet, I mean." She gave me another wicked nudge. "Can't have too much of that, y'know—and you can quote me on that, Gemma Jericho.

"I knew the old Count Piacere well, of course," she said suddenly. "We were neighbors for almost thirty years, and he was even older than I am, though I'm too vain, of course, to admit my age. I always thought forty-nine was a nice number to be, so forty-nine I've remained, and I celebrate the same birthday every year. It's next week, my dear. You must come. I'll send you an invitation."

"Thank you, Countess, I'd be honored," I said, meaning it. This old woman was more alive than many thirty-year-olds I knew. "Tell me," I said, "what was he like, the count?"

"What did he look like? Oh, he was a little man, kind of scrawny, y'know, no meat on his bones. He'd had a thatch of white hair ever since I knew him. Looked like a dotty old professor, and in truth he was a bit dotty. *Scatty* is probably the right word. He never could remember my name, called me Eleonora for years, when of course it's really Margaret. Did I tell you already that everybody calls me Maggie? Oh, right.

"Well, he lived on here after the rest of the family died off one by one, and you know a big house like this with no children around is a lonely place. Never did understand why he didn't marry. I mean, he wasn't, y'know," she bent a finger, "like that. Oh, no, straight as a die, he was. So I think somewhere along the way he was unrequited in love. Now that's an old-fashioned phrase, isn't it? You don't hear that too much anymore . . . unrequited love." She stopped and gave me that piercing look again.

"Have you ever been in love, my dear?" She caught the flicker of surprise in my eyes and nodded sagely. "Well, of course you have. You have that look about you. Not 'a woman scorned,' no, no, not that. But a *sadness* that has something to do with a man. I've been there, my dear, and I know that look, so don't try to deny it. Tell you what, Gemma Jericho, I'm a whiz at the tarot cards. Why don't you just come over to my place tomorrow, the Villa Marcessi, everybody knows where it is, and I'll do you a reading? We'll find out what the future really holds."

"Thank you, *Contessa*—"

"Oh, call me Maggie, please."

"Thank you, Maggie," I said, "but I'm not sure I really want to know what the future holds. I have enough trouble just coping with the present."

"Mmmm, well, we shall see. I think before too long you will find you'll change your mind. Trust me," she added, her faded blue eyes boring suddenly into mine. "I know."

She glanced around as though suddenly noticing

where she was. "Oh my," she said briskly, "I daresay I
should find my host and say hello. Have you met him yet?
No? Well, few people really know him. He keeps to himself pretty much, y'know. But artists are like that, are they
not, my dear?"

And with that she patted my arm, said, "Nice to meet
you, Gemma Jericho," and tottered off on her stilettos to
where the action was.

I watched her go right to the head of the line for the
hot-air balloon, and the next minute she was climbing
into the basket and soaring over the Tuscan hills. Her
flame-colored hair and gold lorgnette sparkled in the sun.
I could swear I heard her laughing, and I thought, There
goes a women who has found the secret of life. I only
wished I might be so lucky. And then I realized I had forgotten to ask her about Luchay.

Alone again, I wandered the winding paths around the
house. Each bend in the weed-strewn gravel pathway was
marked by yet another statue of a god or goddesses, angels or Cupids, as well as a wicked-looking Pan, though
his pipes were broken. I came across a tiled grotto built
into the side of the hill, where icy water trickled into an
ancient stone cistern; then a battered greenhouse with a
long silent pool lined with espaliered peach and apricot
trees, and empty racks where, in the old days, exotic
plants, orchids and passion fruit must have been grown
for the house.

I found yet another old stone building and pushed
open the squeaky door. It was dark in there, and I felt
along the wall for a light switch, praying I wouldn't en-
counter any spiders. Finally I found it and saw that I was
in a *cantina*. The dusty shelves were lined with racks of
wines, all neatly stacked, plus jars labeled Olive Oil, with

the date of the pressing. Someone certainly cared enough to take care of this part of the estate properly.

I wandered on and found myself in what were obviously the old stables, but the stalls were empty, and the old wooden doors hung open. The sweet scent of hay and horses still lingered in the air along with the perfume of the little pink Tuscan roses, but instead of horses there were a concrete mixer and a backhoe, heavy machinery and bags of cement. I stared at the equipment, puzzled, wondering what was going on.

I stood there breathing in the clean, scented air, listening to the silence. And I said to myself, Y'know, a girl could be happy right here on this very spot and never ask for another thing. But I sighed as I said it because I knew it was never to be.

Back on the cool terrace, I leaned against the stone balustrade. I ran a finger over its lichen-covered surface, gazing out over the gardens at an arched pergola smothered under a waterfall of purple wisteria, at white hydrangeas in full bloom and a hedge of lavender abuzz with squadrons of bees. The lavender scent drifted toward me, along with that of tuberoses, as heady as any French perfume. The trauma room seemed as far away as another planet.

I closed my eyes to shut out the view, but it was no good. I knew this feeling from old. There was no doubt about it. *I was in love.* I was in a shimmering, perfumed world, a place of the senses and of the heart, a tiny part of paradise right here on earth, and I never wanted to leave. Sternly I reminded myself I could not afford paradise. And that there was nothing else for it. Villa Piacere must be sold.

CHAPTER NINETEEN

BEN

Ben Raphael was enjoying his party. He strolled along the terrace greeting his guests, only some of whom he knew. He knew all the locals, of course, because he'd been coming here for years. He knew Nico, the butcher, and Cesare, the greengrocer, and Sandro at the little Motto station where he filled up his Land Rover. He knew Ottavio, the farmer from whom he bought fresh eggs; he knew Benjamino at the local cooperative where he purchased wine in plastic casks, then took great pleasure in decanting it into bottles himself; he knew Rocco, who had a truffle dog and who always saved one of the precious fungi for him, and from whom he also bought milk. He knew Flavia at the *gelateria* and her three small children; he even had a nodding acquaintance with Renato Posoli, the local schoolteacher, and Don Vincenzo, the priest. So, though he wasn't exactly a resident, Ben counted himself in with the locals. And that's why he invited them all here to celebrate his American national day: he wanted to share it with them.

Then, of course, since expatriates were notoriously hospitable and he had been invited to dinner at every one of the local big houses, he'd invited them plus all the local aristocracy to his party, as well as the English holidaymakers who took up residence in rented villas and grumbled constantly about the lack of everything, especially hot water, maids, and plumbers, until he wondered why they came back every year and considered this form of torture a holiday.

But then, when you were sitting on your hill of an evening looking at the sun setting over the valley like a misty ball of red wool wrapped in skeins of sherbet-orange, coral, and turquoise, with a glass of the local red wine in your hand, you never wanted to be anywhere else in the world. Especially New York.

He leaned on the balustrade, scanning the grounds for his daughter. There she was, on the swing, all alone. He wondered whether he should go and get her, bring her back to the party, but then thought no, let her come back on her own. He sighed, watching her swinging slowly back and forth, higher and higher, her long blond hair shimmering as she tilted her head to watch the hot-air balloon sail slowly through the sky.

He'd almost not brought her with him. Usually he came here alone. His home was a spacious SoHo loft, though that's not where he'd started out. He had worked his way up and out of the Bronx, the hustler from the neighborhood who had cleverly made his way to the top as a property developer. He had started out with nothing, and by the time he was twenty-seven, he'd had, if not everything, then certainly a lot. And it had gone to his head. He'd thought he was cock-of-the-walk, the young tycoon, and he'd hit the bright lights and the big city like the boy from the Bronx he still was, plowing through the clubs and the women as if there were no tomorrow.

But of course there was, and he had been forced to come back to planet Earth and shore up his crumbling little empire. After that he had never wavered. Work was all. Sure, there were women and fancy dinners and chic little private clubs with velvet ropes, but work always came first. Now his empire was secure again, and he was richer than he had ever dreamed of being.

At thirty, he had married "up," dazzled by Bunty Mellor, the beautiful blond WASP, by her old-money family and the whole ancestral home bit. He was a smart young guy, raw and sexy, and unknown territory for Bunty. *Bunty.* Even her name had enchanted him. Where he came from, girls were called Teresa and Marilyn and Sharon.

He had taught Bunty about sex; he'd introduced her to his old buddies, the ones he'd grown up with and whom he still called his friends, and whom she did not like or understand. And Bunty had introduced him to a life of summer houses in Maine and polo-playing friends in Palm Beach and to charity balls at the Met. It hadn't worked.

And after the divorce, neither had the models, the PR girls, the actresses, the "available" society blondes. Somehow life did not have the *savor* he'd expected from success. Only his daughter was real—and she was a part of him.

Two days before he was due to leave for Rome, he'd gotten the phone call. It was evening, and he was at home. Alone. Music played softly in the background like a chorus to the argument he was having with his ex. She had just broken the news that she was about to remarry the very next week, and he'd said simply that he was glad and he hoped she would be happy this time. And he had meant it. Bunty was spoiled and selfish and rich, but she wasn't solely responsible for the death of their relationship. It had been doomed from the start.

Then she had said that she was going on an extended honeymoon and she wanted him to take Muffie to Italy with him. Muffie! Like Bunty, that wasn't his daughter's real name. She was Martha (for her grandmother) Sloane (for her grandfather) Whitney (for an even richer great-aunt) Raphael (for him), but Bunty had dubbed her Muffie at birth, and Muffie she would be forever.

He loved his daughter, he saw more of her than her socialite mother did, but their deal was that Bunty was responsible for Muffie during that one month in the summer when he went to Italy. It was the only time of the year he got to be by himself. The only time he got to *be* himself. To paint, to read, to absorb the peace. To try to rewrite his life, in a way.

Privately, he felt it was the only time he returned to the man he might have been if he hadn't made all that money and didn't live in that constant head-on battlefield of the business world. And besides, this time there was real work to be done on his vacation. Real getting-your-hands-dirty kind of work, instead of the kind that tarnished your soul. He had been looking forward to it for months.

But Bunty, as always when she wanted something, was firm. So of course he'd taken Muffie with him, and now he was glad she was here. He was enjoying her company, her child's view of Italy, her pleasure in wild strawberries and real pizza and Italian ice cream, her excitement about being in a different country, and her delight at being here alone with him. "It's like an adventure, Daddy," she had said, laughing, and she was right.

He was worried about her, though. Thanks to his ex, Muffie was a spoiled little rich kid, out of touch with ordinary people. Sometimes he thought she seemed to be locked mentally behind the protective stone walls of her grandparents' estate, and that her mother wielded the key that kept her there, imprisoned in the unreal world of the super-rich.

One thing was for sure, he thought, watching his daughter still swinging, idly trailing her toes in the grass. She would see real life with him on this holiday. It wouldn't get any more real than this.

CHAPTER TWENTY

His party was in full swing now, though he noticed there was some contretemps over by the hot-air balloon. He might have known it: Maggie Marcessi didn't want to get off; she wanted another ride and wasn't willing to take her turn. "The more the merrier," he heard her yell over the general noise and laughter. He grinned ruefully; Maggie always wanted what she wanted exactly when she wanted it. It was one of her many failings, which also included her dress sense. But despite that, he loved her.

Maggie had been the first person to call on him the first year he'd rented the Villa Piacere, and she had come bearing a gift: a bottle of rare 1890 port from her late husband's extensive cellar, which she had pressed on him, saying, "I'm sure you'll enjoy this far more than I would. Just don't be like Billy [she always called her late husband Billy, though his name was Benedetto] and save it too long—or you'll be dead like him." Then she'd driven off at breakneck speed, crammed into a Fiat so tiny her head hit the roof as she bounced over the ruts in the driveway and she had to keep the windows open for elbow room.

A rabbit had darted in front of her wheels, and she'd squealed to a halt, backed up, gotten out, inspected the dead creature, picked it up by its tail, and flung it into the backseat.

The next day, her so-called majordomo came by. Actually, the majordomo was a vagrant from the north whom Maggie had rescued many years ago. She had "rehabilitated" him and now called him her majordomo, butler, or chauffeur, depending on which activity he was taking part in at the time. Anyhow, he had arrived the very next day bearing a ceramic terrine and a little note saying, "I do hope you enjoy this rabbit paté—it's fresh!"

Well, that was Maggie for you, and even as he watched, she soared aloft again, laughing and waving to the crowd below. Maggie brought life with her wherever she went, and he loved her for it.

He glanced along the terrace and did a double take. Wasn't that the woman from the Hassler? The enigma in the big dark glasses with the so-what-if-it's-a-party attitude? She certainly wasn't mingling; in fact, she seemed barely to be there. She was staring at the green valley stretched below, seemingly lost in her thoughts. And she certainly didn't give a damn about the way she looked: the crumpled linen dress, the sandals, and the touch of lipstick were an obvious concession to a party to which she had been dragged unwillingly.

He noticed her legs were long and shapely, albeit still pale from an endless New York winter, and that she had a kind of lanky grace. And he also noticed there was a soft look about her mouth, a tenderness as she caressed, with a single finger, the ancient lichen-covered balustrade on which she was leaning.

Somehow he got the impression that this woman was more temperamental than a movie star, more sulky than her daughter, and more unforgiving than even his ex-wife. And besides, she was definitely not his type.

Curious, he strolled toward her. "How d'you like the villa?" he said.

CHAPTER TWENTY-ONE

GEMMA

I was so lost in my thoughts, the voice from behind made me jump. I spun around, silly as a startled colt, and looked right into the eyes of the Michelangelo from Long Island.

I stared at him for a long, silent moment, as though I were looking to see if the pupils were normal or mere clinical pinpoints. Except this time it wasn't the doctor in me that was checking, and all I was seeing was that those eyes were an intense dark greenish hazel with tiny flecks of gold.

He was immaculate in a white linen shirt with the sleeves rolled to show tanned arms sprinkled with crisp dark hair. He wore worn Levi's that fit as though they had been tailored for his narrow butt, and those brown suede loafers I had noticed before, but without socks this time. His hair had a slight wave in it and was brushed back, showing that elegant little touch of silver at the temples. His eyes were narrow under bushy brows, his jaw had a hint of stubble, and his mouth . . . well, it was nice. Actually, it was *very* nice, kind of firm yet sensual, if you know what I mean. He also looked, I thought, like a man who had got where he was going. I saw all this in a flash, though of course I wasn't really interested in him. It was purely clinical. A doctor's reaction, you might say.

"What are you doing here?" I blurted, and knew immediately that I'd blown my cover, because as I remembered from my teen-flirt years, a girl should never let on that she was even aware a man existed.

"Same as you, I guess. Vacation." He leaned companionably on the balustrade next to me. "So how do you like the villa?"

"Like it?" I put my elbows on the stone rail, leaned my chin in my hands, and sighed. "I think I'm in love."

He laughed, showing a gleam of excellent white teeth, and I thought how handsome he was. Too handsome for his own good, probably. Men like him just sailed through a woman's world leaving devastation in their wake. He was so darn full of himself he sent prickles of antagonism up my spine. Yet at the same moment, he made me feel I was the only woman in his orbit.

"That's the way I feel about it too," he said. "It sure beats New York when the humidity's climbing and the heat radiates from the sidewalks and everybody's angry at the weather and at themselves. But *you* know what I mean."

"How do you know I'm from New York?"

He gave me a long quizzical look, one eyebrow raised. "Oh, I guess you just have that New York look about you. Sort of tense, uptight."

"Oh? And you don't?"

"Sure I do. I haven't been here long enough yet to lose it."

He signaled one of the village girls in her frilly apron for more wine, then handed me a glass. I took a sip; it smelled like warm berries and tasted like dark red velvet.

"What do you do, in New York?" He leaned back against the balustrade, his eyes still fixed on me.

"Isn't that precisely the kind of rude question you are *not* supposed to ask at a party?" I took another sip, staring challengingly at him over the rim of my glass.

"Probably, but after all, I've seen you half naked. I hardly feel like a stranger."

That stupid hot blush rose all the way from my chest. "So what do *you* do?" I asked abruptly.

"I paint."

"Then you could work here. The villa could do with a good paint job."

He nodded ruefully. "Okay, touché."

Despite myself, I grinned. "That's all right. I'd heard you were an artist."

He looked surprised, and I added, "My mother asked the headwaiter at the Hassler. She thought you were Italian aristocracy. In fact, she was devastated when she found out you weren't. Nonna is, you see. Italian, I mean, not aristocracy." I was rambling on like a ditsy schoolgirl. "We're here visiting our roots," I added lamely.

"Don't tell me your family is from Bella Piacere?"

"Two generations ago. Momma wanted to come back to see her old village again. Before she dies," I added automatically.

"Fascinating." He looked as though he meant it. "But what *do* you do anyway, besides being a mother?"

"Besides that? I work in a hospital."

"You're a nurse?"

I swung an upward glance at him from under my

lashes, then realized, shocked, that I was actually flirting with him. Old habits die hard, I guess.

"I'm a jack-of-all-trades, really. An emergency room physician. We get everything from the homeless hoping for a bed for the night, to sick babies, to killers cuffed to the gurney, bleeding from multiple gunshot wounds."

He looked impressed. "That's quite a job, even for a jack-of-all-trades."

Out of the blue, attraction flickered between us. I dismissed it immediately. Some guys get all goofy when you tell them you're a doctor; he was probably going through his symptoms mentally and was about to ask me for a free opinion on the state of his health.

Silence hung between us, tangible as cigarette smoke. "Sorry, I'm not much good at party talk," I said. "The only conversations I have are with a daughter full of teenage angst and semicomatose patients in trauma after an incident. An incident," I added thoughtfully. "Now there's a polite euphemism for highway slaughter, street murder, and domestic violence. It covers everything nicely. Like a shroud."

He whistled softly. "That must be one tough job you have, Doc."

I rolled my eyes. "Oh, *puh-lease*—don't call me *Doc*. I feel like I'm on a TV sitcom."

"Sorry, Miss, Mrs. . . . you know, we haven't even introduced ourselves. I'm Ben Raphael." He held out his hand.

"Gemma Jericho." His hand was warm and firm, but not smooth and manicured the way I had expected. The skin was rough, as though he worked with his hands. "Since this is now an even playing field," I said, "may I ask exactly what you do, Mr. Raphael?"

"Oh, *puh-lease*," he mocked me, perfect white teeth gleaming in a smile, greenish eyes gleaming with what might have been malice. "You mean you've never heard of me?"

I opened my eyes wide in faux innocence. "Are you a *famous* artist?"

He heaved another sigh and took a sip of his wine. "No, I'm not a famous artist, and I'm obviously not as well known as I thought I was."

"So?" I let the question dangle, and he laughed.

"I'm a failed artist, or at least an artist manqué."

"What does *manqué* mean?"

"Unsuccessful and unfulfilled."

"Sounds like the story of my life." I took another sip of my wine. I was beginning to enjoy myself. I might even like him, just a little bit.

"So," he said, his arm brushing mine as we leaned over that balustrade again, looking out over that perfect green valley, "you love the villa?"

"Yup, I admit it. I can't remember the last time I felt this way, but I know it's love all right."

He smiled. "I know what you mean. Feel free to come visit any time you like."

"Thank you, I may take you up on that. We'll need to do a proper inspection, get a valuation before we put it on the market."

"Excuse me?"

"Well, I mean, what good is it owning a crumbling villa in Tuscany when you have no money to keep it up? And besides, my life, *our lives* are in New York."

He frowned. "But I'm not planning on *selling* the villa, to your mother or anyone else."

"What do you mean—you're not planning on selling

it? The villa belongs to my mother. The count of Piacere left it to her in his will."

"We need to talk," he said, and took my arm and led me into the *gran salone* with the apple-green Lucca-silk walls and the cushions placed over the worn spots on the sofas.

I frowned, not understanding. "There's really not much to talk about. My mother was informed by Don Vincenzo that she inherited the villa in the count's will. It took several years to trace her, but that doesn't mean the villa was up for grabs. *Signore* Donati has made a mistake."

"I'm sorry," he said, "I didn't mean to get angry, but the mistake is on your mother's part. She's obviously been misinformed."

I thought of Nonna now, of her excitement and her determination to come here, and how thrilled she was to be an heiress; how it had changed her appearance, and how . . . how *gosh-darn happy* she was just to be here. This was *her* village, *her* family friends, *her* inheritance, damn it.

"Look." Ben was serious now, *deadly* serious. "*I own* this place. I bought it last year from the count's estate, signed, sealed, delivered, and paid for via the attorney, *signor* Donati. I've applied for planning permission, and I'm turning it into a hotel. In fact, work is ready to start."

I remembered the heavy equipment in the stable yard. So that was what it was for. My nostrils flared like a horse's at the gate. "I'll fight you on this," I said. "You can't take my mother's villa away."

He shook his head. "Go ahead, but you won't win."

"You'll see. I'll get this villa back!"

He lifted a warning finger, pointed it at me. "Over my dead body."

I glared back, lifted my own finger, pointed it at him. *"Maybe,"* I said. And then, not knowing what to do next, I spun on my heel and stalked regally away.

Pity I tripped over the rug; it kind of spoiled the effect. I heard him laughing as I ran fuming and blushing out into the gardens, in search of . . . of what?

CHAPTER TWENTY-TWO

NONNA

Nonna was sitting at one of the long wooden trestle tables covered with red, white, and blue paper cloths, in the shade of a massive old chestnut tree whose branches spread almost to the ground. Buntings fluttered in the breeze along with the festive little flags; the familiar aroma of burgers blended with the sugary scent of young red wine being poured straight from the wooden cask, and with the hot sweet aroma of fresh-picked tomatoes tossed with olive oil and basil, slathered on slabs of hard crusty bread. Birds twittered hopefully in the trees, surveying for crumbs, and somebody was playing old tunes on an accordion, while those with sufficient wine in them sang along.

It was, thought Nonna, a perfect mixture of the familiar from home—meaning America—and the familiar from her old home—meaning here in Italy. At least she thought that was what she meant, but maybe the wine had gone to her head just a little.

She stared around the table at the weather-beaten faces of men she had known when they were boys, men not much older than she was herself, but whose lives had been lived outdoors, in the vineyards and orchards and fields. They were farmers' faces, lined by the strong sun of summer and the harsh, icy winds of winter, and from worrying about crops and the vagaries of the weather and the need to harvest the grapes before the frosts came. Yet look how they enjoyed life. Just look at them now, singing along with gusto, raising their glasses, eating good food, drinking good wine, enjoying each other's company. Here everybody knew everyone else, they looked out for each other—apart from a few family feuds, of course, but those had been going on for maybe a century and didn't count. The fact that her father had jumped into a freezing winter torrent to save a boy's life did not surprise Nonna. Any other man here, she thought, would have done the same, though at home she could not imagine anyone jumping into the Hudson to save anybody.

And she felt quite different here. Just look at her, a woman who had not worn anything but sensible black for years. Now here she was, in bright green silk from the Rinascente department store in Florence and even a push-up bra the saleswoman had told her she absolutely had to wear with this neckline. And she had to admit the neckline set off the string of pearls rather well; and though the panty hose with the tummy support were killing her, they made her figure look good. She'd always had good legs, she just hadn't thought about them in years. Now, in strappy three-inch heels, they looked, well . . . almost glamorous.

It was true. She did look glamorous. Livvie had told her so, and so had the saleswomen who'd put her outfit together. They had even chosen her lipstick, "Begonia" it was called, as well as a rosy blusher. She had never worn such a thing in her life as blusher, but she had to admit it added a certain youthful glow. In fact, she hadn't felt as young as this in years, despite that lurching heart of hers.

She put all thoughts of rickety hearts out of her mind as she excused herself from the table and walked toward the house. She would take a look at her villa. *Their* villa, because what was hers was also Gemma's and Livvie's.

She stood looking up at all the many windows with the tall silver-blue shutters; at the peeling golden-apricot walls and the shiny terra-cotta tiles of the terrace. A sense of wonderment brought tears to her eyes. *This* was *hers*?

ROCCO

Rocco Cesani parked his rusting white pickup truck at the edge of what once had been a lawn and waited until the cloud of dust settled before climbing out. He dusted off his black suit coat, pulled it on over his short-sleeved blue shirt, pushed up the knot on his blue silk tie, bought specially for the occasion, and whistled for his dog, a white bull terrier with a long pink nose, pink ears, and pink-rimmed eyes, who was known as the best truffle dog in the area. Balancing on one leg, Rocco cleaned first one shoe against the back of his pants leg, then the other. He smoothed back his thick gray hair that bristled like a Brillo pad, put on his old camouflage-green rain hat, ran a finger over his mustache to make sure every whisker was in place, and he was ready.

The dog, Fido, trotted obediently at his heels, glancing neither right nor left. Wherever Rocco went, that was where Fido would go, and hopefully it would be on a truffle hunt, or maybe after rabbits.

"Not today, old fellow," Rocco said over his shoulder.

"Today you will eat American. *Hamburgers*." He rolled his eyes in despair. "Though why they eat hamburgers when they could eat a good steak *fiorentina* I do not know."

He stopped to survey the scene, and the dog sat exactly half a pace behind him. Rocco knew everyone there, except for the English, whom nobody knew because they only came for two weeks at a time in the summer. You never saw them much, though you could hear them all right: the women's high-pitched voices in the *alimentaria* and their kids arguing in the *gelateria* and the men, hot and red-faced from the sun, uncomfortable in the perpetually smoky Bar Galileo, drinking a cold beer with a grappa chaser, waiting for their wives and children.

He knew the *americano* well, though. Ben Raphael came every year. He stayed for a month, sometimes more. Sometimes he even came in the winter, when snow threatened and the Villa Piacere needed cords of firewood to keep the hot water and the fireplaces going. Rocco always brought him a truffle, and the *americano* brought him a bottle of good champagne to drink on Christmas Eve with the traditional Italian supper of fish and mussels and clams.

He thought the *americano* was a good man, though now there were rumors about requests for planning permission and an idea to turn the villa into a hotel. This could not be good. And anyhow, who would want to come to Bella Piacere?

He searched the crowd for a once-familiar figure. And then he saw her, standing alone, gazing up at the villa. He took a deep breath in, then let it out in a soft *aah* of pleasure.

Sophia Maria had changed little since she was thirteen.

She had always been taller than the other village girls, and always with that shiny black hair curling around her shoulders. Now, though, it was swept up in a smart hairdo, and she was elegant in green silk and pearls. Of course he remembered she had always had good legs—and those certainly had not changed. Yet she was somehow different. Was it that she looked American now? That she looked like a rich woman who lived in New York in a fancy house? A woman who might not have time anymore for an old friend? An old suitor, he might have been, had she stayed in Bella Piacere long enough.

There was only one way to find out. "Fido." The dog snapped to attention at his heels. *"Avanti,"* he said, and together they marched forward to where Sophia Maria was standing, all alone.

CHAPTER TWENTY-THREE

NONNA AND ROCCO

"Sophia Maria."

"Rocco Cesani!" Nonna stood with her hands on her hips, staring at him. The boy she remembered as a scruffy urchin in hand-me-downs that were always too small for his sturdy frame was now a stocky, bristle-haired, mustached man, hat in hand, smart in a dark suit. He even wore a tie. A silk one. He looked like a prosperous businessman.

"Rocco Cesani," she said again in a softer tone, watching him taking her in, just the way she had him.

"Sophia Maria Lorenza Corsini." Her names rolled off Rocco's tongue, smooth as liquid gold, as he thought how beautiful she was still, and how elegant she looked, and how glamorous. He told himself quickly that Sophia Maria was obviously a rich woman, too rich for his blood anyhow. But her dark hair still had those silky curls, and the touch of gray only softened the olive tones of her skin, and her eyes still flashed that dark fire at him, the way they had in the schoolyard when he'd tugged at her pigtails. *And* she was still head and shoulders taller than he was.

Nonna stepped forward and swept him into her arms, giving him a faceful of perfumed, lace-covered bosom.

Rocco allowed himself the luxury of being there for a second or two before he pushed himself away. Then he took her by the shoulders and planted a kiss on either cheek.

"Sophia Maria," he said again. "Look what America has done for you. You look like a fashion model."

"And you, Rocco, you look like a man from Wall Street."

They stood at arm's length, he still with his hands on her shoulders, beaming. Each had got the wrong impression of the other. The truth was that Rocco was usually to be found working in his olive groves, and the suit was the only one he possessed, used for weddings and funerals and the annual party at the villa. And Sophia Maria was just Nonna, the suburban Italian-American widow, always in her basic black, who rarely left her little town—except for a Macy's sale—and who was usually to be found slaving over a hot stove preparing that Sunday lunch.

Though he now owned many olive groves and his own *frantoio,* his olive mill, Rocco still lived in the same small farmhouse he always had; he still wore a workman's overalls and boots and still drank with the same cronies every night in the same bar he had been patronizing for over forty years. He had never traveled farther than Florence in his life. Ask him why, and he'd shrug. "There's no need. I have everything I want here," he'd say. And he meant it.

"Sophia, now you are a rich American princess," he marveled.

Nonna blinked. Maybe she should tell him that wasn't

quite true, though of course she was an heiress; but anyhow, right now it didn't seem to matter.

"And you, Rocco," she said admiringly, "are the very picture of the successful businessman."

Rocco shuffled his feet; what could he say when a woman he admired paid him such a compliment, even though it wasn't quite true? He couldn't think of anything, so instead he called his dog. "This is Fido," he said, "the best truffle dog in all of Tuscany."

Nonna raised a skeptical eyebrow. She remembered Rocco had always been prone to exaggeration. "In all of Tuscany?"

"*Sì, sì* . . . well, in the village certainly, maybe in the whole area. But he is the best, no doubt about that. Fido, say hello to Sophia Maria."

The odd-looking pink-and-white dog trotted toward her. Nonna gazed down at him a little nervously, but the dog gazed benignly back up at her, extended his right paw, waited patiently for her to take it, then gave an impatient little *wuff*. "*Ciao, Fido,*" she said, hastily shaking the paw. "*Come stai?*"

Rocco called his dog back, smiling proudly. "He is like my child," he said softly. "Almost as good as the son I never had."

Nonna slipped her arm through his, and they walked together up the steps onto the terrace. "Then you never married, Rocco?"

"Yes, I married. You would not know her. She was from around Montepulciano, a farmer's daughter, a lovely girl. But she never bore a child, and she died ten years ago and left me a widower, alone to mourn her memory."

Rocco crossed himself, and so did Nonna, and then

she told Rocco about her own late husband, and that she had a daughter who was a physician in Manhattan, and also a granddaughter, Olivia.

"A physician," Rocco said, impressed. "And you named your granddaughter for the olive groves of Tuscany."

And then, as they strolled the terrace of the Villa Piacere together, Nonna also told him the story of how her father had saved the old count's life when he was a boy, and that now she had inherited the Villa Piacere.

"Can you believe it, Rocco?" she said, smiling. "This wonderful villa now belongs to me?"

He gave her an odd sideways look, then after a moment he said, "But Sophia Maria, didn't you know that the villa belongs to the *americano*? The very one whose party we are attending? He bought it last year. Signed, sealed, and delivered. So how *can* you be an heiress?"

CHAPTER TWENTY-FOUR

LIVVIE

Livvie was bored. She drifted around the gardens seeking company her own age, but the boys and girls gyrating in the gazebo to Italian pop music stared at her as though she were something from another planet. The girls giggled behind their hands, and the boys grinned and shouted something that sounded like *ciao bella*. She wasn't sure what that meant, but she got the feeling they were laughing at her.

Disgruntled, she drifted back into the villa, swiftly inspecting room after room, stopping to look more closely at the charming murals of the animals and almost jumping out of her skin when the ancient parrot she had thought must be stuffed squawked at her.

She could swear he'd said, "Poppy." "Poppy *cara*." There, he'd said it again. Livvie knew that *cara* meant "dear" in Italian. She reached out to touch his scruffy molting feathers, but he skittered back along his golden perch and she had to lean closer to get a better look at the emerald, ruby, and diamond rings around his legs.

"Wow," she said, awed. "Oh, wow! Poppy *cara* must surely have loved you, little parrot." And then she saw his name on the plaque. "Luchay," she said. The bird batted a beady golden eye at her, then crouched lower, watching her carefully.

"Bye, Luchay," she called as she left. "I hope Poppy *cara* comes back for you soon."

Out on the terrace again, she looked for her mom and saw her talking to a man. It was the guy from the Hassler, the one her mom had called the Michelangelo from Long Island. She wondered what he was doing here. But since he was here, that meant that prissy little kid in velvet would be with him.

She walked to the edge of the terrace, scanning the grounds. Yup. There she was. On the swing, staring into space, all dressed in white and all alone. Great, Livvie thought, grinning wickedly.

She sprang down the terrace steps, then strolled nonchalantly across the lawn. The kid stopped swinging as she approached, and they eyed each other warily. The kid was wearing white shorts, a sweet white top with little ribbon straps, and white sandals. Fresh as a daisy, Livvie thought scornfully.

"Hi," the kid said finally.

"Hi." Livvie walked in back of the swing, and the kid twisted around, following her nervously with her eyes.

"What's your name?" Livvie asked, circling back in front of her again.

"Muffie."

Livvie rolled her eyes. What else would it be!

"So . . . what's *your* name?"

"Olivia."

Muffie said nothing, her eyes on the ground. "I have a golden Lab named Veronica," she offered at last, and Livvie sighed.

"So what? I have a ginger cat that weighs nineteen pounds."

Muffie lifted her eyes to meet Livvie's. "What's his name?"

"Sinbad. But usually he's just called Bad."

Muffie stared at the grass again. "I have a pony too."

Livvie swung herself up onto a branch of the ancient chestnut tree and straddled it. "You *would*."

Muffie bit her lip; she swung a toe through the grass, carving a little semicircle under the tree. Suddenly she slid off the swing. She stepped closer, gazing up at Livvie. "I like your hair. The colors, I mean."

Livvie ran a nonchalant hand through her mostly yellow crop with just a touch of lime at the front. "This is nothing. Usually I have three or even four colors, but Mom said no." She shrugged. "You know moms."

"Oh yes, I *do*," Muffie said fervently. "Believe me, I do."

"I saw you in Rome, at the Hassler." Livvie dangled by her hands from a branch over Muffie's head. "You here on vacation?"

"Yes, with my dad. Mom was getting married again. She said Daddy had to take me with him. I don't think he wanted to. This is his time when he likes to be alone, you see. Just to paint, he says, and to think."

"Why can't he think at home?"

"He says it's too noisy in SoHo, and besides, he's always working."

"Is he rich?"

"Yes, I think so. But Mom is richer, or at least that's what she tells me."

Despite herself, Livvie was impressed. "I never met my dad," she said.

"Oh." Muffie sounded surprised. She retraced the arc in the grass with her toe. "I'm sorry," she added politely.

Livvie shrugged it away. "Anyhow, we're kind of rich now, I guess," she said. "Count Piacere left my grandmother this villa, y'know, when he died. It belongs to us now." She jumped lightly to the ground. "In fact, you might be trespassing. In future you'll have to ask my permission to come here."

Muffie's jaw dropped. "*This* villa? The *Villa Piacere*? But it belongs to Daddy. He bought it last year. He's converting it into a hotel. Everybody knows that."

Livvie stood for a long moment. She glared at Muffie, shocked. "Liar," she said finally. And throwing one last glare over her shoulder, she marched off to find her mother.

CHAPTER TWENTY-FIVE

GEMMA

The three of us held an emergency conference over soothing cappuccinos, sitting around one of the flimsy little tin tables outside the *albergo*. Everybody else was still at the party, and I'd had to figure out the cappuccino machine by myself. I'd blasted enough froth into the cups to send espresso flying in a tidal wave over the edges, but, messy though Nonna said it was, it still tasted good.

"So what's a little coffee in the saucer matter anyway?" I said grimly. "The Villa Piacere is at stake."

"I just couldn't believe it when that kid Muffie told me her dad had bought it," Livvie said. "I told her she was a liar."

"It seems she is not a liar." Nonna poured sugar from a glass canister with a chrome top. "Rocco Cesani also told me Mr. Raphael owns it."

"Oh yeah?" I said. "So how can he own it when the count left it to you? Don Vincenzo saw the will."

"Perhaps there's a time limit." Nonna shrugged helplessly. "Perhaps after a couple of years it reverts back to the estate and they are free to sell."

"A will is a will, and I'll bet that whatever country you

are in, probate cannot be completed until the heir or heirs are found. *Nobody* can just give a villa away, not even a lawyer. And speaking of lawyers, where is that Donati anyway? He's the one with all the answers, and you can bet he's involved in this in some way. In fact, I'm going to call him right now."

I jumped up from the table and ran to my room, shuffled through my bag until I found the piece of paper with the phone number Don Vincenzo had given me, then dashed back downstairs to the phone in the little booth in the hall.

I dialed the number in a town called Lucca and heard that sharp Italian trill as it rang. And rang and rang. My lips clamped angrily together. Where was the bastard? Out spending his ill-gotten gains, no doubt. And more important, where was that will? We hadn't even seen a copy of it yet. All we had to go on was what Don Vincenzo had told us.

"Don't you worry," I said to Nonna. "I'll work it out. Nobody is going to cheat you out of what's rightfully yours."

I called Donati's number every hour on the hour for two days, but without success. By now I was good and mad. Nonna had taken Livvie to meet Rocco Cesani, an old friend of hers, and I mooched moodily around the village on my own.

I wandered into the little church and sat in a worn pew, listening to the hum of silence, watching the dust motes floating in a beam of sunlight, catching the glitter of the brass altar candlesticks.

My mother had been baptized here, I thought, at this

very stone font. She had made her first communion here, dressed in white ruffles and a veil with a circlet of flowers in her hair, like a little bride of Christ. My grandparents were baptized and married here, and their parents before them . . . and who knows how many before that.

When I'd left New York, I'd been just Gemma Jericho, Nonna's daughter, Livvie's mom. Now I was suddenly part of a continuing chain of life I had never contemplated before, never known existed. It made me feel strange, different. As though I belonged.

I bowed my head in thanks, then stepped outside into dazzling sunshine. It was hot, and I needed a cold drink. The Bar Galileo was almost next door to the church, behind the bocce court. I ambled listlessly toward it under the shady umbrella pines. Even from outside the bar I could smell decades of draft beer, and inside was even worse. I stared through the pall of cigarette smoke and the steaming hiss of the espresso maker at the flickering TV tuned to a soccer game. I nodded shyly at the men in workmen's blue overalls who turned to look at me, then backed quickly out again.

Maybe I'd have an ice cream instead. In fact, a *mocha granita* sounded so great I could already feel those tiny iced-coffee crystals sliding down my parched throat.

I was wearing only a sleeveless T-shirt and a pair of khaki shorts, and flip-flops bought in the village grocery store, which seemed to sell everything. Nevertheless, I was hot and sticky by the time I got to the other side of the square and the *gelateria*. I let the glass door swing shut, breathing a sigh of relief as cold air wafted toward me from the freezers.

"Good morning."

I stiffened like a hunting dog pointing a dropped

pheasant. *Ben Raphael.* This was all I needed. I turned to look at him.

He was sitting at a table with his daughter, who was spooning up an enormous multicolored sundae. She got up politely when she saw me, and so did Mr. Raphael. *Always the gentleman,* I thought scathingly, *even though you are a thief!*

"Good morning, Mr. Raphael," I said, icy as the freezer.

"Miss Jericho—*Dr.* Jericho," he corrected himself, "I think we have to talk. I've tried to get in touch with Donati to sort this situation out." He shrugged and held out his hands, palms up. "So far, no luck. What can I tell you except that there must have been some terrible mistake?"

"You bet there has."

"Could I maybe . . . buy you an ice cream? Muffie highly recommends the Everest."

He was my enemy, even if he was too cute for words, and I couldn't allow myself to consort with the enemy. "Thanks," I said, "but I'm the kind of girl who buys her own ice cream."

I heard him sigh as I turned away and ordered my little tub of *mocha granita.* I paused on my way out the door. "For your information," I added, "I have also been trying to contact *signor* Donati. And when I do, he'll be serving notice on you to stop work on the villa. He'll have you out of there before you even know it."

The door didn't exactly slam behind me, but the bell did tinkle very loudly. And then I stubbed my toe on an extra-large cobblestone, and my tub of *granita* flipped out of my hand and splashed onto the ground. I gritted my teeth, staring angrily at it. Then I scooped it quickly up and flung it into the trash can.

I heard the bell tinkle again as the door opened and Ben Raphael stuck his head out. "Like me to get you another one?" he asked, grinning.

"No, thank you," I said, tossing my head like a teenager and stalking huffily away. Damn it, why couldn't I *ever* make a great exit?

CHAPTER TWENTY-SIX

There was an invitation waiting for me when I got back to the *albergo,* written by hand in peacock blue ink and an elaborate flowing script. The thick cream-colored paper had those crinkly-cut edges that told you it was expensive, and there was a crest at the top: a peacock with its magnificent tail spread and wearing what looked to be a diamond tiara.

The Contessa Marcessi requests
the pleasure of the company of la signora Jericho,
la dottoressa Jericho, e la signorina Jericho
at the festivities to celebrate her forty-ninth birthday.
Wednesday July 10 at 7 P.M.
Dinner and dancing. Black tie.

Maggie Marcessi had not forgotten me. *Dinner, dancing, black tie*. What on earth would I wear? I hadn't danced in years. Still, didn't I used to be the Dancing Queen? Who else would be there? I wondered. Surely not Ben Raphael? But yes, of course he would, Maggie Marcessi had been at *his* party, hadn't she? Plus she was his neighbor and had known him for years. Well, that did it. Of course I couldn't go. War had been declared between the Raphaels and the Jerichos, and I was definitely not going to consort with the enemy.

"*Why* can't we go?" Livvie said. "It's a party. There'll probably be hundreds of people there, just like the one at the Villa Piacere. Oh, Mom, come on, I *want* to go."

"I don't see why not," Nonna said, surprising me. "After all, it's only a party, and it's a chance for Livvie to meet some of the local young people."

"*Young* people? Maggie Marcessi must be having her thirtieth forty-ninth birthday. How many *young* people do you think will be there for Livvie?"

"I think we would all enjoy it," Nonna said firmly. "And in fact, I'm calling the *contessa* right now to accept, and maybe I'll ask her if I could bring a friend."

"I didn't know you had anyone special enough to want to invite to Maggie's party."

"She means Rocco Cesani," Livvie said with a knowing little grin at her grandmother. "She's hot for him, y'know."

"Livvie!" Nonna flashed her a warning glare. "Rocco is an old friend. We were at school together. He took us to look at his olive groves and his *frantoio* this morning," she added.

"Bor-ing," Livvie said.

"He produces the best olive oil in the region. He even exports to the United States."

"He lives on a farm," Livvie said, "with a cow and a dog that looks like a pink-and-white sausage that sniffs out truffles. He showed me a truffle." She wrinkled her nose. "It was disgusting. How can people put that stuff in their mouths?"

"Truffles are gourmet delicacies," Nonna said severely. "People in New York pay a fortune to eat them in restaurants."

"More fools them," Livvie said, and I grinned because secretly I thought she was right.

"Anyhow," Nonna said briskly, "it's settled. We're going to the party."

"You *shall* go to the ball, Cinderella," I muttered, still determined not to. I would just have to wriggle out of it somehow.

Meanwhile, Bella Piacere was working some kind of magic on me. I found myself slowing down—so slow, in fact, it was almost a crawl, and soon I expected to be at a total standstill. But I was finally taking the time to taste life. *Real* life. To enjoy dinner in the piazza and go for walks alone in the hills and explore the neighboring villages.

Right now I was in the old graveyard, where the tombs were built into the walls, and stone plaques were carved with their names and dates and angels and cherubs. Framed photographs of the deceased were attached to some of them, and there were little bouquets of real flowers as well as plastic ones, and mossy stone walks and a bell tower.

I sipped icy spring water from the little drinking fountain, then sat on a stone bench with my eyes closed, listening to the birds sing and thinking that this wasn't a half bad place to call your final home. Behind my closed lids I saw a haze of red smudged with purple, like the colors of the big sunsets around here. Bees buzzed in the lavender, cicadas did whatever they did with their little cricket legs that made that summer sound, and something rustled in the undergrowth. I felt myself drifting, sliding gently into sleep.

"Ah, *dottoressa* Jericho . . . the very person I needed to see."

I sat up with a jolt and looked into the pink, smiling face of Don Vincenzo. I managed a startled smile as I brushed back my hair. I hated being caught sleeping; it was so *revealing* somehow. "Why, Don Vincenzo, what a surprise. How nice to see you," I said in scrambled Italian.

"*Dottoressa,* I have what you need," he said mysteriously. At least it was mysterious to me because he was speaking Italian, but I thought that was what he had said.

He fumbled in the pocket of his soutane, which close up and in the strong sunlight shone green with age, with a few spots of what was probably spaghetti sauce dotted here and there. He brought out a crumpled bit of paper, unfolded it, and smoothed it carefully over his knee.

"Here it is, *dottoressa,*" he said, still in Italian, of course. "Donati's new telephone number. I spoke with him this very morning, and I have arranged a rendezvous between the two of you. You are to meet him in Firenze, at the Caffè Gilli in the Piazza della Repubblica, at ten A.M. next Tuesday. Then all will be explained to you."

"Wait a minute." I held up my hand to slow him down. "Are you saying I have *a meeting* with Donati?"

"*Sì, con Donati,* the attorney."

"In Florence?" I quickly ran through the names of the days of the week in Italian in my head. "On *Tuesday?*"

"*Sì.*"

"*Really?*" I was delighted.

"*Sì, dottore* Jericho. Tuesday at ten at Gilli's in the Piazza della Repubblica. *Signor* Donati assured me there must have been some mistake and that he will explain everything to your satisfaction."

"He'd better," I said grimly, thinking of the Villa Piacere in Ben Raphael's hands. Signed, sealed—and delivered by that same *signor* Donati. But I thanked Don Vincenzo warmly and raced back into the village to find Nonna and Livvie and tell them the good news.

The days to Tuesday seemed to tick by slowly, I was so impatient to sort things out and make sure Nonna had her inheritance. We went out sightseeing, saw Nonna's friends, dined under the stars on pasta and tomatoes still warm from the sun with fresh local mozzarella and olive oil that tasted of Tuscany, and ate endless variations of zucchini from the inn's overburdened garden: sautéed, souffléed, broiled, grated, the little flowers stuffed and crisped.

Meanwhile, I seemed to bump into Ben Raphael everywhere: at the daily market, at the *alimentaria,* sipping Campari outside the Bar Galileo, filling up at the Motto station. And each time we encountered each other, we nodded coolly, antagonism crackling between us. But the annoying thing was that now I found myself looking out for him everywhere I went.

Of course, I was not about to tell him I had a meeting with Donati. I knew that would be playing right into the enemy's hands.

CHAPTER TWENTY-SEVEN

At last it was Tuesday and we were on the *autostrada* heading for Florence. It was early, the traffic was light, and the sky already a hard bright blue, promising heat. Livvie and Nonna were talking clothes, planning yet another shopping session for Maggie's party after the meeting with Donati. And I was concentrating on the road signs and worrying about what Donati was going to say.

Don Vincenzo had told me that, as attorney for the old count, *signor* Donati had the original, and as far as he knew, the only, copy of the will. It had not been filed in the probate court because at that time they had still been searching for the heir. Or the heiress, as I'd come to think of Nonna. Funny how I had so not wanted her to come here on such a wild-goose chase, and now I was the one determined to save her inheritance for her. I vowed that whatever it took, the villa was going to be hers. Only trouble was, without a copy of the will we didn't have a leg to stand on.

The beauty of Florence takes your breath away. It's everywhere around you: in the old streets and the stone buildings, in the piazzas dotted with statues, in the markets piled with fruits and vegetables, in doorways draped in jasmine and wisteria. Even Livvie was silenced as we walked down narrow arcaded streets lined with buildings so old, we finally understood how new America really was.

We strolled along the banks of the River Arno, admiring the statues of the Four Seasons on the Ponte Santa Trinità that had been rescued from the riverbed after the War, when the bridge had been destroyed. Now the bridge had been rebuilt, perfectly copied from the original.

The Ponte Vecchio, though, was still the real thing, with its lavish displays of gold jewelry in shops that looked much the same as they had in the fourteenth century—a century I admit never having given much thought to before now.

Lured by the glitter of gold, we paused outside a tiny shop, peering at the antique jewelry displayed in the window. A ring caught my eye: two bands of gold twisted together, centered with a cabochon of clear crystal surrounded by pinpoint-sized diamonds. It was obviously very old, and I wondered if long ago it had been given to a beautiful young Florentine aristocrat by her beloved. For once in my life I coveted something, but I put that desire behind me. I knew it would be too expensive, and anyhow, I had business to take care of.

The Piazza della Repubblica was once Florence's marketplace. Now it's lined with cafés, with tables arranged under blue and yellow awnings. Gilli's had been there since 1793, when it was just a small bar and tearoom. Now it's Florence's meeting place. It was already thronged with Florentines, taking their ease and their morning espresso and *dolce* while browsing through the newspapers and watching the world go by.

At the opposite end of the square, the Rinascente department store was open and doing business. I saw Nonna's eyes light up. No doubt she was remembering the friendly saleswomen who had "put her together" so nicely in the emerald silk and the pearls and the Begonia lipstick. I got the sinking feeling that she was ready for a second go-round and steered her quickly away.

We were looking for a small, very thin man with dark hair and a pencil mustache who was, so Don Vincenzo had informed us, always well dressed. He'd said that at this time of year *signor* Donati would be wearing a summer suit of white linen. "The *signore* is always impeccable," he'd said, "always in the best money can buy."

That little piece of financial information had sent a thrill of apprehension up my spine. Exactly whose money was Donati spending on smart summer suits? I wondered, though I was already willing to bet it was the zillions Ben Raphael must have paid him for the Villa Piacere. Money that definitely did not belong to him.

We checked out every man in Gilli's, both in the old-fashioned mahogany and mirrored interior and under the awnings on the piazza. Of course there were a dozen mustached Italian men in white linen suits, all impeccable and all expensive-looking. I walked along the rows of tables, gazing into their sunglassed eyes. These Italian guys were really good-looking, and every one of them gave me the eye. I'm sure it's just a reflexive thing, a national trait, so to speak, almost like a sort of tic. And I have to admit I kind of liked it. I even smiled back, just a little. I mean, it was enough to give a woman carnal thoughts. Except when that woman was me, of course; the woman who had adopted celibacy three years ago in a promise to myself I would not go back on.

"He's not here yet," I said, returning to the table under the awning.

"He's on Italian time," Nonna said, looking, I thought, far too relaxed for the tense situation. "He'll be here. Don Vincenzo promised."

I wished I were as certain that he would show up, but I ordered that double espresso with the cream on the side, and little sugary pastries topped with raspberries, plus an enormous chocolate sundae and a Coke for Livvie, who was drinking so much of the stuff I feared her teeth would rot in her head before we got her home and to the dentist. Nonna drank coffee and nibbled on a pastry, placidly scanning the morning newspaper while I scanned the piazza for Donati.

Half an hour passed. Forty-five minutes.

"We've been waiting a whole hour," Livvie complained. "So where is he?"

I shrugged as I grabbed my bag. "Beats me," I said as calmly as I could because inside I was really fuming. "I'm going to call him right now." And I marched into Gilli's, found a pay phone, and dialed the number Don Vincenzo had given me. I gave up after the tenth ring. *Signor* Donati was as elusive as a ghost.

Back at the table I chewed reflectively on my bottom lip, thinking about what to do next. "We can't go on like this," I said finally. "I'll just have to speak to Ben Raphael. He's going to have to work it out somehow."

Nonna heaved a sigh that seemed to come from her boots. "And if Mr. Raphael doesn't," she said quietly, "I think I know of another method that might stir him into action."

We waited for her to tell us exactly what action she was talking about, but she quickly changed the subject.

"Don't women say that when all else fails, go shopping?" she said. "Come on, *bambini,* we need to buy ourselves a party dress."

"I really don't want to go to this party."

Livvie glared at me, and I suddenly thought she looked exactly like her grandmother: same hands-on-hips stance, same exasperated look flashing from her brown eyes and aimed at me.

"Aw, come on, Mom," she said impatiently. "It's only shopping. It's, like, just a girl thing, y'know."

"Oh," I said meekly. "A girl thing. Right."

CHAPTER TWENTY-EIGHT

So here we were in Florence. But did we see the Duomo? A brief glimpse. Did we stop to look at the Uffizi? A passing glance. The Piazzale Michelangelo with its statue of David and a view of all Florence? Not even close. No. We shopped. My least favorite occupation and, I had thought until now, Nonna's. Until she had come back to Italy, that is, and since then I hadn't been able to stop her.

We hit the Via de' Tornabuoni at the speed of light, flashing in and out of boutiques so fast I wilted like a flower fading for lack of water. I missed the stillness, the peace, the silence I had become so used to in Bella Piacere, as I sat on little gilt chairs in fancy shops while Livvie and Nonna popped in and out of dressing rooms to get my not very expert opinion on their latest choices.

I was thinking about the villa: about the octagonal room with the ancient parrot; about the faded elegance and the way the apple-green silk walls looked with the sunlight streaming in. The memories sent a shiver of recognition down my spine, a feeling that I had lived there before, though in fact the nearest any ancestor of mine might have gotten to the villa was as a serving maid. Still, the villa was there, at the back of my mind, sleeping and waking, and I realized I didn't only want to get it back for Nonna. I selfishly wanted it for myself.

I thought about how I would corner Ben Raphael tomorrow night at Maggie's party, how I would get him alone out on the terrace, away from the crowd, and then I would . . . I would *what*? Tell him what I thought of him? That I thought he was a liar and that Donati was a thief, or they were in cahoots and were *both* liars and thieves?

Even I knew that approach was going to get me nowhere. I would have to soften things up a little, maybe bat my eyelashes, get close enough so he caught a drift of my perfume . . . What perfume? I didn't possess perfume. Still, that was something I could rectify as soon as we were out of this darned dress shop. Maybe I should gaze into Ben's eyes and appeal to his better nature? If he had one, that is.

Then I remembered him at the Hassler with his little daughter, how tender he had been to her, how caring. Hey, maybe he wasn't such a bad guy after all. Maybe I should give him the benefit of the doubt.

Thoroughly confused, I turned my attention to Livvie, who was twirling in front of me. The aqua-blue dress clung to her like a mermaid's scales, revealing every nubile curve and, even more provocative, every shadow. I had never seen Livvie look like this before, and I suddenly realized she was becoming a woman. *But not yet,* my heart cried, *not yet, please. Stay a little girl just a bit longer . . .*

Nonna came out to take a look. She pursed her lips, clicked her tongue disapprovingly, and shook her head. "Take it off," she commanded.

Livvie groaned. "But, Nonna—!"

"Off, I said."

Livvie twirled imperiously in front of the mirror. "It's time you realized I'm a woman," she said. "I have breasts." She ran her hands proudly over the insignificant twin buds. "I have periods."

"And in that dress you will *not* have your virginity. Take it off," Nonna said.

"Oh, N-o-n-n-a!" Livvie's childish blush almost turned her hair red. She was dying with embarrassment, and I thanked God. She was still a little girl after all.

They browsed the racks some more, with a sweet salesgirl hovering behind making suggestions and finding sizes. I watched Nonna go back into the dressing room with half a dozen more dresses and knew we were here for the long haul. So what was *I* going to wear? Reluctantly I got up and scanned the racks myself. I wished I could wear my doctor's white coat.

"The *signora* will be a size *trentaquattro, trentasei*," the patient salesgirl said, pulling a couple of dresses out to show me. I shook my head. I didn't want to be shown what to wear; if I had to do it, then I would choose something myself, and I would be quick about it. I pulled a beige silk off the rack and held it up against me. It had a V neck, a tight waist, and a puffy skirt. It would do; they said beige was good with everything.

"M-o-m, you can't wear *that*." Livvie grabbed it from me.

"Why not?"

"Because it's, like, *beige,* that's why. And just look at that skirt—you'll look like a bowling ball. Mom, you're in Italy! Why not choose something more colorful? Like, how many women in beige will there be at this party? Not many, you can bet."

Oh God, I thought, now my grown-up daughter is giving me instructions on what to wear. I wished I had never brought her here.

"I don't feel very colorful." I grabbed a soft white chiffon off the rack. It had a high round neck and fell in a straight line just to the knee. "This will do," I said firmly and, ignoring Livvie's protests that I should try it on, and also ignoring the lofty price tag, I told the salesgirl to wrap it up.

"Madame will need sandals," she said to me, and before I knew it I was tottering around in strappy little gold mules with the kind of heels I hadn't worn since I fell in love with Cash. I doubted I could walk more than ten paces in them, but I figured all I really had to do was get from the car into the house and I would be okay.

I approved Livvie's final choice of body-clinging red Lycra—I thought it looked a bit tarty, but I was too worn out to protest anymore—and also Nonna's banana-yellow silk suit with a nipped waist and portrait neckline dotted with crystals, though I did ask her where she thought she was going to wear it back in Long Island. She gave me a withering glance and didn't even bother to reply.

I caught the gleam in her eye, though, and I wondered who it was, besides Maggie Marcessi, she wanted to impress. I remembered the name Rocco Cesani and I wondered, *Could she?* But no, of course not. I pushed the thought that my mother might be falling for an old school friend to the back of my mind. I didn't want to know. Life was complicated enough already.

I thought of Ben Raphael and remembered I needed perfume. I checked my guidebook to find the whereabouts of the famous herbalist and perfume shop that I knew would have exactly what I wanted. It was a scent I had discovered years ago. It had been worn by a patient, an Italian visitor who had come to the ER with a sprained ankle after slipping on an icy winter sidewalk. I'd caught a whiff of it as she bent close to me, and I thought she smelled like the essence of spring. She had told me it was Violetta di Parma and that it was sold mostly in the town of Parma or in special pharmacies, like the one in Florence. I had never owned it, but I remembered the soft, almost powdery violet smell, and also its name.

The Officina Profumo-Farmaceutica di Santa Maria Novella was in part of an old monastery of the same name, tucked away on a street called the Via della Scala. From the glitz of the Via de' Tornabuoni, we stepped back in time into an old-world *farmacia*. Colored potions glistened in bulbous glass bottles on mirrored shelves, and antique wood cabinets were filled with pottery jars. There were ancient frescoes and painted tiles and the scent of herbs and perfumes. Here you could buy remedies to calm your nerves or restore your vitality; you could buy lotions and hand-milled soaps to smooth your skin and creams to soften your face and scents to lend you a certain allure; and all made from ancient recipes written by hand by the Dominican friars of old and preserved until today.

I found the Violetta di Parma and sprayed a little into the air from the tester. It smelled the way I imagined violets picked on a misty spring morning would, and I was in love with it all over again.

We bought a birthday gift for Maggie: a huge basket of soaps and balms and lotions and elixirs wrapped in white tulle and tied on top with a gigantic satin bow. Somehow I thought it looked like Maggie.

Then, laden with our packages, we staggered out of the store, which by now was closing around us for lunch, the way every place did in Italy. We grabbed a taxi and were driven to a small, bustling trattoria, Garga, on the Via del Moro, a narrow little side street jammed with Vespas and minicars, all squashed into impossibly small parking spaces.

Inside it was even more jammed. Customers crowded the rustic entry, stood three deep at the bar, and filled the tables. Cigarette smoke hung in blue curls under the low-beamed yellow ceiling, the scent of wine hung heavy, and conversation echoed from the art-filled walls. There was an aroma of bean soup and the crackle of rosemary-roasted pork and a heady wave of cheerful busyness as we were shunted through the crowd to a tiny table in a side room, jammed so close to the tables next to it I felt like we were joined at the hip.

A bottle of red was plonked on the paper cloth, specials were recounted, our order taken. Bread was brought in a little basket, glasses slammed in front of us, the wine poured, with San Pellegrino *"per la signorina."*

I slumped back in my little wooden chair, glad just to be off my feet, glad to have the shopping behind us, and still totally pissed off that Donati had not shown. But I thrust my worries temporarily away and enjoyed my lunch.

I started with a vast plate of prosciutto with figs so ripe they were at bursting point and so sweet they were almost dessert. Then we all had the rosemary-roasted pork with crispy crackling that melted in the mouth, and after, hot strong espresso to wash it all down.

We collected our packages and pushed our way back through the still-strong crowd into the street, where Nonna had only to raise an imperious arm for a taxi to squeal to a halt in front of us. Then it was back to the parking lot and back to the torture of threading my way through the Florentine traffic, squeezed into narrow streets that had surely been meant for sedan chairs, out of the city and onto the *autostrada*.

Back to Bella Piacere, after having spent an entire day in one of God's most beautiful cities without seeing a single one of its magnificent sights.

CHAPTER TWENTY-NINE

BEN

Ben climbed the round hill in back of the villa carrying a sketchbook and a small box of watercolors. Muffie darted along in front of him, leaping over tufts of grass and hollering when she saw a rabbit. With her shiny, silvery blond hair in a ponytail, long-legged in pink-and-white check shorts, a suntan, and sneakers, she looked like an all-American kid. She was an elf, a sprite, bursting with joy and the freedom of the moment. Ben didn't even have to think about how much he loved her; it was just a part of him. Without Muffie, life would be meaningless.

"Dad," she yelled from atop the hill, "you can see the *whole entire world* from up here." She jumped up and down, waving both arms over her head, a bundle of uncontained energy, making him laugh.

He ran the rest of the way and stood, breathing harder, next to her. "So you can," he said. "You can see *the whole entire world.*"

Muffie giggled as she gave him a nudge. "Oh, Daddy. You know what I mean."

"Okay, so I know. Now what I want you to do is paint it."

"Paint it? *Me?*"

"You," he said firmly. "Here's the sketch pad, the watercolors, the brush. Just paint what you see."

She looked doubtfully at him and then at the expansive view. "But I don't know how."

"You don't know how? Does that mean you can't see?"

"Of course I can see. I just can't paint."

"Muffie, you *can* paint. It doesn't have to be perfect, you just have to enjoy what you're doing."

They lay side by side on their stomachs, and Ben asked her to tell him what she saw. "A cypress tree," she said, pointing. "There, right in the middle."

"So the cypress tree will go in the middle of your painting. Go on, tell me more."

"A church, a village, a farm, olive groves, vineyards on the sides of the hills . . ."

"There you go," he said, turning over onto his back. "Now, get started."

He lay with his arms behind his head, staring idly at the infinite blueness of the sky. It was a blue you never saw in urban areas, he decided. It was as though someone had swept it clean with a broom, making the light brighter, clearer, more intense. The colors held more color, the shadows were deeper, the glare of the sun brighter. And in winter, when the skies grayed and the *tramontana* blew from the Alps and snow fluttered down, there was still a quality of light that intensified things, objects, feelings.

It seemed to him that, like the quality of the light, the quality of life was also different here in Tuscany. It was lived more intensely, more day to day, more of the moment even. Just buying a loaf of bread in the market or choosing a wine or admiring a pretty woman was done with so much more gusto. Every aspect was to be carefully considered, to be tasted, to be admired; every compliment to be chosen with care and thought.

There was no doubt about it, he lived in the moment in Tuscany in a way he never could back in New York. Here he could lie on his back on a grassy hill, staring at the sky and just thinking about his life instead of plunging head-on into it every waking minute of every day and, too often, even in his sleep. Or lack of it.

When he had bought his four-thousand-square-foot apartment in SoHo, he'd thought, This is it; this is the symbol of my success; what more do I need? But it wasn't long before he had discovered that he needed more. A lot more. He filled his days doing what every businessman did: meetings, lunches, negotiations, deals. And he filled his evenings, and sometimes his nights, with a series of pretty women, some of whom made him laugh, some of whom he desired, some of whom he couldn't stand after the first five minutes.

There has to be a different life, he'd told himself. There has to be something more than just this. And that's when he had taken off for Europe, and eventually had ended up in Bella Piacere. It had seemed to him, when he finally closed the deal on the villa, that it was the best deal he had ever made in his life. And now Gemma Jericho was jeopardizing that deal.

Of course, he had gone immediately to the old priest, Don Vincenzo, who had instigated the whole affair by searching out the Jerichos. Don Vincenzo claimed to have seen the will leaving the property to the Jerichos. Then he'd backtracked and said it would be best if Ben sorted out the whole matter with *signor* Donati, from whom he had "bought" the villa.

Bought and paid for, Ben had reminded him, and Don Vincenzo had spread his arms and lifted his shoulders in that expressive little shrug that Ben knew only too well meant that he had been duped.

His thoughts returned to Gemma, that crusty, quirky, offbeat, insecure woman who was devoted to her young daughter just the way he was to his, and who he could tell was also in a love/combat relationship with her Italian mother, who no doubt wanted to see her married. Gemma seemed dedicated to her profession, though he had a hard time imagining her as a trauma surgeon in New York's foremost emergency medical center. She was just too . . . ditsy. Too clumsy. Too . . . restrained. He thought she might have been better off as a librarian. In fact, she looked like a small-town version of a librarian, as seen in the movies.

It was her mouth that got to him, though. He liked how it turned up at the corners in that smiley way, he liked her cushiony underlip and the way she caught it in her small white teeth when she was angry, or thinking bad thoughts. Or maybe it was her eyes that got to him, the way she narrowed them when she looked at him, assessing him with that deep blue glare. Or maybe . . .

"Daddy."

He sat up and looked at his daughter and the painting she was showing him. He shook his head to clear away the thoughts of Gemma.

"Terrific, baby," he said. "That cypress is dead center, and the color of the olive trees is exactly right. Now you understand, it's not always what you see that makes the difference. It's how you see it."

And wasn't that the way of the world, he added to himself.

CHAPTER THIRTY

GEMMA

After all those hours spent shopping, it took me exactly eleven minutes to get ready for Maggie's party. Five to shower, wash my hair, and slather my body with my expensive new lotion. One minute to fluff up my hair and hope it would dry before I reached the party. Three minutes to dust my nose with powder, outline my lips with Nonna's Begonia, and brush the apples of my cheeks with Livvie's tawny blusher. Plus a minute for the mascara and a hint—just a hint, mind you—of bronze shadow, Livvie's again. How come I never knew my daughter had this arsenal of cosmetics tucked away? I was beginning to think there was a lot I didn't know about her. It took another minute to step into the dress and zip it up (forget all the rest—this is when you *really* need a man!) and a second to slide my feet into the strappy gold mules and check the end result in the mirror.

Only trouble was, the mirror was about a foot and a half tall, and I was probably well over six feet in the new heels, and I had to hunker down just to see my head and shoulders. I hitched up a bit to catch the middle part where the white dress floated past my waist. Then I had to tilt the mirror to see the skirt skimming my knees and—the final bit—the gold mules.

I chewed anxiously on my bottom lip until I realized I was biting off the Begonia and stopped myself. I was not happy with what I saw. The dress had looked great on the hanger; it was just that something happened when it was on *me*.

Livvie was right, I thought gloomily, I should have tried it on, but I had been too stubborn and too fed up, and now I was paying the price. It was just a nice dress on the wrong woman. A beauty I was not.

They say there are two things that make a woman beautiful: being in love and being pregnant. I don't know how beautiful I was when I was pregnant with Livvie, but perhaps that was because I wasn't loved. I was on my own, toughing it out, uncertain of my own feelings: about the coming baby, about the future, about myself. But then Livvie was born, and that other cliché—or miracle, depending on how you look at it—happened, and I was in love with her.

It had been different, though, when I was in love with Cash. Then I had felt loved. And maybe that's when the real miracle happened for me too. I walked through life in a state of rapture; I discarded the glasses and bought contacts, took to wearing eye shadow and lacy lingerie. I looked like a woman and not just a doctor, and I *felt* like a woman in a way I have never felt since. And never will again.

I heard Nonna calling me and, still thinking of Cash, I put on my glasses, collected my purse and my wits, and hurried downstairs to meet them.

Amalia and her daughter emerged to admire us in our party finery, and believe me, Nonna was quite something to admire. She was curvy, flamboyant in the yellow, elegant in the pearls, leggy in matching heels. And if this gives you the impression she looked like the bride's mother, believe me, she did not—she glowed like the bride! It was like watching one of those TV makeovers, and I wondered, stunned, if the basic black and the sturdy shoes were gone forever.

"*Che bella figura, signora,*" Amalia cried, meaning she looked elegant and stylish, though I thought sexy was more like it. Now I'm blushing: how can I even *think* such a thing of my own mother?

"Nonna, you look so sexy," Livvie cried, echoing my thoughts, and darn it if Nonna didn't just laugh and pat her dark curls, unfazed. What on earth was going on in my world? I wondered, bewildered.

Livvie, of course, looked like a little siren in the red Lycra and the yellow buzz cut, with a single dangling rhinestone crucifix earring. Just like Madonna's, she'd told me, as if that made it all right. She looked both sensual and innocent at the same time, and I crossed my fingers for the innocence part.

Next to the two of them, in my unsuitable virginal white, I looked ready for the Sunday school outing.

Then I remembered. I ran back upstairs to my room and sprayed myself lavishly with Violetta di Parma. If nothing else, I would smell gorgeous.

We followed a long line of cars up an immaculate gravel driveway lined with poplar trees hung with glowing red lanterns. A bronze fountain sprayed us gently as we stepped out, and a liveried valet whisked away our car.

We stared impressed at the grand floodlit facade of the Villa Marcessi.

It was one of those huge, splendid Palladian villas with a central double stone staircase and symmetrical rows of windows. It was painted a perfect peacock blue that its architect would certainly never have approved of, with architraves and coping stones in creamy marble. Peacocks swept grandly past us on the gravel, their magnificent tails spread. The marble steps were banked with blue hydrangeas, and music drifted from open windows. Through those windows I could see candles glimmering softly in crystal chandeliers and gilded torchères, and menservants in powdered wigs, knee breeches, and peacock-blue livery offering drinks and canapés from silver trays. I'd had no idea that Maggie Marcessi was as rich as this. Now I *really* felt like Cinderella at the ball.

Carrying the birthday gift basket, we climbed the steps to the massive front doors where a pair of liveried footmen waited to take our wraps and the gift, and walked on into the vaulted hall. I stared up at the glorious frescoed ceiling whose faded beauty sent one of those pangs through my heart. Then Nonna went off to find her friend Rocco, and Livvie drifted away, and I was on my own again. I accepted a glass of champagne and stood looking around for my prey. I was here for a purpose, after all.

"There you are, I thought you would never get here!" Maggie Marcessi's fluting English voice came from across the room, immediately making me feel that I was the only person she really wanted at her party. I smiled. *Eccentricity* might be another word for "crazy," but when it's combined with charm, it's a knockout.

She towered over her guests in her silver stilettos, glit-

tering like a Christmas tree in swathes of shocking pink
sequins and a skirt that was a mere fluffy drift of pink
feathers. Her flame-red hair was swept up into its usual
sixties beehive and topped with a diamond tiara at least
five inches tall. Add to that a matching diamond necklace
and enormous dangling earrings, and you get the picture.
And you know what, she still had great legs.

"Dear girl," she said in her best plummy English tones,
kissing me on either cheek and no doubt leaving traces of
her luscious fuchsia-pink lipstick. "How delightful you
look."

"And you, Maggie, you take my breath away."

"Oh, this old thing. I wore it in a Vegas show in, y'know,
in . . . well, I won't tell you exactly how long ago, but *way*
before I met Billy Marcessi, of course. Now how many
women do *you* know who could still get into a stage cos-
tume they wore in Vegas decades ago? Not many, I'll bet."

She stood back, still holding on to my hands, and took
another, more critical look at me. "Too plain, my dear,"
she said, shaking her head. "A woman without jewels is
like a cake without icing." She unclipped the enormous
diamond-and-pearl drops from her ears and thrust them at
me. "These will make all the difference," she said, as I
protested that I couldn't possibly wear her diamonds and
that I would be terrified of losing them.

"Not to worry," she said, giving me an intimate little
nudge. "Plenty more where those came from." Then she
whipped off my glasses and said, "Put these in your
purse, dear, you don't need them tonight. Now, how
d'you like my house?"

"Like you, it's wonderful," I said, cautiously clipping
on the earrings. "Are you really sure about these?"

"Oh, don't keep *on*, dear," she said, taking me by the arm

and leading me through the crowd into a grand *galleria* that was at least a hundred feet long and thirty wide. Tubs of gardenia trees, dropping petals onto the shiny parquet floor, lined walls swathed and looped in peacock tulle. Their scent drifted over us and out through arched French windows that were sheathed in gold silk and hung with giant silk tassels. Between the gardenia trees were giltwood sofas in striped silk, marble plinths with bronze statues of heroic-looking Marcessi ancestors, and inlaid tables with beaded lamps and pretty little boxes and whatnots. A band played on a raised dais in the corner, soft old-fashioned Cole Porterish stuff, and couples were already taking to the floor.

"Let me introduce you." Maggie steered me toward a group of aristocratic-looking people, the men suave in white dinner jackets, the women tanned and glossy, blond and bejeweled. And then she left me to say hello, good to meet you, clutching my champagne glass in one hand, shaking hands with the other, and feeling suddenly very alone.

I soon made my excuses and hurried purposefully away, searching for Ben. I came to the dining room, where chefs were putting the finishing touches to the buffet table, arranging immense silver platters with whole roast suckling pigs garlanded with bay leaves and tiny green apples. There were shiny bronze ducks on golden platters fringed with scarlet feathers, salads strewn with fresh flowers, peacocks carved in ice towering over mountains of fresh shrimp and lobster, and tubs of golden caviar in iced crystal dishes with mother-of-pearl spoons. Peacock-colored tulle was draped from the ceiling like a tent, and waiters in velvet knee breeches and white powdered wigs waited to serve the guests.

It was like a Roman bacchanalia. Everything about the

Villa Marcessi, even the food, was over the top, and I knew there would be no worn rugs here, no cornices in need of fresh gold leaf, no peeling stucco walls. If I had not known Maggie Marcessi was rich, I surely knew it now. The Villa Piacere was a doll's house compared with this.

I knew the old Count Marcessi was long gone, but I'd be willing to bet there were still cellars here filled with his rare wines, and humidors with his Havana cigars, and enormous safes stuffed full of Cellini silver and priceless jewels, like the ones I was wearing, handed down through the centuries. And when the old count had gotten himself a wife who knew how to spend his money, I bet he had himself a wonderful time. How could he not, with a woman like Maggie to show him how to enjoy it?

I stepped through the French windows onto the vast terrace overlooking the Villa Marcessi's immaculate gardens and a lake where illuminated fountains danced to the music. A sudden hot wind stirred my hair. The sirocco, Nonna had told me it was called, blowing in from the deserts of Africa. The peacock-colored tablecloths fluttered and candles flickered as I strolled past the lemon trees in enormous Ali Baba urns.

Dusk was just changing to night, and the hills were as soft as folds of dark velvet. The sky was clear, washed clean by the breeze, and a full moon crested over a distant ridge. Hot night sounds wafted toward me: the whirr of cicadas, the croak of tree frogs, a blackbird's sweet call, the rustle of leaves in the hot breeze. I slipped off my gold mules, and felt the terra-cotta tiles were still warm under my bare feet. It was all so beautiful, and so far removed from my real life, tears pricked the backs of my eyes.

I told myself this was too alluring, too dangerous. It

was a dream life. I had to get out of here, get back to the safety of my own reality; back to the emergency room, doing what I did best. Ha, sure, I told myself bitterly. *Sure*. Just being Doc Jericho, the savior of mankind.

I heard footsteps and quickly brushed away my tears. My enormous diamond earrings jangled as I swung around. Ben Raphael was standing there, relaxed, easy in his white dinner jacket, hands thrust into his pockets. He was so comfortable in his body and so completely at home with himself, I envied him.

CHAPTER THIRTY-ONE

BEN

Ben was determined not to be cheated out of his refuge, but he also wanted to get to know this pesky woman who was driving him crazy, in more ways than the obvious one of the villa.

He'd caught the glimmer of her white dress on the shadowed terrace and a glimpse of her profile in the flickering candlelight. Her blond hair lifted from her brow in soft waves and curled gently behind her small ears—ears that he noticed were loaded down with enormous diamond drops. She was barefoot and slender in chiffon that drifted around her suntanned legs, and he thought that in the white and with that halo of hair, and without the glasses, she looked like a Botticelli angel. Which, of course, she certainly was not. Dr. Gemma had a sharp way with words no angel would have tolerated.

She turned and looked at him from beneath half-lowered lids, her eyes a narrow flash of blue. He frowned; he could swear she'd been crying.

"How d'you like the villa?" he asked, and she tossed her head and gave him that cold sideways look.

"Isn't that where we came in?"

"I thought it was as good a starting point as any."

"Starting what?"

She was as frosty as iced lemonade and just as tart. "We have to talk, you and I."

"Yes," she agreed, surprising him.

She was studying him with those narrowed blue eyes. He studied her back. He thought she had a certain odd allure tonight in that white thing she was wearing, though he'd be willing to bet she was one of those women who looked better out of clothes than in them. She was some tough cookie, though, and boy had she let him know it. She had declared war between them, but now it was up to him to call a truce.

"The Villa Marcessi is beautiful," she said suddenly. "Especially the frescoes in the hall."

He nodded. "They're by Veronese. Did you know that frescoes were painted in a time when most of the population was illiterate? So the artists painted the stories on the walls for them, sort of like picture books."

"I never knew that." They looked at each other for a long moment. Then, "Where's your daughter?" she asked.

"Probably with yours. I saw them together a little while ago, sneaking a glass of champagne."

"And you didn't stop them?" She looked outraged.

"Of course I didn't stop them, there was no need. They took one gulp, choked and spluttered, and then went off to find a Coke. They have to learn, you know, what's bad and what's good."

"Don't you think you should have told them? That drinking is *bad*?"

He laughed. "I think they found out for themselves. Listen, Doc, I'm here to call a truce. Why don't you and

I take a stroll around the garden and talk about the Villa Piacere?"

She stared doubtfully at him, but after all, this was what she had come here for, wasn't it?

She slipped on her gold mules, Ben took her elbow, and they walked down the steps together into the quiet, lantern-lit garden. The wail of a peacock shattered the silence, sharp as a child's cry, and then another and another until the night seemed full of the birds' mournful cries. Ben felt her shiver, despite the hot breeze.

"A ghost walking over your grave," he said, remembering the old saying.

She gave him that icy look again. "Perhaps."

"I want you to know I bought the villa in good faith," he said. "I have all the legal documents. I paid by cashier's check made out to the estate of the count of Piacere. There was no discussion about the will and no word that the count had disposed of the villa in another way. The attorney, Donati, said he was just doing what was expected of him and that the estate would profit from the sale. He said there were long-overdue taxes, plus death taxes. He was glad to get the money and be able to settle the estate. It was all legal, all aboveboard. Trust me, everything was in order. I'm a professional in these matters."

"Except there was a will that Donati never showed you, leaving the estate to my family."

"Do you have a copy of that will?"

Gemma sighed. Somehow she had known that question was coming. "No, I don't."

"Have you ever seen the will?"

She shook her head. "No, but Don Vincenzo saw it. It was after the funeral, and Donati was going through the contents of the count's safe. Don Vincenzo said Donati took out the document. It was the count's last will and testament, in his own handwriting. Donati asked him who Paolo Corsini was, and then he showed him the will, where it said the estate was left to the Corsini family. Donati said of course there was no family left, but later Don Vincenzo found out they had left for America many years before. He vowed to try to trace them . . . to trace Nonna, that is. And eventually, a couple of years later, that's what he did."

"Look." Ben stopped and faced her. "I've tried to contact Donati, but he never answers his phone. I have to say that the ball is in your court, Dr. Gemma. Until you can prove me wrong, I am the legal owner of the Villa Piacere."

She was looking at him as though she were about to cry again, all hurt blue eyes in an angel's face. "I'm sorry." He took her arm, felt her shiver. The same shiver ran through his own bones, but this was no ghost walking over his grave. There was something different about this woman; she brought out a streak of tenderness he had not known he possessed. He ran his fingers lightly down her arm, felt her draw back into herself.

"Gemma," he whispered, "I'm sorry . . . I didn't mean to hurt you."

She shook her head. "That's okay. You're right, I'll have to do that."

He stepped closer, put his hands on her bare shoulders. He could feel the delicate bones beneath, see the flickering of a pulse in her throat. Her eyes reflected the sparkles from her diamond earrings, and suddenly he wanted to kiss her. In fact, he'd wanted to kiss her from the moment he first saw her. He wanted to know how a woman like this kissed. He wanted more, he wanted to *know* her, to know what she was really like, what her secrets were, why she walked around like the ice maiden, deliberately frumpy, deliberately denying herself pleasure.

He put a hand on the nape of her neck, eased his fingers into her soft blond hair, felt the moist heat there. He pulled her closer, saw her mouth open in a soft oh of surprise. And then he was kissing her.

CHAPTER THIRTY-TWO

GEMMA

Do you know what it feels like to kiss a man for the first time in three years? It's an electric shock jolting through your veins; it's points of light behind your closed lids; it's knees that are suddenly wobbly as a kitten's and a willpower that has melted into a warm hot glow between your legs. It's like discovering sex for the first time—only better, because now you know what it's all about and *why* you are feeling like this.

I was like the heroine in a Jane Austen novel, weak and about to succumb to an attack of the vapors—except I wanted more. More kissing, more of this feeling. . . . I never wanted it to end.

His lips were firm on mine, pressing open my mouth, exploring me gently with his tongue. Oh, God, I knew you should never do this on a first date—kiss open-mouthed, I mean . . . at least not in my youth, you didn't. But I wanted to, I just *wanted* to. And yes, I admit it, I wanted *him*. His rough bluish-stubbled chin scraped against my skin. I pressed my body against his long lean length, ashamed of how much I wanted him. I had been celibate for three years, and in the space of thirty seconds I was a goner.

He lifted his mouth from mine and I stared breathlessly into his eyes. I know I should have pushed him away, I *know* it. I was compromising my whole future here. But did I do it? *No.* His fingers tangled in the hair at my nape, pulling me back to his mouth. And I was lost in a rapture I barely remembered. *Oh God,* I thought, *oh God,* as my mouth linked with his and I tasted his tongue, sweet, smooth, slippery. Just as I wanted it to be.

Fireworks exploded in the night sky, in a shimmer and glitter of rockets and sparkles and flowers and stars. For a moment I wondered if it was just in my head. Then I realized it was for real, and the fireworks were to celebrate Maggie's forty-ninth.

I forced myself back to my senses, pushed him away, stepped back, smoothed my ruffled hair, hardly daring to look at him. When I did he was smiling at me.

"I didn't mean to do that," he said.

"Thanks for the compliment."

"What I meant was, I wanted to do that so badly I couldn't stop myself. I think I've wanted to kiss you since the first time I saw you."

I remembered that look he had given me in the Hassler restaurant, when I had felt like the only woman in the room. He was giving me the same look now, and I wondered, confused, what to do about it. This man was my enemy, he was about to take away my mother's inheritance. This was worse than consorting with the enemy— it was almost *sleeping* with him.

Fireworks still crashed through the night as I bent to pick up my little gold purse, which had slipped to the ground. I took out my glasses and put them on. They were a barrier between me and him, but now I could also see him clearly—and oh, *darn it,* he was just as good-looking, just as relaxed, just as *sexy*. I had to get out of here before it was too late.

"I'll find Donati, you'll see," I said breathlessly. Then I turned on my spindly little gold heels and stalked away. And for once, I did not trip. I did turn back to look, though. He was wiping my lipstick off his mouth with a handkerchief, smiling to himself. *Like the cat that got the cream,* I told myself furiously.

Oh darn it, I had made a fool of myself again after all.

CHAPTER THIRTY-THREE

MUFFIE

Muffie Raphael followed Livvie out onto the terrace to see the fireworks. She had been following Livvie all evening, hoping Livvie would talk to her, but Livvie just pretended like she wasn't there. Muffie had even sneaked a mouthful of champagne when Livvie had, and then coughed it up all over her awful pink dress.

Livvie had stopped on the edge of the terrace, half hidden by one of those giant pots with the lemon trees. She was very still, not looking at the show in the sky but staring out across the dim gardens where the lanterns glowed like scarlet balloons in the trees. Lanterns as red as the dress Livvie was wearing, Muffie thought enviously.

She smoothed her hands over her own pink taffeta, hating the ruched bodice with the frills around the armholes and the wide pink satin sash and the damn black patent leather Mary Janes her mother always insisted she wear. She wasn't allowed to choose anything for herself, and by now she had given up trying. "Mother knows best" was a constant refrain in their household, and if it wasn't Mom, then it was Grandmother. Everybody knew best, except Muffie herself. And her dad, though he didn't seem to know what girls her age wore anyway.

She hovered just a step behind Livvie, hoping she would turn and say hi, but Livvie didn't. She just kept on staring out at the garden, as if there was something really interesting there.

Muffie pushed past the pot with the lemon tree and stood next to her, looking at the fireworks exploding in showers of peacock blue and silver. Livvie did not so much as acknowledge her presence. Muffie followed Livvie's gaze and saw her father with his arms around a woman. She drew in her breath sharply. "Oh my God," she whispered, and Livvie finally turned to look at her.

"*Your dad* is kissing my mom," Livvie said coldly.

"Your *mom* is kissing my dad," Muffie retorted.

"My mom does not kiss men—not since Cash," Livvie said.

"Well, it looks as though she *likes* being kissed." Muffie leaned over the balustrade to get a better look.

"How would you know? Have you ever been kissed?"

"Well, no. Yes . . . but only in party games, y'know. . . ."

"Huh," Livvie said, though her own experience was not much greater. "So you don't know then."

"Do you?" Muffie looked longingly at Livvie. She wanted to hear about being kissed, about where to buy clothes like the ones Livvie wore, about her hair . . . about Livvie's entire sophisticated, worldly life that was so different from her own. Stuck in the big house in Connecticut where you had to make appointments for your friends to visit and nobody ever just dropped by. Mostly, she only felt really alive when she went to stay with her father in SoHo and he took her out to funky little restaurants and to Broadway shows and helped her with her math homework, which was the bane of her life—she simply had no head for math. He'd laughed at her, told her he didn't know how a daughter of his could not know how to add correctly, and then he'd shown her how. She loved her dad more than her mom, if truth be known. But the real truth was, she wanted freedom.

"Your mom looks pretty tonight," Muffie said.

Livvie nodded gloomily. "The thing about my mom is she has no idea that she's pretty. Like, it just never occurs to her. Sometimes I wonder exactly what she sees when she looks in the mirror, though she hardly ever does. She never has the time."

"I love your dress," Muffie said.

Livvie looked her up and down. "Where did you get *that*? You look like somebody's bridesmaid."

Muffie nodded glumly. "I know." She was silent for a moment, then she said, "How do you do your hair like that, the color, I mean?"

"Easy." Livvie's eyes lit up, and she grinned suddenly. "Want me to show you how?"

"*Really? You'll show me? Really?*" Muffie's eyes sparkled.

Livvie nodded. "You bet I will, Muffie," she said, throwing a friendly arm around her shoulders.

CHAPTER THIRTY-FOUR

ROCCO AND NONNA

Rocco Cesani looked smart in his black suit, white shirt, and the black tie Sophia Maria had said he should wear, though it made him feel as if he were going to a funeral instead of a party. For once he was not wearing his hat, and also for once his dog was not with him, though Fido was, in fact, waiting in the truck. Rocco mingled with the other guests, sipping a glass of champagne—good champagne, he knew the difference—and checking out Maggie Marcessi's home.

Like the Villa Piacere, he'd known this house forever. He had played there with the gardener's kids when he was a child. As a lad he had waited on tables and helped in the kitchen for a hundred parties, though the only one as grand as this had been Maggie's wedding, when she'd worn billows of white satin adorned with pearls and diamonds until he hadn't been sure which was the bride and which the wedding cake.

He had poached pheasant and rabbits on this estate, knew that the best truffle spot was in the lower copse under a small, squat oak tree—and that he and Fido were the only ones who knew that. For years he had supplied the house with the best milk from his special white Chianina cow, which he kept in a barn and groomed every day. He had attended Count Marcessi's funeral ten years ago wearing this same suit and tie and had stood in the reception line to kiss his widow's hand afterward. He had supplied the suckling pigs for tonight's feast, as well as the first-pressing "virgin" olive oil from his best grove. He was a man of many parts, and he knew many of the people here tonight, and many others knew of him.

He saw Sophia Maria edging her way through the throng. *"Madonnina mia,"* he whispered to himself, *"che bella."*

She walked toward him smiling, and he held out his hands and took hers. Then he bent and kissed them. *"Principessa,"* he said smiling, and Sophia Maria swept him a little curtsy and said, *"Principe,"* and then he led her onto the dance floor and swept her into a waltz.

Sophia Maria liked the way his hand felt in the small of her back as he guided her confidently around the floor. Being head and shoulders taller than he was, though, she had to look down at him when she spoke. He gazed up into her eyes, and they smiled.

"Rocco," she said, "you remember what we talked about the other day?"

"The Villa Piacere, *sì* . . ."

"I think it is time for action, Rocco."

He stopped and looked at her. He rubbed two fingers against the side of his nose in an Italian gesture that said it would be done, and nodded solemnly. "Trust me, Sophia Maria," he said.

The waltz finished, and they left the dance floor. They sat close together on one of the little giltwood sofas. A footman offered them champagne, and another came by with tiny blinis mounded with caviar, and they sipped their champagne and nibbled the caviar, heads together, plotting.

Fireworks lit the night sky, and Maggie Marcessi swept by in a flurry of feathers. "Bloody Italians," she said, "they never get the timing right. They were supposed to go off at midnight while the band played 'Happy Birthday.' *Attenzione,* everyone, it's too late to do anything about it now, so you may as well enjoy it while you can—as the actress said to the bishop." And she waved her arms in the air, directing traffic onto the terrace amid *oohs* and *aahs* as showers of golden rain descended from a sky suddenly studded with sparkling diamonds.

Sophia Maria's eyes, brown like Rocco's own, reflected the fireworks' glitter as they met his, and he took her hand and smiled.

CHAPTER THIRTY-FIVE

MAGGIE

Maggie saw Gemma running up the steps from the garden. Mmm, she thought, I wonder where she's been, and with whom. She snagged Gemma's arm as she hurried by. "Enjoying yourself, my dear?" she said.

"Oh, oh . . . yes. Thank you, Maggie, it's a lovely party."

But nothing escaped Maggie's experienced eye. "It looks to me, Gemma Jericho," she said, "as though *you* have just been kissed. And *well* kissed, judging by that look in your eyes."

"What look?"

Maggie's laugh boomed out. "You can't fool me, my dear. Come, let's go to the powder room so you can fix your lipstick, and then you can tell me all about it. Girl to girl, y'know. Oh my, isn't this exciting."

The boom of a gong echoed from the walls, making them both jump half out of their skin. Maggie glared at the young footman, who was one of her six gardeners in his day job. "Silly boy," she murmured, "I warned him not to whack the thing so hard."

"*Signore e signori,* dinner is served," he said, and the

party crowd swerved away from the terrace and headed for the dining room.

GEMMA

The powder room was large and luxurious enough for a five-star hotel. I sank onto a little brocade bench and stared at myself in the pink-lit mirror. Even in that rosy light I looked pale, and my mouth had that chewed-up look that moments of passion give you.

"Mmm," Maggie said thoughtfully, looking at me, "maybe you need more than just lipstick; you look as though you need a cold shower."

"Oh, Maggie," I said, and to my horror tears trembled on my lashes again.

"What is it, girl? You can tell Maggie." She squeezed onto the bench next to me and took my hand. "Don't worry, no one will come in, they're all eating," she said encouragingly.

"It's . . . complicated," I said, and she patted my hand.

"Isn't it always?"

"Yes, but this is *really* complicated. It's just that something happened to me three years ago, a man . . . my lover. Oh, I'm not telling this at all well. I just never talk about it, you see. But Maggie, I loved him so. It came to an end. My heart was broken, and I swore I would never, *never* look at another man again. I told myself I didn't need *any* man, I was going to dedicate my life to my profession, I was going to save other people's lives. I would just raise my daughter, care for my mother, go to work every day . . . and that would be it. No more highs, maybe, but no more terrible lows either. Life would go on."

I looked into Maggie's sympathetic blue-shadowed eyes. "I erected a barrier against the world," I whispered sadly. "I was the woman with ice around my heart—"

"And no man was ever going to melt it." She finished my sentence for me, and I nodded. "Until tonight," she added shrewdly. "Let me guess who it was. Ben Raphael."

"I made a fool of myself, Maggie," I whispered. "Damn it, I let him kiss me—and damn it even more, I liked it."

"Of course you did. There's nothing wrong with a good kiss, my girl, and I'll bet Ben's a fine kisser. But you mean to tell me you haven't kissed a man in *three years*?"

"I promised myself to be celibate."

She nodded briskly. "Well, my dear, perhaps it's time to come out of the nunnery. I don't know what happened between you and your man, and right now I'm not going to ask, because I can see how upset you are. But life goes on, Gemma. And you must get on with living."

She took a little gold compact from her beaded purse and offered it to me, along with her fuchsia lipstick. "Come on now, girl, dry your tears, powder that nose, put on some fresh lipstick, and let's go and have ourselves some dinner. And then it's dancing until dawn."

She waited for me at the door. "And next week, I promise to read your tarot cards," she said with a sly wink. "Then we'll see what your future really holds."

CHAPTER THIRTY-SIX

BEN

The morning after the party, Ben woke late. It would be nice to be able to say that his first thoughts were of Gemma, but in fact, they were not. He would think of her later on, but in a completely different context from the previous night.

The sun blasted through the tattered brocade curtains that were so thin with age they were almost like net. He was hot, and in fact his first thought was simply that he needed a shower.

He put on a robe and walked barefoot down the hall to his daughter's room. Her bed was empty. The pink taffeta dress was in a crumpled heap on the floor along with one of the despised black patent leather Mary Janes. He thought he was going to have to do something about Muffie's clothes; she really hated the stuff her mother bought for her. He guessed she would be down in the kitchen with Fiametta, the housekeeper. She would be eating the toasted *ciabatta* bread with Fiametta's homemade strawberry jam that they ate every morning, along with a glass of cool sweet milk from Rocco Cesani's special cow.

He wandered back down the hall and into his bathroom. It was so big you could have held a party in there.

The claw-footed tub was an antique in situ; the shower apparatus was a convoluted curve of brass that ended somewhere about the middle of his chest; and the showerhead was a huge brass sunflower with lethally sharp-pointed petals and pinprick holes that emitted a spray suitable for a birdbath.

The entire bathroom had probably been redone around 1904. There was a green-tiled corner fireplace with an ornate mirrored overmantel, the floors were of worn parquet, and the tall uncurtained windows overlooked the front entrance, giving visitors a direct view of the showerer. But what the hell, he wasn't expecting anybody.

He stepped into the tub, warily dodging the brass sunflower petals, and turned the elaborate four-pronged brass tap marked *caldo*. There was a distant clanging in the pipes. He waited patiently. Things took a while to work around here. He bent over to adjust the tap, yelping as the brass sunflower fell off and a jet of water, icy enough to have come from a subterranean spring, hit him in entirely the wrong place.

He gritted his teeth. Okay, so it would be a cold shower. He soaped up. There was more clattering in the pipes, a grinding noise. The cold jet thinned to a brownish trickle. Then nothing. *Zero*.

He smacked the brass pipe with his fist, but all it coughed up was another meager brown trickle. He was covered in soap, and it was a *desert* in here.

Cursing, he dried off, then went to investigate. Only to find there was not a drop of water in the entire house.

"Nothing can be done, *signore*," they told Ben when he finally got the water department on the phone. "It's hot, too many tourists are taking showers, there are too many swimming pools. That's the way it is in the summer. You will just have to be patient, *signore,* the water will come back eventually."

"Yeah, but when exactly is *eventually*?" All he got was a laugh in reply.

"*Piano piano, signore. Con calma.* Soon enough it will be back."

Ben put down the phone and stared thoughtfully at it. He'd been coming here for years, and nothing like this had ever happened before. He got the picture now: it was water blackmail, and money was the answer. He would have to take a trip into town, go to the bank, and try to deal with the bureaucrats. He thought about it some more, fingers drumming impatiently. Odd, though, that this had happened only after Gemma Jericho and her family came to town.

He threw on shorts, T-shirt, and sneakers and clasped his old steel watch around his wrist. The watch almost qualified as an antique, he'd had it so long. He'd bought it when he was twenty years old and just hitching himself up the ladder by his bootstraps, along with a pair of cheap silver cuff links he thought would help him to present a successful facade. Not that the watch and the cheap silver cuff links made any difference, but he hadn't known that then. He'd still had a lot to learn. And probably still did, he thought, sighing.

He walked to the window, pulled back the curtain, and stared out. Even the fountain had died.

He wondered about Gemma Jericho.

CHAPTER THIRTY-SEVEN

GEMMA

I paced my room at the Albergo d'Olivia, arms clamped across my chest, frowning. We had gotten home late after dancing till dawn, and to my surprise, I had slept like a log. If it hadn't been for Ben, I would have felt like the Dancing Queen again. At least I hadn't lost my touch in that department. I awoke at midday to the sound of birdsong and the aroma of lunchtime cooking wafting through my open window. And the first thing on my mind was Ben. And that kiss.

Oh God, I shouldn't have done it, I really should *not* have kissed him. I had broken every promise I'd made to myself; I had proven that Dr. Gemma was just a weak, silly woman after all. How about that, Gloria Steinem? So much for the power of feminism. And anyhow, hadn't *she* gotten married recently, after telling the rest of us women that we didn't need a man to be fulfilled? Huh!

"Gemma?"

I opened the door and looked at Nonna, fresh and clear-eyed in a crisp blue cotton shirtwaist and white sandals, with her hair curling around her shoulders. Just like the old photograph, I thought, astonished that she still had the power to astonish me.

"Where's Livvie?" Nonna said.

"She's in her room, I suppose."

"No, she isn't."

"Then she's probably gone off to meet the Raphael girl. You saw how buddy-buddy they were last night."

"A nice child." Nonna approved Livvie's choice of friend, though of course Livvie had not had a choice, because as I had expected, there were no other young people at Maggie's party.

"Take your shower at once, Gemma, it's late. Then come on downstairs," Nonna told me. "We'll have coffee together."

"Mom," I said, "I'm thirty-eight years old. You can't tell me what to do." All I wanted was to go back to bed.

"Of course I can. I'm your mother, aren't I? Now hurry up, Gemma. This may prove to be an interesting day."

And leaving me wondering what the hell she could mean, she went downstairs, and I obediently stepped into the shower and washed away the sins of the previous night.

LIVVIE

Livvie had walked down to the main road to meet Muffie at eight o'clock that morning. They had hitched a ride with a farmer, sitting in the back of his dusty old truck with two squealing and decidedly smelly pigs, and had been dropped off in Montepulciano.

Muffie sniffed, horrified, as they walked up the steep

hill to the main piazza. She wrinkled her nose. "Now I smell worse than the pigs."

"Like, shut up about it, why don't you?" Livvie said. "Don't be such a baby."

Muffie trudged along, trying to keep up with Livvie's long stride. "I'll take a shower as soon as I get home," she said, and heard Livvie's irritated sigh, so she shut her mouth firmly and vowed not to say another word about how bad they both smelled.

In the piazza, Livvie headed straight for the café/bar. They sat under an umbrella out of the hot sun, and Livvie ordered *"Due cappuccini, per piacere."* Muffie looked impressed, and Livvie said, "I speak quite a bit of Italian, y'know."

"Do you know how to ask for the stuff in the *farmacia*?" Muffie whispered, looking around to make sure no one heard.

"Of course I do. Anyway it'll be written on the box, so we won't have to ask for anything."

"Oh. Okay."

"You gonna buy some new clothes today?" Livvie spooned the froth from the top of her cappuccino and slurped it up.

Muffie did the same. She patted the pocket of her shorts. "Got the money right here."

"Good. Hurry up then with the coffee. We've got lots to do."

Muffie's tummy was making hungry rumbling noises, and she thought longingly of Fiametta's toasted *ciabatta* and fresh strawberry jam, but she drank up obediently, burning her mouth in the process. Then the two of them hurried off in search of the pharmacy, and after that the local boutiques.

Two hours and a lot of hard work later, they emerged from a funky little shop called La Gatta Cioccolata, clutching plastic bags. They were heading down the hill back to the piazza when Muffie grabbed Livvie by the arm.

"Omigod," she gasped in a tone Livvie recognized as urgent. "There's Daddy."

Livvie immediately shoved Muffie into the doorway of a handy *pasticceria* and told her to sit at a table all the way at the back, while she kept watch. Muffie did as she was told, breathing a sigh of relief when at last Livvie waved that the coast was clear.

Then they bought a couple of ham and cheese pastries and walked back to the main road. There they stood, thumbs hopefully out, munching their pastries, hot, smelly, and sticky. They were soon picked up by a couple of French tourists, who seemed very much amused by them and who were kind enough to drop them back at the gates of the Villa Piacere.

"Okay, Muffie," Livvie said, as they flung their parcels onto Muffie's bed. "We know your dad's in town, so this is as good a time as any to do it."

Muffie stared fearfully at her. "Oh, yes," she breathed. "It is."

CHAPTER THIRTY-EIGHT

BEN

Ben jolted up the rutted drive to the Villa Piacere, making a mental note, as he always did, that he really must get the drive leveled and truck in some fresh gravel.

He swung the old mud-green Land Rover around the dead fountain and threw it into park. Still no water. Scowling, he strode up the steps and into the hall. Fiametta would be gone by now, and he was worried about Muffie being alone for so long.

"Muff," he yelled, "where are you, honey?" He waited a few seconds, then called again. "Hey, Muffie, I'm home."

The house had the silent feel of emptiness about it, and he was suddenly worried. He strode into the kitchen. No one there. He checked the terrace and the swings. Empty. He checked the octagonal room, where Luchay gave him a beady-eyed glare and then put his head back under his wing. He took the stairs two at a time and hurried along the hallway to his daughter's room.

"Muffie, are you in there?" He knocked loudly, then tried the door. It was locked. A dozen possible scenarios rushed through his brain, all of them bad.

"Muffie," he yelled again. "Are you in there? Answer me."

"I'm here, Daddy."

"Jesus!" He sagged against the door frame in relief. Then anger took over. "Then why didn't you answer me? You must have heard me. Right?"

"Right, Daddy."

"So? Open the door then."

He waited. Nothing happened. He put his ear to the door, heard whispering inside. What the hell was she up to? "Who's in there with you? I'm warning you, Muffie, if you don't open this door at once, I'll have to break it down."

More whispering. He heard her footsteps crossing the floor and the key turning in the lock, then her footsteps running back away from the door. He flung it open, stared at his daughter.

"Jesus Christ, Muffie," he roared. "What the hell have you done?"

Muffie's long blond hair had gone. It looked as though someone had put a pudding bowl over her head and just clipped straight around it. It stuck out around her ears in stiff points, and it was pale green. She was wearing skintight Lycra shorts and a teen-pop-diva top that left her navel bare, except for the glittering gemstones that surrounded it. *And* she had a clip-on gold ring in her nose.

Muffie just stood there, looking nervously back at him. And next to her, looking guilty as hell, was Gemma Jericho's daughter, the post-punk Manhattan street kid.

"Muffie, your mother will kill you," he groaned. "After she kills me, that is."

"Then she can kill me too," Livvie said, staring nervously at the floor. "I told her to do it."

"No, Livvie did not. I *wanted* to do it. I'm sick of looking like, y'know, a jerk." Muffie had rebellion in her eyes. "I'm sick of pink taffeta and Mary Janes and living behind locked gates. I asked Livvie to help me—so she did. It's all my fault," she added, and a tear trickled down her cheek. "I didn't mean to upset you, Daddy, but, like, you know . . . I just had to do it."

Damn it, Ben thought, not only does she *look* like the Jericho kid, now she's *talking* like her.

"I get your point," Ben said at last. "But don't you think this is a bit extreme, Muffie? You could have just asked me to take you shopping."

"*You* could have suggested *taking me* shopping," Muffie retorted. "But you didn't. All you ever think about is the villa."

Ben knew she was right. It was all he thought about these days. "Okay," he said, "but I'm very, very angry with you both. And I'm not letting you off the hook so easily. Livvie, get your things, then both of you come down to the car. I'll be waiting for you." He paused on his way out. "And Muffie?"

"Yes, Daddy?"

"Ax the nose ring."

CHAPTER THIRTY-NINE

GEMMA

I was in the *alimentaria* looking to buy an Italian pain reliever to chase away my hangover and my blues, aware of half a dozen sets of eyes watching me as I made my purchases. The *signorina* advised me I needed a remedy for my *fegato,* my liver (the Italians seemed to blame every illness on the liver). I smiled at the silent, black-shawled old women lingering in the store and no doubt waiting to talk about me once I left. I hoped I had made their day.

"*Ciao, dottoressa,*" they muttered in a ragged chorus as I waved good-bye. I laughed. I kind of liked that everybody knew who I was and what I was doing. It was like a security blanket, almost the way the trauma room was.

I had just stepped out the door when I saw Ben Raphael's mud-green Land Rover bouncing over the cobblestones in the piazza; he definitely needed a new suspension. He stopped in front of the *albergo,* and I quickened my footsteps. Had he come to see *me*?

I saw him get out of the car, fling the door wide, and haul out my own daughter. And then . . . was that *Muffie*? My heart did another little jiggle, not a good one this time. *Oh God, Livvie,* I thought. *What have you done now?*

I caught up to them, and my eyes met Ben's. His were hard and angry. Mine were wary.

"Do I have to tell you what happened?" he said in a cold voice.

I glanced at Livvie, then back at him. "I think I get the picture."

"Your daughter is responsible for this." He thrust Muffie forward so I could get a better look. I took in the pale, spiky green hair, the outfit, the platform shoes. I thought the henna tattoos on the backs of her hands and the dried-blood-color nails were a nice touch. She had joined the ranks of the *Nosferatu* extras.

"Livvie?" I looked sternly at her. There was no doubt from her hangdog look that she was guilty.

"I just wanted to help her, Mom. I mean, like, I couldn't let a friend go through life looking like *Pollyanna,* could I?"

"It's true." Muffie stared earnestly at me. "I hated the way I looked. I wanted to look like Livvie, to *be* like her. I'm sick and tired of not being a real person."

"A *real* person?" Ben said, baffled.

"Well, I wasn't a real person," Muffie said stubbornly. "I was Mom's little girl, the one she likes to show off at parties, the perfect little lady. Well, y'know what, I'm not perfect and I don't want to be perfect, and Livvie is my friend and she's not guilty of anything. I *asked* her to do it."

"Actually," I said, and I couldn't help but grin, "the pale green is rather fetching, with her suntan and all."

"I might have expected you to take that stance," Ben said angrily. "I don't know how you propose to punish your daughter for what she's done, Dr. Jericho, but I'm warning you to keep her away from Muffie. I don't want to see her near my place again."

His place! We glared at each other furiously. "I'll deal with Livvie in my own way," I said. "And let me remind you that *your* place is actually *my* place."

He gave me a final angry glare. Then he told Muffie to get in the car and got in next to her. The tires squealed as he swerved around the piazza, and we saw Muffie's hand, with the henna tattoo and the dried-blood nails, sticking out the window as they raced away. She was waving to us.

CHAPTER FORTY

"You are in the wrong," Nonna said.

The two of us were in the little dining room at the inn, having dinner at one of those tables with a bright green cloth and a frilly pink carnation stuck in a San Pellegrino bottle. I had banished Livvie to the kitchen, where she was to help out cleaning and preparing vegetables and salads and doing dishes until such future time as I relented.

I ran my teeth down a succulent artichoke leaf that I had already dipped in the dressing, a vinaigrette made from the local olive oil and a little red wine vinegar. It was an artichoke I had no doubt my daughter had washed and helped prepare, but the thought gave me no pleasure. I could hear squeals of laughter coming from the kitchen, and I wondered whether Livvie was actually enjoying herself instead of suffering for her misdeeds.

"I'm wrong about what?" I said.

"It *was* Livvie's fault—or at least her responsibility. She's older than Muffie, and she knew better. You owe Ben an apology."

"I *do*?"

"Don't be snippy, Gemma. Of course you do. Livvie was wrong, and *you* were wrong to confront him like that.

You should have accepted responsibility and apologized then and there."

I nibbled thoughtfully on another tender leaf. "It's still not his villa, though."

"Listen," Nonna paused, her fork with a circle of sautéed zucchini halfway to her mouth, "we may be at war with Ben, but we are still civilized. Right is right— and the man was *right* to be angry with Livvie, and with you for being so intractable."

"Intractable?" I felt as though I were back in third grade—*Gemma is intractable, needs to pay more attention in class. . . .*

Nevertheless, I couldn't sleep that night thinking about what Nonna had said. I was out of my virginal bed at dawn, pacing the floor one more time, arms clamped across my chest again, staring out over the silent piazza and the fountain with the chipped cherubs and the dolphins; at the church just beginning its early morning honey-colored glow as the new sun struck it; at the empty bocce court with the umbrella pines waving gently in the dawn breeze; at the Motto station, where young Sandro Maresci, the proprietor, was just parking his truck, making an early start on his work; at the silent Bar Galileo where a lamp still burned over the door; and at Don Vincenzo waddling down the steps from his house next to the church, also getting ready to open for early business.

In Manhattan at about this time, I would be sitting on the subway, staring out the windows and seeing only my own weary reflection. I would be mulling over the past night's dramas and turmoil, my head full of the cries, the wails, the smells, the desperation of the emergency room. And I'd be worrying about Livvie, about what was to become of her with her mother so busy all the time. Just the way I was worrying now. Except now I was with her, and she was in more trouble than she had ever been.

Nonna was right. *Ben Raphael* was right. And I had to swallow my pride and go and apologize to him.

I waited until the more or less civilized hour of ten o'clock. Then I drove up the hill to the Villa Piacere. I parked behind the fountain, where I was surprised to see that no water was spouting from Neptune and Venus. I climbed the stone steps and rang the bell, even though the door stood wide open. "Hi," I called tentatively.

I shifted nervously from sandaled foot to sandaled foot. I had dressed carefully for my apology scene. Clean white cotton shirt, short khaki cotton skirt that showed off my newly brown legs, and thong sandals.

"Hi," I called again, ringing the bell one more time. Nobody answered, so I stepped into the hall and stood looking hesitantly around. Somebody must be here. I mean, the door was *open*.

I peeked into the octagonal room where Luchay was perched on top of his golden cage, sharpening his beak against one of the jewel-encrusted gold finials. A half-finished canvas was propped on an easel, with brush and palette and oil paints on a table next to it. It was a painting of this very room, and I was thinking how good it was when Ben Raphael said suddenly, "Come to inspect your property again?"

I rolled my eyes. Here I was on my best behavior, ready to humble myself and apologize, and he was already on the attack. Reminding myself that I was supposed to be Miss Sweetness and Light, I turned to confront him.

"Hi," I said, giving him my best dazzling smile, the one that made the patients feel better, or so they said.

Didn't work on him, though, no siree. He gave me that cold-eyed look and asked me again why I was here.

I gulped, got up my courage, and said, "I've come to apologize. I was wrong. It was Livvie's fault. She's the older girl, and she should have known better. I want you to know that she's being punished. She's on kitchen duty at the inn until further notice."

There, I'd done it. I glanced hopefully at him from under my lashes. I had to admit that he looked good, in a fresh blue shirt, paint-spattered jeans, and sneakers. And his mouth, such an attractive mouth, damn it, was twitching at the corners.

"That must have taken a lot of effort," he said.

"Yup. But I did it."

He turned away. "How about some coffee?"

"Wait a minute. I need to know if you accept my apology."

"I accept your apology, though I still don't know what I'm going to do about my daughter's hair, nor what her mother is going to say when she sees it."

"It'll soon wash out," I said. I had to admit it would be quite a shock to the society dame and her friends, but actually I thought it didn't look half bad.

I followed him into the kitchen, where a pot of coffee waited on top of the stove. He poured two cups, asked if I liked cream and sugar, then carried them outside. We sat in a sunny little paved courtyard by the kitchen door, under a blue awning that cast a shadowy twilight over us, almost as though it were evening. We sipped our coffee in silence. I could smell roses.

"I guess it's not entirely Livvie's fault," Ben said, and "Don't be too hard on Muffie," I said, both at the same time. We grinned at each other. "You first," he said.

I considered what to say. "You know what, Ben," I said finally, "our daughters are alike. They both have parents who are too busy for them, even though *my* excuse is that my job is an essential one, and *yours* is probably that hundreds of people are dependent upon you for their livelihood. Our lives are too busy, and theirs are not full enough. And *you* and *I* are alike. Both too concerned with our own lives."

"I wonder what would happen if we both just quit."

"I can't do that."

"Why not?"

"I need to work. I have to make a living. I'm not independently rich, like you."

"I wasn't always rich." He was sipping his coffee, looking curiously at me, as if to see what made me tick. I wished *I* knew what made me tick; Lord knows I *should* know by now.

"What happened to your husband?" he said.

"Ha! He-who-is-better-not-spoken-of, you mean. He left before Livvie was born. He's never even seen his daughter."

"Fool. He's missed the best thing in his life."

"Well, we certainly don't miss him." I was brisk again, fortified by the jolt of caffeine.

"So? What happened after that?" He stretched his long legs out in front of him, looking sideways at me. "You ever fall in love again?"

Heat flashed up my spine, and I felt my face flush. God, could this be early menopause, or were my hormones raging for a different reason? I hated myself for blushing, and I saw his little smile as he caught that.

"I was too busy to fall in love. I had to finish med

school, as well as work. You know, that 'reality' sort of thing."

"And after med school and work? You fell in love?"

Our eyes met. "None of your business."

"Jesus," he groaned. "You know what it is about you? You're hermetically sealed in your own neat little Ziploc bag, the one you shove in the freezer every time reality—a man—*me*, for God's sake—every time I get near you. What's *wrong* with you anyway?"

I stared at him, wide-eyed, shocked. Nobody had ever talked to me like that. Ever.

He grabbed my hand and led me back through the kitchen and down the hall, through the doors to where his Land Rover was parked.

He held the car door open for me. "Get in," he said.

"Where are we going? Where are you taking me?"

"I'm kidnapping you," he said, pushing me into the car. I wasn't sure I really cared. I was too numb with shock.

"We, Gemma," he said as we drove off, "are going to see Real Life. The one with the capital letters. You say you want this villa? You want to live here in Tuscany? Well, what do you *know* about it? What do you know of the *real* Tuscany? I've been coming here for years. This is my refuge, my *place*. God knows, every time I plan to come here I ask myself whether I'm not just running away from life. And then, when I'm here, I *know* I'm not.

"Look out the window, Doctor. Tell me what you see. An empty white road and a little path wandering up the hill; poplars casting their shade; sun, wind, the elements that give us the grapes and the wine and the sunflowers and . . . oh hell, woman, just look at it, absorb it through your pores. *Feel* it. Feel *something,* for God's sake."

I stared out the open window, not knowing what to say. The countryside slid by like a magic show, shadow and light, colors, scents that were not the hospital. I stole a glance at him.

"Where are we going?" I asked again as he swung the car up the hill and through a lopsided wooden gate to a small farm, a hodgepodge of lean-tos and sheds, a cow barn, and a small stone farmhouse.

A pond the size of a beach blanket floated two or three optimistic ducks. A couple of dogs came nosing at us as we got out of the car, the bitch no more than a couple of years old and already obviously into serial breeding. A pretty white cow peered at us from inside the barn, her liquid dark eyes fringed with the longest lashes.

"We're here for what she produces," Ben said, grabbing a bottle from the backseat.

We walked through the knee-high grass to the rear of the stone barn. "This is Rocco Cesani's cow," he said. "I don't know if she's aware of the prestige that carries, but the milk she gives is superior." He opened the lid of a refrigerated steel vat, turned a tap, filled the bottle, capped it, and we were back in the car again.

"Milk delivery, Tuscan style," he said, as he handed me the bottle to taste.

It was thick and creamy; rich as ice cream with the tang of vanilla and sweet hay. It was milk heaven, the way we never, *ever* taste it in this era of 2% fat, homogenized, pasteurized, decreamed, transparent "milk," and it gave me a creamy mustache.

We saw Rocco coming through the field with pink-and-white Fido. He was wearing a pair of shorts that hung around his sturdy knees, a ragged T-shirt, his old rain hat, and green rubber Wellingtons. He waved his stick in greeting, and we waved back, called our thanks, and were on our way.

"Where now?" I asked, suddenly enjoying myself.

Ben flashed a grin at me. "Getting interested, huh?"

"Maybe."

"We're off to market," he said.

It was a Sunday morning, and the piazza by the church in the nearby village was thronged. The church bells clanged the time for services meant to sustain the spirit, while the stuff of life went on under its stained-glass windows.

We browsed our way along the stalls, delightedly checking the produce. There was the *signora* who specialized in *lamponi*—raspberries, lustrous as rubies and picked that very morning. The *signora* herself was not your usual idea of a market vendor. She was of a certain age, blond and charming, smart in a Versace silk scarf. She told us about her berries and about her special raspberry mustard and raspberry vinegar.

Three packets of berries and the mustard later, we were at the fish stall staring into the bright eyes of salmon and trout, striped bass and eels. We browsed through the vegetables, admiring a kind of broccoli they told me was called Romanesque, swirling minispires of beautiful apple-green florets that I had never seen anywhere else, and we bought radicchio and butter lettuce and goat cheeses and pecorino.

The woman at the bread stall spoke English. She was olive-skinned with bright Gypsy eyes. She told me she and her husband had looked for their farm for seven years. Now they had found it, and they were growing their own grains, grinding them on their own mill wheel, and baking their own breads in their kitchen ovens. "My husband bakes our bread with love," she said, clutching a hand to her heart. And I believed her. I bought a heavy rustic loaf, and we tore off delicious chunks to eat as we pushed our way through the crowd en route to the next stop, the bar.

It was already well populated with locals—the real Italian locals, that is, plus the imported locals from Britain, Holland, Germany, and America, who had left urban delights behind for the simpler pleasures of a country villa, a rural market, and a Sunday espresso with a cognac. First, though, we picked up custard-filled pastries called *sfoghiate* from the *pasticceria* opposite. Then we joined the crowd, sipping our coffee—large with hot milk on the side for me, so I could judge how milky I wanted it; straight for Ben. We tried not to breathe in the cigarette smoke, an impossibility, and Ben shouted *ciao* to the proprietor and other acquaintances as the church clock loudly chimed the hour. Then we shuffled our way out through the throng and back to the car.

"Rural pleasures," I said, giving him a long glance from under my lashes, the way I remembered from my old teen-flirt days. "I'm all for them."

"Have you ever really *seen* Florence?" he said.

I shook my head. "Then that's where we're going," he said, putting the Land Rover into gear.

And you know what? I would have gone anywhere he wanted to take me. I hadn't had this much fun in a long time. I was on a magic carpet ride.

CHAPTER FORTY-ONE

Lavender clouds puffed in dainty scallops above the hills, with here and there fat towers of puffy white cumulus. Beams of sunlight forced their way through, painting the skyscape with a golden wash and tinting the sluggish River Arno amber.

I was walking down the Lungarno delle Grazie, somehow *hand in hand* with my sworn enemy, and thinking blissfully that I had never seen a lovelier sight than the river and the old stone buildings, and the man I was with.

I couldn't explain it. Was it just that I was in Italy? Or that I was a weak little woman? Or maybe that, hey, I was just enjoying myself? Nothing serious. No going back on my vow or anything drastic like that. Just having fun for a change. Oh, what the hell, why didn't I just enjoy it?

For someone seeing Florence for virtually the first time, I had the perfect guide. Ben knew all the details, the dates, the history of every great building and every statue.

We stood in the Piazza Santa Croce taking in the amazing proportions of the enormous square lined with thirteenth-century buildings. Then Ben said, "I have something special to show you," and he led me into the church.

Our footsteps echoed in the lofty silence as we walked

to the basilica. And there, my friends—was the tomb of Michelangelo. I got that same feeling I'd had in Rome when I saw the ruins of Marcus Agrippa's temple. The shock of how ancient it was, how much a part of life, even of our lives today, had hit me in the solar plexus as well as the brain. Well, that's exactly how I felt now.

I thought of Nonna at the Hassler and the Michelangelo of Long Island, and I laughed.

"What's so funny?" Ben whispered.

When I told him, he laughed too and said, "I'm glad to know at least you were thinking about me." Our eyes met over Michelangelo's tomb, and I do believe, for a breathless moment, the world stood still.

The baptistery looked like an octagonal wedding cake with its walls of white Carrara and green Prato marble, and I craned my neck until it ached gazing up at the astonishing mosaics on the inside of the dome, crafted by Venetian masters in the thirteenth and early fourteenth centuries.

Next we stood awed in front of the great East Door of the Duomo, the cathedral (by Lorenzo Ghiberti, 1378–1455, Ben told me, and he also told me that an admiring Michelangelo had dubbed it "The Door of Paradise"). There were ten bronze panels depicting what Ben described as "the Bible's top ten stories," but what was even more interesting were the twenty-four heads of artists of that era, including Ghiberti's own self-portrait.

Then Ben took my hand again, and we walked, single file—there was room for only one person at a time—up a spiral stone staircase so tight and narrow it terrified me into claustrophobia. By the time we reached the top, after what seemed like miles, my heart was pounding for all the wrong reasons. I stared over the narrow ledge, at Florence far below and Tuscany beyond and the river threading through it all, and then the world dissolved into a whirl of color. I shrank back against Brunelleschi's great dome.

"I can't *stand* heights."

Ben was leaning over the edge, taking in the view. He turned and grinned at me. "Scared, huh?"

"Right," I whispered, and seeing my agonized face, he took pity on me and took my hand and guided me down those endless narrow, worn stone stairs, back to the safety of the street.

Then, to calm my shattered nerves, my guide—who was, believe me, acting like Mr. Charm himself—took me to the Caffè Rivoire in the Piazza della Signoria, an old art nouveau–style tearoom, where, since there was a sudden chill in the air, we drank hot chocolate and shared a rich pastry confection, getting sugar all over our faces, just as though we had been doing this together for years.

I had expected Ben to be prickly, antagonistic, angry. What, I wondered, was going on? But I really didn't want to know. I was happy. And I certainly wasn't thinking about the past—or the future. This was what was called "living for the moment." And there's a lot to be said for that. Sometimes.

Even though the grand piazza is now almost entirely a parking lot, you can still sit and look out at the fourteenth-century Palazzo Vecchio, which Ben told me was the very heart of Florence, and at the marble Fountain of Neptune. Relaxed, content, I wondered why the sound of a fountain on a sultry summer afternoon was so seductive.

We didn't talk much. We were too busy looking at Florence and, stealthily, at each other. I was just saying that the hot chocolate was like sipping molten gold, when quite suddenly Ben said to me, "Did you take a shower today?"

I knew it had been a long day, but surely things couldn't be that bad. He wasn't smiling either. He was, all of a sudden, deadly serious.

"Of course," I said primly. "Didn't you?"

"Yes. But with great difficulty."

I could not imagine what he meant.

"There's been no water at the Villa Piacere for the past two days," he said. "I had to carry water from the old cistern into the house so we could bathe and make coffee."

I wondered what this little piece of personal information had to do with me, or the fact that we were sitting in Rivoire's drinking hot chocolate and, I had thought, having a good time. "I'm sorry," I said politely.

"The man at the Water Board told me there were too many tourists taking showers, too many swimming pools; he said it happens all the time."

"And does it?"

"It's never happened before."

His eyes locked onto mine. In other circumstances, I might have considered drowning in them, the way heroines do in romance novels, but he obviously did not have romance on his mind.

"It never happened before you and your family came to Bella Piacere and claimed that you owned the villa."

It was my turn to lock on to his eyes. "Are you . . . can you *possibly* be saying that *I* had something to do with it? That *I* sabotaged your water supply?"

I guess honest righteous indignation told him he was

wrong, because he sighed, then apologized. He said he didn't know what had happened, but that he'd handed over sufficient lire in what the Water Board had told him were "unpaid back expenses" to have his supply returned by tomorrow.

"Well, good," I snapped. "Then you can take a shower in peace."

"I'm sorry," he said again, taking my hand across the table. "Of course you didn't have anything to do with it. You're too noble. You're a doctor. You wouldn't stoop to sabotage, even though you do want to get me out of the villa."

"I want to find Donati and show you the will and get you out of the villa honestly," I said. "And that's the truth."

CHAPTER FORTY-TWO

We were in the Oltrarno—literally the "other side" of the river, in an area of small *botteghe,* musty-smelling little workshops where artisans carved wood into glorious curlicues for mirrors and overmantels and where elaborate gesso frames were made, then gilded, ready to enhance old, and sometimes new, paintings. Where the softest leather was crafted by hand into smart bags and exquisite gloves; where marble tables were inlaid with patterns of mother-of-pearl and malachite and lapis. Where goldsmiths fashioned rings to be sold on the Ponte Vecchio and the Via de' Tornabuoni, and ceramics were painted in the same designs they had used for centuries.

A lone tree rustled in the sudden wind as we wandered happily down the narrow twisting streets, peering into windows and deciding what we would buy if we were rich. Of course, Ben *was* rich, but that didn't seem to matter: the game was the thing.

We bought a bag of ripe black cherries from a vendor, and I bit into one, sending out a sudden squirt of rich juice. Ben wiped the cherry juice from my chin, then licked his fingers. I felt myself melt inside. It was one of the sexiest things that had ever happened to me. We just looked at each other, and then he bent his head and kissed my juicy lips. I shivered as *I* looked at him, thinking how I would like to be in love again. *Crashing into love!* Wasn't that a line from a Marc Anthony song? It described the way I was feeling—hurtling, *crashing* . . . into love. That is, if I could just allow myself. But of course, I could not.

A distant rumble of thunder broke the spell. Huge raindrops bounced off the cobblestones and our heads. We ducked into a doorway, and Ben said, "How come we never noticed it was going to rain?" and I wanted to say, Because we were just too caught up in each other, that's why, but of course I didn't. And then his arms were around me, and we were kissing again, but *really* kissing this time.

His mouth pressed on mine, parting my lips, drinking me in until I was breathless, dizzy with delight. My stomach did double flips, and the cherry juice seemed to have slipped all the way down to between my legs. I wanted this man. *Really* wanted him. I clung to him, tasted him, wrapped myself closer. I smiled, remembering the Romans I had seen embracing in doorways. Now I was one of them, and I quickly tried to tell myself that of course it was really Italy that was seducing me, not this man. This lovely man whose body was hard against mine.

When we surfaced, he stroked back my hair. His face was so close I breathed his breath. "Your hair is standing on end," he said wonderingly, and I put up my hand to feel it.

"Like a curly blond halo," he said. "My Botticelli angel." And then he kissed me some more.

The next time we came up for air and to try to regain our equilibrium, Ben looked up at the lowering gray sky and said, "This storm is here to stay. We'd better get out of here."

"But where shall we go?" I clutched his hand, teeth

chattering from nerves and the sudden damp chill. The sultry heat had disappeared with the first clap of thunder, and now the rain came steadily down, interspersed with flashes of blue lightning. I hate thunderstorms; the power of nature terrifies me.

"Scared?" He raised an eyebrow with a smile.

"Yes," I admitted, for the second time that day.

"Don't worry. I'll take care of you," he said. "But we'll have to make a run for it."

By the time we got to the end of the street we were soaked. An opportunistic vendor in a kiosk had put out a display of umbrellas, and we bought one, then huddled under it, searching the empty street for a cab.

"We'll have to walk," Ben decided, and when I asked him where we were going, he said, "To a place I know." So we sloshed off through the puddles again.

Ben held the umbrella, and I held his arm, but he was taller, and the wind was blowing hard now, and it was blowing the rain on me. Ben stopped suddenly and looked around. "I need to ask directions," he said.

Wet and shivering, I said, "But you *know* Florence. This is your turf. Why do you have to ask directions *now*?"

He gave me a pitying glance. "Because we're lost, of course."

I drooped under the umbrella. I hated to think of what I looked like by now.

We asked directions in stumbling Italian from a man just getting onto his Vespa, only to have him answer, in our very own American accents, with a decidedly poor-tourist-fools glare, that we were walking in the wrong direction. We must go back, cross the river again, walk a couple of more blocks, and we would be there.

So back we went, umbrella thrust forward, sloshing through a torrent of water, back over the river (gray and sullen), down a deserted street—and there it was. Cammillo's on the Borgo San Jacopo. Paradise!

Only we were not exactly a paradisial sight. My shirt was plastered to my back—and front, my feet were soggy, and my hair had that just-washed-dog look.

Cammillo's yellowish walls reflected the lamplight, and it smelled of flowers and wine and herby sauces. The trattoria was as old as the rest of Florence and had been serving good food to its customers for decades. It had a glass door with a lace curtain, and a bell that jingled as we entered. They knew Ben there, shook his hand, took our umbrella, and sympathized with how wet we were, then ushered us to a table in the back room.

We laughed as we looked at each other, then said what the hell and patted ourselves dry with Kleenex, under the disapproving stares of a couple of country-club American matrons, who obviously thought we were bringing down the tone of the place.

"They have no sympathy for a couple who have braved the storm to get here," Ben whispered to me.

"Not only that," I whispered back, twisting rainwater out of my sodden locks, "*their* hair is immaculate."

All of a sudden I remembered Livvie and Nonna. "I'd better call home," I said guiltily, meaning the inn.

"Me too."

"You first," I said, in what was becoming our usual repartee. So he disappeared and came back a few minutes later, smiling.

"Guess what, it's not raining in Bella Piacere. Anyhow, Fiametta is taking Muffie over to Maggie Marcessi's to spend the night."

"My turn." I got up and squelched through the restaurant to the phone. I had no trouble getting through to Nonna. "What rain?" she asked suspiciously. "It's not raining here."

"Mom," I said with a sigh, "there's a terrific thunderstorm. It's a washout here in Florence. I don't know when I'll be back. Anyhow, I'm here with Ben Raphael, and we're trying to sort things out."

"About the villa, you mean?"

"Of course that's what I mean, Mom." I crossed my fingers because this was a lie. "Tell Livvie she's off kitchen duty for tonight," I added. "She can keep you company."

"Okay. But Rocco Cesani is coming over for dinner also."

"Then there'll be three of you, Momma." I thought about Rocco, suddenly suspicious. "You wouldn't know anything about the water being shut off at the Villa Piacere, would you, Mom?"

"Water? Of course I know of no such thing," she said briskly, but I couldn't help wondering if her fingers were crossed too.

Ben held my chair for me. "Everything okay?"

"Fine." I was still thinking about Rocco Cesani and the water.

"I ordered red wine," he said, filling my glass with a fruity young Chianti. We attacked the delicious bread as ravenously as if we had not eaten all day, which come to think of it, apart from a couple of pastries and a few very juicy cherries and, almost, each other, we had not.

We ordered hot, homey spaghetti bolognese to start, and ate it holding hands across the tiny lamplit table, steaming slightly as we dried. Ben's hand was warm on mine. Watching him, I wondered what he was thinking.

CHAPTER FORTY-THREE

BEN

Ben was thinking that Gemma's hair was drying in little golden spirals, like a fancy poodle's, but that he couldn't tell her that, because he knew she would take it the wrong way and be insulted. He had learned the hard way to be careful with her; now he knew that beneath that wary doctor's exterior lay the heart of a sensitive woman.

She licked the spaghetti sauce from her lips. Lips, he noticed tenderly, that lifted at the corners in that sweetly touching way that made her look as though she were smiling even when she was mad as hell. It sent a dagger of passion through him, and he wanted to kiss her again, to hold her. At this moment he didn't give a damn about the Villa Piacere and the water; he didn't even care if she was guilty of sabotage.

"What next?" Gemma asked, and he laughed, enjoying her enthusiasm. "How about a salad?" She shook her head. "Okay then, a veal cutlet for you and boned squab for me."

"*I* want the squab." Her narrow blue eyes were laughing at him, and he grinned back.

"Waiter," he said, "two boned squab, please." Then he

poured the last of the wine into her glass and ordered a second bottle.

She raised an eyebrow. "It's been a long time since a man tried to get me drunk."

"I'm not trying to get you drunk, Gemma." It was true, he didn't want her drunk; he wanted her alert, smiling, clinging, loving.

The American country-club matrons got up to leave. "Please call us a cab," they said to the manager, who shrugged and raised his hands palms up and said, "Sorry, *signore,* but it's raining. There are no cabs."

Ben and Gemma smirked at each other. "I like to think of them walking through the rainstorm," she whispered, "and arriving back at their hotel looking exactly the way we did."

"Kind of, that'll show 'em, huh?" he said, and she laughed out loud as though he were the wittiest guy in all Italy. God, Ben thought, you had to love this woman, didn't you?

They had chestnut-flour fritters for dessert, filled with ricotta doused in rum, an old country recipe, the waiter told them. And then they had espresso, and contemplated each other silently.

"I wonder if the rain has stopped," Ben said, praying it hadn't. And "I wonder what time it is, " she said, glancing at her serviceable doctor-style watch with the big numerals and the second hand swishing around, ticking away their time together.

As if it were God himself answering, a clap of thunder rattled the windows.

Ben paid the check, and they stood in the doorway staring at the solid sheet of rain. Lightning fizzled and thunder rumbled around as they clung together. Ben told her it would be dangerous even to attempt to drive in such a storm, and anyhow, the car was parked at the other side of the city.

"The only sensible thing to do is find a hotel," he said.

Gemma clutched his hand, terrified of the lightning, and scared of what he had just suggested. "A hotel?" she whispered, searching his face.

"Is that okay with you?" he asked, and kissed her gently on her rain-wet cheek.

CHAPTER FORTY-FOUR

GEMMA

We didn't bother to run; there was no point. We just skidded through the puddles back to the riverbank, and, just the way it used to happen with Cash, we almost fell over a tiny hotel. A sign blinked green outside, VACANCIES.

There was a glass door with a brass handle and a shiny brass plate with the name HOTEL DOTTORE. We laughed, and Ben said it was obviously meant to be. Hand in hand, we pushed open that door and went inside.

Don't think I didn't ask myself what I was doing. Of course I did, but wine warmed my veins, and excitement gripped my loins, if that's what that sexy part of us is called. I was falling, tumbling, hurtling—*crashing* into love. Me, the ice maiden . . . the one whose vow was about to be broken. Oh—but it couldn't. *I* couldn't. *Of course* I couldn't. I'd just remembered I was wearing my old cotton underpants, the ones that had been laundered a thousand times. And Ben was a man of the world; obviously he was used to making love to expensive blondes in lacy lingerie. But it was too late. He was giving me that look that made me feel I was the only woman in the room. And this time I was.

Our window overlooked the rain-swollen river, but

now Ben closed the tall shutters. We were alone together, in a tiny room with a large bed with a carved gothic headboard. Ruby lamps cast a pink light over us as we stood there staring into each other's eyes.

"You're so wet." He stroked back my hair tenderly.

"You too." I lifted my face, waiting for his kiss. I no longer gave a damn about my hair, or my underwear. I wanted this man.

I slid out of my wet shirt like a stripper on opening night, unzipped my skirt, let it fall around my ankles. He had his shirt off by now, then his jeans. We were barefoot, half naked, wet.

He strode away from me into the bathroom, and I stood there admiring the way his lean, muscular back sloped to his butt. Such a sweet butt, I thought tenderly.

He came back with a towel and began to briskly dry off my hair. I bent my head feeling like a pet dog, and I giggled. Then I took the towel from him and dried his hair, then his chest, and then . . . lower . . .

He picked me up and carried me to our pink silk bed, threw back the covers, and then threw me onto it. I laughed again as he flung himself over me, kissing my face, kissing my hair, sliding the straps from my shoulders and finding my nipple with his tongue. I was shocked to hear myself moaning, an otherworldly sound coming from somewhere deep and primitive inside me. I found myself reaching out for him, sliding my hands down his smooth hard body, over crisp black hair, and then the round softness, and then the delicious hardness.

He groaned too, and whispered, "I'm making love to an angel, my Botticelli angel."

I almost looked around the room to see if someone else were there. Could he possibly mean me?

But we were kissing again, joined at the mouth, body, hip, my long length stretched taut while he lapped me as though I were the fountain of youth and he was a desperately thirsty man, and I arced and twisted, begging him shamelessly not to stop.

When he finally pushed between my legs, he held himself there for a moment, above me.

"Scared?" he whispered, looking deep into my eyes.

It was the third time he had asked me that today. Third time lucky. "No," I said.

Remember the electricity the first time he kissed me? Well this was like being struck by forked lightning. I raised myself up for him, felt him thrust into me, felt my juices flowing around him, heard my own cries of pleasure. His body slammed into mine and I was over the top, tumbling down the other side of paradise.

Much later, we pulled away from each other and lay, side by side, soaked with the sweat of love, slippery with its precious juices, hands linked just the way our bodies had so recently been. I didn't want to let go of him. My body was tingling again. I wanted more.

I turned my face to look at him, just as he turned and looked at me.

"Botticelli," he said, *"angel."*

I thought, I needn't have worried—he hadn't even noticed my old cotton underpants. And then we made love some more.

I awoke to darkness. Chilled, I touched his sleeping form, moved closer, hugging spoonlike around him. Rain spattered against the windowpanes, and thunder still rumbled distantly. I had no idea what the time was. All I knew was that I didn't want this night to end.

I don't like the night. I have always been afraid of the dark and slept with a light on. Night is so dense, it touches you, whispers seduction in your ear. I can *feel* night. It's a time of soft moans, unuttered dread, a soundless scream. Or else it's the magic time of making love with a man you want, a man you're crashing into love with. Night, I thought now, when you're holding the man you loved, is the best time of all.

The next time I awoke, a gray light filtered through the shutters. I wondered for a second where I was. Then I turned my head and looked at Ben's still-sleeping face. Such a handsome face, I thought, mentally tracing the line of his firm mouth with my finger, the jut of his blue-stubbled jaw, the wide swerve over the cheekbone. I wanted to lick every little bit of him.

Pins and needles stabbed through my right arm, which was crushed beneath his body, but I didn't care. He could crush all of me if he wanted. Outside our window, life was returning: muted bird chatter, the faint hum of traffic, the clatter of a motorcycle on the cobblestones. That cool dawn breeze. I thought about Bellevue, and about Patty, about my long silent journey home on the subway, almost too weary to shower, too tired to eat. But the one thing I did not allow myself to think about was Cash.

I sighed. I was a woman whose hard edge had suddenly slipped, along with the memories of her job and her responsibilities. I turned to Ben, pressed closer, feeling his warmth. I had always liked making love at dawn.

CHAPTER FORTY-FIVE

We breakfasted like naughty children, on *semifreddo* at Riccis in the Piazza Santo Spirito, looking out at the exquisite little church and surrounded by frescoes and mahogany and polished brass, as well as by smart Italians drinking espresso on their way to work. Now, *semifreddo* is a custard-based ice cream made with chocolate chips and frozen whipped cream, and it's about as sinful as you can get, a fact I thought appropriate to the moment.

We were not exactly the perfect couple: I had no makeup on, not even lipstick, because my mouth was swollen from his kisses; and though my shirt and skirt were almost dry, they looked as though I had slept in them. Which, of course, I had not, but judging from the skeptical looks of those around us, others were not of the same opinion.

Ben looked much better than I, and I wondered how it was that after a night of passion, men always emerged looking refreshed and at peace with the world, while we women had to worry about a sore chin where his stubble had grazed us, and the tender bruises along our inner thighs, and the fact that we looked as though we had just

fucked all night, which, even if we had, we didn't neces-
sarily want the rest of the world to know.

"Hi, angel." Ben spooned a little dollop of *semifreddo*
into my smiling mouth, and I felt suddenly all right again,
and I didn't give a damn about the way I looked, or about
other people.

"Botticelli," I said, licking my lips. "Where on earth
did you get that idea?"

"Oh, from a painting . . . a lot of paintings. You know
the ones, with the sweet-faced, impish-looking angels
with masses of curly golden hair."

"Aren't they usually plump, though?"

He laughed and fed me some more ice cream. "Better
eat up."

"Time to get back," I said regretfully.

"Real life again, huh?"

"I have my responsibilities."

"Me too."

He looked seriously at me. "Are you all right with this,
Gemma? I mean, with us?"

"Oh, sure." I shrugged uneasily. It wasn't the woman's
place to make the next move, was it? I was so out of practice, I didn't know where I stood. "You know," I said
awkwardly. "These things happen."

"Do they?"

I glanced away, remembering my unseemly behavior.
Unseemly. God, I was talking like Jane Austen again. My
wanton, shameless behavior was more like it.

"I guess so," I said casually. And he looked away from
me, down at the little marble table.

"You're right," he said, getting to his feet. "I guess it's
time to go."

And we made our way back to where the Land Rover was parked, and drove, almost silently, back to Bella Piacere.

Oh God, Cash, I thought, suddenly bereft. What have I done?

CHAPTER FORTY-SIX

BEN

Back at the villa, Ben unplugged his electric razor. He plugged it in again, switched it on. Nothing. He flicked the light switch. Same thing. Now he had water but no electricity.

He grabbed a towel, wrapped it around his middle, and stomped downstairs to the phone. There was only one in the entire house, and it was in the library. He flung himself into a chair, looked up the number of the electricity company, then dialed it. Scowling, he put the phone to his ear. Nothing.

Now he had no telephone either.

He went into the kitchen to find Fiametta. The door to the courtyard was shut, the kitchen silent and dark. The usual pot of coffee was not brewing on the stove, and there was no smell of toasting *ciabatta*.

He went outside and sat at the table where he'd had coffee with Gemma—was it only yesterday?

His mind was suddenly full of her: of her scent, the way her skin had felt under his hands, the little lift at the corner of her mouth. Her smiley mouth, he thought tenderly, smiling himself, remembering how she had looked with her wet halo of hair as she'd patted the raindrops off at Cammillo's, and remembering how she had denied she was scared when he was going to make love to her, her cries, her long slender legs wrapped around him. Remembering her, her joy, her lust, made him hard, and he smiled ruefully.

Gemma was a complicated woman, hot one minute, freezing him out the next. It was just his bad luck to complicate his life with a woman when all he had come here for was peace and quiet: to paint, to begin work on turning his villa into a hotel, and to escape exactly these sort of complications, which always messed up his life. Yet now he couldn't get her out of his mind.

Still, there was work to be done. And come to think of it, he couldn't hear any sounds of machinery coming from the stable yard.

He ran back upstairs, threw on some clothes, then hurried out to the old stables. The backhoe, the digger, the concrete mixer were gone. All that was left were sacks of cement and a pile of builders' sand. He stood for a minute, arms folded, an angry scowl on his face. Then he walked back around the house, got in his Land Rover, and drove to Maggie's to pick up Muffie.

He found them on Maggie's immaculate back lawn. Maggie was teaching Muffie how to play croquet. The sun glinted off his daughter's pale green hair, and he groaned; he had forgotten about that. Plus she was wearing a brief little skirt that came almost up to her butt and a skimpy red top with sequined straps and clompy platform shoes that made her two inches taller. His kid looked like a minihooker. He wondered about the Jericho family.

"Hi, Daddy, we're playing croquet." Muffie ran to be

kissed, and he picked her up and swung her around. Tacky-looking or not, she was his daughter and he loved her.

"Hi, honey," he said. Then "Hi, Maggie."

"Hi, yourself, Ben." Maggie whacked the ball with the mallet, then stood back and watched it swing in a perfect arc through the little hoop. She grinned, pleased with herself, then turned and looked him up and down. "Have a good time last night, Ben?"

She had that knowing look in her eyes. Maggie had a nose for intrigue. She always knew when something was going on, and usually what it was and with whom. Plus she was a born gossip.

"For two days I've had no water," Ben said, ignoring her query. "Today, I have no electricity, I have no phone, and the heavy equipment has been removed from my yard. Fiametta did not show up for work, nor did the construction crew. I am virtually cut off from the world—the local world—and I am totally pissed off—'scuse me, honey," he added in an aside to Muffie, "with the locals. I'm being sabotaged, Maggie, and I thought you might know something about it."

Maggie opened her blue eyes wide. She patted her hair, adjusted her rope of pearls, and got ready to make another play, feet apart, hands clasped near the top of the mallet, swinging it gently. "Why should I know anything?" She jabbed at the ball and clipped it on the side, sending it careening over the lawn. "Damn it," she said.

"That was God's retribution," Ben said, "for lying. You *do* know what's going on, don't you? And you know it has something to do with the Jericho women."

"Oh, Daddy," Muffie interrupted, "you *always* want to blame the Jerichos for everything."

Maggie gave Ben a whack on the shins with the mallet, smiling wickedly as he yelped with pain. "That's for calling me a liar, Ben Raphael. I know nothing about your diggers and backhoes and your electricity. However, you and Muffie are welcome to stay here until you get it sorted out." She gave him a sharp sideways look. "Which no doubt you will. In due time."

"What do you mean, 'in due time'?"

"Ben, my dear, this is Italy. *Rural* Italy. Don't you know by now it works on its own time schedule? All I can suggest is that you go and talk to the mayor. He's usually to be found in the Bar Galileo about now, having his first grappa of the day. Why don't you ask *him* what's going on?"

Guido Verdi, the mayor of Bella Piacere, also had a day job, working his own small vineyard where he grew Trebbiano grapes that he sold on to the large vintners. He owned two acres of chalky hillside, where his vines grew in neat rows, each with a rosebush planted at the end. The roses were not just for ornament's sake, though he enjoyed their flowers, but because bugs would attack them first, thus giving him warning before they reached his precious vines. In his own world, Guido was a success. He owned a small farmhouse, much like Rocco's, had a wife, a son, and two grandchildren, and he was mayor of his village. He was a happy man, and every day at eleven, he headed into Bella Piacere and the Bar Galileo.

He was sitting in his usual green plastic chair, watching a soccer game on the old TV with the black-and-white confetti picture. He was enjoying a shot of grappa and a cold Peroni, his favorite beer. With him was his old friend Rocco Cesani. Having come straight from the fields, both were in their usual work attire of tattered shorts, T-shirts, and Wellington boots.

When Ben walked in the door, which was propped open with an empty beer keg, Guido and Rocco had their heads together, laughing. Carlo, the bar owner, was rinsing glasses behind the Formica counter, and Ben noticed there was no shortage of water here, or electricity. The three glanced his way, threw him a polite nod, then returned to a rerun of Firenze versus Milan.

Ben dragged up a chair and planted himself between them and the TV. "*Signor* Verdi, Rocco," he said, "I'm here on important business. Water at the villa was cut off for two days. Now there is no electricity, no telephone, and my heavy machinery has disappeared, along with the contractors. I demand to know what's going on."

The two men glanced slyly at each other. They shrugged their shoulders, lifted their hands, palms up, in perfect synchronization, then said as one, "Perhaps it's just bad luck, *signor* Ben. Maybe there is some mistake with the bills. . . ."

"They told me that at the Water Board in town. I paid the so-called overdue expenses. Now what am I supposed to do? Go to the phone company? The electricity company? The contractors? Pay more 'overdue expenses'?"

The mayor shrugged. "If that is what needs to be done, *signor* Ben, then that is what you must do."

Ben looked them both in the eyes. They glanced uncomfortably away. Ben knew they knew more than they were saying, and *they* knew *he* knew it.

"Everything can be worked out, *signore*," Rocco said soothingly. "It is only a matter of time."

"How *much* time, Rocco?" Ben banged his fist on the

back of his chair and then wished he hadn't; it hurt like hell, matching the whack on his shin Maggie had given him.

Rocco just gave him that shrug again, that little expressive lift of the shoulders, the sly smile that said more than words. *"Signore,"* he said, "this is Italy."

Ben got to his feet. He placed the chair carefully back where it came from. He called the bartender for more grappa for the mayor and for Rocco. He stopped at the door on his way out. "No, Rocco," he said, seething with anger, "this is *not* just Italy. It's *sabotage.*"

And then he went off to find Gemma Jericho and her troublesome family.

CHAPTER FORTY-SEVEN

GEMMA

I was stretched out on the old wicker lounger in the garden at the inn, staring up at the tiny hard green grapes dangling over my head, and the dust and pollen and other no doubt allergy-making material floating in the filtered beams of sunlight, doing absolutely nothing at all. My mind was empty; my body was drained; my emotions numb. My arm slid from the lounger and just dangled there; it took an effort to lift it back up again.

I wasn't thinking about Ben; I was thinking about Cash. About the time he took me to meet his family in Texas. Of course, Livvie was with us. Cash had said he wanted to show off his ready-made family, and young Livvie was so excited about the plane ride.

Cash and I had been together for almost a year, not exactly living together except on weekends, when we really felt like a family, and Sundays at Nonna's took on a whole new meaning. It was as though there was a future, beyond just Sunday lunch.

Cash was in an off-Broadway play, I was working hard, and whatever time we could manage in between our odd schedules, that's what we had. We loved, we lived, we took care of Livvie, together. The idea of being apart never even occurred to me. This was it. The end. The ultimate. I was so in love with him, and with my new life.

A man who looked like an older version of Cash met us at the Dallas/Fort Worth airport. Cash's father, of course. His hair was silver and not the sun-streaked blond Cash's was, but his eyes were the same light blue, and they were crinkled at the corners, from staring out over his acres at the ranch, I guess. He hugged me, then took Livvie in his arms and said, "You too big to be carried, young lady?"

I still remember Livvie's confident laugh as she said that of course she was, but she still liked it, and then they walked hand in hand to his big Chevy Suburban, white and dusty and crammed with bits of machinery and lengths of rope and other masculine stuff. He and Cash and the car were so macho I could almost smell testosterone in the air. And I loved it. Oh, how I loved it. I had never felt more secure in my life.

"So you're a doctor," Matt Drummond said to me, smiling at me in the rearview mirror.

"That's me." I was suddenly shy.

"I always told Cash to find a clever girl," he said. "Brains beat beauty every time."

I stared horrified at his reflection in the mirror. Did I look that bad?

"But Cash got lucky," he added. "He got both." We all laughed then, and Livvie asked when could she see the horses, and how many acres, and did they have a dog—a big one, she hoped.

We drove for what seemed a long time and finally turned in through a gate with wooden posts and an iron arch on top with their brand, an entwined D & R, inscribed in iron letters. The blacktop road led through acres of gentle grassland rimmed with dusty hills, and about a mile along was the house. A typical low-slung ranch house, built of wood with a tile roof, painted white with green trim, with lots of shiny clean windows gleaming in the sunlight. And Marietta Drummond waiting on the porch to welcome us.

"Welcome, welcome," she called, her arms open wide, all ready to hug us. After we hugged and Livvie was made a fuss of, we were shown the house and our rooms. Ours was Cash's old room, complete with pennants and high school swimming trophies and his framed graduation diploma from Texas A & M. How he had ever emerged from this secure family, this secure way of life with a certain job running the ranch that seemed tailor-made for him, and decided to become an actor, I would never know. Had it been me, I never would have left.

It was so lovely, just being there with him as his girl-friend and future wife. We were not officially engaged; no ring as yet; but it was "in our stars," Cash said, and I knew that was true. We had talked about the house in the country and promised Livvie the biggest dog she could think of—the Newfoundland for which Sinbad was now a surrogate. I had planned to change my life, move to Connecticut, get a job in a local hospital, one that would have easier hours, giving us more time together.

Cash, beautiful Cash with his golden hair and eyes already crinkling like his father's, with his body that fit so well with mine, and his passion for me . . . and mine for him. I never wanted anyone else, I told him. And I meant it.

It was different making love with him in his schoolboy bedroom, in his family home, with his parents just down the hall. We were quieter, of course, almost stealthy, gig-gling guiltily as we wrapped ourselves around each other, so tenderly, oh so very tenderly. So much in love.

The next day we rode the range, pretending to be cow-boys. Cash looked perfect in the role, and Livvie was a natural, but by the end of the day I had a sore butt and a headache from the sun, and I knew why they wore those big hats and got the crinkles around their eyes. To Livvie's delight, one of their five dogs had attached him-self to her and hung around with her wherever she went; and that night there was a gargantuan barbecue with all their friends and family and neighbors invited. It was like old home week in Texas, with the guys in white Stetsons and the women in pointy alligator cowboy boots, and we were welcomed as part of the family.

That was the night Cash made his announcement. He had been offered a job, a movie—his first. It wasn't the lead, but it was a good role—and not playing a cowboy either. He was to play a Hollywood gumshoe in a noirish script, sort of Raymond Chandler style. He said, of course, that meant he would have to move to Hollywood.

"Only temporary, of course, honey," he added, putting his arm around my waist and squeezing hard. "I'm a stage actor at heart. I'll soon be back."

I felt a little lump in my throat at the thought of losing him, even temporarily, to Hollywood. But we had so much, and our love was so strong, I knew nothing could go wrong.

Could it?

I was torn from my reverie of Cash and the past by the sound of Ben Raphael's voice. My heart was pounding like a young girl's in the throes of second love as I hurried to meet him.

He was sitting opposite Nonna on the hard green leather sofa. His arms were folded across his chest. He looked up as I came in, and he did not smile. *Oh God,* I thought, *now what?*

I saw Amalia hovering around in the hall and Laura, her daughter, standing there with her mouth open, not even pretending not to listen.

"Mrs. Jericho," I heard Ben say, "I have reason to believe you are behind my troubles at the villa."

"What are you talking about?" I stood next to Nonna, my hand protectively on her shoulder. "Is this about your water supply? *Again?* I already told you we had nothing to do with it."

"Right. And I suppose you, along with your accomplices, Rocco Cesani and the mayor, Guido Verdi, have nothing to do with my electricity being cut off, and my phone being cut off, and my contractors disappearing and taking my heavy machinery with them?"

For a moment I was too stunned to speak. I noticed Nonna was silent too and thought how shocked she must be, with Ben accusing her like that.

"I'm here to tell you that if this sabotage continues, I will be forced to take legal action," Ben said.

That tipped me over the edge. It was as though last night had never happened. We were strangers, enemies, at war with each other. "And if you continue to slander my mother—and me," I said haughtily, "I too will take legal action. *Mr.* Raphael."

He got to his feet. Somehow he looked very tall in that low-beamed ex–cow barn of a room with the old iron feeding troughs on the wall. "You can't intimidate me," I added hopefully.

He looked at me, a long look with those greenish-gold eyes that I could not read. "I apologize if I sounded . . . impolite," he said stiffly. "But I meant what I said."

We looked at each other again. I felt Nonna's eyes swivel back and forth between us in the long silence. Then he turned and walked away.

Oh God, I thought. *He just walked out of my life.*

CHAPTER FORTY-EIGHT

"What's going on between you two?" Nonna said.

I shrugged. "As you saw—nothing. Absolutely nothing."

"Ha, I know what I saw." Still sitting on the hard green chair, cool in her blue cotton shirtwaist, she looked levelly at me. "You might have told me something was going on. We could have approached this whole matter differently."

"What *matter*? You mean the villa? Jeez, Momma, don't tell me you had something to do with this after all!"

"*I* didn't do anything. Anyhow, my feeling is that Ben Raphael is only getting what he deserves. If the locals have turned against him, what chance does he have of succeeding around here with his plans for a hotel? In *my* villa," she added.

I ran my hands frantically through my hair. This was crazy. I wished with all my heart I was back in the safety of my trauma room, just dealing with life and death, which was the thing I did best, instead of all this. It was too complicated, too emotional, too . . . fraught.

I fished in the pocket of my shorts and found the car keys. "I'm off to see Maggie Marcessi," I said, heading out the door.

"What are you going to do there?" Nonna hurried anxiously after me.

"Get my tarot cards read," I said.

"Well, dear girl, this is a surprise." Maggie was arranged on a squashy chintz sofa, legs propped on the glass coffee table, in the "small" *salone*. Her color scheme today was violet: a print dress with a hemline well above the knees—she was so proud of her legs—and a deep V neck adorned in the cleavage with an amethyst butterfly pin. A ruffle trailed from neck to hem, and a sash wrapped her plump waist. The shoes were lavender lizard mules and, like everything else she wore, very expensive.

She patted the sofa for me to sit next to her. "You look very pretty," I said, sinking into the feathery cushions.

"I believe in color coordination, dear. It always works. I'm into colors, y'know, as well as tarot. And tea leaves, I'm quite good at those too."

She patted her red beehive hairdo studded with sparklers of the diamond sort and gave me that shrewd look. "I've been expecting you," she said.

"Really?"

"Ben was here already."

"Oh." I stared uncomfortably at my feet in their old sneakers.

"You smell nice, dear," she said after a while.

"Violetta di Parma," I said. "Violets."

"I know."

"Maggie," I heard the desperation in my voice, "I want you to read my tarot cards."

"Of course, dear girl. You want to know your future. And maybe some of your past also." She got up and went to a small antique escritoire, took out the cards, and called me to come sit at the table under the window.

"Well now," she said with a mischievous cackle of laughter. "Let us see what we shall see, shall we?"

"I think I already know it," I said, but she shook her head.

"Fate is fickle, my dear, remember that. None of us ever knows exactly what is around the next corner." She gave me the cards to shuffle. "Now, let's begin."

She laid out the cards, staring thoughtfully at them. "Mmm," she murmured. She placed more cards on the table, murmuring comments about each one, none of which made any sense to me.

"What does it all mean?" I asked, and she began to tell me about the Greater Arcana and the Lesser Arcana, poking a jeweled finger at the Joker, or Fool, which I just knew she was going to say was me.

"You're fooling yourself, my dear," she said, looking at me over the tops of her little gold bifocals. "It's a failing you have, not looking reality in the face."

"But I face reality every day of my life." I was thinking of the hospital.

"Not your own, my dear," she said quietly. "Never your own. See here." She pointed to another card. "I see a place of pain and disruption, a great river still to be crossed."

She glanced curiously at me, but I shrugged and said skeptically, "You already guessed that."

"I see trouble ahead," she said, "difficulties. . . ."

Now I was wishing I'd never asked her to read the cards.

"Aha!" she exclaimed, delighted. "A dark man." She beamed triumphantly at me. "Ben Raphael. Of course!"

"Maggie, can you really see stuff in there, or are you just putting me on?"

"Of course I see things in the cards. I'm a bit of a witch really, you know. At least my second husband used to call me that. Oh, now look, Gemma. You have a date with destiny."

"I'd rather have a happy ending," I said, ever hopeful, but Maggie said that that was up to me.

"Try again next week, darling—the cards are sure to have changed by then," she said with that mischievous little grin.

We had tea then, though I refused her offer to read the leaves. We ate plain English cookies, and she asked me where things were at between me and Ben.

"At a standstill," I told her. "Worse. We're at war." And I told her what he had accused us of.

"Do you think he might be right?" she asked, curious.

"Of course not! I would *never* do a thing like that!"

Maggie sipped her tea thoughtfully. "Think about it, my dear. There's an old saying, you know, about not cutting off your nose to spite your face. Now I know something happened between you. I read it in Ben's face and yours. Make peace with him, my dear, that's my advice."

I thought about what she had said, driving home in the car.

CHAPTER FORTY-NINE

Two days passed with no word from Ben. I moped in my room with a summer cold, caught no doubt in the rain, struggling to balance my conscience with my actions, and failing. Making love with Ben had definitely not been the right thing to do. I had broken my vow. I had taken a chance again. But it had been so delicious, so sensual, so scary, that feeling that I was crashing into love. Could it be love? The way it had been with Cash? Of course not. It was just a brief affair. And it was over.

I remembered our latest confrontation and knew that Ben believed I had something to do with his troubles at the villa. It was all Donati's fault, and the bastard had disappeared without a trace. He was ruining my life.

Angry all over again, I raced downstairs to the phone and tried Donati's number again. Of course, no one answered. There was now no doubt in my mind that Donati had pocketed Ben's money and disappeared with it, as well as with the only copy of Count Piacere's will. And that my only chance of sorting this out once and for all was to go to Ben, tell him this, and suggest we employ a detective to find Donati. "It's the only way to find the truth," I would tell him. Surely he would see the sense of that.

I hung up the wall phone and saw Amalia hovering in the hallway, pretending to dust. *"Buona sera, dottoressa,"* she said. "I hope your cold is better." She was speaking in Italian, but I had enough of an ear by now to get the gist of what was going on. I said thanks, but no, and pointed to my red nose and watering eyes.

"I saw the *signor* Ben this morning," she said casually, and my ears pricked up. "He was in Rome for a couple of days," she added, "on business. He's back now, though."

"Oh, *grazie,*" I said, because I couldn't think of anything else. But my mind was ticking over, fast. I thought about calling him, but remembered he had no phone. It was four in the afternoon. Nonna and Livvie were out on a sight-seeing trip, taking in the fabulous gardens of La Foce, near Pienza. Now was my chance. It was now or never.

Nonna had the car, so I would have to walk to the villa. I checked the weather; a cloud covered the sun, and it wasn't quite as hot. I got out of my bathrobe for the first time in two days, put on shorts and a white T-shirt, dabbed on sunscreen, combed my unruly hair, powdered my nose, decided against the lipstick, and slammed a straw hat on my head.

I sprayed Violetta di Parma lavishly all over and headed out the door. To my date with destiny, I thought, remembering Maggie's tarot cards.

The villa was farther than I remembered, *and* it was on top of a hill. It was also hotter than I'd thought, and by the time I got there, my shorts were rubbing my legs and my T-shirt was sticking to my back with sweat.

The Land Rover was parked by the fountain. He was home. "Hi," I called, striding into the cool hall. "Hi there,

Ben, it's me." I walked through the French door onto the terrace, calling hello.

Ben was sipping a cool drink, and next to him was a tall, icy Scandinavian beauty. Her pale blond hair was pulled back from a perfect face, she wore huge dark glasses, and she was immaculate in white linen. Even her toes in her expensive sandals looked perfect, lacquered a pale shiny peach. She was glamorous, sexy, and a dead ringer for a blond Nicole Kidman. And Ben might as well have been Tom Cruise, that's how remote he seemed.

That rainy night in the cool white bed in the old hotel with the ruby lamps and a window overlooking the River Arno seemed light-years away.

Ben got to his feet, while the blonde just stared, as though she had never seen anything quite like me. He said, "Gemma, this is Luiza Lohengrin."

I felt plain just being next to her name! "Excuse me, I didn't m-m-m-mean to in-in-interrupt," I said, smiling as though I hadn't a care in the world. "See you later, Ben." Damn it, I was *stammering. I should never have come.* Then I flung around and walked straight into the French door, which had swung closed behind me.

I bounced off it like a rubber ball. *Oh God, oh God, I was dying here.* I shoved my sunglasses back up my horribly painful nose and stalked regally away.

I heard Ben call after me, but I was out of there, running down that rutted gravel drive, tripping over the clumps of weeds, and cursing myself for being a stupid fool. Of course he didn't give a damn about me . . . he never had . . . just look who he was with now . . . and it had taken him all of *two days* to find her.

Well, fuck him! I marched on, wounded, alone. I

should never have done it, never have made love with him, never have let him into my life. Those ruby lamps had shed too romantic a glow on that cool white bed, our hot bodies. Oh God, I couldn't bear to think about it. I was so *humiliated*.

I looked back at the Villa Piacere, serene in its shady bower of trees with the Tuscan hills encircling it. When I'd first seen it, I'd thought it was paradise.

Well, now paradise was lost.

Back in the safety of my white room, I flung myself onto the bed and my fury turned into tears. I was thinking of Cash now. I hadn't cried in a long time; too long, I guess, because now the tears wouldn't stop. They spurted from my eyes and trickled into my ears, soaking my pillow, but this did not soothe my battered soul one little bit. Tears did nothing for me.

After about an hour of crying, I sat up, blew my nose, struggled to my feet, and went to the gigantic old armoire that filled one white wall. I found my duffel and took out a sweater I treasured. Soft cashmere. Light gray. *Cash's* sweater.

I held it to my face, seeking his scent the way an animal might, but it had been so long, the smell of him had disappeared. All that was left was the gray wool. And memories. I pressed the sweater to my face and cried, softly now, into its folds.

By the time Nonna returned with Livvie later that evening, I had showered off the sweat and grit and stresses of the day and composed myself. Nevertheless, one look at their horrified faces told me they knew something was wrong. I guess it was the swollen red eyes and the battered nose, lit like Rudolph's.

"Mom." Livvie was at my side in flash. "What happened? Are you all right?"

I could see she was on the verge of tears herself, at my state, and I hugged her to me and told her I would be fine.

"What happened, Gemma?" Nonna said, very quietly for her. For once she wasn't playing the Italian matriarch, and I knew I must really have her worried.

"I have to get away from here for a while," I said, trying to keep the wobble their sympathy evoked out of my voice. "I mean . . . I just have to . _ it's necessary."

For once Nonna didn't question me, she just nodded and said, "We'll leave tomorrow. I've always wanted to see the Amalfi coast, and it'll do Livvie good to be at the seaside for a while."

CHAPTER FIFTY

The Amalfi coastline south of Naples is a narrow torture of hairpin bends hanging over a sheer drop into the sea, but I hardly had a chance to see its beauty. It was hell just avoiding those trumpeting *camion* tearing along the road as though they owned it, as well as the tour buses plodding down the very middle, though I did manage to eyeball the half-naked, sun-browned youths on old Vespas heading for the beach. Even in my state I noticed them, so you can imagine how gorgeous they were.

Crazy Italian drivers in small Fiats darted past us on the bends, cars swung in front to park, pedestrians walked nonchalantly under my wheels; ice cream vendors jutted their carts into the road, and dogs ambled lazily through the traffic. Many, I noticed, were limping.

Livvie and Nonna were asleep in the backseat. The drive had taken hours, and now we were stuck in traffic in a small coastal town, a one-lane crawl in the heat. We had been nose to tail forever, it seemed. I wound down my window and hung my elbow out, praying for a breeze, glancing in the rearview mirror at my mother and my daughter.

I looked anxiously at Nonna. There was a grayness to her face I hadn't noticed before, a waxiness to her skin. I told myself it had been a long drive; it was probably just fatigue and the heat.

I was leaning wearily on the wheel, waiting for the traffic to move through the little Italian beach town, dwelling on what was wrong with my life, when I noticed an old man. He was hobbling down the broken sidewalk carrying a magnificent white Persian cat.

His walnut face cracked in a toothless smile as he held the cat up high for the passing motorists to admire. The cat's hair was pure white, thick and soft; the old man's was straggly, sparse, streaked in shades of gray. The cat's huge blue eyes surveyed us languidly; the old man's boot-button eyes gleamed with pride in a face of a thousand wrinkles. He was gnarled, stooped, a peasant and poor, yet he had tied a red ribbon bow around his cat's neck and brushed her long fur until it was satin. As I watched, he placed the cat carefully on the seawall.

He turned, beaming, to face the snarled traffic. *"Guardate,"* he called out to us. *"Guardate tutti, la mia principessa. Vedete quanto bella è."* Look, everybody, at my princess. See how beautiful she is.

Heads stuck out the windows of crawling cars, and eyes widened as people looked. The old peasant waved an arm, pointing proudly at his cat, and people laughed and called out to him, *"Quanto bello, è allinare una principessa."* How lovely, she is truly a princess.

The old man took his bow humbly. *"Grazie, grazie, signori."*

And the cat stared calmly back at us, her admirers. She extended a languid front paw as though inspecting her manicure, yawning as she accepted her applause.

I was suddenly stricken by the pathos of this little vignette, by the old man's pride, his love, his need to share the only beautiful thing in his poor life. He was not holding out his cap. He was not begging. He asked nothing in return, only our acknowledgment of his cat's beauty.

As the traffic moved slowly on, leaving the old man and his *principessa* behind, tears slid down my hot cheeks. I was crying for the old peasant and his beautiful cat, and for all my own accumulated sadnesses: the daily struggle, the emotional letdown of the emergency room when a life had slipped away from me and I had to acknowledge that I was only human, only a doctor, not a god. I was crying for the loneliness I had striven to push away as though it didn't exist and that now, because of Ben, I knew was a fact. And I was crying for Cash and for Ben and my own lost loves.

It was a kind of epiphany. Because of an old man and his love for his beautiful white cat, I was finally able to see my own life in its reality. And for the first time I asked myself, Is this all there is?

If there were only one good reason to come to Italy, I knew this might have been it.

CHAPTER FIFTY-ONE

We were at the San Pietro, a small, luxurious country-style hotel miraculously pinned to a steep cliffside in Positano. This was a simple kind of luxury: a cool white interior, masses of fresh flowers, and a jaw-dropping fall into the sea hundreds of feet below. My spacious bedroom, its floor tiled for coolness, led onto a flowery balcony and a sunlit panorama of blue sea. The bathroom window was part of the tumbling green cliffside so you could lie in the tub and watch little boats whizzing by far below.

It was that magical time just before dusk slides into night, with the sea a deep underlit blue and the sky an opaque chrome gray. We were sitting on a beautiful bougainvillea-covered, lamp-lit dining terrace, but I noticed that Livvie was not looking at the view. She was staring morosely into her glass of lemonade, looking suddenly lost.

I realized that for Livvie this scene, all this beauty, was not enough. She was bored; she needed other young people; she needed action. I sighed, not knowing what to do.

The charming headwaiter beamed at us; he told us we need not simply choose from the menu. "Please, *signore*," he said, waving his arms wide to demonstrate what he meant, "tell me what it is you want, and you will have it. We are here to make your dreams come true."

I wish, I thought somberly, but Livvie said, "Okay, I would like some Cream of Wheat, please." I glared at her. I knew she was putting them to the test.

"But of course, if that is your dream." He looked sad that Cream of Wheat was all she desired, and Livvie's own face fell. I could tell she was already regretting it.

"Well, maybe I'll have pizza," she said in a small voice, and he smiled at her and said, "Your wish is my command, *signorina.*" Minutes later he appeared bearing a thin, biscuity pizza margherita, fresh from the glowing wood-fired oven at the end of the terrace. I could tell Livvie was impressed, and she smiled and said thank you, remembering her manners for once.

I don't recall what I ate, only that it was delicious. And that there were fireworks over the bay as we dined, reminding us of the Fourth of July party at the Villa Piacere, and reminding me of Ben. As if I needed reminding.

Later I climbed exhausted into my huge bed. The beautiful linens smelled of the fresh wind and sunshine, and the cicadas made a racket outside my open window that somehow I found soothing. It was a hot night, and I was naked under the sheet. I pushed it back, lying there in the starlit dark with only the sound of the sea and the crickets and my own thoughts for company. I wasn't used to sleeping naked; I hadn't done it in a long time. Well, not since last week . . . with Ben.

And that was a lifetime ago.

CHAPTER FIFTY-TWO

LIVVIE

The morning was sunlit, with a promise of heat to come. Bougainvillea crisscrossed over Livvie's head in a blaze of purple and hot pink and salmony orange, and below, the sea sparkled with a cool blue glitter that looked tempting. She was on Nonna's terrace, breakfasting on a feast of fresh fruit, tiny croissants, and crusty bread with freshly squeezed orange juice. Nonna was pouring coffee, hot and strong, from a large silver pot, and Livvie noticed that all her mom wanted was coffee. Nonna had said she was still in a funk, and it was about love again, only this time it was Ben as well as Cash.

She thought about Muffie. She wished the kid could have come with them; at least then she would have had someone to talk to, because right now she was going out of her mind with boredom. She and Muffie weren't exactly friends—more like allies—but she liked that Muffie had had the guts to do what she did *and* to stand up to her father, though she was willing to bet Muffie wouldn't have done it had her society mother been around.

She stared gloomily at the translucent blue sea. Even the thought of swimming in it was no fun, not without someone her own age to share it with, someone to dunk under the miniwaves, someone to float on a raft with, the way she could see people doing far below their terrace. Maybe she should just get on one of those rafts and float away on her own sea of loneliness. Is that what she was feeling? Lonely? Bored? Restless? Who knew? She didn't know herself what was wrong with her.

None of them had brought bathing suits, so now they had to go into Positano to buy some. Livvie thought at least that would be a diversion: shopping was always good. Maybe they'd have some real funky stuff in the village. Ha, some hope!

It was already hot when they took the hotel shuttle the couple of kilometers into Positano. The village sprawled down the hill in a series of charming narrow cobbled streets, with stone archways spilling peach- and rose-colored blossoms. Holidaymakers were already sipping coffee under yellow umbrellas in terraced cafés, and tourist shops had hung out their wares: sun hats, bathing suits, cotton sarongs, and T-shirts that said POSITANO on them. There were ceramic shops with the local blue and yellow pottery; craft shops with carved olive-wood bowls and napkin holders; art shops with large paintings of the Bay of Salerno, glittering and even more blue than the reality below them; and fun little shoe stores and boutiques.

Livvie bought a minuscule red bikini that she knew Nonna disapproved of; her mother bought a blue one-piece tank suit that Livvie said was boring; and Nonna bought a white strapless little number with draping over the stomach that her mother said made Nonna look like fifties movie star Rita Hayworth. Then Livvie said, "Omigod, *red, white,* and *blue*! We'll look like *the flag*!"

While Nonna and her mother fortified themselves with

more espresso in one of the outdoor cafés, Livvie mooched alone down to the harbor. And it was there she saw him. Balanced on the hull of a Riva speedboat, lazily polishing its brasswork.

He looked, she thought breathlessly, exactly like his speedboat: slender, sleek, lithe. *Omigod,* all those words she had never thought applied to a man surely did now. All the guys she knew at home were sort of geeky, still growing into themselves. Everybody knew girls were much more advanced than boys the same age. But this one was older. *And* he was a golden boy: blond sun-bleached hair to his shoulders; lean golden-tan body with muscles that rippled as he moved; a dusting of golden hairs along his arms, his legs, his chest, even on his taut tan stomach.

He turned, caught her looking at him, and stared back at her with eyes the color of the sea behind him. *"Ciao,"* he said, and Livvie thought it was the most wonderful word in the world.

"Ciao," she said back, suddenly shy and also suddenly too aware of her long skinny body with its as yet too small breasts. She only hoped she wasn't going to be like her mom and have to stuff her bra with panty hose. For once she felt uncertain about the way she looked.

He was still staring at her. *"Che bella,"* he called, doing that kissy thing with his fingers and smiling with a flash of terrific white teeth. Livvie bit her bottom lip and stared down at the ground, embarrassed. Compared with the guys she knew, this one was A MAN.

"You wanna rent?" he said, waving his arm to indicate the glossy speedboat. "I take you to Capri, only half an hour."

She edged closer, shading her eyes with her hand as she looked up at him. "You go to Capri?"

"I go anywhere—with you," he said, giving her that smile again. "To Capri for the shopping—everybody goes."

A whole half hour in his company—a half hour there—*plus* a half hour back again. Whatever it cost, it was worth it. "How much?" Livvie said. She gasped, though, when he told her the number with all the zeros. "I'll be right back," she said.

"Gotta ask Mamma," he called mockingly after her as she fled up the steep, narrow street back to the café.

"We've got to go to Capri," she informed her mother and Nonna, still breathless. Almost as breathless as they were when she told them the price of the Riva and its captain. She looked pleadingly at her mother and saw the sudden softness in her eyes that meant she was about to give in. "Oh, thank you, thank you, Mom," she cried, hugging her.

"Tell him to pick us up at two o'clock at the San Pietro," her mother said, smiling at her.

"Two o'clock at the San Pietro," Livvie told him, even more breathless from the run back down the hill.

"Okay." He was still polishing his brasswork, and she watched for a minute. He was, she decided, Absolutely Perfect.

"What's your name?" she said at last.

"Tomaso." He flicked her a knowing little smile. *"E tu?"*

"Livvie."

He nodded. "Okay, Livvie, two o'clock."

"Okay," she said, still lingering. "Well, *ciao* then."

"Ciao." He whistled as he worked.

Back at the hotel, Livvie changed into her new bikini and sarong, then, with her mom and Nonna, took the outside elevator eighty-eight long meters down through sheer rock to the tiny cove with a sunbathing platform built out over the sea. A huge shallow cave was in back of them, with a bar and a beach attendant who bullied the guests, deciding, like a miniemperor allotting his lands, who got the prime spots along the edge of the sea and who had to sit two or three rows back. Of course, when Nonna informed him in Italian who she was, they were given three sun loungers on the water's edge. Crisp white towels were spread over their loungers, orders were taken for lunch, which had to be sent down from the kitchen upstairs, and requests for cold drinks were filled.

Feeling as if the work of the day had been done, Livvie arranged herself on her cushioned lounger. She lay on her stomach, staring at the glittering bay, idly playing with the fringe on the towel, and thinking about Tomaso. TOMASO. Two o'clock seemed an eternity away.

CHAPTER FIFTY-THREE

GEMMA

Why did I agree to go to Capri this afternoon? All I really wanted to do was lie here and stare at the sea and think about absolutely nothing. *Zero*. My mind is too full to cope anymore. Numb would be the right word to describe my feelings right now. And I need to stay that way.

I glanced worriedly at Livvie; I so wanted her to enjoy this trip, and in a way she was, but she was lonesome and, I guess, lost. Lost in the young teen way of longing for something but not knowing exactly what; of knowing things but not knowing enough; of longing for experiences and being afraid of them; of presenting a streetwise facade to the world, when she was really just as vulnerable as any other kid. Life was so tough when you were a teen.

Did it get any easier when you were older? I asked myself. Look at the mess I was making of things. I was hardly a great example.

I watched as Livvie and Nonna went off to the beach bar to have lunch. I wasn't hungry. Mostly I was just running on high-octane caffeine. I saw Livvie slip her arm through Nonna's. They smiled at each other, and I felt a little better. I wondered what the speedboat ride would be like, and Capri. I hoped the trip would perk Livvie up a bit, snap her out of her boredom.

I needn't have worried. Livvie was waiting on the edge of the little jetty at one fifty-five, hands shading her eyes, staring out to sea like a New England sea captain's wife waiting for her man to return from a long journey.

We had changed from our bathing suits into shorts and shirts and sun hats, and I was looking around at the Italian women, so chic and somehow "together," every sleek hair in place, red lipstick perfect, golden tan smooth, wondering where I'd gone wrong. I recalled the icy Scandinavian blonde on Ben's terrace with her perfect peach-polished toes and her cool white dress, and jealousy stabbed me again. I hate jealousy. It was beneath me to feel this way, but damn it, that's how I felt.

I turned to Nonna. "I need to go shopping," I said firmly.

She flashed me an astonished glance. "Well, it's about time."

Livvie leaned forward eagerly as the speedboat hove into sight. The engine cut, and it slid silently alongside. I saw her face fall as she stared at the person piloting it.

He looked like Hemingway's Old Man of the Sea: long, wild, curly gray hair and burned-bronze muscles, eyes permanently narrowed from years of gazing over tempestuous oceans, and a face worn into creases from the sun and the wind.

Livvie said, "But I thought—"

What had she thought? I wondered. And then I saw what. Or rather *whom*.

Blond, beautiful, and *sexy*. A lethal combination. I looked worriedly at my daughter.

"*Ciao,* Tomaso." She smiled, and he nodded *ciao* back to her as we walked carefully down the slippery little steps. Tomaso helped us into the boat, the Old Man of the Sea revved his engines, and we slid away from the jetty with a throaty roar. He gave it full throttle, and we were speeding across the glittering blue sea past a panorama of towering cliffs matted with greenery, past secluded sandy coves and tiny seaside villages with seemingly no road leading down to them, past giant rock formations and deep dark caves and a cruise ship, with its sails unfurled, sleeking grandly across our path.

Tomaso, who I now realized was the reason we were in this boat and on our way to Capri, climbed like a monkey along the side. Spray dotted his golden body with crystal. He balanced like a circus performer on the hull of the speeding Riva. Then he stripped off his shorts.

He wasn't *exactly* naked; I mean, he had on one of those brief little bathing suits European men sometimes wear, the kind that leave nothing to your imagination. He posed there for a second, then lay down on the front of the boat, legs stretched out, arms propped behind his head, as he gave himself up to the sun and the wind, the spray and the speed.

Livvie's eyes met mine, and we smiled, the kind of smile that said we had a little secret between us and that I knew where she was at and she knew what I was thinking.

We were in Capri in a flash, hair whipped by the wind that had also put a sparkle in our eyes. Although in Livvie's case, it was probably just Tomaso. The Old Man of the Sea cut back his engine to a muted purr, and Tomaso rose from the deck. He posed for a second, then dived into the blue, blue sea. He emerged seconds later, climbing back onto the deck, shaking drops of water from his golden body, sleek as any dolphin.

I glanced at my daughter and saw that helpless lost-puppy look in her eyes that I knew from my own teen years. And I knew she was in love, for the very first time.

CHAPTER FIFTY-FOUR

It's no hardship to shop in Capri. You name it, there's a boutique selling it, from the grand names to the smaller but still exclusive Italian shops, from the local vendors to the ice cream parlors. We inspected baby-soft cashmeres in delicate sugared-almond colors and tucked linen dresses in pretty pastels, snug, strappy little dresses in supple silks, south of France bathing suits, wraps and shawls in pashmina and lace, beaded handmade sandals, beautiful shoes and bags, glittering real jewels, and even bigger and more glittery fake jewels. But let's face it, I was not the world's greatest shopper. I had difficulty choosing. Lack of experience, I guess.

Just the act of shopping was exhausting. We were in this chic boutique where an obviously rich old Italian woman, thin, with lacquered blond hair and a rapacious look in her eyes, was trying on the entire shop while the patron danced attendance. I picked out what I thought was a nice top: blue flowers on white, very pretty.

In a flash, the old woman snatched it out of my hand. She said something to the patron, who shrugged help-lessly and whispered to me that the woman wanted it. Nonna said scornfully, "Let the old warhorse have it. She needs dressing up," and we exited to outraged cries.

Next I was trying on this Lycra top. The chiffon scarf the boutique owner had wrapped over my face to protect the garment from my nonexistent makeup blinded me, the plastic ticket dug into my back, the sleeves were somehow twisted—it was a form of torture, and flustered I asked myself one more time, *What am I doing here?*

Discouraged, I walked out. And then, across the street, I saw the dress I had tried on in Rome. The silky chiffon one that I had thought looked okay on me in an odd kind of way. Red and sexy and exactly the kind of dress I had nowhere to go in. The one that cost a fortune. I went in and bought it. And to go with it, a pair of shoes with heels that I knew were too high, red with pointy toes that I knew would kill me but made my legs look surprisingly good. They were my own little ruby slippers, ready to take me to the Land of Oz. So there I was, inches taller and somehow curvier in this delicious frock, and suddenly feeling like a woman again.

"Maybe this shopping game isn't too bad after all," I said.

"It's the success that counts," Nonna said knowledgeably, because hadn't she become the champion shopper?

Anyhow, I ran back to Malo, the cashmere shop, and handed over my poor AmEx card for an ice-green sweater that was maybe the softest thing on earth, then dashed back down the street and picked up a simple white skirt, except it fit like a glove. I treated myself to some expensive new underwear—I was never going to be caught on the hop in my old cotton undies again, I told myself, but then I quickly reminded myself that I certainly was not. I was the ice maiden, wasn't I? Yeah, that's right. So I bought lacy bras and panties, and I picked up a few shirts and some cute shorts and a couple of cotton sundresses, and by then I knew I was broke.

Especially when Livvie just had to have a green dress that was the color of Muffie's new hair and that was actually *pretty*. It was a real girly dress, cut on the bias with skinny little straps. It clung softly to her young body, somehow making her look older instead of younger, the way I thought it would have. We bought a pair of the handmade beaded sandals to go with her dress, and a smart suit in lavender linen for Nonna. Then we had a quick pistachio ice cream cone. (I had learned from Flavia at the *gelateria* in Bella Piacere that if you're buying pistachio ice cream in Italy, the thing to remember is that the good stuff, the kind made from real pistachios, is a kind of sludgy green. If it's that bright shiny green, it's made from colorants and fake flavors.) This one was *perfect*. And then we were back at the harbor, where our Riva was waiting. As was Tomaso. The real reason we were here.

CHAPTER FIFTY-FIVE

This time Tomaso was driving. His father sat up front, winding ropes and studying charts and doing other such nautical things, and Tomaso invited Livvie to come sit next to him.

I watched the back of my daughter's cropped yellow head, trying to fathom what she was thinking. Nonna nudged me, raised her brows, and nodded in their direction. *"Amore,"* she whispered. I sighed. I knew she was right. "Now she can really get into trouble," Nonna added.

"Not if I have anything to do with it, she won't," I whispered back, glaring at Tomaso's exquisitely muscled back. There's just something so beautiful about youth, though, about the lean spareness of the body: every rib, every vertebra shining subtly, every effortless muscle delineated under the flesh, the torso tapering like a Greek, or maybe I mean Italian, statue, the beautiful taut muscular butt, the strong legs. I couldn't blame Livvie; she had never seen anything like this. But, I asked myself, exactly *what* did Tomaso see in my little girl?

A companion, I thought wistfully. Someone to joke with, to flirt with, to pass long, hot, sunlit summer days with. But not the nights. No, *definitely not* the nights.

"Mom," Livvie said when we arrived back at the San Pietro, "can I go out with Tomaso tonight? He knows this perfect little club; he says it's just great."

She looked hopefully at me. I was on the verge of saying no, but she was suddenly so all sort of shiny and expectant. "You can't go out with him alone. It has to be in a group. And he has to have you home by eleven," I said sternly.

"Oh, Mom." She was breathless with excitement, smiling. "Midnight."

"Eleven-thirty. And no later."

"Thanks, Mom." She grinned and threw her arms around me in a giant hug. "I'll wear my new dress."

Livvie was in the sea-foam-green dress, with a touch of bronze eye shadow and a pale lipstick. I looked at her and thought, amazed, *My daughter, the young mermaid, is going out on a date with her merman.* Her first *real* date. I gulped back the panic, told her to remember her manners and who she was and that Nonna would kill her if she didn't behave and that I would cry, and she said, "*Omigod,* Mom, I'm only going to a club." And then she grinned and said, "I'm gonna dance my feet off—and I'll be with the best-looking guy in town."

And when Tomaso came to pick her up, in the smallest car I ever saw, about the size of a golf cart, red with rusty-looking blotches on it, I knew she was right. Dressed, he looked almost better than half naked, in a white short-sleeved shirt and snug-fitting white pants. Forget Fabio, this guy could have walked down any runway in Milan or Paris.

"If she has to go out on a date," Nonna muttered, "it might as well be with a guy who looks like that."

Tomaso's friends, a young man and a very pretty girl, struggled out of the backseat and came to shake our hands. Then Tomaso helped Livvie into the car. He made sure she was comfortable and closed the door as though he were locking up some precious jewel—which he was. *My kid.*

I crossed my fingers and hoped Nonna was right. This was worse than my own first date.

Nonna and I dined alone on the terrace. I stared at the lights of Positano twinkling around the curve of the bay, wondering what Livvie was up to.

"No use worrying," Nonna said crisply. "You raised her properly, didn't you?"

"Yeah, but so did you, and look what happened to me."

Nonna pursed her lips, assessing me. She called over the waiter and ordered two vodka martinis. "With Grey Goose Vodka," she added, causing me to shake my head with wonder and ask how she knew about vodkas.

"I read a lot," she said. "Anyhow, I thought we both could do with a drink. You've been through a lot lately, Gemma."

"Yes." My voice sounded small as I suddenly choked up. I took a sip of my martini.

"You want to tell me about it?" Nonna was suddenly my mom again, with the same anxiety in her eyes that I had when I thought about Livvie. Moms were still moms, however old you were. And I was the same tongue-tied, embarrassed daughter, confessing her sins to her mother.

"I think I'm in love with Ben," I said. "I don't want to be, but I'm afraid I am."

"Afraid? That's a very dramatic word, Gemma."

I looked despairingly at her. "But that's just what I am. Afraid."

"Because of Cash?"

Oh God, just his name could jolt my heart. I took another sip of the martini and nodded. "Mostly."

"Mostly? So what's the rest? The other reasons?"

"Well, for instance, I hardly know him. And somehow I always make a fool of myself when I see him, and—" I stopped. There was no way I could tell *my mom* about that night in bed with Ben, and how I had felt. "And anyhow he has another girlfriend. I saw them together, at the villa. Plus he hates me because he believes I'm sabotaging him. He thinks *I* had his electricity cut off, and his phone, and his water, and God knows what else."

"He thinks *that*?" Nonna sounded astonished.

"It's war between us, y'know." I finished the martini with one moody swirl down the throat. A thought occurred to me. I glanced suspiciously at her. "You wouldn't know anything about that, would you?"

"Very little," she said airily, summoning the waiter and ordering a bottle of the local rosé, well chilled.

"But you do know *something*."

"Perhaps Rocco knows. This is, after all, a local matter."

"Oh, of course, and nothing at all to do with *you*."

"Well. Maybe. Just a little."

I leaned my elbows on the table and put my head in my hands. "*M-o-m!* What have you done now?"

"Only tried to get my villa back," she said spiritedly.

"The locals decided to help me, that's all. After all, I am family from Bella Piacere."

"Yeah, and Ben is the *americano,* the foreign inter-loper, who was doing very nicely, thanks, until you came along."

She leaned across the table and looked into my angry face. "Are you forgetting that I am the heiress? That Ben is living in what, by rights, is *my* villa?"

"No, Mom, I'm not. But *sabotage?*"

"Okay." She gave in suddenly. "For your sake, I'll tell Rocco to call it off."

"Rocco! I might have known he had something to do with it."

"But remember, I'm doing this for you. Because you have been through bad times, and I think maybe now you are finally ready for the good times again. I would rather give up my villa and have you happy again, Gemma." She clutched my hand across the table, worry in her eyes. "And that's the truth."

I took Nonna's hand and kissed it, and she gave me that radiant smile, the kind I knew she must have flashed at my father when she first met him, the same one she was using now on Rocco Cesani. Plus the one I had rediscovered that I myself possessed. "Don't worry, Gemma, I'll take care of things," she said. "And now let's order. How about wild mushrooms sautéed in a little olive oil to start, with a slice of pecorino cheese? Then the gnocci, light as a feather and with just a little tomato sauce. Then maybe a nice fish, or how about veal?"

I let her go ahead and order, sipping the chilled wine that was more red than rosé, but light and sparkly on my tongue. When the food came, I just picked at it. Of course it was wonderful, but my taste buds had quit, along with my appetite. I knew I had to snap out of this, but not tonight. I just didn't have the energy.

After dinner, Nonna went to her room, and I took my book and sat on one of the comfortable white sofas in the lounge. Waiting for Livvie. It was ten o'clock, and I was already counting the minutes.

CHAPTER FIFTY-SIX

NONNA

Nonna called Rocco on the phone. It rang and rang, and she was just about to give up when he answered.

"Pronto," he said gruffly.

"Rocco Cesani, were you sleeping?" she said accusingly.

"Sophia Maria, I was thinking about sleeping. It's tenfifteen, and I have to be up early."

"You work too hard, Rocco. It's time you let your workers do more. All you should be doing is taking care of business."

Rocco pushed away his bowl of soup. Sophia Maria was still under the impression that he was a big success, an olive oil entrepreneur. He supposed, her being a rich woman, she didn't understand how the other half lived, and that he actually had to work in his *frantoio*.

"I have news for you," Rocco said. "The *americano*'s building permits for the new hotel . . . somehow they have disappeared! And tomorrow the road to the villa will be dug up by order of the local council. Maintenance work, they will say."

For a moment, Nonna was tempted. But she said,

"Rocco, listen to me. *E' importante. Urgente.* Cancel the roadwork, refind the lost permits. We can no longer go on with our plan."

"What are you saying? What about your villa?"

"Forget about my villa. This is something I have to do for my daughter. She is in love with the *americano,* but he believes she is sabotaging him. You see what I mean, Rocco. She tells me he hates her because of that."

"E' amore." Rocco sighed resignedly. Fido leaped onto his lap and licked his face, then jumped onto the kitchen table and lapped up the rest of Rocco's garlicky soup. That dog loved garlic. Rocco smiled fondly at him. He knew all about love. Anything that dog wanted, he could have.

"Si, è amore," Sophia Maria said now over the phone, and he smiled.

"Then there is nothing more to be said."

But Nonna had quite a lot more to say. "Tomorrow first thing," she instructed him, "you will go to the villa. You must speak with *signor* Ben personally. Tell him that Gemma was not responsible for the sabotage, that it was you and I, and the others in the village. Apologize, Rocco. Tell him it was all a mistake, it's over."

Rocco frowned: apologizing was not in his nature. Still, he rubbed his nose with his finger in that familiar gesture. "It will be done," he promised.

"And also," Nonna said, "make sure you tell him where Gemma is."

"Okay."

"Good. And then I will return home very soon."

"I will be waiting for you, Sophia Maria," Rocco said, smiling.

CHAPTER FIFTY-SEVEN

LIVVIE

Livvie sat next to Tomaso at a tiny table in a hot, crowded, smoky little club, sipping a Coke and trying to look casual, while all the time she was so aware of his leg pressing against hers, she could almost have fainted. The couple who had been in the car had disappeared as soon as they arrived. Nervous, she gulped the last of her Coke. Her straw made that slurping sound, and she frowned, embarrassed. It made her look like a silly little kid, and Tomaso was so . . . adult.

"How old are you anyway?" she asked suddenly.

"Cosa?" He smiled into her eyes in the smoky twilight, not understanding.

"Quanti anni hai?" She pointed a finger into his chest. *"Tu . . .* you," she added.

"Ah, parli italiano adesso." He flashed her that dazzling smile. "Now you speak Italian. *Ho sedici anni."*

"Sedici?" It sounded more like *seduce* than a number.

"Sixteen," he said, surprising her; she'd thought he was at least nineteen. *"E tu?"*

Livvie knew she couldn't possibly tell him she was

only fourteen; he'd probably drive her home immediately. "Fifteen," she said.

He gave her a long look. *"Più o meno?"* He waggled his hand. "More or less?"

"More," she said firmly. *Omigod,* lying in Italian was hard work. And flirting was almost impossible. Except when they were dancing, which they were doing now.

She was a better dancer than he was. She sparkled on that tiny dance floor, moving with the hip grace of a streetwise Manhattanite. What's more, she knew all the latest moves, and now she taught him. With hip-hop and her favorite boy bands blasting, Livvie was queen, just like her mom before her; but when they played those slow, smoochy Italian summer pop songs, Tomaso was king.

He held her close to him, one hand low on her back, the other clutching her hand under his chin. It was just, like, oh, gosh . . . so *sexy.* His beautiful golden body was so close to hers she could feel him tremble. *Omigod!* She jumped back, not sure whether to be shocked or excited, and he pulled her firmly toward him again.

"Carina," he whispered in her ear, and a lot of other lovely words she didn't understand. Then before she knew it, their noses bumped, his lips were grazing hers, and the strobe lights were going off in her head as well as on the dance floor. *Omigod,* she couldn't wait to tell her friends back home, they had talked of this so often, and now she was actually *doing it. Kissing.* She just had to tell *somebody*; even Muffie would do.

The music stopped, and she opened her eyes. She hadn't even realized they had been closed! Tomaso still had his arm around her, his face close to hers. "Come, *ca-*

rina," he murmured, taking her hand and leading her out of the club, into the almost tropically hot night.

His hand felt rough against her soft one, and Livvie thought worriedly that maybe she would have to do some weight lifting, something to harden her up, make her seem more adult. They stopped outside a waterfront café. Tomaso waved and shouted *ciao* to the young people hanging out there, and they yelled back, "*Ciao,* Tomaso. Who's the girl? She looks like a pop singer with that yellow hair."

"E' Madonna," Tomaso yelled back, and they all laughed.

Livvie glanced at them from under her lashes; she didn't know what they had said, and it made her uncomfortable. She was just praying she hadn't inherited that blushing thing from her mom.

Tomaso took her over to meet his friends. He introduced her to a group of boys and girls, some of whom looked her own age. They smiled and were friendly and curious, and they liked it when she told them her grandmother was Italian. But mostly she just sat with another Coke in front of her, careful this time not to slurp, holding hands with Tomaso and basking in the knowledge that she was "Tomaso's girl." She liked very much that little electric tingle his fingers transmitted to hers, that superawareness of herself that she had never felt before, as though every nerve ending had suddenly acquired new meaning.

The hot breeze would have ruffled her hair if she'd had any more than half an inch, and she licked an ice cube, enjoying the contrast against her hot tongue.

The church clock struck the hour. She counted contentedly along with it; she never wanted to leave this place, her new friends, and Tomaso. *Omigod,* the clock had just struck *twelve!*

She leaped to her feet. Panicked images of her angry mother and—even worse—Nonna rushed through her head. "I have to go. I promised to be back at eleven-thirty."

Tomaso took her arm. "Of course, *carina*. I will take you home." He winked at the others and said something in Italian that Livvie didn't understand, but that she would bet was that American girls had to go to bed early, or something dumb but true like that.

She almost ran up the steep cobbled streets to where Tomaso had parked the car on the main road at the top of the village. He held the door open for her. Then, as she bent to step in, he unfolded her again and took her in his arms.

"Carina," he murmured. "Livvie."

His beautiful face hovered over hers, and their eyes locked. She watched fascinated as his mouth came closer. He was going to kiss her, properly this time. And she didn't know how to kiss. Still, she had talked about it forever with her friends; it should be easy. And then her eyes had somehow closed all by themselves, and her mouth was linked to his, and she was dying of love . . . or whatever it was she was feeling.

"Carina," Tomaso murmured, when he finally took his mouth from hers. She gazed bleary-eyed at him, and then for some dumb reason, she said, "Thank you." And he smiled and said, "Thank *you, carina,*" and then he helped her into the car.

In five minutes they were back at the hotel. She was scared stiff because she had promised her mom she would be home by eleven-thirty, and she just knew her mom would never ever let her out on her own again, and *omigod,* what was she going to do if she could never see Tomaso again?

She flung open the car door before either the doorman or Tomaso had a chance, throwing him a fast good-night over her shoulder.

"Livvie, wait." He came after her, caught her at the elevator that led down the cliff to the front hall. "Tomorrow, Livvie? The same time?"

His eyes were pleading, and so sea blue she could just die. "Okay," she said weakly. Then she pressed the button, and he disappeared from view. And probably from her life, she thought miserably, because now she was in real trouble with her mom, she just knew it.

GEMMA

I was pacing the San Pietro's terra-cotta-tiled floor, trying to cast myself back into the role of a teen and telling myself that of course everything was okay and that Livvie had not (a) been seduced, (b) gotten drunk, (c) been kidnapped, or (d) oh God, *please not,* been in a car accident.

The memory of that narrow curving road threading around hairpin bends made me sick to my stomach. Where *was* my kid? I wanted her here, home, safe, with me. I knew I was only going through the first-date trauma every parent goes through, but that didn't make waiting any easier.

I paced some more, nodding *ciao* to the desk clerk and the barman, trying to concentrate on admiring the way the vines trailed across the ceiling, bringing the outdoors inside, and the profusion of flowering plants and cascading bougainvillea. I told myself sternly to seize the moment: admire the beauty, the candlelit terraces, the flower gardens, the lights of a passing cruise ship on the horizon, the glitter of Positano . . . where my daughter was . . . *and she was late.* Damn it, she was *definitely very extremely late,* and now I was really worried.

I paced back to the elevator, the door sprang open, and there she was, barefoot, with her new beaded sandals from Capri clutched in her hand, biting her lower lip just the way I did when I was anxious.

"I'm sorry, Mommy," she said, hanging her head the way she used to when she had been a naughty little girl. "I'm really sorry. It wasn't . . . I mean, nothing bad happened. It's just that I forgot the time. We were sitting at this café with his friends, and somehow the time, like, just skipped right by me."

She glanced up at me from under her lashes, and I saw myself in her so clearly, I felt a pang of pity for her. I held open my arms and said simply, "Get over here, daughter."

Livvie ran into them, and we hugged each other tight, and then she pushed me away just a little and said, "Mom, he kissed me . . . and Mom, I was so scared."

We both laughed and hugged some more, and I thought, *Thank God everything is all right: she hasn't been seduced or kidnapped or in an accident. And she had actually told me about her first real kiss.*

"Come on," I said, and we walked, arms around each other's waists, out onto the terrace, where we leaned on the balustrade and I listened while she told me about her evening. It was, I thought, exactly the way things should be between a mother and daughter. At least for now it was.

CHAPTER FIFTY-EIGHT

ROCCO

Rocco bumped slowly up the gravel driveway in the white pickup, with Fido bouncing and skittering in the back, frantically trying to keep his footing, giving the odd quick, sharp little woof as though to tell Rocco to stop it. Rocco parked in the old stables, got out, and stood looking around the deserted yard. The dog jumped out the back, trotted over to him, then sat patiently at his side.

It was *perfetto*, Rocco was thinking. He had done a perfect job. It could not have been bettered. And all for nothing. Plus now he was going to have to swallow his pride and apologize to the *americano*. Well, maybe not *apologize*, exactly.

Ben walked around the side of the villa and saw Rocco standing in the yard with his cartoon dog. He wondered what he was up to this time. *"Ciao, Rocco,"* he called.

"Signore, ciao." Rocco whipped off the old ex-army hat that he wore, sun, rain, or hail. He held it over his chest, standing at attention like a soldier confronted by a general.

Odd, Ben thought, he usually just ambled around, and

never did more than touch his hand to the brim of that hat. Something was up.

"What can I do for you today, Rocco?" he said, looking stern because he knew Rocco was involved in his troubles somehow.

"*Signore,* I have the good news." Rocco gave him a beaming and very false smile that showed all his teeth. "They tell me the building permits are not lost after all."

"Is that right?" Ben leaned against the stone wall, arms folded.

"Is correct, *signore.* Not only that, the council have decided there is no need for the maintenance work on the road to the villa. It will not be dug up."

"And why is that, Rocco, d'you suppose?"

Rocco gave one of those enormous expressive shrugs, arms wide, shoulders high. "As you say in America, it beats me, *signore.* Maybe is just sometimes God is good to us."

"I'm all for that, Rocco," Ben said dryly, accepting it for the apology he knew it was meant to be. "Let's hope the Almighty is also taking care of my phone and my electricity and water."

Rocco beamed again. "I can guarantee it, *signor* Ben. *Domani.* All will be fixed." He hesitated, glancing out the corner of his eye at him. "One other thing, *signore.* It's about . . . well, it's personal . . . about the *dottoressa.*"

Ben straightened up. He took a couple of steps toward Rocco, and the dog growled. Ben stopped and looked at the pair of them. "What about the *dottoressa?*" he said. "You know where she is?"

"I know. And I know also that she did not sabotage your villa, *signore.* She is innocent of all your charges."

"I never charged her with anything."

"That's not what I heard, *signore*."

"So if the *dottoressa* is not guilty of sabotage, Rocco, then exactly who is?"

Rocco scratched his head; he shrugged again, smiling. "Who knows, *signore*? Who knows?"

"Only the good Lord, I suppose," Ben said, and Rocco beamed in relief. He was off the hook; he hadn't even needed to lose face and apologize. Before too long the *americano* would have his services restored to the villa, he would reunite with the *dottoressa,* and Sophia Maria would come home. Everything was good again.

"The *dottoressa* is in Positano, *signor* Ben," he said, and noticed Ben glance quickly at his watch. "She is at the Hotel San Pietro with the daughter and Sophia Maria. It's not such a long drive, *signore,* you could be there in . . . oh, six hours maybe."

Yeah, in my dreams, Ben thought, as he shook Rocco's hand and they slapped each other on the back. Ben said, "Thank you," and Rocco said, "For nothing." Then Ben said, "My good old friend Rocco," and Rocco said, "Next season, *signore,* you will see the largest truffle ever found in Tuscany. Fido will find it specially for you, and I will carry it here myself, personally."

"Glad to hear it, Rocco." Ben was already heading back to the villa to tell Muffie to get ready; they were going on a trip.

CHAPTER FIFTY-NINE

BEN

All the way on that long drive south past Rome, then on to Naples, Ben told himself he was crazy to be doing this. He hardly knew the woman. And anyhow, *she* was crazy, always tripping over her feet and walking into doors. God knows how she managed in that famous emergency room. And then, of course, she had walked in on him with Luiza. Just her typical rotten timing, he thought. So why, he asked himself for the hundredth time, if she gets you so damned irritated, are you trekking all the way to Positano in an old Land Rover to apologize?

He groaned out loud, and Muffie, stretched on the backseat, bored, hot, and fed up with being in the car, sat up and took notice. "What's the matter, Daddy?"

"Just traffic, I guess." But his daughter was smarter than that.

"It's Dr. Jericho, isn't it?"

"Isn't what?" He looked at her in the rearview mirror and decided he was getting used to the green hair. It looked almost normal to him now.

"Oh, Daddy, *you know*." Muffie giggled and put her head back down again. "Men," she said loudly, and he grinned. This trip to Tuscany was not all in vain; his girl was growing up.

Which still didn't explain why he was chasing halfway across Italy after a woman who was so difficult, so contrary, so . . . *ornery,* she baffled him. The truth was he had never met a woman like her. He'd never met a woman who did the difficult job she did, and never met a woman who cared less about the way she looked.

Yet in Florence, sitting in Cammillo's with her narrow blue eyes laughing at him and her quirky mouth tempting him, he had never seen anyone look more honestly beautiful. She had struck a chord within him, made him look at himself, at his relationships.

He wasn't a selfish man. He treated his women gently, courteously. He had cared about the women he dated, and he had cared about his wife. Been madly in love with her, he'd thought then. But he had never felt like this before.

So how *did* he feel? He contemplated that, idling in traffic in a little coastal town called Piano. Odd name for a place, he thought, though he knew it meant "slowly" in Italian, and since they had been stuck for more than ten minutes, it couldn't have been more appropriate.

Damn it, he didn't know what he felt for Gemma; only that he wanted to be with her. He wanted to hold her in his arms, make love to her, protect her from all those minidisasters she seemed prone to. And there was something else. He wanted to melt that freezer she called a heart. Gemma Jericho was a problem. And a mystery. He needed to solve both.

CHAPTER SIXTY

GEMMA

I was awakened from an afternoon nap by a knock on my door. It was Nonna, with a gleam in her eye that made me suspect she was up to something.

"Let's get dressed up tonight, have some champagne, celebrate," she said. "Wear the new red dress, why don't you?"

"Wait a minute," I said, still bleary-eyed. "Exactly *what* are we celebrating?"

She gave me a little smirk and a nudge with her elbow. "The end of the sabotage," she whispered, and then she laughed. "Anyhow, Gemma, this is your chance to wear it, so why not?"

An hour later I was checking my appearance in the tall mirrors that gave me a more than adequate view of my newly tanned self in the red dress and the ruby slippers that were meant to take me to Oz. The soft chiffon clung where it should and left bare what was nicer left bare. There was no doubt about it, the Italians knew what they were doing when it came to clothes. I sighed, thinking gloomily that

I'd better make the most of it; it was probably the last chance I'd get to wear it. Soon—too soon—we would be returning to New York. To work and the daily grind.

You mean to the life you love, I reminded myself. *The one where you have eliminated all romantic and emotional complications.* Yeah, right, I whispered. Back to the woman with the ice around her heart. Remember?

I didn't have a lipstick that went with the dress, so I put on my usual paleish neutral, which was entirely unsuitable, and a dust of blusher on my pale gold face. A swish of mascara, a wet finger to smooth my eyebrows, a fluff of my hair, and a squirt of Violetta di Parma, and I was done. Oh, wait a minute: my glasses. There, now I was ready. To celebrate the end of the sabotage of the Villa Piacere and, if I were truthful, the end of Nonna's dream of being an heiress.

Livvie knocked on the door, then bounced in. "Mom, can I borrow your new white skirt?"

This is too much, I thought, startled. *Now my daughter's borrowing my clothes. She's growing up too fast. I want her to stay a little kid. I liked that, it was so much easier. Now there's kissing and clothes and teen stuff to get through.*

"It'll be too long for you," I said, being used to my daughter's micromini-length apparel.

"That's okay." Livvie held the skirt up against her. "I'm thinking of changing my whole look. Y'know, like more grown-up. I want to be totally unique."

She disappeared with my new skirt, and I wandered upstairs to meet Nonna. She looked quite at home, propping up an international bar.

"The heiress looks pretty good tonight," I said, hitching onto the stool next to her.

She gave me that Sunday up-and-down look, critiquing me mentally, I could tell. Then she said, "I hate the lipstick."

"Jeez, Mom, what about the dress?"

"The dress is perfect. And the shoes." She turned to the barman and ordered what seemed to be becoming our usual drink: a martini with Grey Goose Vodka, while I stared down at my feet. The shoes were already squinching. Pride was painful, I remembered, knowing that some poor woman must have coined that phrase.

Livvie glided slinkily toward us. My white skirt fit her perfectly. With it she wore a simple black roundneck T-shirt and the flat beaded Capri sandals. If not for the henna tattoos, thankfully already fading on her arms, and the cropped yellow hair, she might have looked almost normal.

The skirt reached to her knees. "I've never seen you without legs before," I said, grinning, and she said, "Oh, Mom, don't start," and Nonna told her she looked almost ladylike and ordered her a Coke.

"A telephone call for the *signorina,*" the barman said, passing Livvie a phone.

"For me?" Astonished, she took it and said hello. "Oh, okay," she said, sounding subdued. "Okay. Yeah, well, maybe. *Ciao.*"

She handed back the phone and took a sip from her Coke while we stared expectantly at her. "Well?" I said.

"Oh, it was just Tomaso. Maybe he can't make it tonight, maybe he can. We'll see."

That silenced us. I didn't know what to say, and of course Nonna had not been privy to our woman-to-woman conversation last night, so she did not know the full details of the Kiss, and the perils of first love, especially when you were only fourteen. So Nonna said, "Good, that means you can celebrate the end of the sabotage at the villa with us," and Livvie gave her the kind of look that said what did she care, and I sighed, looking forward to a silent, grim "celebration."

CHAPTER SIXTY-ONE

We had just settled ourselves at our usual table overlooking the bay, with the sky all golden-orange from the sunset, when *"Bene,"* Nonna said, sounding like the cat that got the cream. I followed her eyes. Muffie Raphael was standing in the doorway.

Livvie yelped in delight. She threw her arms around Muffie as though they were bosom buddies and said, "Great to see you." And Muffie grinned back at her and said, "Me too."

I looked at the pair of them: Muffie in totally inappropriate white Lycra shorts and a top with sequined straps and all that spiky pale-green hair; and my daughter, a simple blonde in the white skirt to her knees and a plain T-shirt and flats. *Omigod,* I thought, quoting Livvie, the girls have changed roles. Muffie has become Livvie—and Livvie has become Muffie.

Then I realized that if Muffie was here, so was Ben. And suddenly there he was, in rumpled shorts, looking hot and tired and sweaty. And *I* was looking positively gorgeous in my new red chiffon and smelling of Violetta di Parma. Had we reversed roles too?

My pulse jumped up a dozen notches; I didn't know what to do. I ran my hands agitatedly through my hair and said, "Oh, goddamn, what's he doing here anyway?" and I scrambled to my feet with somehow the idea of running away. Then I told myself I was never going to run away again because when I did I always tripped or walked into doors or something, and I sat down again quickly.

The waiters looked suspiciously at Ben and Muffie as they made their way along the terrace of elegant diners. I almost laughed. *Scruffy* and *offbeat* might have been apt words to describe their appearance, but y'know what? It did not take away from Ben's fatal charm one bit, especially when he looked into my eyes and made me feel, all over again, that I was the only woman in the room.

"Gemma," he said, holding out his hand. Somehow I struggled to my feet. I took that hand, and we walked together back along the terrace, followed by the interested gaze of the other diners.

A trio was playing a song I thought I knew; soft, romantic, sexy. Ben pulled me to him into a slow dance. The lights were low. We were the only couple on the floor. I could smell my own perfume and his sweat. I thought it was the sexiest smell in the world.

This is all wrong, I told myself, looking into his eyes. Did I tell you they were gray-green with little gold flecks? Did I tell you that his hands were hard, firm? Did I tell you that I knew his body as well as I knew my own, and that when you dance a slow dance with a man whose every movement you recognize, you realize that you are a woman and, possibly, a very weak one? And that even though I knew I shouldn't be doing this, that I should have sent him packing with a cold good-bye and maybe even a Get lost—I was not about to do that.

Ben felt my sigh and lifted his cheek from mine. "I'm

here to apologize, Gemma," he said. "Luiza is just an old acquaintance. I've known her for years. There's nothing between us. Never was. This was all my fault."

"Well, maybe not *entirely* your fault," I murmured, linked to his eyes by what I knew must be electricity, and not wanting to hear another word about the gorgeous Luiza.

His sexy eyes swept me up and down, and I didn't care that the pointy-toed shoes were killing me. I hardly even felt the pain. "I like you in red," he whispered, his face so close I could feel his breath.

"Gemma," he murmured, his lips hovering over mine, "I drove here as soon as I found out where you were. I asked myself all the way on that long drive why I was doing it. And when I saw you sitting on the terrace, with your upswept glasses and your red dress and Botticelli hair, I knew why."

I looked at his mouth, then into his eyes, and okay, this time I really was drowning in them. "Bet you didn't recognize me," I said stupidly, and he sighed.

"Why do you always interrupt me?"

"Sorry. What were you saying?"

"Damn it, I think I was saying I missed you, you crazy woman. Maybe I'm falling for you, Gemma Jericho."

I was never a girl who could accept a compliment easily. "Get outta here," I said, grinning like a fool. "You hardly know me."

He pulled me so close I was positively crushed against him. He rested his chin against my forehead, and I heard him mutter, "Whatever am I gonna do with her?" Then he looked at me again and said, "Just think of all the good things about you I still have to find out."

The trio swept back into that song again, and now I remembered it. It was Marc Anthony's "You Sang to Me." The one where he's "crashing" into love. I was afraid he was singing about me, doing exactly what I had vowed never to do again. In that song Marc Anthony also says he's not afraid to love, but oh, *I* am. And besides, I didn't want to crash into love with a man who was virtually a stranger; a man I had broken a vow to make love with; a man who might just possibly wreck the carefully controlled life I had fashioned for myself.

The music had stopped, and Ben was leading me out of there, away from the curious diners. Away from Nonna and Livvie and Muffie, who I hoped were enjoying their end-of-sabotage celebration dinner, and out into the night.

"Where are we going?" I asked.

"My place." He handed me into the dusty Land Rover. "The Hotel Sirenuse, just down the road. There was no room at this inn."

I glanced nervously at him from under my lashes. This was my last chance. I could get out of the car and walk away without even a good-bye. But I didn't. Instead I kissed him, and he gave me that deep, knowing look, and in minutes we were at the Sirenuse.

CHAPTER SIXTY-TWO

We were in a room overlooking the sea and the village of Positano. Ben closed the curtains, shutting out reality, the way he had in Florence. He looked into my frightened eyes. "Why?" he said, after a long moment. "*Why* won't you let me into your heart, Gemma?"

"I will," I said. "I have." But I was lying, and he knew it.

He ran a finger lightly across my chin and over my cheekbone. He took off my glasses and stroked back my hair with both his hands, holding it tight against my scalp until I thought I must look a bit like Fido, but he didn't seem to think so, because what he said was "Beautiful, so beautiful."

Then he stepped quickly away and began to pull off his clothes. I gasped. I mean, this was a bit quick, wasn't it? Whatever happened to foreplay?

"Got to take a shower," he said. "Don't go away." He turned at the bathroom door and caught me ogling his delicious body. *Bug-eyed* might have described me, and he laughed. "Please," he added, "don't leave me."

I didn't. In fact, what I did was slip off the red dress and my Oz shoes and the lacy new underwear that, on second thought, maybe I should have kept on and flaunted for him. But I left it all in a little heap on the floor, and then—maybe I shouldn't have done this either, but I did—I followed him into the bathroom, and into that shower.

Making love under running water is like having your breath taken away twice over. Water is in your eyes, in your mouth, in your hair.

"It's the rainstorm in Florence all over again," Ben said, kissing me gently, "only this time we don't need an umbrella."

I was the aggressor, shamelessly reaching for him. I don't know where this trait comes from—or maybe I do. It's just that I had suppressed it for so long, and now I was going for the brass ring. I soaped his long strong body, massaging him, digging my nails into him, and then I knelt in front of him and took him in my mouth. He tasted like wine and roses and sex and everything wonderful. He was groaning, pressing my head into him, and I wanted to laugh, I was so happy. I thought maybe this is really what I was put on earth for, to pleasure a man, to take pleasure from him. But then I knew that it was all part of life, part of loving, of living, of being a woman who, even though she shouldn't, was maybe, just maybe, *crashing into love* with a man.

He picked me up, backed me against the tiled shower wall, bent to kiss my nipples until I groaned with pleasure. "I can't wait," he said, lifting me up and onto him. "Gemma," he cried, as I wrapped my legs around him and he held me there, thrusting into me, looking into my eyes, and we were drowning this time in each other's. Thrills of orgasms rushed through me, one after another, and I heard him cry out, felt him inside me, warm, wetness, wonderful.

I unfolded my legs from around his waist, and he held me until I could stand, then he leaned both hands against the shower wall, breathing hard, staring at me.

The shower still gushed water, streaking our sweat-slick bodies, and he said, "I guess that's what missing you can do to a guy." And I said I thought it was probably that, and he laughed.

He wrapped a big white bath towel around me, then picked me up and carried me to the bed. We lay side by side, just holding hands. Outside the window I heard a snatch of music from a sidewalk café; a burst of laughter, the clatter of heels on terra-cotta tiles.

"What are you thinking?" He rolled on his elbow and looked at me.

"I'm thinking," I said slowly, "about crashing into love."

"Me too," he said, and he took me in his arms again, and this time we were more gentle, more caring of each other. He took his time and I took mine. I never knew it was so easy to become a shameless hussy.

CHAPTER SIXTY-THREE

BEN

Ben lay awake listening to Gemma's soft, even breathing. He thought it was probably one of the few times he had seen her quiet, and certainly one of the few times she hadn't been coming back at him with some quip, or else tripping over something. He grinned in the darkness. He really liked her. Plus she was one of the sexiest women he'd ever known. She had a wonderful instinctive sexuality; certainly nothing she had learned from the pages of *Cosmo,* and certainly no faking. She enjoyed herself, enjoyed his body, and God, he surely loved hers. And though he still couldn't fathom why, he really cared about her.

Did he mean he loved her? Was he *in love* with her? She had certainly brought something new into his life that he didn't want to lose. He supposed, when he thought about it, it was innocence.

And that was pretty remarkable when you thought that Gemma looked death and human destruction in the face every day. But she still came out a winner. Winning over death.

He touched her warm thigh and she moved sleepily closer, wrapping herself around him. His arm was crushed under her shoulders, and it felt as though she weighed about three hundred pounds instead of being the skinny long thing she was. He needed to move, but he didn't want to disturb her, she slept so soundly. Inspecting her face in what was by now the half-light of dawn, he saw the red bump on her nose where she had walked into the French door. Laughter rumbled in his chest.

"What's so funny?" Gemma muttered sleepily.

"*You*, sweetheart," he told her. "Now go back to sleep." And she did. Even though he wanted to make love to her again, wanted to feel her clinging to him, wanted to taste her and probe her mouth with his tongue and feel the luxury of being deep inside her.

He sighed, staring up at the ceiling. Oh God, was he *really* in love this time?

CHAPTER SIXTY-FOUR

GEMMA

Much later that morning, back at the San Pietro, we had established our territory of seafront loungers spread with fresh white towels. We rented rafts and floated out into that blue, crystalline water, paddling lazily alongside Livvie and Muffie, who were splashing each other and falling off their rafts, shrieking.

I thought it was a good thing Muffie had shown up, because Livvie had told me that last night Tomaso had not. I had caught the stunned look in her eyes that told me she was feeling bad about this, and I guessed she was wondering *why* she had kissed him. Now she assumed Tomaso didn't want to see her again, and she was feeling just the least little bit "cheap."

So I'd said as cheerily as I could, "Never mind, hon, there's plenty more fish in the sea." Livvie had given me a look I knew well (because it was so like mine) that said, Mom, give me a break, there will never be another fish like Tomaso. So Nonna had bought ice cream sundaes, which, as usual, was all she could think of to cheer Livvie up, and now she seemed to have, at least temporarily, forgotten him. I just hoped he hadn't left a permanent bruise on her vulnerable young heart. But then, don't we all learn about love the hard way?

I glanced up as a helicopter clattered overhead, hovering like a bright insect over the water. I held my breath as it made straight for the cliffside, then suddenly dropped and made a perfect landing on the helipad near the rose garden. *Wow,* I heard Livvie and Muffie saying. I noticed that they spoke the same language these days. Then I heard Ben say, "Well, what d'ya know? Guess who that is."

I didn't have to guess: even from a raft floating off the coast of Italy I could see the sun sparking off the diamonds.

"Hey, it's Maggie," Livvie yelled, and she and Muffie paddled rapidly back to the jetty to greet her.

Ben grabbed a corner of my raft. He swung it around until I faced him. Lying on our stomachs, we smiled up at each other, one of those deep, intimate smiles that passes between lovers.

Life was pretty good, I thought. In fact, it didn't get much better than this, floating on an air mattress on a cool silvery-blue sea with your lover. I mean, what more could a woman ask? Especially one who was not thinking about her past. *Oh God, the past. And Cash. What was I doing?* I sighed. I knew exactly what I was doing. *I just couldn't help myself.*

"Yoo-hoo." Maggie waved at us from the edge of the jetty. "Stop smooching and get back here," she called. "I heard you had all snuck away to Positano, and I've come to join you."

We paddled lazily back, hands linked across the tiny stretch of water between us. That is, until Ben gave me a sudden shove and tipped me off. He dived right in after me and caught me just as I was coming up, spluttering, from the depths. I yelled at him and pushed him back, and then we were both under the water, kissing madly, arms and legs entwined. I couldn't breathe, but I thought, Well, if I'm going to go, this is as good a way as any, just as we bounced to the top again, shrieking and laughing. I heard Livvie yell, "Oh come on, Mom, quit that," and I rearranged my face from its silly grin because I could tell I was embarrassing her.

"So," Maggie said, when we were finally all sitting around a table in the beach bar, sipping glasses of cold rosé and nibbling on fresh fruit. At least the grown-ups were. The girls were drinking Coke and eating fries and grilled cheese sandwiches. I envied them, but thought I had better watch my figure now that I was into lacy lingerie and sex.

"So," Maggie said again, "the reason I am here is a little matter of arbitration."

We looked inquiringly at her. As usual she was quite a picture, in turquoise and fuchsia stretch capris, a matching top, several gold necklaces plus a whopping pearl one—to say nothing of the usual glittering rings and the pins that adorned her hair.

"Arbitration?" Nonna looked interested.

"Reference the Villa Piacere," Maggie said.

Nobody looked at each other. Nobody spoke. I picked at a piece of melon, glancing out the corner of my eye at Ben. He was sipping his wine, staring out to sea.

"We all know the facts, so there's no need to go over them again," Maggie said briskly. "What we need to do now is find out who the villa really belongs to. I've hired a detective to track down Donati." She glanced at her diamond watch. "He'll be reporting back to me this evening with the first of what you might call clues to Donati's whereabouts."

Livvie bit into her sandwich. "Wow, Muffie," she mumbled, "we are gonna be, like, y'know, *spies*."

I told her sharply not to talk with her mouth full, and she and Muffie giggled together. "Then what?" I asked, stealing a french fry.

"Then you and Ben will follow up the detective's clues and track down Donati. I'm sure you'll find him," she added.

"I'm glad you have such confidence in us," Ben said dryly, and my mouth twitched at the corners.

"New careers," I said, "the entrepreneur and the emergency doc, chasing a thief across Italy."

"Just like in the movies," Muffie said, breathless with excitement, plus the fact that she too had a mouthful of sandwich. I sighed and temporarily gave up on the mom and manners bit.

"There's just one thing." Maggie looked sternly at us over the top of her extra-large, extra-dark sunglasses with the Versace logo in gold on the sides. "If you find the will, and the Corsinis are named as heirs, the villa belongs to Sophia Maria. If you don't find the will, it belongs to Ben."

"Winner takes all?" I looked questioningly at Nonna.

"Winner takes all," she agreed.

"Maggie," Ben said, exasperated, "you are a rich forty-nine-year-old woman who misses the action and loves interfering."

"Right on every count," Maggie agreed.

"Winner takes all?" I said, pinning him down.

He sighed. "I guess so. But believe me, you're never going to find that will."

After lunch the chairs had been turned away from the sea to face the latest angle of the sun. We sank into them, each lost in our thoughts, and perhaps because I'd had so little sleep the previous night, I dozed off.

I awoke a couple of hours later feeling great. Thanks to Maggie, the problem with the villa would be solved one way or the other, and thanks to Ben, I felt like a woman again. Life, I decided with that little smile that seemed permanently stuck on my face, was pretty good. Right now.

Always that little get-out clause, I reminded myself. And always the memories of Cash, my true love. Which also reminded me that reality and my job at the hospital were almost around the corner. Time was passing: our summer vacation in Tuscany was almost over. And when it was, what then? I decided quickly I wasn't going to worry about that now. I was going to take what I could get, while I still had it.

We gathered our scattered belongings and trailed slowly up the steps to the elevator carved into the cliff. It was too small for all of us, so I went first with Ben and Nonna, and Maggie came up next with the girls. Ben went off to make sure there was a table large enough for us all for dinner, and then I heard Nonna say, "Well, well, just look who's here."

I turned and saw Tomaso walking toward us, just as the elevator doors opened again and Livvie stepped out.

I held my breath. I wanted to run to her, to hold her hand. But Livvie didn't need me. She stuck her chin in the air and gave him the kind of look I knew so well: sideways, lids half lowered, yellow head tilted arrogantly back.

"Like, what are *you* doing here?" she said.

"I came to apologize," Tomaso said, and I guess somebody had told him the correct phrase to say in English. "Last night, there was work to be done, with my father."

"Sure. That's okay," Livvie said, obviously not meaning it.

Muffie hovered at Livvie's side, staring at the golden-tan vision. Livvie put an arm around her shoulder and said, "This is my friend Muffie. She goes where I go. Right?"

"Right," the sea god said humbly.

"Okay then, eight-thirty," Livvie told him. "We'll meet you at the same café. Right?"

"Right," he said. "See you then," and with a funny little bow in our direction, he turned and walked away.

"Wow," Muffie said, her eyes sparkling. "Like, y'know, we've got *a date*." And giggling, the two of them linked arms and hurried away to talk over the latest developments.

"Somehow," I said to Nonna, "I don't think I have to worry about Tomaso anymore."

"Thank God for that," Nonna said, crossing herself.

CHAPTER SIXTY-FIVE

Ben and I had decided to take up the detecting business on our own, and Livvie and Muffie, who fancied themselves as the latest incarnation of Bond girls, were left indignantly in Positano with Nonna and Maggie.

We drove back to Tuscany in the bone-rattling Land Rover, with me complaining all the way about why a rich guy like him had to drive such an ancient vehicle, and him asking why a poor woman like me drove an expensive rented Lancia.

Maggie's detective had given us an address in Lucca, where Donati had supposedly been sighted. Lucca is a charming walled city northwest of Florence, all alleys and piazzas, famous for centuries for its silk manufacturers. In fact, some of the mulberry trees that had fed those silkworms still grow on top of the old walls, which are wide and grassy as a city park. But the address Maggie's detective had given us turned out to be an antiques store, and no one there had ever heard of Donati.

Our next clue was that he was in Gali, a small Tuscan town set in the middle of Chianti country. There was a central square with narrow streets leading off it like spokes of a wheel, fancy tourist-oriented grocery stores selling wild boar, the specialty of the region, and a scattering of cafés. This time the address turned out to be an ice cream parlor. And of course, there was no sign of Donati.

Next there was word he would be at a roadside fruit stand near Montepulciano. Wrong again!

We were sitting in the Land Rover, axle deep in grass and weeds, outside a ruined olive mill that had been the latest Donati clue. We stared despondently at the pile of gray stones; it was obvious nobody had been there in decades.

"Where the hell is this detective getting his information?" Ben asked.

"Where did Maggie get the detective?"

"We've driven all over Tuscany looking for Donati," Ben said. "I'm tired. I need time to be alone, with just you."

"Just me?" My eyes sparkled, and he leaned over and kissed me, long and lingeringly.

"I want you, Gemma Jericho," he whispered, nuzzling my ear.

I shivered with delight, but at the same time I was asking myself why he wasn't telling me he loved me. Of course, I didn't *want* him to tell me, because that meant commitment and I could never commit to anybody. It was better this way: companions, friends, lovers.

"Do you think this is right?" I said wistfully, still thinking, the way a young girl does, that sex equals love. "You know I can never fall in love with you," I added, because I needed to make my position clear, to myself as well as Ben.

"Gemma, give me a break," he said. "What's wrong with our falling in love?"

"Oh . . . it's just that . . . I'm never really going to do that again."

His golden-flecked eyes stared deep into mine, as though he were trying to divine my mixed-up thoughts, my guilts, my past.

"You're crazy," he said after a long moment. "How can I love you when you are really *so damn crazy*?"

"I don't know." My voice sounded small, terrified, even to myself. "Yes, I do know. And it's just better not to."

He took his arms away, and it was like the end of the world: I knew he was finished with me, at a loss with what to do with me.

He got out of the car, walked around to my side, and opened the door. "Come with me," he said, holding out his hand.

And I went with him, the way I had that first day when he took me to buy milk, and to the market, and to Florence, and then to bed. I would trust him with my life, I thought. Except my life was not mine to give.

We walked, fingers loosely linked, past the old mill and the giant olive press, now a rusted tangle of metal and broken wheels, to the crest of the hill. Tuscany lay below us in all its green and gold beauty, the same as it had for centuries. Timeless, ageless.

The wind tugged at my hair, and I had the feeling that nothing here would ever change: that the grapes would always be grown in long symmetrical rows on the hillsides, and that they would be picked in October, and the wine would be made and celebrated. That the olives would be plucked from their burdened silvery trees and their oil pressed, tasted, and admired. That milk would be taken every day from the pretty white Chianina cows, and it would always taste of cream and sweet grasses. That there would be concerts in the piazzas, and big family weddings in the local churches, and *bambini* would be born and baptized and confirmed and married, all in that same little church, and then they would raise their own *bambini*, in exactly the same way. A life without change, Amen, I thought wistfully. And oh, how I loved it.

"Gemma, tell me what's wrong," Ben said.

I felt myself choking up, and shook my head. He took my chin in his hand and kissed me gently. I clung to his mouth. I didn't want him to move away. I didn't want to talk. I only wanted to kiss, to feel the warmth of his arms around me, his body next to mine.

"Sweetheart," he said, "dear love," and he stroked back my hair, kissing me endlessly until we were drowning together, helpless against the tide. We sank to our knees, still kissing, his hands still on my face, and I felt myself sinking back into the soft springy grass.

"Beautiful," he murmured, inching his lips down my neck, "so beautiful, Gemma." And this time I had no jokes to hide my fear. I was alone with him, lying face-to-face on that grassy hill, with all of Tuscany stretched below us and only the azure sky above. Alone in our own paradise.

Our kisses were gentle, tender, questing; searching for each other and finding it in our linked mouths, in the matched passion of our bodies. He unbuttoned my shirt and slid it off, tugged at my skirt, unhooked me, slid me out of my underwear until I was naked and vulnerable under that blue sky. And then he was naked too, and we were rolling together, like Adam and Eve, and I was thinking how beautiful he was, how hard his body, how smooth his skin, how gentle his touch, how wonderful his mouth was as he tasted me.

And even as he took me over the edge, I wanted him

again, I wanted more; immediately. "Now!" I cried, and I heard him laugh.

"You're wanton, shameless," he whispered, running the tip of his tongue around my ear as he thrust himself into my welcoming body.

"Oh yes," I cried, "oh yes, yes, I am." And then I was falling into that wonderful fathomless place where only lovers can go; where my body and his fit like pieces of a jigsaw puzzle; where what he was doing to me sent shudders of passion through me.

And I knew then that soon I would have to tell him the truth: exactly what had happened with Cash that had turned me into an ice maiden, unable to love a man.

CHAPTER SIXTY-SIX

We lay, still entwined, for a long time after we had made love, just holding each other. I felt as though I had been on a long journey of the spirit, as well as the body. Ben and I had traveled together to a place only those passionate about each other can reach, and I knew it was for the last time.

My body rested against his, absorbing every inch of him: the way his skin felt, his taut bicep where his arm gripped me; his breath on my closed eyelids, the sweetness of his hip against mine.

He was half sleeping, and I raised my head to watch him, just as thunder rumbled distantly around the hills. "Why is there always a storm when we make love?" Ben murmured, his eyes still closed. "It must be all the electricity we send out." And he laughed, still happy.

Raindrops flicked our faces, and I stuck out my tongue to catch them the way I used to when I was a kid.

"Better go," Ben said, as thunder rumbled again. "The heat's been building all day and we're in for another of those summer storms."

He pulled me to my feet and held me at arm's length, looking at me. I ran my hands worriedly through my hair, knowing that he must see every flaw, from the appendix scar to my too small breasts and my sticking-out bottom that I had always wished were less instead of more.

"Beautiful," he said. "Gemma Jericho, you are beautiful and you know it."

"No I don't," I said, pushing him away and reaching for my shirt. "I'm just your average too tall, too skinny—apart from my butt—doctor."

He said, "You know what? You're right." And we threw on our clothes and, laughing, ran hand in hand through the raindrops back to the car.

We held hands all the way back to the Villa Piacere, and I thought to myself, I really don't have to tell him. At least not yet. I want this for a little while longer, just a bit. Until we find Donati and get Nonna her villa back anyway.

"What will you do if you get the villa?" Ben asked, reading my thoughts as we bounced up the rutted drive-way.

"Sell it to you," I said promptly, and he barked with laughter.

"The doc turns businesswoman," he said. "But let me warn you, I'm better at it than you are."

The Neptune fountain in front of the villa was gushing again. "I see the water's back on," I said with a sly grin.

"Yeah. Now let's try for electricity."

We ran up the steps and into the big front hall. Ben jiggled the switch, and the chandelier blossomed with light, then sank rapidly into a flickering glimmer.

"I guess you can't have everything," I said smugly, but I was shivering. "It's cold in here."

"There's an answer to that," he said, and in minutes we were standing under that big brass sunflower shower, skin turning pink from the hot water, dodging the pointy edges

as we kissed. Then, warm and wrapped in white terry-
cloth robes and Ben's white athletic socks, we ran back
downstairs to the kitchen in search of food.

A fresh-baked *ciabatta* waited on a wooden board.
There was thin Parma ham and fontina cheese and fresh
tomatoes, sliced and sprinkled with black pepper and
olive oil and lemon juice. Ben picked out a bottle of Anti-
nori Chianti Classico Riserva, grown in one of the famous vineyards we had driven past just a couple of days
ago in our search for Donati, and we piled it all onto a
huge tray, along with a slab of fresh butter that smelled
sweet and creamy, the way fresh butter should. We added
mustard, a bread knife, and glasses and headed for the octagonal room.

Ben put a match to the kindling already arranged in
the grate, waited a minute, then added a couple of small
logs. Flames licked eagerly upward, sending a glow of
comfort through me. Next he lit the candles in the Venetian glass candelabra on the coffee table. Then he
arranged our picnic.

The storm was passing, and a thin ray of evening sunlight filtered through the window, resting on Luchay, who
stared inquiringly at us from one beady dark eye. And
also on a cat stretched across the back of the brocade
sofa, the one scratched so long ago by those Siamese in
the wall paintings. Only this cat was black as night, with
silken fur that glistened in the sun's ray, and he had yellow eyes. I went over and touched him gently. He sniffed
my hand, then gave me a lick and went back to his
snooze.

"I didn't know you had a cat," I said.

"That's Orfeo, my housekeeper Fiametta's cat." Ben

poured the wine and handed me a glass. It tasted the way I thought wild berries would, but with a dry, silken edge.

"And so is Luchay," Ben said, looking pleased with the wine.

"The parrot belongs to Fiametta?"

"Not exactly. She's looking after him for the owner, who's in the U.S. at the moment. It's a long story."

I slid off the sofa and sat cross-legged next to him on the rug, nibbling on the delicious bread and cheese, sipping my wine. "Tell me," I demanded, "about Luchay."

"You know, of course, that parrots can live to a great age," Ben said. "Much longer than mere mortals, and Luchay is very, very old. The story goes that he was brought to Europe from the Amazon by a sailor, a rough, cruel man, who, when he couldn't sell him, was about to wring his neck. The parrot was rescued by a young girl. She was alone, destitute, helpless as the baby parrot she had just risked her life to save. Her name was Poppy Mallory, and the parrot became her only friend, her only companion.

"She named him Luchay—*luce* in Italian meaning "light"—because he brought a ray of light, of hope, into her poor life. He was someone to love, to share her pain and small pleasures with. Someone to care about.

"The story, told to me by Fiametta, is that Poppy went on to win fame and fortune, and tragedy. And that as her fortunes rose, and she bought herself jewels and fine things, she also bought them for Luchay. His cage is pure gold, the rings around his legs were commissioned by Poppy from Bulgari and fashioned from real emeralds and rubies and diamonds.

"Luchay remained Poppy Mallory's only true friend

through her years of notoriety as the madam of a grand bordello in Paris and the lover of a man who, despite himself, was born to be a Mafia boss. They said that Poppy knew everybody's secrets, but only Luchay knew hers."

My eyes were wide as a child's being told a bedtime story. "But what happened? Why is Luchay here at the Villa Piacere? And why is his portrait on the wall?"

"A few years ago, long after Poppy died, an advertisement appeared in the international newspapers seeking her heir. She had left a substantial estate. Answers came from around the world: everyone wanted a share of that money, legitimate or not. Among them was a young woman by the name of Aria Rinaldi, who lived in a crumbling old palazzo on a canal in Venice. Fiametta's mother had worked for the Rinaldi family for many years. And somehow, now Luchay belonged to Aria.

"Aria loved the parrot the way Poppy had, and in many respects they were similar. They were both lonely, beautiful young women, except that Aria came from a different class. She was a young woman of breeding, but her family was poor, and she was expected to marry well to save their fortunes. When Fiametta's mother told her about the Mallory ad and the search for the heir and her connection to it, Aria saw a way out of an arranged marriage. If she inherited the money, she would be free."

"And did she?" I was so absorbed in his story, I had forgotten I was holding a piece of bread halfway to my mouth.

"It's all documented in a book called *The Rich Shall Inherit*. It's Poppy's story, and Aria Rinaldi's, and the story of all the other contestants for the inheritance, one of whom was a killer. And of course, it's Luchay's story. I'll buy the book for you, and you can read it for yourself."

"And how come Luchay's portrait is on the wall?"

"Poppy lived in Italy on and off for years; Fiametta's mother was a local woman from Bella Piacere. Poppy had met the Count Piacere, and she came to stay here at some point in her travels. The old count was more than half in love with her, they said, and he wanted to paint her portrait. When she said no, he painted Luchay instead, adding him to the family menagerie."

I looked at Luchay, imagining all the secrets tucked away in his small head. "Poor Luchay," I murmured. "Poor Poppy Mallory."

The parrot cocked his head to one side. "Poppy *cara*, Poppy *chérie*, Poppy darling," he said clearly.

The black cat slid silently from the sofa. He put a soft paw on my thigh, indicating that he wished to sit on my lap. Used to the ways of Sinbad, I obediently stretched out my legs, and he climbed, purring, onto my knee. He turned around a couple of times, then settled down, tail tucked under his nose.

I watched Ben pour more wine. I so loved the way he looked, the way he moved. And I loved his hands. Lightly tanned hands with dark hairs curling over that big steel watch. Hands that worked magic on me. I smiled as I watched him. "Now tell me about you," I said, knowing I was putting off that evil moment when I would have to tell my own story.

"You know it all by now." His greenish eyes glinted in the firelight. "Or most of it. The rest is pretty routine stuff . . . poor boy from the Bronx, worked two jobs when I was still in high school, hit the streets running—never stopped since."

"That's short and sweet," I said, wanting more. "What about your mother, your family?"

"Dad died when I was three. Mom worked all her life. She was a waitress at the local diner, worked both the lunch and the dinner shift. She was pretty, kind of fragile-looking, and too thin because, like you, she was always running from one job to the next. I had no brothers or sisters." He raised a brow. "Can't you tell I'm an only child?"

"You mean by your ego?" I said, and he laughed.

"My biggest regret in life is that Mom died before I made a dime. I wanted so badly to take care of her, get her out of the Bronx, buy her a house, shower her with gifts—the way Poppy did with Luchay." He shrugged. "But life isn't like that. We rarely get to repay those kinds of emotional debts."

I nodded. I knew what he was talking about.

"You know about my ex-wife, Bunty. I already told you about her. And since then I've been kind of playing the field, I guess. But now . . ."

Our eyes met.

"Now," he said softly, "I feel the need to have someone there to say good-night to, last thing before I fall asleep."

"Someone . . . ?" I sounded breathy, unsure of myself.

"Someone like you."

He took the wineglass from my numb hand and set it down on the coffee table. Then he took that same numb hand and held it to his lips. "I love you, Gemma."

He loved me. Ben *loved* me. He was looking at me, waiting for me to say I loved him too. But I couldn't let this happen. I couldn't do it. I couldn't break my vow.

"I love you, Gemma," he said again, looking puzzled. "I only wish I *knew* you."

Oh God, I knew what was coming.

"I told you Luchay's story and mine. Now you have to tell me yours."

I turned away. "I don't want to tell you."

"Why not?"

"Because then you won't want to know me anymore."

He shook his head. "Of course I'll want to know you. For God's sake, Gemma, what is it? What happened to you? You *have* to tell me."

CHAPTER SIXTY-SEVEN

A sudden draft fluttered through the room. The candles flickered, and then with a little hiss they went out. There was no moon tonight, and the tall windows reflected only blackness.

Ben stirred the fire with a long iron poker and threw on another log. I saw his profile against the leaping flames, and then he turned and looked at me. He saw the desolation of my soul reflected in my eyes, and with a look of great tenderness, he came to sit next to me. He propped more cushions against my back, and we leaned against them. He took my hand and said, "It's all right, Gemma. Whatever it is, it's all right, I promise you."

I wished it were true.

"The hardest thing about being an emergency room doctor," I said in a quiet, distant voice I hardly recognized as my own, "is telling the victim's family the bad news. This is sort of like that. I've never talked about this with anyone before, not even Nonna, or my best friend, Patty. I just couldn't, you see, because then they would know how guilty I was."

Ben's hand gripped mine tighter, and I felt a kind of strength running from him to me. "But now," I said, "because of what happened between us, because of *us,* I know I have to tell you. To explain about Cash."

"Cash and I met by chance," I said, "in a Starbucks, and I guess I was in love right away. He was younger than I by about six years. Not a lot, I suppose, but I was in my thirties and he was still in his twenties. I always thought that someday he would dump me for a younger woman, a gorgeous nineteen-year-old with no emotional baggage and no children. But then when I knew him better, I told myself Cash wasn't like that. He was different, special."

I stared silently at the dark windows, empty black spaces in those walls full of color and life, and suddenly I was there, reliving my life. *Our* lives. Cash's and mine.

I told Ben about our first meeting, how I had given him my bag and with it, symbolically, my entire life. I remembered the fun times, sandwiched between my crazy hours and his off-Broadway theater groups. The wonderful day at the little New England inn. About how gentle and understanding he had been with Livvie, who adored him and couldn't wait to call him "Pop." About our plans for the house in the country, the enormous Newfoundland dog for Livvie, my new life as a local doctor, Cash's potential success on Broadway.

When you are young and in love, everything is possible. And this was the first time I had ever really been in love, the first time I knew what love was all about. How it touched your heart as well as your body, how it took over your mind so you wanted to think of nothing else, wanted no one else. Forever.

Nobody told me that forever did not exist.

I told Ben how happy we were on that plane ride to Dallas and how easily Livvie had fitted in with Cash's family; how kind they were to us, how accepting. And then Cash's bombshell news that he was going to Hollywood to become a movie actor. "Movie star, you mean," I remember saying, because with his looks and his talent, how could he lose?

"The three months he was away were the longest of my life," I said to Ben. "And there had been some long ones before that, when I was alone and going to med school and having a baby. Loneliness takes many forms, and some of us deal with it in different ways. I chose to fill my life with work. There were just me and Livvie and Nonna. Until I met Cash.

"Anyway, finally Cash finished his movie, but he lingered a few more weeks, 'taking meetings' with agents and producers and directors, lining up the next job. 'A job' was what Cash called it. It was work, just like anything else, he said, only it called for more of *himself*, more input, more soul-searching in order to transform himself into someone he was not. 'An actor's life is not easy,' he said. 'Sometimes I think we're all schizophrenics,' which of course clinically was not correct, but hey, I couldn't play the know-it-all doc all the time. I was just glad he was home."

I fell silent again, staring at the blank windows in the firelit octagonal room, thinking about Cash being home and how it had felt to have him back with me, with us. Somehow he'd enfolded us into his life, taken us out of the strict day-to-day routine I had fashioned in order to keep myself going. We laughed more, we went to the zoo, we ate in funky little barbecue places and tried Indian food and saw shows his friends were in. I was drawn into his world, into the impromptu after-show parties, where we drank cheap wine or too-sweet Cosmopolitans, and I found myself being jealous of the pretty girls who were struggling to take their first steps up the ladder to what they just knew would be fame and fortune. I wasn't jealous of their looks and their uninhibited sexuality, I was jealous of their freedom. They made me realize that I had never been free. I had gone from high school to married woman to mother to doctor with never a break. I had never been just me, alone.

I looked at Ben. He was still holding my hand, staring down at it, serious-faced and silent. Waiting for me to continue.

"When Cash came back, my world was lovely again," I said, half smiling as I remembered. "You know the old cliché about rose-colored glasses, well that was me. I saw everything through that lovely pink haze. My job seemed easier because I was able to put less of my own emotions into it, I suppose. Even the rotten winter weather was okay. I could cope with freezing and snow and those winds careening down the avenues almost taking my nose off.

"Anyhow, this night, a Saturday, I was to finish my shift at midnight. It had been the usual mayhem in the ER, but for once instead of crashing, I was awake, alert. Cash was having dinner with his new agent, who had come specially from Hollywood to see him. 'It's important,' Cash had said. 'The agent thinks I'm on my way, Gemma.' I can still see the look on his face as he told me, that sort of triumph mixed with awe that precedes a momentous life-changing act. And I wished him good luck, and he laughed and said, 'Never say that to an actor, honey. It's always "break a leg." '

"'Okay, so break a leg then,' I told him. 'Then I'll fix it for you.'

"We hadn't made arrangements to meet, because he didn't know how late he was going to be, and anyhow I was usually too exhausted after a Saturday-night shift. But now I wanted to see him, to hear all about the new offers that I secretly feared would take him away from me. I called him on his cell phone. He was just leaving the restaurant. 'Good news, honey,' he told me. 'Everything's great in Hollywood.'

"'I'm glad, Cash,' I said, though I heard a little snaggle of resentment in my voice. 'Hey, listen, I'm not so tired tonight. Why don't you come and pick me up? We could grab a cup of coffee somewhere, and you can tell me all about it.'

"I heard his laugh, that great laugh that had so intrigued me when I first met him. 'Be there in fifteen,' he said. 'See you then, honey.'

"'I can't wait,' I said, and I was smiling, because it was true.

"At the stroke of midnight, I handed charge of the trauma department over to my colleague and went and scrubbed the hospital smell off my hands and face. I took off my white coat and my stained green scrubs, brushed down my jeans and sweater, powdered my nose, and put on lipstick. I actually remembered to comb my hair. Then I said good-night and went out through those automatic glass doors to wait for him.

"Of course it was raining again; didn't it always on a Saturday night? And now the rain was turning to sleet. I shivered, turning up my coat collar, snuggling my cold nose into its faux fur depths. Maybe there was something to be said for mink after all, I was thinking as the minutes ticked by. And ticked by . . .

"I called Cash again. There was no reply, but he was absent-minded and often forgot to switch on his phone. I paced up and down outside the hospital, watching for his little red sports car.

"I heard the wail of police sirens and the blare of the fire rescue trucks, but that was nothing unusual around there. Nor was the paramedic ambulance that sped away into the night. I peered down the street, but I could see nothing. I bumped into Patty, who said, 'Hey, I thought you'd gone home twenty minutes ago.' I told her I was supposed to meet Cash. He was coming to get me, but he was late, darn it. And she said, 'Well, better come back inside instead of freezing out here. Let's get a cup of coffee.' So I went back in with her.

"A few minutes later we got the call. Patty said they were bringing in a road accident victim with major head and chest trauma. I heard the wail of the ambulance siren. And something in my heart told me that it was Cash.

"I ran and put on my white coat—my doctor's coat— my official badge that meant I knew what I was doing. Stupid, I know, but somehow it mattered, it made me more able to cope.

"The paramedics ran with the gurney, one holding the plasma bottle aloft. Cash was strapped to that gurney. His arm dangled over the edge, fingers curled like a child's. I saw his beautiful blond hair—his 'Malibu surfer's' hair— tangled in a mass of blood. *Oh dear God*, I thought, *it can't be true . . . this cannot be for real. . . . Please, someone, tell me I'm dreaming. . . .*

"And then Cash opened his eyes. I could swear he was

smiling. 'Sorry I'm late, hon,' he whispered, and then his eyes closed again, shutting me out from his world of pain.

"I helped lift him from the gurney onto the table. I was checking his vital signs while they cut off his clothes, trying not to think that this was the man I loved, my lover. Patty was right there with me, my whole team was there. They were silent for once, working steadily, doing what they knew how to do best.

"Cash had skidded on the slick road, hit a truck—one of those huge shiny steel tankers, the kind you can see your car reflected in when you drive up behind them. Only Cash hadn't seen it in the sleet.

"His car was an old sports model, too old for air bags. His skull was fractured. The steering wheel had crushed his chest. I intubated him, watching his lifeblood gushing out through the plastic tube, his vital signs slowing down on the monitor. He had a pulmonary injury. A rib had penetrated the chest wall, punctured the lung. *Princess Diana died like this,* I thought. *She died exactly like this.*

"Don't die! The scream was locked inside me. *Don't fuckin' die.* But Cash was choking to death on his own blood. And all my training, all my experience couldn't save him. And that's what I did every day, for god's sake. Saved people."

I stopped and looked bleakly at Ben. "But I couldn't save the man I loved."

I heard Ben's quick indrawn breath. I wasn't crying. I couldn't cry anymore for Cash. I was drained dry.

"Gemma, I'm so sorry." He lifted his shoulders helplessly. "It's not enough to be sorry, I know that, but I don't know any other words to express what I feel. *How* I feel. Except to say that I recognize your pain. Your loss. Your helplessness."

I stared at him, and for a second his strong dark face blurred into an image of Cash; so blond, so young, so handsome. They were intertwined somewhere in my heart, in my head . . . except that I had no right to this new love.

"Not only did I not save him," I whispered, "I *killed* him. Cash would be alive today if I had not made that phone call, not asked him to come and pick me up. He wouldn't have been on that road, in back of that tanker. He would have been home, waiting for me."

There was silence. Head bent, shoulders slumped, I watched the black cat uncurl itself from a cushion. He walked over to Ben, inspected him carefully, sat in front of him. His yellow eyes slid from Ben to me, then back again. And he waited.

Ben sighed, and I knew it came from somewhere deep inside. He wasn't foolish enough to say, Look it wasn't your fault, it could have happened anywhere, anytime, you were not really responsible. He was a man who understood the facts. A businessman like him knew all about responsibility and the bottom line.

"So—afterward," I said, and heard my voice tremble slightly, "I decided to dedicate myself to my job. I had not been able to save Cash, but I would do my utmost to save anybody else coming through those hospital doors. I would work as many hours as I could, as hard as I could, do everything I could. It was a sort of penance I set myself. I had killed my lover, and now I would have no other lovers. There was to be nothing else in my life but my family and my work. I *needed* nothing else. In a way I suppose it was like dedicating my life to God, hoping He might forgive me for my terrible sin. And so that's exactly what I did."

"And has God forgiven you?"

I shook my head. "I don't know."

"You certainly have not forgiven yourself."

"I kept myself so busy I didn't have time to think about guilt. I thought my hyperlife could blot out Cash's death. But inside raged guilt and fear and helplessness. And anger. So much was happening underneath my normal day-to-day persona, things I didn't want to acknowledge, didn't want to know. I *hated* myself. *Hated* what I was—the fraud I was. The doctor who couldn't save the life of her own lover."

He was stroking my hand, soft, gentle strokes like the lick of the black cat's tongue. "You must have been very lonely."

"Lonely? I didn't have time to be lonely. I was just so damn busy."

I turned to look at him then. Firelight flickered over his face, his good, handsome, strong face.

"Trouble is, Ben," I whispered, "I still love him."

CHAPTER SIXTY-EIGHT

That night Ben and I slept in his bed, wrapped in each other's arms. His warm body comforted me, his tenderness enveloped me, I felt treasured, and I loved that feeling. But I still loved Cash. I still grieved for him, as I knew somehow I always would. Even though Cash was dead, he was still part of my life, and I would never let him go. I felt his presence all around me, as a muted gentleness, a softness in the air I breathed, a treasured memory of love and beauty.

When I awoke, Ben was gone. My throat tightened with fear that he had left me, and then I asked myself, Why shouldn't he leave me? Hadn't I just told him I loved another?

I climbed out of the big sagging old bed that we had shared so innocently together, and went to the window. It was a glorious morning. Everything smelled fresh after the rain; rose-colored oleander tumbled over the walls, and those tiny pink Tuscan roses I had come to love scented the air. With the high blue sky and the silence, it felt like the beginning of the world. Instead of the end of it.

I stood under the cold shower, pulling myself together, telling myself I was doing the right thing. I mean, how could a woman who felt the way I did about one man possibly tell another man she loved him? Even though her body did, and her senses, and every damned little nerve ending she possessed.

It's sex, that's all, I told myself, as I threw on some clothes. It's because you didn't make love for three long years, and you were weak and succumbed. And now you can't stop. You don't want to stop, you want to keep on making love to him.

I heaved a giant sigh. Ben was right: I was crazy. How could he possibly love me? And come to think of it, he hadn't said he loved me since I'd told him about Cash. In fact, he hadn't spoken about Cash at all, he had just held me, let me weep on his shoulder, his stubbled face pressed against my tear-wet cheek. He had stroked back my hair, undressed me, put me to bed, covered me gently with a lavender-scented linen sheet. He'd climbed in next to me and held me close, and, still crying, I had fallen asleep in his arms.

This is the end, I told myself, hurrying down the stairs in search of him. I would tell him I was leaving right away, that I wouldn't fight him any longer for the villa. My summer in Tuscany was almost over. Soon I would return to New York and that same old reality. Back to the emergency room, back to Livvie's school, Nonna's Sunday lunches. My heart sank at the thought of losing all this beauty. But it wasn't meant for me.

I found Ben in the stable yard, checking the lack of progress on the remodeling of the stables into guest cottages. His eyes met mine. There was no smile, he just said good morning, and I said good morning back, nervous as a new kid at school. I suddenly felt I didn't know him; I didn't know what to say. I heard a telephone ringing.

He fished a cell phone from his pocket, said, "Yes, hi," and "Is that right?" He wrote something on the back of an old receipt and said, "Okay, Maggie. Just tell the famous detective he'd better not be giving me the runaround again. See you soon."

He clicked off the phone and looked at me. "I'm off to Rome," he said. "Back on the trail. Want to come?"

"Do you still want me to?" I held my breath, waiting for his answer.

He shrugged, put the phone back in his pocket. "It's in your interest, after all."

"That's not what I meant."

We looked at each other. Things had changed between us, there was no doubt about that. He nodded. "You know I do," he said.

We didn't talk much on the drive down, and certainly not about Cash. Nor about love. By some unspoken agreement, we did not mention the previous night and my confession that I still loved Cash. I put my head back and closed my eyes and pretended to be dozing. It seemed like the easiest way to avoid a confrontation.

It was high season, and there were no rooms at the Hassler. We were at the Crown Plaza Minerva, overlooking a pretty piazza with, in the center, Bernini's exotic statue of an elephant supporting an ancient Egyptian obelisk, and, across the way, the beautiful thirteenth-century gothic church of Santa Maria Sopra Minerva. And right around the corner was that ancient temple built by Marcus Agrippa whose ruins had stopped me in my tracks and which had been my first real taste of Rome.

Our suite was smart in forest green and burgundy, a

modern setting in an ancient refurbished palazzo. I looked around, thinking I was getting too used to the suite life and had better get my head back into reality and start thinking about the trauma room again because it was looming ever closer.

I stared at the two beds, wondering if Ben had asked specially for them. Obviously we were to sleep separately tonight. I began to unpack my small bag, but Ben told me there was no time to waste, and soon we were in a cab on our way to Trastevere.

Trastevere is across the Tiber, that great green river that bisects Rome. Manual workers, artisans, and poor laborers had once lived in its narrow alleys and tiny squares, but now almost every street was crammed with tiny mom-and-pop-style *trattorie,* every square a backdrop to espresso cafés, and every alley a haven for a somnolent population of cats.

The cab dropped us at the entrance to a dingy cul-de-sac littered with orange peels, plastic bags, and old newspapers. The crumbling buildings leaned into each other, blocking out the light, and the tiled roofs were a grim forest of TV antennas.

I stepped gingerly through the debris. "I don't get it," I whispered, because somehow the dark, creepy alley lent itself to whispers. "Why would Donati be living here? He's a rich man. He stole all that money from you, and probably more from the count's estate."

From the corner of my eye I saw a gray shadow run past. I yelled and threw myself, panicked, at Ben. "*Omigod,*" I said, quoting my daughter.

"Don't tell me you're scared of rats?" Ben untangled my arms from around his neck.

I shuddered. "I never could stand them, even in the lab.

It's just something about their tail. Plus they carry disease, bubonic plague and . . . like that."

"And when was the last case of bubonic plague you heard about?"

"Well, 1480, somewhere around there, I guess," I admitted. "But I still hate rats."

We were now standing outside a narrow five-story building. Its dirty yellow stucco outer coat had peeled away in giant layers, revealing raw-looking wounds of old brick beneath. A battered wooden door with a massive iron ring for a handle led into a small hallway, where a bare staircase zigzagged to the top, and a grimy skylight let in no light at all. There were no other windows, and when the door closed behind us, we were in darkness.

I felt my throat constrict in that old panic about the dark, until Ben found the light switch, took my hand, and led me reluctantly up the rickety stairs.

"This can't be the right place," I muttered. Then the light went out, and Ben disappeared. Darkness pressed against my eyelids, touched my hair, shivered down my spine.

"Where are you?" I whispered urgently, just as the light went on again.

He was leaning over the stair rail looking down at me. "It's on a timer," he said. "You'll have to make a run for it."

I shot up those splintery wooden stairs, arriving just as the light went out again. "I hate this," I muttered. "I just hate it."

"Aw, come on," Ben said. I could see his teeth gleaming in the darkness and knew he was laughing at me.

In front of us was a chipped brown wooden door with a metal number plate. Ben was already trying the handle.

"Shouldn't we knock first?" I asked nervously. But then it opened, just like that.

I followed Ben cautiously into a small attic room. A couple of tiny dormer windows poked out over the street. There was a rumpled bed in one corner, a tiled counter piled with dirty glasses and plates, a littered table in front of a stained brown velvet sofa, and a dusty wooden floor with a red shag rug. And no Donati.

"Let's go," I said, already backing out of there, but Ben held up his hand for silence. I watched, astonished, as he tiptoed toward the only closet. Did he really think Donati was *hiding* in there? He flung open the door.

We looked at the white linen jacket swinging on a metal hanger. "That's your best imitation of Inspector Clouseau yet," I said, giggling.

"Y'know what, Doc, you can be a real pain sometimes." He was already going through the jacket pockets. "And anyhow, didn't Don Vincenzo tell you that Donati always wore white linen suits? This is his all right."

He moved to the pile of old papers on the table. "See, Donati *was* here," he said triumphantly, showing me a torn scrap of paper with the penciled letters DON.

"You call that evidence?" I thrust it back at him.

"Sure it's evidence. Donati was here, but he's flown the coop. Once again, we're too late."

"What do you mean, *once again*?" I stumbled behind him back down the filthy stairs. "We've never been anywhere near Donati."

The heavy front door slammed behind us. I turned and saw a man standing at the end of the street. He was small and thin, with a pencil mustache, a panama hat—and a white linen suit. For a fraction of a second, our eyes met. Then he slid out of sight around the corner.

I was already running, yelling his name, but Ben over-took me. He was around that corner seconds before I got there. I shaded my eyes, searching the empty street. It led to a tiny piazza with alleys leading off in every direction. I leaned, panting, against the wall and saw Ben walking back toward me. "Was it Donati?" I gasped.

"I'd be willing to bet on it," he said.

Defeated, we hurried around several corners until we came to a friendlier area with a little bar, where we had icy shots of grappa and boiling espressos piled with sugar. Numbed by the grappa and focused by the caffeine, we found a cab and drove silently back across the Tiber to our new haven on the beautiful Piazza di Minerva.

I hurried into the shower, washing off the memories of rats and grime and torn pieces of paper with maybe Donati's name on it. When I emerged, Ben was not there.

I fell naked onto the bed, staring blankly at the ceiling. I had ruined everything. Plus we were no nearer finding out who really owned the Villa Piacere than we had been on day one. I was still lying there staring at the ceiling when I heard the door. Ben was back. There was a question in his eyes as he looked at me, and his arms were full of roses. Dozens of them, hundreds maybe, in every possible color, from pale lavender to pure peach to lemon and copper and scarlet.

He flung them on the bed, and I sat up, startled. I touched the soft petals, smelled their fresh scent. "It's a whole garden," I said, awed.

"I'm wooing you." He was on his knees next to the bed. "I figured it was the only way to get to you. I love you, Gemma."

I melted inside; I hadn't expected such tenderness, not after what had been said. I was kneeling on the bed looking down at him, and he was kneeling on the floor looking up at me. I felt as though we were in a scene from a Broadway play ... guy loves girl, girl loves someone else. ...

"How do you know it's love?" I said, uncertain.

"Gemma! I have *feelings* for you!"

Despite my vows, I inched to the edge of the bed, drawn toward him.

"When we make love," he said, finally speaking the question that had been in his eyes when he entered the room, "and you say you love me, do you mean it?"

I stared at him, and traitor that I was, I was thinking about Cash, how I had yelled that I loved him when we made love. But now ... "I didn't mean it," I admitted.

He took my hands in his, and we just knelt there, looking at each other. He sighed. "I can see I've got my work cut out to convince you."

"You mean you're going to keep trying?" I couldn't keep the catch of amazement out of my voice. Or—universal traitor that I was—maybe it was hope.

He grinned at me then. "I'm a street kid from the Bronx," he said. "You don't mess with us guys."

All of a sudden I slid off the bed on top of him, slamming him to the floor. I heard the crack of his head against the wooden night table and his groan. Then I was bending over him, shrieking "*Omigod, omigod*, are you all right?" and dabbing at the trickle of blood sliding into the silvery bits of his hair, the ones that gave him that distinguished look, which is a long way from the Bronx street kid he used to be.

"Jesus Christ, Gemma," he said, wrapping his arms around me. "You're even a disaster when you're on your knees! What the fuck am I gonna do with you?"

I chewed worriedly on my bottom lip. "I don't know," I said, stumped.

I heard that rumble of laughter in his chest, then he hauled me from the floor and pushed me back onto the bed, onto the bower of roses.

"I'm crushing my flowers," I murmured.

"That's okay." He was already kissing me.

"I can't, y'know . . . love you," I said, because it was true.

"Remember me?" he said, covering my naked body with kisses. "I always win."

CHAPTER SIXTY-NINE

Come twilight we emerged, like a pair of bats, in search of dinner. We wandered through Rome's crowded streets, and Ben held my hand. I felt good, female, sensual. My red chiffon dress floated around my knees in the still-hot breeze, I was Violetta di Parma'd all over, my new lipstick had a nice ripe-berry glow, and even my ruby slippers weren't hurting. In fact, I was totally into that chic Roman woman walk, striding confidently over those lethal cobblestones without once getting my heels stuck.

We strolled down Via della Gatta, named for the small marble statue—ancient, of course, as everything is around here—perched on the cornice of a roof and looking more Siamese than alley cat. Then along Via del Gesù, which turned out to be a Fifth Avenue of shops for ecclesiastical garments in bougainvillea colors: cerise cardinals' capes and purple bishops' robes, lavender and pale-green vestments, and gold silk embroidered chasubles. We decided that the Roman clergy must be very well dressed.

In a tiny square in front of a small floodlit palazzo adorned with frescoes, we came across the perfect restaurant: small but busy, and most of it already occupied by a congregation of nuns, noisy as a flight of magpies beneath their new-style wimples. A young priest headed the main table, and I could tell instantly that priests were different in Rome. This one was a hunk, better looking than most movie stars and twice as sure of himself. A definite "Thorn Bird." Now I knew why they had a Fifth Avenue for the clergy.

The owner showed us to a table and told us that the young priest had just been ordained and that they were celebrating.

We ordered wine and studied the menu, trying not to stare. The waiter brought bread, olives, *bruschetta*. A fork rang against a glass, and we turned in midbite to look. The young priest was on his feet, and as the nuns bent their heads meekly, he began to say grace.

Ben looked at me. "How can we eat when he's praying?" he whispered, as I hastily bent my head too.

The prayer was a long one. I glanced up at Ben. He guiltily put down the olive that was halfway to his mouth. Another minute passed: the priest was still intoning, and a reverent silence reigned over the restaurant.

"He's never going to shut up," Ben whispered.

"Just wait a minute," I whispered back.

The minute went by, then another, and another. Five minutes, and nobody was even so much as lifting an eyelid, never mind a head.

We were trying to choke back our giggles, but it was impossible, so Ben threw some money on the table, grabbed my hand, and we slid stealthily out of there.

"*Buona sera*"—a nuns' chorus followed us, wishing us good evening.

We were still laughing when we arrived at Nino's on the Via Borgognona.

"You're looking very 'girly' tonight," Ben complimented me when we were seated.

"Surprise, surprise, I used to be a girl," I told him, but I was glad I had dressed up in my new red chiffon, because Nino's was a place where chic Romans congregated.

It was old Rome, all cream walls and dark wood and ancient white-aproned waiters who let you know that they knew more than you did and that anyhow they had seen it all before. Ben told me Nino's baby artichokes Roman-style were a treat not to be missed. I saw them on the antipasto table, tiny purple morsels perched on their uppers, stems in the air, lathered in olive oil and garlic, and looking like a miniature forest on a plate. Plus, Ben said, their steak *fiorentina* was not bad either, and their simple tuna with warm cannellini beans was to die for.

The food might be Tuscan and nothing really fancy, but the diners were something else, everyone from rock stars and businessmen and Roman society to ordinary tourists like ourselves. I *loved* it.

Ben was concentrating hard on the menu while sipping a local Frascati. I had only recently discovered that Ben was a wine buff. A connoisseur, in fact.

"The Frascati's nice," he said, surprising me.

"Nice? What kind of word is that to describe a wine?"

He threw me a grin that threatened to melt my suddenly too soft heart. The same heart that had the ice around it, never to be melted. He looked so gosh-darn cute in a thin black leather jacket and a blue shirt. I wanted to touch him, but I didn't.

"Okay," he said, swirling the inexpensive wine from the Roman hills in his glass and sniffing it. "So this is a fruity little number with a delicate nose." He paused to take a gulp, and I sincerely hoped he wasn't going to spit it out again in professional wine-taster fashion. Thank God, he just swallowed it, frowning with pretend concentration.

"A bit short on the palate," he declared. "But nice. Yes, quite definitely nice."

We laughed again. Despite the elusive Donati, and the knowledge that soon I would return to my real life, my spirits soared. I was in Rome with my lover, enjoying a fruity little wine and the prospect of some delicious food. And later . . . Well, I won't go into what I had in mind for later. But my toes curled just thinking about it.

I had already decided on the artichokes, and then pasta with a porcini mushroom sauce, and I was gazing around the room smiling to myself because I liked what I saw. It's so *satisfying,* don't you think, to see people enjoying themselves, each table into its own conversation, its food, its wine?

I was sitting facing the entrance so I saw her come in. My heart dropped. It was the beauteous blond Luiza Lohengrin, on the arm of a much older and not so lovely man, one of those sleek mogul types who looks as though he owns a mega-yacht, with drooping eyes that slide right over you, letting you know he could buy this place—and probably you too—if he wanted. Not only that, but Luiza was wearing *my* dress. *Worse,* she looked better in it than I did, all long tanned legs and perky breasts and wisps of red chiffon.

Of course she zeroed in on Ben, greeting him with kisses on both cheeks. She threw me a cold smile, taking in the matching frock.

"It's so nice to dress down on these warm nights, isn't it?" she said, knowing I was no competition.

Her companion had not even bothered to stop by our

table. He was already over in an important corner, looking bored and checking out who was there. Luiza told us
he was a famous movie producer, then she kissed Ben
again, lavishly and lingeringly on the mouth this time,
while I pretended not to look. She said *arrivederci* to him
and left me agape, wondering what had happened to our
lovely evening.

"Want to know a secret?" Ben had mischief in his
eyes. "Her real name is Monica Grimm." I stared at him,
then we both burst out laughing, and I swear I felt Monica
Grimm's jealous eyes boring into my duplicate red chiffon back.

CHAPTER SEVENTY

It was 1 A.M. and the piazzas were still thronged. Everyone was out enjoying the beautiful night: babies, children, lovers, grandparents, the young and the old. The city was their living room. In the Piazza Navona, street entertainers performed magic tricks and swallowed branches of fire, the magnificent Bernini fountains splashed, and artists offered to paint our portrait.

We walked the way lovers do, aimlessly, thoughtlessly, just enjoying the moment, past illuminated monuments and into a secret little square we just stumbled on, silent as a ghost scene and yet with the clamor of the city only a minute away. There was a tiny church; its doors were still open, and old women slowly climbed the steps. From within I caught a glimpse of flickering candles.

We sat side by side on the marble steps outside the church, and I slipped off the pointy-toed shoes that by now were killing me. Sighing with relief, I stuck out my legs and wiggled my toes in the air, hoping my circulation would return.

I felt Ben turn to look at me. I looked back at him. Silence hung between us. It was a moment of such aching tenderness, I almost wanted to cry. Because soon there would be no more magical moments like this, sitting on church steps on a hot summer night in Rome, alone but together.

"I have to go back soon," I said. I didn't need to tell him that I meant not just to the hotel but to New York. I looked away and we fell silent again.

"Gemma, we have to work this out," he said after a while. "You know that."

"I'm not just being perverse, Ben," I said quietly. "I just can't live with this burden of guilt, and that's the truth. And the other truth is that I'll always love Cash."

His eyes were filled with a deep understanding. "And I hope you always will," he said. "Death does not kill love."

"I get the feeling there's a *but* in there somewhere."

"The *but* is that life must go on, Gemma. You know that."

"But . . ." I gave a little half laugh, half sob at coming up with my own *but* to combat his. "Cash died *because* of me. *If only* I hadn't asked him to come and get me, *if only* I had just gone home the way I usually did . . ."

"You of all people, in your job, must surely realize that accidents are made up of *if-only*s. That's the very nature of an accident, Gemma. It's no one's *fault*. It just *is*. And now you're floundering under a double burden of guilt."

I hung my head again, silenced.

"So when you made love with me? When you said you were crashing into love? What about that, Gemma?"

"I meant it. But I still knew it could never be."

He held out his arms and I fell into them. I pressed myself against his chest, longing for the love he offered, to which I knew I had no right.

"We're not burying Cash with our love, Gemma," Ben whispered. "We're allowing him to live again, to be remembered, to be spoken of. We're bringing him into our lives, and Livvie's and Nonna's and Muffie's. He's too good and you loved him too much for him to be shut away forever. Let him live again, Gemma, in your mind and mine. Then maybe you can be free."

I thought about the times I had met Cash's actor friends, how I had envied the girls their freedom, and that I had never had that kind of freedom. Well, this was my chance. Did I go for the brass ring? Or didn't I?

"Tell him," Ben said, clutching me to his chest, "tell Cash what you feel."

And right there on the church steps in the silent little piazza in Rome, I threw back my head and yelled in a voice choked with pain, *"I love you, Cash. Goddamn it, I love you."*

And then the tears flowed and I cried into Ben's shoulder. And though the past would always cast its shadow over my life, I felt the beginnings of *freedom*. That there was hope for a new hope.

CHAPTER SEVENTY-ONE

ROCCO AND NONNA

Rocco was perched on the old stone wall that encircled one of his olive groves. He was shaded by a the gnarled branches of a tree that had been planted by his great-great-grandfather, and though it no longer bore fruit, he would never cut it down. That tree was a symbol of his family's history. The Cesanis had grown olives for centuries and always would.

It was lunchtime, that long two hours in Italy when everything closes down and everybody eats a huge meal. Then they have a little siesta, and perhaps a little loving too. Except Rocco, of course.

He was eating a huge sandwich he'd fixed himself—slabs of garlicky wild boar sausage, a chunk of pecorino cheese, and a thick slice of raw sweet onion stuffed into a heavy rustic bread slathered with mustard. A flask of red wine made from Sangiovese grapes grown in his own small vineyard perched beside him on the wall, and Fido sat hopefully at his feet.

It was a day like any other: nothing different, nothing unusual, you might say. Except what was going on inside his head. Normally he would have been content listening to the chatter of the birds, identifying each one by its cry, hearing the rustle of wild creatures in the hedgerow— creatures that Fido never rushed to try to annihilate as most dogs would. Rocco would never admit this to anyone, but despite the fact that Fido was a bull terrier, a breed with an awesome reputation as fighting dogs, Fido was a coward. He avoided confrontations, slinking away with his tail between his legs. If it were not for the apparent evidence against it, Rocco might have wondered if Fido were a bitch. But no, Fido's equipment was all there.

Not that this mattered, because Fido, with his long pink nose, had a speciality that made him king of all dogs in this region. "Rocco Cesani's Great Truffle Hound" everybody called him, and for Rocco that was like winning Best in Show at Madison Square Garden.

He flung the dog a slab of sausage, grinning as Fido snapped it out of the air, swallowed it in one great gulp, then sat back again waiting for more. Rocco always shared his lunch with his dog.

But today his mind was not on his lunch, or on Fido. He was watching the road that led around the valley and up the hill to Bella Piacere. Sophia Maria had telephoned him last night from Positano to say that she was returning home.

It was the word *home* that had sent an arrow through his heart. Sophia Maria had called Bella Piacere "home." Could that mean, despite the fact that she was a rich American widow, as well as an heiress, that she might be thinking of living here in Bella Piacere again? But what if she were not the heiress? What if she did not own the villa? Would she still contemplate staying here, back in her old home? *With him?*

He caught the glitter of sunlight glancing off a windshield. It was the silver Lancia. His heart sank again as he thought about how rich she must be to drive such a smart car. She could not possibly care about an ordinary man like him, who had rarely even left his home village. And besides, he wasn't even sure that she and Fido liked each other. Still, he knew where *his* heart belonged.

He threw the rest of the sandwich to Fido, took a long gulp from the wine flask, brushed the crumbs off his shirt, and tugged his hat more firmly over his brow. There was work to be done.

Maggie was driving the Lancia with Nonna beside her and the two "daughters" giggling and talking girl-stuff in the back. Mostly about Tomaso, Maggie suspected. The two of them had certainly led the poor boy a dance, showing up for a date, then not showing up for a date, plus wherever Livvie went, she had insisted Muffie go too.

Sophia Maria had said Muffie was the best chaperone Livvie could ever have, and there was no chance of her getting into trouble, so apart from insisting they be back at the hotel by eleven each night, Nonna and Maggie had left them to their own devices. Until Tomaso had given up on his romantic quest for summer love and Livvie had reverted to being a kid again, who enjoyed floating on her raft for hours at a time with Muffie next to her, every now and then pausing to eat that terrific pizza that Maggie was sure had put more than a few pounds on her own ample thighs.

As they wound slowly up the white road that curved around the hillside, Maggie thought about Gemma and Ben, and what she had told Gemma she had seen in the tarot cards. The truth was, she was no expert at tarot, and maybe she had fudged it a little to get the result she desired. But then, she had always been an interfering woman. How else would she have gotten where she was today without a little manipulation of "fate"?

"I wonder if Ben has asked Gemma to marry him," she said to Sophia Maria.

The two girls lounging in the back sat up quickly, ears tuned.

"She'll turn him down," Sophia Maria said. "She's too dedicated to her work to marry again."

"She won't marry him," Livvie said. "Not after Cash."

"Who's Cash?" Muffie asked, and Livvie said she would tell her later.

As they drove into the village, Sophia Maria spotted Rocco's white pickup parked outside the Bar Galileo. She smiled. She had missed Rocco: missed their plotting, missed the challenge of the wild convolutions of Rocco's mind that it took a fellow Tuscan to understand, missed his down-to-earthness, though she had not missed his dog.

She saw Rocco coming toward her. He looked the way he always did, unless he was in his party and funeral suit: in baggy shorts and his camouflage rain hat. She thought he was a very modest man, although he was surely very rich with all those olive groves and his own *frantoio*.

The girls piled out of the car, hauling their bags after them, and Maggie asked if Nonna would mind if she took the car back to her villa and returned it later. They waved good-bye, and then the girls went into the *albergo* in search of Amalia and Laura and some lunch, while Sophia Maria, for that was how she thought of herself now, walked across the piazza to meet Rocco.

She could see his beaming smile from fifty paces, the

one that showed all his teeth and that also, when he really meant it, lit up his eyes.

Rocco smoothed his mustache. He took a step toward her, shaking his head with wonder at how lovely she looked with her clear skin and her shiny hair and her sun-tanned legs.

"Sophia Maria," he said.

"Rocco."

She held out her hand, and he took it. Then they went and sat on the old iron bench under the umbrella pines that shaded the dusty bocce court. Fido sat beside Rocco, head down for once.

"What's the matter with the dog?" Sophia Maria asked.

"Maybe he missed you."

She glanced sideways at Rocco. He wasn't joking or smiling now, and she interpreted that to mean that Rocco had also missed her.

"I missed Fido too," she said.

Rocco smoothed his mustache. "Maybe Fido thinks he shouldn't be here, sitting next to such a rich American lady. Maybe he thinks he is not good enough to be in such company."

"Or maybe Fido thinks he is too rich to associate with a modest widow," Sophia Maria countered, "who may or may not inherit a villa and who anyhow has decided to spend whatever money she has left and enjoy life. While she can."

Rocco thought about what she had just said.

"The excellent truffle dog of a modest producer of olive oil, owner of several olive groves—but excellent groves, mind you, and his own *frantoio*—and also owner of a small farmstead with a vineyard and one splendid cow that provides the best milk and *panna* in Tuscany, might think himself lucky to be in the company of a modest widow from America who is spending all her money in order to enjoy it. While she can."

Sophia Maria sat with her ankles crossed, her hands folded in her lap. It was her turn. "Fido might also have to think about being in the company of a woman who is *forced* to enjoy life. *While she can.*"

Rocco swung around, startled. "Sophia Maria, what do you mean?" So she told him about her heart and what the doctor had said.

"And your own daughter, the doctor?" Rocco demanded. "What did *she* say?"

"She said nothing because I did not tell her. Nor am I going to. You, Rocco, are the only one who knows about this besides me. And that's the way it's going to stay."

Rocco slid his hand along the bench toward her. She reached out and took it. "Of course, I told the doctor I was going to live forever and that he was full of medical nonsense, as all doctors are. And he said, 'Perhaps you will, Mrs. Jericho, perhaps you will.' And you know what, Rocco? I believe I will."

"Bene." He squeezed her hand, and Fido gave a low growl. Rocco stared at his dog. The coward of the area was growling, actually *growling* because he was holding Sophia Maria's hand. Fido's lip lifted in a snarl, and he gave that low, threatening growl again, staring hard at Rocco.

"Poor Fido," Sophia Maria said in a soothing voice, "I think he's jealous."

Fido stopped snarling. He turned and looked at her. He

put his head on one side, his pink nose twitched, his pink-rimmed eyes beseeched. Then he took a running jump at her.

Sophia Maria held open her arms and caught him, and then Fido was licking her face, whining, and wriggling his tail with happiness. "Rocco," she said, "I think the dog wants me to stay."

"I believe he does, Sophia Maria," Rocco said, scratching his bristly head.

They looked at each other for a long time, searching each other's familiar faces grown older for an answer. Rocco did not even have to ask the question.

"I will, Rocco," Nonna said firmly. And then she gave a great sigh of relief and said, "Now I've really come home."

CHAPTER SEVENTY-TWO

GEMMA

We were back home once again. Ben swung the Land Rover into the long driveway leading to the villa. The old car shimmied over the ruts, and I hung on tightly, trying not to bounce against the roof. "You need to get either a new car or a new driveway," I complained.

"I love this car."

"*Love* it?" I gave him my skeptical look.

"It's a guy thing. We love our cars, the older the better."

"Okay, then how about a new driveway?"

"What if the villa ends up being yours? Then you'll be the one paying for a new driveway."

"I can't afford it," I said, and he laughed.

In the cloud of dust just ahead of us I made out Rocco Cesani's white truck with Fido in the back. As we circled the Neptune fountain, I saw that Nonna was sitting next to Rocco. I thought for a second about how close the two of them seemed, and how nice it was for her to have reunited with her old friend.

Maggie was waving at us from the top of the steps, and the two girls came running barefoot over the lawn. Rocco helped Nonna out of the truck, like the true gentleman he

was, but of course I had my own door open and was out
of the Land Rover before Ben could even get to me. I
guess I was just out of practice in the having doors
opened for me way of life.

In moments we all had hugged and kissed and said
how much we had missed each other. They asked about
Rome and Donati. Ben drew a finger across his throat and
shook his head, and everyone's faces fell.

"Not to worry," Maggie said cheerfully. "I think tomorrow we shall have better news."

She did not amplify that statement, and to tell you the
truth, I almost didn't want to know. I figured she was
about to send us to some village in the back of beyond
where there would be no espresso bar and we would end
up sleeping in a barn with the cows. Actually, maybe that
would be fun . . . tumbling in the soft sweet hay, with
Ben.

Enough of those carnal thoughts, I told myself. But
you know what, every time I looked at that man I got carnal thoughts. I wondered if this was normal.

We were all sitting on the terrace, refreshed with iced
tea and Fiametta's fresh-baked cookies, which Nonna had
to admit were almost as good as her own. Fountains tin-
kled soothingly, hummingbirds hovered near the
bougainvillea, and to my surprise, Fido came to lie down
next to Nonna. He rested his head on her feet and heaved
a deep sigh of satisfaction.

"Mom, I think that dog has fallen for you," I joked.
She lifted her chin and gave me a long look that I might
almost have said was smug.

"Of course he has," she said. "Fido has decided that we
should get married."

"You're going to marry *Fido*?" Livvie said.

"Of course not, Olivia," Nonna said. "Fido has given his approval for Rocco and me to be married."

"*Wow*," Livvie and I said together. A very *stunned* kind of wow.

"A wedding!" Maggie's shriek of delight split the silence that followed. "How wonderful! Congratulations! Now I'll have Sophia Maria for a neighbor. Oh, I can't wait. Will the wedding be soon?"

Rocco gave us his toothy smile. "We thought maybe next month," he said, looking modestly down at his wellies.

Livvie threw her arms around her grandmother. "I'm so happy for you and Rocco," she said. Then she glanced hopefully at me. "Does that mean we get to stay longer?"

"Congratulations," I said, still weak from the shock. "But remember, we're going home next week. Nonna, what about your house, your life there?"

Nonna ignored me. She said to Livvie, "Of course you will stay for the wedding. Your mother will telephone her hospital and tell them she is taking extra vacation time. She'll tell them it's an emergency," she added, laughing.

I heard the happiness in her laugh, and with a pang I realized how rarely I'd heard it back home. I thought about how narrow her life was there, how devoid of companionship, how lonely she must have been, just waiting for Sundays to come around when she would see us again. I thought of how tired she had looked and, sometimes, how sad.

"I'll call them," I said, getting up and giving her a big hug and a kiss. Fido gave me a warning growl, but I told him he'd better get used to it. After all, I knew her first.

Rocco took my hands in his rough ones, and I looked

into his kind, humorous face. "I will take care of her, *dottoressa*," he said quietly. And I knew he would.

That night we celebrated Sophia Maria's and Rocco's engagement at a *trattoria* opposite the beautiful San Biagio Church in Montepulciano. Rocco presented her with a fine gold ring, worn thin with age, with a tiny ruby at the center.

"It was my great-grandmother's," he told us. "I thought I would never find anyone worthy of such a ring, but Sophia Maria is more than worthy. She deserves more than I could ever give her."

Nonna blushed, and I decided blushing was definitely a family thing. We admired the pretty ring, and Nonna said she would never remove Jack Jericho's wedding band and that she would just wear all the rings together.

We toasted that sentiment in a Vino Nobile di Montepulciano, rich, dark red, and tasting to me of sun-warmed grapes and vanilla and oak, and we feasted on light-as-air ravioli and lamb roasted over branches of rosemary.

Ben tried to hold my hand under the table, pretending not to notice the girls' knowing smirks, and after a couple of glasses of the Nobile, I let him. Truth was, I wanted to do more than just hold his hand, but decorum and the presence of my mother and daughter thankfully held me back.

Afterward we zigzagged lazily down the hill through the little town. Nonna was in front, her arm linked in Rocco's, and I was just thinking about how different her life would be, and how I would miss her, and how terribly she would miss Livvie, when I saw her stumble. Rocco grabbed her, then he half led, half carried her to a chair on a café terrace.

"Momma, what's wrong?" My fingers were already on her pulse. It was rapid, and she had that gray, waxen look I'd noticed before.

"It's nothing, I'm just tired." But she put a hand to her heart as though she felt pain there, and my own heart leaped in response. "I'm fine, Gemma," she murmured, "I just need to rest awhile. And I've been forgetting to take the beta-blockers."

"Beta-blockers!"

"Dottoressa." I felt Rocco's hand on my bare arm. He looked as panicked as I felt. "She is ill," he said quietly. "She told me about it. Her doctor told her it was a congenital heart condition."

Dear God, I thought, *my own mother has a congenital heart condition and I didn't know about it? What kind of doctor am I?* And then I thrust away the panic and became that fine-honed speed machine I told you about.

Within minutes the paramedics were loading Nonna into the ambulance, and I was climbing in next to her. I glimpsed Livvie's terrified face and called out to her not to worry.

The Ospedale della Croce Rossa was white-tiled and immaculately clean. Nurses in rubber-soled shoes sped silently past, taking care of business, and a burly, bearded Italian doctor who reminded me of Pavarotti was already waiting for us with his team. Within minutes Nonna was lying on the table under a glare of white lights. People were clustered around her hooking her up to monitors, checking her heartbeat, her pulse rate, her brain activity.

The others were here by now, standing silently in the big empty waiting room, freezing in the air-conditioning.

Rocco stood in the corner shifting nervously from foot to foot. Livvie clung to Maggie, sobbing, and Muffie huddled frightened next to Ben. I went out to tell them that Nonna was doing all right.

"Will she be okay, Mommie?" Livvie whispered.

I kissed her tenderly and said, "I hope so, sweetheart. I'm right there with her."

"Then I *know* she'll be okay," she said, so trustingly I felt myself wince at the memory of that other time.

"Dio mio." Rocco paced the floor, lost without Fido at his heels. The dog wasn't allowed in the hospital, and he'd had to stay in the truck. I thought Rocco looked lonely without him; a simple, tough, wiry Italian man who, after her long widowhood, had brought my mother happiness again. I put my hand on his shoulder, let it linger there. He gave me that same beseeching look Livvie had. "She'll be all right," he said, trustingly.

Then I was out in the white-tiled corridor, and Ben was at my side. "Are you okay?"

I nodded. "I just can't allow myself to think this is happening to my mother. I have to keep my mind on that doctor track, just *concentrate*." I leaned wearily against him; his arm was strong under mine.

"I'm here for you," he said gently.

An hour later I was standing next to my mother's bed in the Coronary Care Unit. She was hooked up to machines, and there was a drip in her arm. The color had returned to her face, and thank God she did not look like a gray ghost anymore. In fact, she had that familiar combative look in her eye.

"Why didn't you tell me?" I said, seething with relief

and indignation. "I'm your daughter. I'm *a doctor*, for God's sake."

"Just because you're my daughter, I don't have to tell you everything." She adjusted the blue hospital nightshirt.

"You told Rocco."

"I'm going to *marry* Rocco."

"Momma, how can you even *think* of getting married, of staying *here*—?"

"Don't be ridiculous, Gemma. Of course I shall stay. I'm happy here. Besides, this was just a little blip in my heartbeat, nothing to fuss about."

The Pavarotti doctor came in just then. *"Bene,"* he said genially. "You feel better."

Nonna inspected him, decided she liked him, and said yes she did feel better. No thanks to him, of course. She would have gotten better perfectly well on her own. All she had needed was a cup of coffee.

He held out his hands helplessly, palms up, and said to me, "My own mother is the same." Then he added, more seriously, *"Signora* Jerico, there is nothing more we can do. Life must be lived day to day. And of course," he added with a jolly smile, "a woman like you, it will probably take years to kill you."

"Ha!" Nonna said tartly and with all her old spirit. "With a woman like me, it will take decades."

I thought she was probably right.

CHAPTER SEVENTY-THREE

Ben and I were in the old stable yard watching the return of his backhoe and the cement mixer and the digger. *"Ciao, signore, ciao, dottoressa,"* the drivers called cheerfully, as though the machinery had never disappeared and was now, like magic, reappearing. *"Domani, signore,"* they said, "we begin work." And Ben nodded and said that was good.

We were surprised to see Maggie, in high-heeled pink mules, coming down the path waving at us. It was only noon, practically the crack of dawn for Maggie.

"I have it," she said, giving us that infamous smile that I knew hid a thousand Machiavellian secrets—like, for instance, whether or not she could really read those tarot cards. She flourished a rusty-looking iron key. "The key to Donati's office in Florence," she told us, looking very pleased with herself.

Ben gave a low whistle. "Maggie, you're a genius."

"Well, of course I am. My detective got it from Donati's landlord."

"The landlord *gave* the detective the key?" Even I thought that sounded doubtful.

"Not exactly. Let's just say the detective 'happened by it.' "

"How?"

She gave us that smile again and said, "Ask me no secrets, I'll tell you no lies. Here's the address." She passed Ben the piece of paper. "Now all you have to do is go there and search his office."

My eyes swung nervously from Maggie to Ben. "Isn't that called breaking and entering, in police language?"

"Hardly 'breaking,' my dear," Maggie said soothingly. "*Entering* maybe. But that's all right."

"Is it all right?" I asked Ben.

He gave me a grin that matched hers. "Who knows?" he said, "but I'm game if you are."

Donati's office was on a mean little street near the station, tucked away behind a dry cleaner's and a funeral home. The looming buildings blocked out the sun, and I shivered, suddenly chilled. Ben shoved the giant key into the lock.

"What if he's in there?" I said, still nervous. He gave me a definite James Bondish look (one brow lifted, a quizzical little smile), then he pushed open the door and slid inside. I slid after him, into total darkness. "Jesus," I whispered, shocked. "We really are breaking and entering."

He grabbed my hand and closed the door behind me. We stood for a long minute in the darkness. I scrunched up my eyes, listening hard. I could swear I heard someone *breathing* in there. Then I realized it was me. "Can't we at least put on the light?" I whispered.

But Ben had already left me. He swung a flashlight around, and I caught a glimpse of a heavy wooden desk with one of those green shaded lamps, a leather chair, and a layer of dust. It was obvious that nobody had been here for a long time, and I thought, relieved, that at least Donati wasn't about to spring out at us from the darkness.

Ben was already opening drawers and filing cabinets, whisking through them fast. Nothing. The thin beam from his flashlight fastened on a green iron safe standing in the corner. It wasn't large, just about big enough to put your jewels in, if you had any.

"How about a little safecracking?" he said.

My teeth chattered with fright. I had never done anything illegal in my life, unless making love in the back of a car is illegal, that is. "We don't know how to open it."

He gave me that arched Bond eyebrow again and knelt in front of the safe.

"Ben, we *can't* do this. Please, let's just *go*." I held my breath as he put his ear to the safe, twirling dials and listening, just the way they did in caper movies. I was stunned. "Where did you learn safecracking?"

"I'm a kid from the Bronx, remember? You learn a lot of stuff on the streets."

"Apparently not enough," I said, because he was having no luck. The safe remained firmly closed.

He took a small Swiss Army knife from his pocket, flipped it open to the little screwdriver, then proceeded to remove the screws from the hinges. "Any kid could have opened this," he said, forcing the door wider.

I dropped to my knees beside him and we stared at the bulky document tied loosely with pink tape and with a broken red wax seal.

The *ah-aha-aha* wail of Italian police sirens suddenly split the silence. We looked at each other open-mouthed. The sirens stopped, and the door burst open.

We were caught red-handed. Stealing Count Piacere's last will and testament.

CHAPTER SEVENTY-FOUR

I scowled as I glared between the bars at Ben in an identical little holding cell opposite. He wasn't even looking at me. He was peering down the dimly lit corridor to where a guard sat. On the table in front of the guard was the evidence, still bundled in its pink legal tape.

"Damn it," I said, shivering with chills and fury, "we didn't even get to see if the count had left the villa to Nonna."

Ben shrugged. "At least we found the will."

"Yeah, and now we'll have to find Donati to prove he's the real criminal and not us."

"I wouldn't bet on that. Donati knew the game was up long ago. He just took my money and ran. We'll never see him again."

"I wish you'd told me that earlier." I slumped onto the hard wooden bench, staring at my feet. I noticed my toenails needed polish.

Ben had called Maggie, and we were waiting for her to arrive with a lawyer. He told me that she had laughed and said not to worry, my dears, she would be there in a flash with her own attorney. "The very best, of course," she had said. I surely hoped she was right and not just consulting those tarot cards again. I stared angrily at my unpolished toes.

"I guess this is as good a time as any to ask if you've decided you love me."

"What?" I looked at Ben in disbelief.

"Well, things couldn't get any worse. So I may as well hear the bad news now." He was leaning against the bars, and there was a kind of desperate look in his eyes. "Cash is in our past, Gemma," he said softly. "It's time to go on living."

The ice around my heart was melting into puddles of what was surely warm maple syrup. Cash, I thought. Oh, Cash, my love . . .

"Marry me, Gemma," Ben said.

At least I think that's what he said. I was so dazed I asked him to repeat it.

"Marry me, Gemma," he said again.

I gulped. "Why? I mean, why do you want to marry *me*?"

"Because you're crazy, you're funny, you make me laugh, and I love your hair."

"My hair?" I ran my hands frantically through the hated blond halo.

"I always wanted to marry a Botticelli angel."

"I'm no angel . . ."

He gripped the bars of his cell tightly, looking at me. "Damn it, Gemma," he groaned, "why are you making me work so hard? I love you. All I'm doing is asking you to marry me."

"In a *jail cell*?" I gripped my own bars angrily. "I mean, couldn't it at least have been on the church steps in Rome? On a café terrace drinking champagne? In the garden at the villa by moonlight?"

"It could," he agreed, "but I'm asking you now."

I looked doubtfully at him. I wanted to love him, I wanted to be able to say it, to be free to say it. And free to love again.

"I know all your secrets," he said. "I *know* you, Gemma, and I love you."

I began to cry. Of all *times*—when the man I now knew I loved had actually asked me to marry him, even if it was in an Italian jail cell. The mascara I wish I had never worn was running down my face as I sobbed uncontrollably. Ben just stood there, watching me. He didn't say, Hey, babe, it's okay, everything's all right. He just stood there and waited for me to stop. Which eventually, I did.

"Okay, so now you're over that," he said calmly. "Are you going to marry me, or not?"

"Not," I whispered, confused, but he looked so stunned, I guess maybe I didn't get it right. "Try me again with that one, will you?" I said.

"Tell you what," he said with an exasperated look, "why don't *you* ask *me* this time?"

My knees finally gave way. I sank to the stone floor and pushed my hand through the bars toward him. "Ben Raphael, I love you," I said. "Will you please marry me?"

And he gave a great shout of laughter and said, "Darn right I will, Gemma Jericho."

I had asked a man to marry me and he had said yes. I was the happiest woman in the world. I thought of my dear love Cash. I would always share my love between him and Ben. But I was alive again, and all of us who have suffered a loss know this moment when there comes a turning point and life goes on.

And my lovely Ben, my savior, my new best friend,

my lover and fellow criminal, keeper of my secrets and master of my soul and my body, will be my husband.

Ben took a little velvet pouch from his pocket and pushed it across the strip of floor between our cells.

I wriggled my arm through the bars, trying to reach it; it was just a finger breadth away. "Damn," I muttered. Wiggling both hands I almost had it. *Yes!* I edged it toward me. My fingers encircled it.

"Open it," Ben said, kneeling opposite me in his cell.

The metal bars cut into my arms as I jiggled the pouch open and saw the ring. It was the one I had so admired and longed for in the old jewelry store on the Ponte Vecchio. The one with the twisted bands of gold, centered with a cabochon of clear crysal surrounded by pinpoint diamonds. The one I just knew had been given to some beautiful young Florentine aristocrat by her long-ago beloved.

"How did you know?" I whispered.

"Never underestimate the power of daughters."

"Livvie told you?"

He nodded. "I wish I could put it on your finger. And then I would kiss you."

We knelt there, in our jail cells, staring longingly at each other. I looked down at my beautiful engagement ring still on the floor. I nudged it toward me until I got close enough to push it onto the proper finger. I held out my hands through the bars to show him. It sparkled softly in the dim light.

"Did I really ask you to marry me?" I said.

Ben nodded. "And I said yes."

"Then shouldn't I be the one giving you the ring?"

"That's okay. I'm trusting you'll keep your word."

I sighed happily, trying to wiggle my hands back

through the bars. "Oh," I said. "Ow." I tried to pull my arms toward me. *"Ouch!"* I said.

I was kneeling on the floor of the cell, with my arms poked through the bars.

Ben clapped a hand to his forehead. "Don't tell me," he said. *"You're stuck."*

"It could happen to anyone. You put your arms through bars, you're gonna get stuck."

"Pity you didn't think of that earlier."

"But then I wouldn't have been able to put on your ring."

"True."

"What am I going to do now?" I asked meekly.

By the time Maggie had arrived, they had cut me out of there with a heavy-duty steel cutter that I thought was going to saw my arms off. And the cost of the "operation," I was warned sternly by the chief of police himself, would be paid for by me.

It turned out that of course Maggie knew the chief. She explained to him in her delightful English-Italian mix that we had only been searching for what was rightfully my property, and that Donati was the real criminal who had taken the *americano*'s money and run. We apologized sincerely for wasting police time and appreciated the trouble they had taken, and of course we would pay any necessary costs.

She had us out of there in a flash and into her "best" car, a big old yellow Rolls that dated from the fifties and floated along the bumpy little roads as gently as a baby's pram. The butler/majordomo/chauffeur drove, and Maggie sat beside him with the count's last will and testament, still folded neatly, on her knee. I was dying to know what was in it, but I didn't want to seem pushy. Not when I had just become engaged to the man whose villa I might, or might not, now own.

"Ben and I just got engaged," I said instead.

"In *a jail cell*?" Maggie sounded so Oscar Wilde that I laughed. "So you finally asked her, Ben?" she added.

"I did. And she asked me. We both said yes."

"Well, of course it was written in the tarot cards. Congratulations, my dears, we will have champagne tonight to celebrate. And caviar. I do so love caviar, don't you?"

I eyed the document in her lap anxiously. "Maggie?"

"Yes, my dear?"

"Do you think . . . I mean, could you just look at the will and see—"

"Of course." She ripped off the pink tape and rustled through the stiff parchment covered with spidery hand-writing. "Piacere wrote it himself," she said. "And he signed it. *And* it was witnessed."

She skimmed the pages, then she looked up, beaming. "Winner takes all," she yelled, delighted.

"Maggie," Ben said, exasperated, "exactly *who* is the winner who takes all?"

"Why, Sophia Maria is, of course."

CHAPTER SEVENTY-FIVE

Nonna had decided she wanted a true old-fashioned Italian wedding in the village square at Bella Piacere. That way, she said, everyone could come.

She had what she called a "final shopping blowout" in Florence, where, to her delight, she hit the sales. "Dolce e Gabbana," she told me proudly, showing me the dress and the matching shoes. If I'd had any shock left in me, I would have fainted. Whoever thought my mom would even know about D & G, let alone wear it for her wedding?

Then my friends Patty and Jeff arrived from New York, thrilled to be part of it all, happy for Nonna, and dying to meet Ben.

"Hey, 'hag,' you're looking pretty good," was Patty's greeting to me. Then she saw Ben and added, admiringly, "And now I know the reason why."

We had all moved into the villa, and now we put Patty and Jeff in a corner room in one of the little square towers. It had windows on three sides looking out at the overgrown garden at the front and the villa's tiled roofs to the left and the Tuscan hills to the right. Jim said it was a pity it wasn't going to be a hotel anymore because it was just about perfect, and that we would have to throw them out of there to get rid of them. But I told them that we would have to sell the villa.

"Sell it back to Ben," Patty said. But Ben had already bought and paid for the villa once, and that would hardly have been a good business deal for him.

After the wedding, Nonna and Rocco were to drive in Rocco's truck to Forte dei Marmi, a pretty little beach resort, for their two-day honeymoon. Fido was to stay with Maggie, and Guido Verdi, the mayor, who was also to be Rocco's best man, was personally going to take care of the cow. But by then, of course, Livvie and I would be back in the wilds of Manhattan. Our bags were packed, and we were leaving paradise the day after the wedding.

Livvie hated to leave. When she wasn't busy organizing the wedding flowers, which Nonna had put her in charge of, as well as her own and Muffie's wedding outfits, she moped around with a sorrowful look on her face. I had also caught that same wistful expression in Ben's eyes.

And me? Had I let myself, I could have broken down and cried buckets of tears at the thought of leaving Bella Piacere and our lovely villa, but I reminded myself that this was Nonna's moment, and that I had no right to spoil her happiness. Still, even though I now had Ben, how would I manage in New York, back in my daily life in the trauma room, without Nonna always being there, without seeing her every Sunday?

The day of the wedding arrived at last. Clear and blue and hot, with no hint of those warning purple clouds. But then, of course, it would not have dared to rain on Nonna's wedding day.

The whole village had joined in the planning. Trees and shrubs in giant planters blocked traffic from entering or leaving the village and lent a verdant garden look to the cobbled square. Buntings were strung from the umbrella pines and along the street, fluttering in the sirocco, which was blowing heat from the Sahara again, and banners with Bella Piacere's emblem and Count Piacere's coat of arms hung from lamp standards and in windows.

Ancient speakers like giant megaphones had been attached to roofs at each corner of the square, and long trestle tables were covered in red-checked paper cloths, with bunches of wildflowers picked in the hills by Livvie and Muffie stuck into yellow pottery jugs. Flimsy folding chairs listed rockily, and round red paper lanterns swung overhead. Children in their Sunday best chased each other, knocking over chairs and hiding under the tables. A black dog lifted its leg in one corner, then went sniffing after a crowd of other dogs, and the tabby from up the hill took a position in a sunny spot on one of the tables.

Old women in their black and shawls, who remembered both Nonna's and Rocco's mothers, climbed the steps into the church, crossed themselves, and took up their usual seats near the front. The bridal couple's old school friends were there, in colorful silks and good suits with huge pink carnations pinned to the lapel, and so were their smart sons and daughters and packs of grandchildren, plus the village's young marrieds with their new babies. Rocco's olive grove workers were there too, and all the local farmers, and the owners of the vineyards, as well as the local gentry, most of whom had known Rocco all their lives.

A wooden platform for dancing had been built over the bocce court, and musicians were setting up the drum kit and testing their accordions and fiddles. Rocco's special white cow was tethered under the trees with a trough of sweet hay to keep her happy, busily whisking away the flies with her tail and watching the world go by from her long-lashed liquid-brown eyes.

The simple honey-colored church, with its brass candlesticks burnished to a fine gleam, was filled with flowers of every sort and color, and the heavy smell of incense mingled with that of tuberoses and lavender. The *signora* in the pink linen dress, who was also the local librarian, pounded out snatches of Bach and Vivaldi on the old pump organ, while one unfortunate lad, sweating up in the loft, worked the bellows, and a crop of choirboys, big-eyed Italian movie urchins, all jostled and sniggered, undaunted by Don Vincenzo's warning glares.

Don Vincenzo had bought a new soutane and shined his shoes, and Rocco was smart again in his black suit and the blue silk tie Nonna had given him. His bristly hair was gelled flat, and not a whisker was out of place on his mustache. He waited at the altar beside Mayor Guido, and with Fido, who, with special dispensation from Don Vincenzo, sat at his master's heels, looking worried in a large pink satin bow.

I took my seat at the front, as nervous as if I were the bride. And, in the white dress I had bought in that mad moment in Florence without ever trying it on, I could have been. It was the one I'd worn to Ben's Fourth of July party. I'd looked so gawky and odd in it then, but now, with my new suntan and Maggie's diamond drop earrings and the sexy "look of love" that hung around me tangible as smoke, somehow I looked kind of cute.

Maggie was over the top, as usual, in her favorite peacock blue, a shimmery sequined dress that would have looked good on a movie star half her age, and all her best diamonds, plus a gigantic aquamarine tiara. She sat beside me, mopping her tears with a tiny linen handkerchief, though the ceremony hadn't even started yet. "I can't help it," she boomed over the roar of the organ, "I always cry at weddings. Except my own, of course."

I heard the rustle of silk and the sound of footsteps on the stone floor, and I turned to look. Ben was giving Nonna away, and they stood together, caught for a moment in a muted ray of sunlight that filtered through the stained glass.

The bridesmaids, Livvie and Muffie, wore pale celadon-green cotton T-shirt dresses they had chosen themselves, and Livvie had colored their hair a delicate lemon color. They were barefoot and each carried a single tall sunflower, held like a candle in front of them. Today they looked less like *Nosferatu* extras and more like frescoed cherubs.

Sophia Maria was the star of the show. Hair pulled softly back, begonia lipstick perfectly in place, in a pale silk dress splashed with watercolor flowers, low-cut with a little "shrug" around her bare shoulders for the church, and a tiny hat with a flutter of spotted net over her eyes, she was . . . just lovely. She carried a simple bouquet of those little pink Tuscan roses and white hydrangeas and cream lilies from the villa's gardens, and she had the happiest smile on her face.

I looked at Ben as he walked my mother down the aisle. He looked so good, all dressed up in a dark blue suit, my heart flipped and my knees turned to jelly all over again.

I ran my hands through my hair, completely wrecking the careful job Livvie had done combing it into place, and the gardenia I had tucked behind my ear fell over my glasses.

I thought about how much she had changed, from the lonely suburban widow to this pretty, happy woman. Had I changed too? Yes, of course I had. I still looked the same, and I was still "the walking disaster area," as Ben called me. But I had changed inside. Now I saw the world through clear eyes, unclouded by regrets and sadness. Like Nonna, I was taking my happiness where I found it, and for as long as it lasted. And for both of us, I hoped it would be forever.

The choir sang, the vows were said, the organ pounded out the wedding march, and *signor* and *signora* Cesani emerged from the church to the pealing of a cracked bell, with smiles big enough to match the quarter moon. The sirocco blew, hot and spicy, the sun settled over the velvet hills, the birds fell silent, and the crickets started noisily up. The voice of a fellow Tuscan, Andrea Bocelli, singing "Time to Say Goodbye" came at full tinny blast over the loudspeakers as Rocco turned to his bride and planted a big kiss on her mouth. Then, "Let the party begin," he cried.

I hugged Nonna so tightly, she complained I was crushing her dress, but our eyes met in the long, loving look that I knew just as well as I knew that other combative look she so often gave me.

"Good luck, Momma," I said in a voice choked with tears, and she said, "I have everything I want, daughter, including luck."

Then it was Livvie's turn to kiss her. She said sadly,

"What shall we do on Sunday now, Nonna, without you there?"

But Nonna just nodded wisely, and said, "We shall just have to see about that, *ragazza*."

I congratulated Rocco and warned him he had better look after Nonna. He gave me a wink and that beaming toothy smile, smoothed his mustache, and said, "You betcha," in something approximating English. Fido scratched at his pink satin bow and allowed us to pat him, and Livvie even kissed his pink nose, which made him sneeze. Then champagne corks were popping and platters were being carried to the table, and the party began.

CHAPTER SEVENTY-SIX

Everyone in the village had contributed to the wedding feast, and Nonna herself had made the sauce for the pasta, from the abundant delicious tomatoes in the *albergo*'s back garden. Ben had provided unlimited champagne and wine, a local Rosso di Montalcino, as well as beer, and the Bar Galileo was open and free to all. Fiametta had baked the wedding cake, five tiers, alternating red, white, and blue icing for the United States and green, red, and white for Italy. On top was a little model of a wedding couple, with a pink-and-white sugar dog that looked exactly like Fido.

With a blast of tarantellas from the loudspeakers, the feast began. There must have been at least ten courses, starting with *bruschetta*: that good, coarse, crusty, saltless Tuscan bread, from the local baker, dipped in Rocco's own best olive oil and topped with chopped sweet tomatoes and fresh basil, anchovies, and olives.

Huge platters of antipasti were passed around by the women. There was homemade fennel sausage and *salame di cinghiale*, the strong wild boar salami; mortadella and smoked red peppers; ham and shaved Parmesan cheese. Then gnocchi, light as little pillows, bathed in sweet butter and sage; and the best ham from Parma, with figs so

ripe they burst with juices; a salad of arugula and baby
lettuces fresh-picked that morning. Then *involtini di
vitello,* veal rolled in ham and sage leaves, served with *fa-
gioli*; then Nonna's ravioli stuffed with ricotta and
spinach and covered in her tomato sauce, which gained a
round of applause and shouts of *"Brava, brava, signora
Cesani,"* amid much laughter.

Next came the *arrosto di maiale*, loin of pork roasted
with rosemary, whose aroma was enough to make me
drool, served with polenta and porcini mushrooms.
Bowls of fresh fruits were brought out, more wine corks
popped, and long wooden boards covered in green lemon
leaves and an assortment of local cheeses were carried in,
plus huge plates of cookies.

Couples were already dancing on the wooden platform
under the umbrella pines, and children held hands and
whirled around together until they tumbled, laughing, in a
heap. Livvie and Muffie chased after the toddlers, helping
out the mothers who were taking time out to enjoy the
party. Babies cried and were fed; guests yelled to each
other across the tables and poured more wine; the dogs
barked; the cow gave an irritable moo; the loudspeakers
blasted; and over all was a buzz of laughter.

Patty and Jeff, holding hands as always, sat in amazed
silence. "It's like Sunday lunch, only bigger and better,
and with sound effects," Patty said.

Don Vincenzo sipped a grappa; his wire glasses slid
down his nose, and there was a contented smile on his
chubby face. Then Maggie invited the mayor to dance
and almost caused a major upset with his wife, who bristled with jealousy. And Nonna—well, Nonna was Sophia
Maria, giddy and glamorous and feminine.

And Ben? He snatched me in his arms and spun me

around that wobbly wooden floor, humming along in my ear to Paolo Conte's song *"Gli impermeabili,"* which apparently means "Raincoats," a most unlikely title for one of the most romantic songs we had ever heard. It's a story about lovers and a room with lowered shutters on a rainy night, the touch of a hand on a bruise, and it reminded us of our night of love in rainy Florence.

New York and our own future seemed a long way away, yet even as we danced I remembered that our bags were packed and we were to leave the very next day.

"Kiss me," Ben whispered, and our mouths met in a long clinging kiss that I hoped would never end. Until I heard the applause, that is, and Livvie's voice saying, *"M-o-m!"* Of course I was blushing as we swung apart. But then it was time for the wedding cake and speeches.

Somebody turned the loudspeakers down, and Paolo Conte's soft, quirky *"Mocambo"* blurred. Nonna and Rocco stood there while the crowd applauded and whistled and stomped their approval.

Rocco spoke first, saying what he had to say in both Italian and English, having been coached by Nonna. "I am very happy," he said, beaming. "I have my Sophia Maria by my side. I have my new family. I have my friends. I have my dog. We are both very happy."

Nonna tapped the microphone, testing it. She smoothed down her skirt and patted her little veiled hat to make sure it was still at the correct angle. Then she gazed around like a queen at her subjects.

"Amici," she said, *"mia famiglia di Bella Piacere . . .* friends, dear ones, you and my village have always been in my heart. Even though I left so long ago, I never forgot you. Bella Piacere and you people were among the best

memories of my life, even though my life was a good one in my wonderful country, America.

"But now I am older. I needed to come home again. And the count and Don Vincenzo gave me that opportunity, though of course that crook Donati almost succeeded in cheating me out of my inheritance." Boos mingled with laughter, and she smiled.

"And my daughter, the *dottoressa,* ended up in jail, almost a criminal herself," she added. Everyone looked my way, and there was more laughter.

"In the middle of my own happiness with my new husband," Nonna smiled at Rocco, "I also want to thank my family, Livvie and Gemma, for . . . for just being my family. And also to thank Gemma for expanding it so nicely by promising to marry Ben, and thereby giving me a second granddaughter, Muffie. And who knows," she added, lifting a nicely penciled eyebrow, "maybe even more grandchildren.

"My only sadness is that tomorrow they are to return to America." She stopped here and gave me that long hard look.

"*Bambini,*" she said, and I said to myself, *Uh-oh, here comes trouble. . . .*

"*Bambini,*" she went on, "the Villa Piacere legitimately belongs to me. But now I am giving it to Gemma, and to Ben."

Startled, I looked at Ben.

"So now they have no excuse not to stay here," Nonna said firmly. "Gemma, you can become the local doctor. We need one around here. Ben can run the villa as a hotel, which he had already planned to do anyway, and he can get on with his painting and become another Michelangelo. And Livvie and Muffie, you two can go to school in Florence." The crowd applauded and whistled some more. "That way, I get to keep you all, and you get to keep the villa." She beamed. "It is, I think a fair trade."

My eyes met Ben's. Could we?

I thought about the Saturday nights at Bellevue: the mayhem, the ugliness, the tragedy. My daughter growing up a teen diva, the danger.

And Ben remembered clawing his way to success and the striving to stay there; his daughter growing up a spoiled rich kid, the danger.

Could we leave that harsh, sophisticated urban world behind and face the new reality of a simple life, where the change in seasons is marked by changes in crops and food as well as in the weather; where the wine harvest punctuates the year, and the olive crop is more precious than pearls? Where a great day out is a drive to Florence to sip cappuccino at Gilli's, making small purchases of a special cheese or a pair of beautiful shoes, finding an old painting in a backstreet junk shop or considering the purchase of a spanking new silver Vespa? Life with a permanently stumbling water supply and erratic electricity; of the cold winter *tramontana* blowing from the snowy mountains, and the long, languorous, hot summer months; of chestnuts in autumn and *Panna cotta* at Christmas and special cake at Easter? Where the latest movie may take several years to appear in the tiny local cinema; where books and music are the diversions, along with an evening glass of wine on the terrace, and where the view and the man you are with are all the magic you need? Ben held out his arms, and I walked into them.

Oh yes, we could.

EPILOGUE

Three months have passed. I'm here at the villa, my new home, lying in the dark that used to hold such terrors for me, wallowing in the big old bed that sags in the middle from age, safe in my husband's arms.

We were married a week after Nonna and Rocco, in a small ceremony in one of Florence's prettiest churches, where I wore jasmine in my hair and we promised to love, honor, and care for each other, forever. I used not to believe in that word—*forever*—but now I know it means for as long as you both shall live. I thought of Cash, and I smiled. I knew how he would approve. I only wished the old man with his beautiful white cat, his *principessa,* could have been at the wedding with us too, because he had shown me how to change my values, helped change my life.

Livvie and Muffie were asleep down the hall. Nonna and Rocco were cozy in their little farmhouse with Fido; and Sinbad, whose flight from New York had not fazed him one little bit, was curled up on my feet.

It's October and cold. Tonight we lit the fire and roasted chestnuts, and tomorrow we will rise early. We'll drink coffee with milk from Rocco's cow and eat Fiametta's toasted *ciabatta* with strawberry jam, and then we'll go and help pick grapes in our own little vineyard.

Luchay is still with us, and I have yet to read his full story, along with Poppy's. Maggie is already planning big Christmas festivities, and Ben and I are planning what to do with our villa.

I look at the sleeping face of my lovely man, and I want so badly to kiss him. I brush my lips over his, so softly, but even in his sleep his arms grip me tighter, until I'm pressed close to him, as close as you can get. The scent of his skin is in my nostrils, the texture of his flesh is smooth under my hands, and the love I feel for him is so tender, I never want to let him go. I kiss him some more, until he wakes and kisses me back.

I want you to think of this story I have shared with you as a minimovie of my life, perhaps with music by Paolo Conte and a song by Marc Anthony that seems to have become my theme: "You Sang to Me," the one about *crashing into love*. I love that image. I hope it stays with me—with all of us—for the rest of our lives.

And what shall we do with the villa? Shall we try to restore it to its old glory, turn it into a hotel? Ah, well, of course that is another story.

I know someone has said this before, but life, here in Bella Piacere, is beautiful.

THE HOTEL RIVIERA

CHAPTER ONE

LOLA

It was late September when I first met Jack Farrar, one of those balmy, soft-breezed south-of-France evenings that hinted summer was finally over. And though I didn't yet know it, it was a meeting that would effect great changes in my life.

My name is Lola Lafôret—and yes, I know you're thinking I must be a stripper. Everybody thinks that. Actually, what I am is chef and *patron* of the Hotel Riviera, and I used to be the much more normal Lola March from California before I married "the Frenchman." But that's a long story.

It's been six years since I welcomed my first guests to the Hotel Riviera, though "hotel" is far too grand a title for this old villa. It's a casual sand-between-the-toes, cool-tile-floors, kind of place. There are just eight rooms, each with tall French windows opening onto a terrace spilling over with bougainvillea and night-scented jasmine. You'll find it on a spit of pine-covered land off the Ramatuelle road near Saint Tropez, down a long sandy lane shaded with umbrella pines and alive with the chirruping of *cigales*. We have our own little private beach here with sand as pale as platinum and soft as sugar, and in summer it's dotted with marine-blue umbrellas and sunny-yellow loungers, and the golden-tan bodies of our guests. Small children run in and out of the lacey wavelets while grown-ups sip iced drinks in the shade, and in the heat of the afternoon they retreat to their shuttered rooms to nap, or to make love on a cool white bed.

Imagine a sunny, sea-lapped cove, gift-wrapped in blue and tied with a bow like a Tiffany box, and you'll get the feel of my little hotel. It's a place made for Romance with a capital R. Except for me, its creator.

Somewhere in the process, my own Romance withered on the vine. Somehow it was never my "Frenchman," Patrick and me dining alone on the candle-lit terrace with the moon throwing a silver path across the dark water, and champagne fizzing in tall glasses. It was never Patrick holding my hand across the table and gazing into my eyes. Oh no. I was always in the kitchen cooking delicious feasts for lovers who had the romance in their lives I so badly wanted, while my own "lover" took in the delights of summer in St. Tropez nightlife.

When I met and married Patrick six years ago, I thought I had found "true love." Now, I don't believe that such a thing exists. Yes, I admit I'm wounded, and I know I have always had a penchant for rogues, and that those straight and true guys, strong-jawed, steady, the good providers, are definitely not drawn to me. I seem to attract riffraff like summer flies to a glass of wine.

Which brings me back to Jack Farrar again.

So, there I was, alone on the terrace, taking a breather before the first dinner guests arrived. It was my favorite time of the year, the end of the long hot summer season when the crowds are gone and life drifts back into a more leisurely pace. The sky was still a flawless blue and the breeze soft against my bare arms as I sipped a glass of chilled rosé, gazing blankly out over the pretty bay, brooding over my problems.

I'm a woman in limbo. And here's the reason why. Six months ago my husband Patrick climbed into his silver Porsche, *en route*, he said, to buy me a birthday gift. As usual, he'd forgotten my birthday, but I guess someone must have reminded him. He was wearing dark glasses and I couldn't read the expression in his eyes as he lifted his hand in a careless goodbye. He wasn't smiling, though, I do remember that.

I haven't heard a word from him since. Nobody has. And nobody seems to care, though I went *crazy* trying to find him. Of course, the police tried to trace him, his picture as "a missing person" was posted everywhere and they followed clues leading as far as Marseilles and Las Vegas, without any luck. Now the case is on the back burner and Patrick is just another missing person. "Missing husband" is what they mean. It's not unknown around here when the summer beaches are crowded with gorgeous girls and the yachts filled with rich women for a husband to go missing.

You might have thought Patrick's friends would know, but they swore they didn't, and anyhow they were always Patrick's friends, not mine. In fact I hardly knew the guys he hung out with, or the women. I was far too busy working at making our little hotel perfect. And Patrick had no family; he'd told me he was the last of the Lafôrets who had lived and worked their fishing boats in Marseilles for decades.

Speaking of boats, I'm back to Jack Farrar again.

A small black sloop had drifted across my line of vision. Now I don't like *my* cove to be disturbed by holiday-makers partying all night, with disco music pounding across the water and shrieks and screams as they push each other into the water. I took a long hard look at the sloop. At least this wasn't one of those mega-yachts; in fact I didn't believe they would allow such small fry into the St. Tropez marina, even if its owner could have afforded it, which, from the look of his shabby boat, I doubted. And which was probably why he'd chosen to anchor in *my* protected little cove with a free view of *my* pretty little hotel instead.

The black sloop cut across the horizon, sails slackening in the tiny breeze, then tacked into the cove where, as I had guessed, it dropped anchor.

I grabbed the telescope at the end of the terrace and got the boat in focus; the name *Bad Dog* was inscribed in brass letters on her bow. I moved over an inch and got a man in my sights. Muscular, broad in the shoulders, powerful chest tapering to narrow hips. . . . *And oh my God he was totally naked!*

I knew I shouldn't but okay, I admit it, I took a peek—actually a long look. I mean, what woman wouldn't? After all, he was just standing there, poised for a dive, almost flaunting his nakedness. And I must say, the view was *good*. I'm talking about his face of course, which was attractive in an odd sort of way. Actually, I thought he looked like his boat: tough, workmanlike, rather battered.

I watched the Naked Man make his dive, then cut cleanly out to sea in a powerful crawl until all I could make out was a faint froth in his wake. From the corner of my eye, I caught a movement on the sloop; a young woman, all long legs and long blond hair and wearing only a bright red thong was stretched out on a towel in the stern, catching the final rays. Not that she needed them; like him she was perfectly toasted. Spread her with butter and jam, I thought enviously, and she'd be perfect for his breakfast.

The Naked Man was swimming back to the sloop and I got him in my sights again. And that, you might say, was my big mistake.

He climbed back onto the boat, shook himself like a wet dog in a cloud of rainbow-colored droplets, then flung out his arms and lifted his head to the sun. He stood for a moment, beautiful, hard-bodied, golden from the sun and the sea-winds, a man at one with the elements. There was something so free about the gesture, it took my breath away.

I followed as he padded aft, saw him reach for something. A pair of binoculars. *And then he had me in his sights, caught in the act of peeking at him.*

For a long moment our eyes met, linked by powerful lenses. His were blue, darker than the sea, and I could swear there was laughter in them.

I jumped back, hot all over with embarrassment. His mocking laughter drifted across the water, then he gave me a jaunty wave and still laughing, stepped into a pair of shorts and began unhurriedly to clean his deck.

So. That was my first meeting with Jack Farrar. The next one would prove even more interesting.

CHAPTER TWO

I beat a hasty retreat into the dining room in back of the terrace, and began hurriedly to check the tables, polishing a knife here, adjusting a glass there. I checked that the wines were cooling, checked that the linen napkins were properly folded, checked my long ginger hair in the mirror behind the bar, wishing I could call it copper or even red, but ginger it was. I wished one more time that I had exotic almond-shaped eyes instead of my too-round ones, wished I knew a recipe to get rid of freckles, that I was taller and leaner and maybe ten years younger. I was thirty-nine years old and, after the events of the past six months, I decided gloomily I looked every year of it.

I wasn't exactly into a glamorous mode either, in my baggy hounds-tooth chef's pants and shrunken white tee, with no lipstick and even worse, no mascara on my ginger-cat lashes.

Horrified, I realized I was looking at exactly what the Naked Man had seen through the binoculars. I thought worriedly I really must make more effort but that anyhow he certainly wasn't interested in me, then I forgot about him and headed for my true domain.

The jewel-colored bead door-curtain jangled behind me and I was in my favorite place in the whole world, my big tile-floor kitchen with ancient beams and a row of open windows overhung with blossoming vines.

I'd known the first day I saw it, this had to be MY kitchen. It had stolen my chef's heart even more than the magical view from the terrace and the sandy winding paths, the shady pines and the wild overgrown gardens. More than the cool upstairs rooms with their tall windows and lopsided shutters, and the downstairs "salon" with its imposing limestone fireplace that was far too grand for such a humble seaside villa. More than any of that, this kitchen was *home*.

It was the place where I could put all thoughts of sophisticated city restaurants behind me and get back to my true foodie roots, back to the simple pleasures of local produce and seasonally grown fruits and vegetables. Here, I would grill fish that swam almost at the bottom of my garden and pick the herbs that grew almost wild to flavor my dishes. I knew I could relax and be myself in this place.

It all seemed so perfect. But first "true love" disappeared; then Patrick had disappeared, and now my only love left was my little hotel. Oh, and Scramble, who I'll tell you about later.

My private life might be a mess, but all was well in my culinary world. Sauces simmered on the stove; fishes shone silver and bright-eyed in the glass-fronted refrigerated drawer; perfect little racks of Sisteron lamb awaited a hot oven, and individual *tians* of eggplant and tomatoes were drizzled with succulent olive oil from Nice, ready to be popped into the oven.

A fifteen-foot pine table stood under the windows. On it a couple of *tartes tatin* cooled alongside a big blue bowl of sliced ripe peaches marinating in vermouth. Next to them were the spun-sugar cage confections, a remnant of my old "grand" restaurant days and with which I liked to top my desserts because I enjoy the delighted *ooh*s and *ahh*s they evoke from my guests. Oh, and as always, a tray of my signature nut-topped brownies, my American specialty that I like to serve with the coffee.

You'll find no huge white plates centered with tiny "culinary arrangements" here. Our food is simple but lavish, our plates are locally made stoneware, the color of good honey, and we garnish them with only fresh flowers and a sprig of herbs.

I dropped a kiss on my assistant Nadine's cheek in

passing. She's been with me since the beginning, all six traumatic years, and I love her to pieces. She's a local woman, dark-haired, dark-eyed, olive-skinned, with a raucous laugh and a sense of humor that's gotten us through many a kitchen disaster. Along with her sister, she takes care of the housekeeping as well as helping in the kitchen, while I deal with the food, the marketing, the menus and the cooking; and Patrick supposedly took care of the business end, though from our meager bank account, I'm not sure how good a job he'd been doing.

Petite dark-haired Marit, straight out of culinary school and a new recruit this season, was chopping vegetables, and Jean-Paul, the seventeen-year-old "youth-of-all-work" was busy cleaning up. The real season was over; it would be an easy night with just the remaining hotel guests and perhaps a couple of last-minute strays who might wander our way.

I slid a Barry White album, my current favorite sexy man, into the CD player, grabbed a brownie, pushed my way back through the jangling beads and came across Scramble. Okay, so Scramble's not a dog, she's not a cat, or even a hamster. Scramble is a hen. I know it's crazy, but ever since she emerged from the shell, a soft fluffy yellow chicken cradled trustingly in the palm of my hand, I've adored her, and I'd like to believe she loves me too, though with a hen it's hard to tell. Anyhow, the fact is I'm the only woman who cried the whole way through *Chicken Run*. And though you might think it's a sad state of affairs, giving all my love to a hen instead of a husband, Scramble deserves it more. She's never unfaithful, she never even glances at anybody else, and she sleeps in *my* bed every night.

She's quite big now, soft and white with yellow legs,

ruby crest and wattles, and beady, dark eyes. She was scratching energetically in the big terra cotta pot with the red hibiscus outside the kitchen door that she'd claimed as home, preparing to settle down for the night, or at least until I go to bed when she'll join me on my pillow.

I gave her an affectionate little pat as I passed by, which she returned with a hearty peck. "Ungrateful bird," I said. "I remember when you were just an egg."

I cast a cautious glance at the black sloop as I walked back along the terrace. Lights twinkled and banners fluttered festively. I wondered what the Naked Man was up to, and whether he might row the boat's little dinghy into my cove and join us for dinner on the terrace.

I sighed. I wasn't betting on it.

CHAPTER THREE

"That's a pretty little sloop," Miss Nightingale called. "Rather different for these waters, don't you think?"

"It is, and I hope they're not going to play loud music and interrupt your peaceful dinner," I said.

"Oh, I shouldn't think so, my dear, it doesn't look the right boat for that sort of thing. It's more of a proper sailor's boat, if you know what I mean."

I smiled at my favorite guest. Mollie Nightingale was a retired British schoolmarm, and by way of being my friend. Nothing had ever been said, but it was just there between us, that warm feeling, a kind of recognition I suppose you might call it. She had certain qualities I admired: integrity; an offbeat sense of humor, and a personal reticence that matched my own. Miss Nightingale kept her own counsel and I knew little about her private life, just the woman she was here at the Riviera. A woman I liked.

She had been my first guest, the week the Hotel Riviera opened for business, and she had been back every year since, coming late in the season when prices were lower and she could afford to stay for a month, before heading home to her cottage in the Cotswolds and her miniature Yorkie, Little Nell, and another long English winter. Meanwhile, she lived out her annual dream here, alone at a table for one, with a small carafe of local wine and book to hand, and always with a pleasant word and a smile for everyone.

Miss Nightingale was, I would guess, somewhere in her late seventies, short, square and sturdy, and tonight she wore a pink flower-print dress. A white cardigan was thrown over her shoulders, though it was still warm out, and as always she had on her double row of pearls. Like the queen of England, she always carried a large handbag which, as well as a clean linen handkerchief and her money, also contained her knitting. Now, I'm not sure if the queen of England knits, but Miss Nightingale, with her determinedly gray hair set in solid waves and curls, and her piercing blue eyes behind large pale spectacles, was a dead ringer for Her Majesty.

She was usually first down for dinner, showing up about this time for a glass of *pastis*, a little self-indulgence to which I knew she looked forward. She'd mix the anise-liquor with water in a tall glass, then sip it slowly, making it last until dinner, which I also knew was the social highlight of her day.

I sat with her while she told me about her outing to the Villa Ephrussi, the old Rothschild house with its spectacular gardens up the coast near Cap Ferrat. She always liked to tell me about the gardens she had discovered, she was a keen gardener herself and her own roses had won many local prizes. In fact, she was often to be found pottering about the gardens here, straw sun-hat slammed firmly over her eyes, pulling up a naughty weed or two, or snipping back a recalcitrant branch of honeysuckle that threatened to overwhelm the already out-of-hand bougainvillea.

Settled at her usual table, the one at the end of the terrace nearest the kitchen, glass of *pastis* to hand, she gazed at the spectacular view and heaved a satisfied sigh.

It was that special time in the evening on the Côte d'Azur, when the sky seems to meld with the sea and all the world turns a shimmering silver-plated midnight-blue. In the sudden breathless silence that always comes when day turns into night, the chatter of high-pitched French voices floated from the kitchen, and a tiny lizard swished by, pausing to stare at us with jeweled yellow eyes.

"Divine," Miss Nightingale murmured. "How you must love it here, my dear. How could you ever bear to leave it?"

Without realizing it, Miss Nightingale had struck right at the heart of my dilemma.

I do love it here. The trouble is I do not love my husband. All I feel for him right this minute is anger because I believe that when Patrick left that morning he knew he was not coming back. He simply left me without a word, left me not knowing where he was, what had happened to him, or even if he were safe. If he'd run off with another woman, or decided just to wander the world the way he used to, at least he should have told me. And if he was in some kind of trouble, then he should have shared that with me too, and not just left me alone like this. Not knowing.

"The Hotel Riviera is my home," I said to Miss Nightingale. "It's my own little piece of paradise. I'll still be here when I'm an old, old lady, still looking after my guests, still cooking, still drinking rosé wine and not believing how blue the late evening sky can be just before night falls. Oh no, Miss Nightingale, I'll never leave here, even if Patrick never. . . . ."

"If Patrick never comes back." She eyed me sympathetically from behind her large glasses. "My dear, do you think he's run off with another woman?"

I'd thought of that possibility so many times, lying in bed, tossing and turning, and I'd decided it was the only answer.

"Miss Nightingale," I said, genuinely lost, "what do I do now?"

"There's only one path for you to take, Lola, and that's to move on with your life."

"But how can I? Until I find out the truth?"

She patted my hand, gently, the way she might an upset schoolgirl. I almost expected her to say "There, there. . . ." but instead she said, "The answer to that, my dear, is you must find Patrick."

I wanted to ask her how, where do I start? But my other guests were showing up for pre-dinner drinks and a chat with the "patron," so I pulled myself together, dropped a kiss on her powder-scented cheek, and with a whispered "Thanks for being so understanding," went to greet them.